For Lin

GLEN

*Dick Fordyce
(Kingston 2025)*

GLEN

A Novel

Rick Fordyce

iUniverse

Also by Rick Fordyce

I Climbed Mt. Rainier With Jimi Hendrix's High School Counselor and Other Stories of the Pacific Northwest

On the Wide African Plain and Other stories of Africa
(forthcoming)

Glen

Copyright © 2008 by Rick Fordyce

All rights reserved. No part of this book may be used or reproduced by any means, graphic, electronic, or mechanical, including photocopying, recording, taping or by any information storage retrieval system without the written permission of the publisher except in the case of brief quotations embodied in critical articles and reviews.

This is a work of fiction. All of the characters, names, incidents, organizations, and dialogue in this novel are either the products of the author's imagination or are used fictitiously.

iUniverse books may be ordered through booksellers or by contacting:

iUniverse
1663 Liberty Drive
Bloomington, IN 47403
www.iuniverse.com
1-800-Authors (1-800-288-4677)

Because of the dynamic nature of the Internet, any Web addresses or links contained in this book may have changed since publication and may no longer be valid. The views expressed in this work are solely those of the author and do not necessarily reflect the views of the publisher, and the publisher hereby disclaims any responsibility for them.

ISBN: 978-0-5954-9767-6 (sc)

Print information available on the last page.

iUniverse rev. date 02/19/2015

To Mother, Father, and David

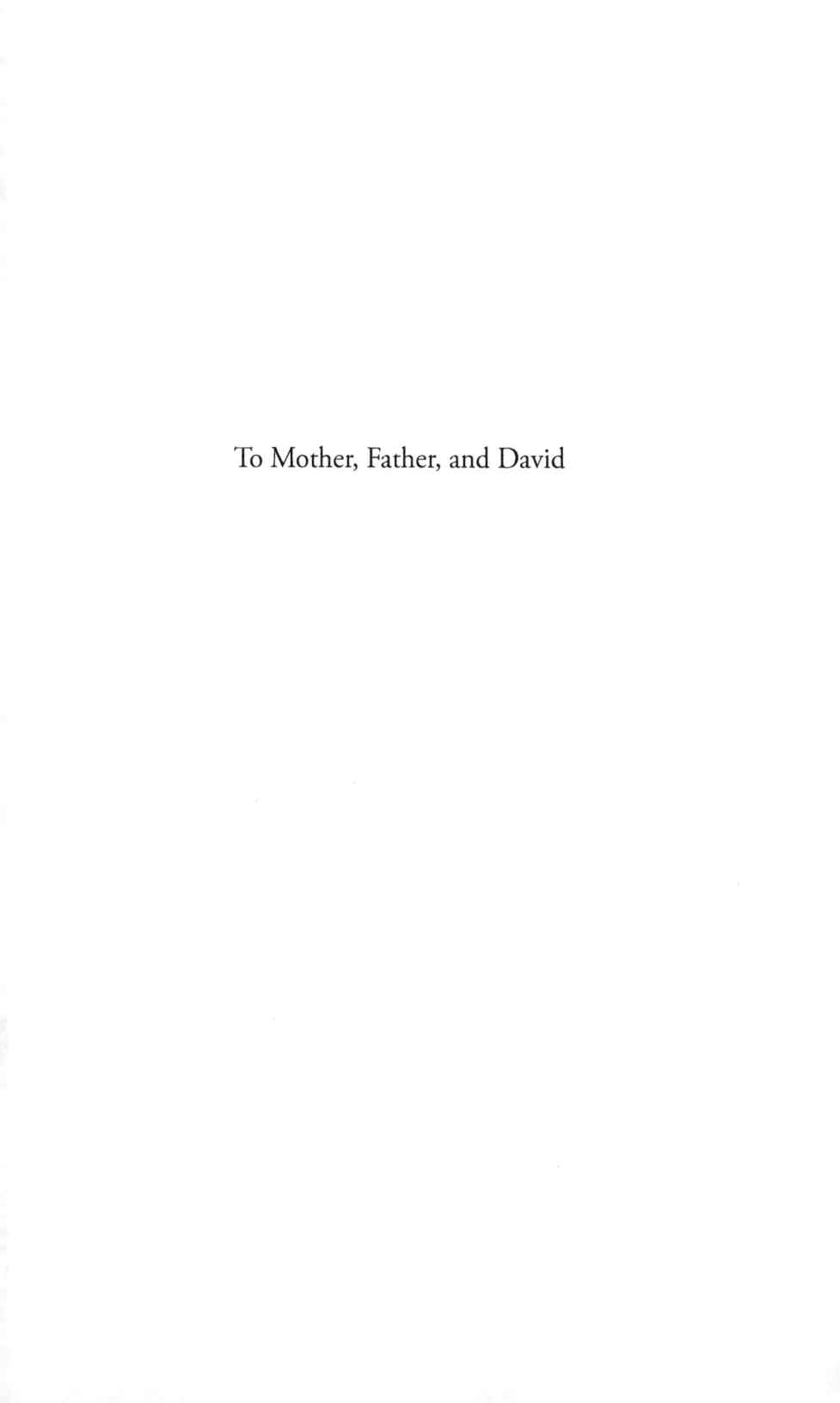

McDonalds is our kind of place
It's such a happy place
A clean and snappy place
A hap, hap, happy place
McDonalds is our kind of place
It's such a happy place
McDonalds is our kind of place

The African ran swiftly down the village road leading from the compound to the house of Mr. Andoah who worked in the clinic. Barefooted children, carrying buckets of stream water in the early morning light, turned, still sleepy-eyed, toward the fast moving man, as the goats and chickens wandering in his path leaped over a ways. As he approached Andoah's, his legs a blur of motion, his arms pumping furiously, he began to cry out in a high piercing scream: "Kwaku!—Kwaku! Come quickly ... Mr. Glen ... He is not well ... His head—Blood—There is no breath!"

Part I
NORTHGATE

*   *   *

He's crying again, Phil ... can you get him this time?
He is? I wish the doctor could find what's wrong.
He can't; there isn't anything. Remember? Sometimes they just cry a lot.

ONE

The three young boys were marching slowly into the wind across the snow-covered field when they spotted Tommy and Michael and Alan coming from Belmont Lane onto the field's opposite side. They lowered themselves into the snow and prepared for the ambush.

"Wait 'til they're by the fence," said Paul, taking aim with his hand.

As the children watched their friends move into easy range in front of the fence behind the Stanwood's house, the wind momentarily died and Paul yelled out: *"Now!"*

The cries of 'pow, pow, pow, pow' rang across the field toward the startled young explorers who, seeing they were under fire and obviously hit, dropped into the snow in writhing death. Then from one of the other houses at the edge of the field came the call of a woman's voice: *"Glen ... Glleeeennnnn! ... Lunch!."*

"Your mom's calling you, Glen," said Paul, one eye still on his fallen targets.

"—*Okay!*" Glen shouted back toward the house. "I got to go," he said to his heavily clothed friends.

Across the field, Tommy, Michael, and Alan were now brushing off snow and running over to Paul and Harry and Glen. "Hey! You got us!" Tommy yelled excitedly as he approached through the foot-deep snow.

"Yeah!" Glen said, smiling broadly, his eyes wide beneath the wool cap, his nose red and running. "We got you good!"

* * *

When he was five years old, Glen lived in a large northwest city with his parents and younger sister in a rented house that was at the edge of some woods with several small fields. The winters were usually wet and gray, but seldom cold, so it was rare when snow fell and stayed on the ground. When it did, though, the many children in the neighborhood would come out excitedly to play, and for Glen and the children his age the woods and fields were the most fun to explore.

Glen's mother had called Paul's to check on with whom and where they would be going to play, and for how long, and then Paul, who was seven, and Harry, who was six, came and got Glen. "Look at the creek and then I want you over in the field," Glen's mother had said to the boys as they stood in the cold air of the front porch, reminding them of what they had already been told several times before.

They had entered the woods on the trail off Glen's street and Glen was excited that Paul and Harry were taking him along because they were older and didn't have to take him. But they liked Glen because he played hard and tried hard and somehow always managed to keep up. He didn't hold anyone back, which was most important.

Paul had led, followed by Harry, with Glen coming last, which actually made it easier because the snow was already broken up. Once, Glen even happily yelled out, "this way!", and took off through the trees, and Harry and Paul, seeing it was an even better direction, turned and excitedly followed. But most of the time Paul led, and Glen brought up the rear; and they trudged through the heavy snow bundled dry and warm. And although the sky was gray, the forest glowed light with the snow, almost bright, and the silence gave it all a familiar and magical feel.

The exploring was as much a duty as play: snow had come to the woods, their woods—although they were actually owned by an old man who lived alone in a small cabin on the far side and who would sometimes chase them away if they ventured too close—and now they were checking on their woods. Yes, most definitely; snow had fallen in every direction. Just about the same amount everywhere: at the big stump with the two deep notches, like eye slits, that was twice as wide as they were tall; at the small stream in the gully which was the most fun because of the steep sides they had to scramble down without sliding into the water—although it was more a ditch at the bottom than a stream (but any water-soaked feet would not be approved of later at home). And finally, the ancient logs of the collapsed bridge that had once crossed the narrow ravine.

Standing above the logs, the ravine and the bridge blanketed in snow, the stream barely a trickle on the frozen floor, for Paul, Harry, and Glen, the woods were safe and secure. And now it was time to go to the field.

They came from the trees to the field's edge where the wind whipped across the flat and snow again swirled down from the low gray above. Stepping into the drifts, they struggled toward the houses on Belmont when, in the distance, Paul spotted the three slow-moving figures.

TWO

In the spring, long after the snows had melted and the new green had emerged, Glen's family moved from the house on Belmont to a larger rental that was very near to a new style for arranging businesses for shopping. Less than a year before, on what had once been a kind of swamp near some main roads in a section of the city that was rapidly expanding in new residential homes—as were many of the cities throughout the country during that first decade after the second world war—a group of local merchants had decided to expand together by building two long rows of connected stores with a covered walkway in between and surrounded by large parking lots. Because it was located in the north end of the city, they called the new collection of stores Northgate, and that spring, when Glen's mother would take him along, Glen would go to the world's first shopping mall.

With so many mothers soon coming to shop with their children, the mall owners decided to put a small amusement park at the end of one of the parking lots, with a few small rides and game booths and refreshment stands. (In the most-northern lot, from the fading echoes of the area's indigenous past, they placed an enormous totem pole—its brightly-painted Thunderbird head and spread wings at the top seeming to watch, like a towering sentinel or masthead of a great ship, over the forested, still mostly-undeveloped lands to the north.) The amusement park was nothing like the large parks a few miles away on Highway 99, with their towering roller coasters and haunted houses, but to now six-year-old Glen, it was still exciting and fun, even if he just rode the merry-go-round or the small Ferris Wheel.

And so once or twice a week, usually in the afternoon after first grade, Glen would climb into his family's old Studebaker with his mother and little sister, Cindy, and ride to Northgate, where they would first visit the stores offering the items Mrs. Gray was seeking that day, and then, if there was time and their mother wasn't too tired, visit the amusement park where Cindy and Glen would each get one ride and often some candy or a soda.

* * *

With all the new families with young children, there soon were many newly-constructed schools throughout the growing residential areas, but the nearby elementary school where Glen's mother had enrolled him for kindergarten, and then first grade, was old and dark and made of brick, and it looked old.

Glen soon became friends with many of his classmates and would often visit them at their homes after school to play, or they to his. They mostly lived in Glen's neighborhood, or within a few blocks, except for one somewhat smallish boy, Gordon, who had become a particularly good recess playmate, who lived in the opposite direction from the school in a neighborhood of extremely large homes sitting on wooded lots that lined a tall bluff that overlooked the nearby Inland sea of Capers Sound.

The vast majority of the houses throughout the city, and for that matter the entire region, were small and of modest design, and the families of low or moderate income, except for a very few isolated neighborhoods where the wealthy lived. And in the case of *The Vistas*, the neighborhood where Gordon lived, the very wealthy; and the large wooded lots on which the box-shaped, three-story houses sat were like small parks.

Back then, in that area of the country, most all of the children of the wealthy attended the same public schools as everyone else, and the schools and homes and all the different neighborhoods were all near to each other and interconnected. So it was not out of the ordinary when Glen's mother drove him into the nearby gated community to drop him off at Gordon's home to play one day after school. (Later, as an older boy, when the first images of the civil unrest storming the south began appearing on the evening news, Glen asked his father about poor neighborhoods in Sealth, the city where Glen and his family lived, and about the Negroes of Sealth, and his father, with the unmistakable and impression-setting-tone of sincere concern toward the southern struggle, quietly responded that there were some streets toward the center of town where the city's black people primarily lived, some just down the hill from Fifteenth Street, where the homes were of terrible poverty.)

Coming up the long driveway in the Studebaker that late fall day and pulling under the pillared canopy, Glen and his mother were met by Gordon and his mother coming out the large front door, with Glen jumping excitedly out of the car almost before it had come to a complete stop. After greeting an equally excited Gordon, who immediately yelled for Glen to follow, they ran toward the side of the house and down the long lawn of the gently sloping backyard while Glen's mother remained on the front porch to talk briefly with Gordon's. Running across the damp green grass, which ended at a grove of tall shrubs and trees, Glen suddenly yelled: "Wow!" as he could now see where they were headed through the trees.

From back at the house a woman's voice called out: "Gordon—stay on this side of the fence." It was Margaret, the house cleaner and part-time nanny, who was watching with folded arms from the wide patio in the cool November air.

"Okay!" Gordon yelled back, and then excitedly to Glen, "Come on. I'll show you a really neat place." And they headed onto a well-worn path that wove through the thinly scattered growth. Soon there was much daylight coming through the trees and the trail suddenly stopped at a low fence, and, approaching slowly, they saw the edge of the bluff just beyond the fence and beyond the bluff the immense open expanse of the sea. The steep bluff dropped easily a hundred feet down to the rocky shore and dark waters of the sound that stretched to each side for as far as they could see and straight across for many miles to the forest covered hills of the western peninsula. And there, towering above the hills, the snow-covered peaks of the Astoria Mountains rose into the gray sky. Far out on the water, like an elongated cake on a barge, the white sides and top of a ferry approached from the peninsula, while to the distant north, a huge freighter, its stacks spewing dark smoke, steamed toward the open straits and the ocean beyond. Standing silently below the tall madrona grove at the top of the bluff, Gordon and Glen were but two finite specks in the immense swirling current of the surrounding terrain.

Then, once again from behind came the woman's voice. "Gordon ... your mother has cookies back at the house for you and Glen when you want them." Margaret had wandered down from the house to keep an eye on them.

"Okay!" Gordon yelled.

"Wow!" Glen said from behind the fence, his eyes wide, stretching forward to see as far over the bluff as he could. "This is the biggest cliff I've ever seen!"

"It's my favorite place," Gordon said.

"I like it!" Glen said excitedly, as broad a smile as possible crossing his face.

"Come on!" Gordon suddenly shouted. "Let's get cookies!" And together they ran back into the trees.

* * *

"What's wrong, sweetheart?"
"A nightmare, momma."
"Another bad dream?"
"Uh huh. Will you stay? ... Please?"
"You want me to stay? All right, just for a while. Move over."
"Thanks, momma."

* * *

 The two old men climbed down off the northend bus and saw the light was green and hurried across the busy street and got to the other sidewalk just before the cars began to come. They took a few steps and looked into the gray sky:
 "Oh, George, it's true—look what they've had made! This totem, so tall, a Potlach! We are such old men!"
 "And it is a long-house, Arthur! A great long-house!"
 "A long-house with stores."
 "I don't know this story, but look at these animals—this carver, he must have been a Sahk-TAHBSH. Do you ever see the Sahk-TAHBSH clan, anymore?"
 "No, not even since they moved to Lummi. When I was a child, my father told me he remembers when they lived on the inside, across the water by the bluff on the cove. But that was a very long time ago."
 "Arthur, did you bring money for the movie?"
 "...No."

THREE

When Glen was in the third grade his family moved again, this time to a new and larger home which they were able to purchase, a few miles further across the city. The two-story house, with its neatly trimmed lawns and gardens, was one of many in a new development that was still under construction near the shores of a large lake, and much closer to the electrical utilities company where Glen's father was employed as an engineer.

The deep, blue lake, which was several miles across and many miles long, was separated from Glen's new home by a tree-covered ridge, with the new development on the floor of a small valley that had yet another stream running through one side and more fields. In one of the fields, half buried in dirt, sat the rotting, grass-clogged shells of several old horse-drawn wagons that had once been part of the valley's original farm. The owner of the land, now in his eighties, still lived in his original homestead on the nearby shore of the lake where he still kept horses and several more functioning wagons.

One warm August evening that first summer, as Glen came out the door of his new home, from up the street he heard the strange yet unmistakable sound of horse hoofs clopping on pavement, a sound he had only heard before on pony rides at the city zoo and on the many westerns that appeared daily on their black and white television in the basement recreation room. And there, sitting at the reins of an old wagon moving slowly up the street, was the man who once owned the farm and the land where the development that contained Glen's new house was now being built.

In his tennis shoes, summer shorts, and tee shirt, Glen stepped out to the driveway as the horse and wagon slowly moved by, passing in front of several of the neighbors cars parked on the dirt shoulder across the street before disappearing around the long curve at the end of the block. Glen thought briefly about fetching his bicycle from the garage and attempting to follow, but quickly concluded that the wagon would soon be beyond the allowed boundaries of his unsupervised terrain; and he drifted back toward the porch, the sound of the clopping hoofs slowly fading in the August air.

* * *

In the middle 1950s, throughout the city's large northern end, there were many other forests and fields and streams, nestled between the growing residential and commercial districts, most of which Glen explored throughout his grade school years, until they were almost all gone: sold, divided into lots, and developed.

* * *

They didn't recognize these boys; they were not from their street and were at least two or three years older, sixth or seventh graders. But then Glen and Steven had never before ventured this far into these woods. Had they overextended the boundaries of the new freedom that had been granted with increased age? Now the boys were coming toward them; that's right, just keep walking, ignore them, mind your own business. But they seemed suddenly very alert, glad to see them; there was that unmistakable look of trouble: like on the faces of the older boys at school who were regularly seen being taken down to the principal's office; and then came the fear. What? What did these boys want? Oh, fine, you are not going to let us pass. No, Steven and I are not from around here—on 102nd; yes, that's where we live. In the bag? My lunch. No—no! Don't! Give it back! NO! ... The ground is muddy ... it is very muddy ... my pants ... my face ... my coat ... my new coat ... MY NEW COAT! LEAVE ME ALONE! ... Wait for me, Steve! ... WAIT! ... I don't know which way—I don't know. Run—RUN! ... I know I'm crying ... I know ...

FOUR

Compared to the elementary school, the junior high school was immense, and with a seemingly much greater diversity of students—at least as to income, as the students were still vastly Caucasian. But the range of economic backgrounds was enormous: wealthy kids from homes with maids along the lakeshore mixed with those from pockets of near Appalachian-like poverty, all within the vastly blue-collar neighborhoods of the area; and everything in between.

Although he by no means excelled at them, the still averaged-sized—and in the summer sandy-haired (although with the constant crew cut it was difficult to tell)—Glen, enjoyed sports, and in the summer before that first year of junior high, he turned out for the local Pop Warner football team. This resulted for the first time in his being pulled away from his family, and greatly broadened the range of influence of his peers.

In the early days of the season, in the mid-August heat, Glen would usually leave the practice field in the late afternoon with two teammates headed in the same direction, one of whom, Clark, would always have a crumpled pack of cigarettes he had stuck under a nearby rock or bush, and, after they were down the street and away from any adults, he would pull them out.

"Hey—give us one," the other kid, Fairfield, said on the season's first walk with Glen and Clark, his helmet at his side, his wide shoulder pads bulging from under the jersey on his skinny frame, his rubber cleats stirring the dirt shoulder of the residential road.

"Glen don't smoke," Clark laughed back in his whining, surprisingly low voice, his face caked with dirt from the hot practice, a cloud of dust trailing his feet as well. "He don't smoke—and he don't like clouds."

"Clouds?" Fairfield said in his high, cracking voice.

"Yeah, clouds ... Girls, stupid."

"I smoke," Glen lied, his voice also high and cracking; he had snuck one from his parents a few times but had lasted only a few puffs. "Give me one."

"Clouds?" Fairfield said again, confusedly. He was nowhere near as tough as Clark but at least he knew how to deal with him.

Clark lived with his mother in a small house near Northgate in one of the oldest blue-collar neighborhoods in Sealth, which was also the same neighborhood that had produced Tommy Johnson and Ed Norton and Carl Diminski. But whereas Glen and his friends were anonymous new seventh graders at the three year school, Tommy Johnson and his friends were ninth graders and well known. As true greasers from the 1950s they were relative anomalies with their hair combed back and up in front in a wave, like 'Kookie Burns' of the popular television series *'Seventy-Seven Sunset Strip'*. And with hand-sewn precision they had meticulously tapered in their Levis blue jeans to make them skin tight and wore scuffed-up pointed, black-leather shoes; but mostly it was an unfathomable air of toughness that seemed to radiate from somewhere deep inside. There were street fighters at the large, aging, brownstone school, and then there was Johnson and Norton. They were friends and had enough mutual respect that they never had to fight one another (or maybe they had once already at a younger age) and seemed simply to enjoy their somewhat legendary status. But they were not bullies: they were genuinely friendly and fair with everyone; even with Fairfield and Glen and the other seventh graders. It is just that it was innately known; you could sense it: like you could sense the seriousness of the vice-principal with the ruffled suit and sagging eyes who you saw in the crowded hallways only briefly, most often from a distance, always moving; that if you offended either—Johnson or Norton—you risked great damage, both physical and emotional. Of course, one look at Tommy Norton, whom it was widely rumored regularly lifted weights and was of a low, wide, muscular frame, told you all you needed to know about personal safety. As for Diminski, his status was legendary not for being tough, but because he had grown his hair somewhat long and combed it down in front, as was rumored to be a style in England and other parts of America. And longer hair then, at that school in that neighborhood, was daring unto its own. And Clark was an unusual combination of the two, as he, also, had much longer than average hair—although not as long as Diminski's—and was muscular and tough, or at least he was known as tough.

"Yeah, clouds—chicks," Clark said from the side of the road with the unlit cigarette in his lips. "The new '*Crabs*' song; don't you know? 'Get Off My Cloud'. So the guy is like saying: 'Get off my chick—get off my cloud'." Clark struck a match and lit the cigarette.

"Wow—really?" Fairfield said in awe.

Clark looked at him with contempt.

"Boy ... I never knew that," Fairfield said, seemingly speaking to himself as much as to Clark.

Walking with his two friends along the tree-lined street in the afternoon sun, Glen didn't say anything; he instead concentrated on the burning cigarette that Fairfield now held and was about to hand him and hoped he would be able to inhale without coughing.

* * *

    Along with a more varied peer pool, skintight pants, and scruffy shoes, there was also, for the first time, the boy-girl component at the junior high school, and, after more or less observing for a year, Glen developed a significant crush in the eighth grade on a girl who was in several of his classes. Following through, however, proved more difficult than he had imagined from his observations of various other couples at the school. Eventually, however, after many months of showing up around her locker and making clear his interest—at times by just smiling and saying 'hi' (but more often by the anthropologically-confirmed adolescent-ritual of 'clowning around')—he worked up the nerve one afternoon to ask if he could walk her home from school. And so began a lengthy teen-age courtship from winter through spring of long walks, school-sponsored weekend dances—which included the heart-stopping slow-numbers—and the previously mentioned ritual of nervous clowning.
    By late spring, word filtered back to Glen that if he did not soon 'pin' her—ask her to go steady by presenting her with a 'pin'—usually an inexpensive necklace or tie-tack or other small ornament—she was going to give up and say good bye. So Glen went quickly to the recently opened clothing store at Northgate that catered primarily to teen-agers, and picked out a new necklace, one with the recently popular Maltese Cross, and presented it to her the next day in front of her house after the walk home from school, while asking if she would go steady with him. And Karen Greene said yes to Glen Gray and they both stood for a moment looking at each other and then Glen put his arms around her and they held each other just like one of the many slow dances they had been a part of that winter and spring. Then, from the open kitchen window, Karen's mother called to her; and they quickly disengaged and left for their homes and spent most of the remaining day and night within the safe confines of their sociologically-stumping bedrooms, simply observing the wonderfully altered universe they now inhabited.

***

Between the increasingly numerous teen-age clothing stores along the old, pre-mall commercial stretch of nearby Perkins Way, and those at Northgate, as well as the shady, grassy parks on the shores of the lake, Glen and Karen logged many miles on foot that summer, holding hands, embracing, and, when Glen and a neighborhood kid got the door put on their ramshackle tree house, and the ladder improved, kissing.

The dating highlight that summer, though, was the all day 'teen fair' being held downtown in the old municipal armory that the local rock and roll radio station, KMR, put on, to both celebrate and capitalize on the rapidly increasing cultural influence of pop and rock music. And so on a cloudy Saturday in mid-July, Glen and Karen caught an early bus to the armory grounds at the edge of Sealth's downtown (a largely industrial area rumored to be the future site of a World's Fair, with the expectant result of enhancing Sealth's present minor national-status) and there immersed themselves for six straight hours in a teen-age ecstasy of local rock bands, food, games, and fellow teens from all over the city dressed in the latest fashions, all under one enormous roof. Then there were the carnival rides and game booths outside that were erected each summer for the city's youth, and by the end of the day, Karen and Glen couldn't imagine life providing greater pleasure, as they rode the noisy city bus back in the early evening, arm in arm on the back bench, happily exhausted.

***

As July turned to August, though, Karen, apparently, could imagine life providing greater pleasure, and one warm crowded day at Thornton's Beach on the nearby lake shore, when Glen had half-unknowingly snubbed her by going first to lay down with some other friends instead of her, she came marching over and gave him back the necklace.

Now came a painful new sensation: the sinking of the heart, the sudden shattering of the previously invincible universe, the vile spew of inner chaos. Too dumbfounded to speak, Glen just stared blankly at her now more-beautiful-than-ever, one-piece-clad rear, disappearing back into the crowded beach, as the many jeers and laughs from his buddies who had witnessed the event seared like salt on an open wound.

Days of desperate negotiating got her back for almost a week, but by the following Friday, in the loud, back-beat-thumping darkness of the end-of-summer teen-dance at the community center, the very place where their teen-age love had most fully blossomed, she ended it for good, saying simply that she wanted to date other boys. Now the sinking returned with a vengeance: it was not humanly possible that life could be this painful, he thought.

Outside the dance in the warm night air, Glen wandered numb through the jam of parents picking up children, over to a boy he barely knew who was smoking a cigarette off to the side with a few other kids.

"Can I have one?" Glen quietly asked. But instead of giving him one the boy made him pay a dime and then after getting it lit, before he could take even two drags, Glen saw his father's Buick turning into the parking lot and he quickly threw the cigarette to the ground.

* * *

"Are they on?"
"No—but Mom, come quick, they're almost on—hurry."
"I'm coming, Cindy ... I'll be right there ... I'm coming
"Hurry, Glen!—they're almost on! Oh ... That's them—they're on! THEY'RE ON!!"
"God ... is that them?"
"Which one's Ringo?"
"The drummer."
"Look at that hair!"
"Can you hear the music? I can't hear the music."
"Look at the girls!
"Mom ... Look—look at Cindy!"
"Good heavens, is she crying?"
"DON'T LAUGH!"

FIVE

Glen picked up the telephone as soon as it rang: "Hello?"
"Glen—it's Pete. We'll be by; quarter to eight."
"Okay." Glen hung up and went into his bedroom and looked again at the shirts hanging in the closet. He thought for a moment and then took off the plaid burgundy shirt he had on and exchanged it for the green corduroy one. He tucked it into his jeans, gave his collar-length hair one last look in the mirror, then headed for the front door.
"Where are you going?" his sister Cindy asked, coming out of the kitchen with an apple.
"Out."
"Again?"
"Again," Glen said and then to his mother who was in the living room reading with his father: "Going out, Mom."
"Okay, dear, have a good night."
On the front porch, he took out a cigarette and waited in the early June light for Pete and Tim. There were several kids playing

on bikes on the gravel shoulder across the street, just as Glen had done only a few years before, and a few houses down, the buzz of Mr. Caldwell mowing his lawn filled the warm evening air.

Later, riding across the city's north end in the back of Pete's car, Glen unbuttoned his shirt and pulled out the tail with the air too warm for corduroy, even with all the windows rolled down and the wind rushing hard against his face.

"So, what did you get, Rainier?" Glen asked Tim, who was riding up front with Pete, and whose brother, Dean, had bought them the beer.

"Yep," said Tim, his tall, skinny frame turned toward Glen.

Glen had grown considerably during high school—so much and rapidly that his parents had become concerned enough to voice their worries to Dr. Anderson, the family physician, who assured them it was nothing abnormal—to where he now towered over many of his classmates. But unlike skinny Tim, Glen was full-boned and broad-shouldered and with girth and plenty of weight. (Given his size, there had been one tryout with the High School football team, instigated, somewhat oddly, by Mr. Stevens, Glen's science teacher, with whom he had developed a minor rapport. It was Mr. Stevens's hope that the team would be a means of both broadening and adding balance to Glen's high school experience. But after a week of the hot grueling practices, Glen realized it was a far cry from the Pop Warner teams of earlier years, and, with the rapid decimation of the initial excitement and fire, he limped into the trainer's room from the painful foot blisters he had acquired and turned in his equipment.) (The crew cuts required for the basketball team had, in Glen's self-conscious adolescent mind, immediately eliminated that possibility.)

"Dean said he was getting Rainier for himself," Tim said from the front seat of the car, "so he just grabbed another case ..." He turned a little further toward Glen. "Six bucks—give me two."

Glen pulled two dollars from his pocket and handed them to Tim. "It's not half bad," he said, taking one of the bottles and a can-opener from Tim, the wind still streaming steadily through the window, his straight, sandy hair blown back. "Seems like I've just been drinking a lot of 'Oly' lately." The bottle fizzed when he pried off the cap.

"Yeah?" said Pete from the drivers seat, glancing into the rearview mirror, his curly hair blowing slightly in the wind, his black, horn-rimmed glasses spread loudly across his face but not having hindered his appeal to the girls of their high school. He drove the old Ford steadily down the wide arterial, his elbow out the window, heading west into the setting sun, the large totem pole at the entrance to Northgate passing by on one side. "Yeah, me too; 'Oly's' cheap—but it's good, too. If we get more later we can get 'Oly'."

No one responded to the 'Oly' plan but it was understood that it was unanimous.

"I sure hope the Garden is cooking," Tim said emphatically as the houses and cars and people in their yards passed by.

"It should be," said Pete. "Friday night—end of school year." With his elbow still out the window, he glanced rhythmically back and forth from the road to the houses, the houses to the road. "Mark said him and Felton hit on Tuesday. He said they'd never seen so many girls on a week night."

Tim looked over, his face seeming to light up; and he took a drink from his beer. *"Oh yeah,"* he half spoke, half sang to himself.

Glen smiled hearing Tim and drank from his beer. "There's supposed to be a lot of people at Darren's, too. There'll probably be a lot of girls there. He knows Nancy Stewart real well. She always brings tons of her friends from Roosevelt."

"Christ ... Roosevelt," Tim echoed from the front seat, sounding humorously disgusted, the car now stuck at a busy intersection. "You have to be some kind of rocket-scientist for those ladies."

"Hey, no shit," said Pete, and he accelerated with the green light, the six clanging-cylinders of the engine straining from the driver's imagination.

The road crested a small ridge and the hazy outline of the distant mountains were now visible below the reddening sky of the setting sun. "Those rich Laurelhurst girls—Lordy." Pete shook his head. "Hey, what say we get some smokes before the Gardens. I'm almost out."

Golden Gardens Park, on the rocky shores of Capers Sound, ebbed and flowed greatly, like the sound's twelve-foot tides, every few months between crowds of high school and college kids, and the police. (Capers Sound: The first glimpse of shoreline and smell of saltwater never failing to unleash in Glen a flood of childhood memories of hazy summers on the inland sea: from the oily ferry docks of Sealth's downtown waterfront, to the tree-covered islands of the Juan de Fuca archipelago a hundred miles to the north, and every driftwood-lined bluff and beach in between.) At Golden Gardens, the large numbers of kids drinking and hanging out would bring the police after a while which would send the kids away which eventually would draw fewer, then no police, which would result in the kids gradually coming back and the cycle repeating itself. The park was a great gathering place in the city's north end, especially in the evenings in the spring and summer when the days lengthened and the sun set further and further north over the Astoria Mountains across the dark waters of the sound. The long parking lots sat directly on the water separated from the nearest residential areas by a heavily forested greenbelt, so the police, when they came, had to drive in from Ballard, a mile or so away.

The Fairlane wound through the trees down the steep hillside and when they came to the hairpin at the bottom they quickly saw that the police had not been around in quite a while. The parking lots, roughly divided into the hot rod section near the main entrance, and everything else south of there, were overflowing in a sea of people and cars.

Pete pulled into the hot rod lot to have a look around and began the slow crawl through the jam of cars and people and the noise and smoke. There were many kids walking around with beer cans and sitting on car hoods and on the grass strip between the water and the lot, and every now and then some adults or a family with small children would accidentally wander through, usually quite quickly.

Most of the hot rods weren't the true roadsters of the late forties, but more regular sedans of the mid-to-late fifties, and some early-sixties, that were heavily modified to be loud and fast. The noise at times was deafening and they never went anywhere without a momentary igniting of the oversize rear tires which accounted for much of the smoke; although some also was from the many small beach fires in the gravelly shore that extended north beyond the lots.

Not surprisingly there were no places to park in the hot rod area so Pete continued slowly through, but when he got to the end he suddenly popped the clutch on his aging wreck which made the car lurch; and Tim whacked him on the shoulder and some kids standing nearby yelled.

"Shit, Pete—fool!" Tim said and tried to pinch Pete's neck.

"Over there," Glen said from the back, pointing to a parking spot that had just opened in the other lot. Here the cars were slow station wagons and family sedans, a lot of them borrowed from parents; and Pete backed into the space. Across the lot was the sea and beyond the sea the mountain peninsula with the still snow-tipped peaks and the now orange sun descending rapidly toward them.

They got out with their beers into the warm evening air, Tim and Glen lighting cigarettes, and stood beside the car looking at all the people. Some girls drove by in a white Rambler and Pete and Tim and Glen all looked hard but no one did anything and they looked at each other and grinned and thought they could probably do better later and took drinks from their beers.

Some girls walked by.

"How's it going there?" said Pete, smiling hard.

But they gave no response other than a quick glance as Pete held out his beer, still smiling; and he could see now that they were somewhat older, possibly even in college, and definitely uninterested, and, shrugging, Pete turned to Glen.

"Hey—over there," said Glen, nodding toward three girls sitting on a curb a few cars down. They weren't smoking or drinking anything and from a distance seemed mildly amused at the surrounding chaos, and one of them, with light, straight hair, and shorts and a sleeveless top, leaned back and the light of the setting sun caught a corner of her face, and Glen walked toward her. "Hi," Glen said, glancing at her and moving as though he was just passing by; but he suddenly stopped and came over to the curb.

"Hi ..." she said and smiled; and Glen could see the depth of her eyes and smoothness of her skin, and he gestured with his hand, asking to sit. Hesitating only briefly, but still with a grin, she slid over to make room and Glen sat down and Pete and Tim came over and said hello and sat beside the other two. One, very attractive and with dark hair, seemed fairly tall and athletic—although it was difficult to tell from her sitting position on the curb—and the other was thinner and had more reddish hair and was wearing glasses.

"Where are you from?" Glen asked, thanking God for beer as he took a sip. She was pretty, he thought, and seemed cool.

"Up north," she said. "We go to Ingraham."

"Oh yeah?" Glen smiled. "Ingraham, how's Ingraham?"

She glanced down, smiling. "Oh, it's not that great." She looked at her two friends, grinning, then to Glen. "Where do you go?"

"Lincoln," Glen said.

"Yeah? What year?"

"Juniors." He held his beer out to her.

She pushed her hair back and took the bottle. "We're all sophomores," she said, taking a small drink, then handing it back and glancing around again. A car screeched its tires and everyone looked. "Actually, we've only been down here once before."

"Really? What's your name?"

"Julie."

"I'm Glen."

She smiled slightly and looked away. Pete was talking to the tall, dark-haired one. She was quite attractive. All three were dressed similarly in cut-off jeans and sleeveless tops and open-strap shoes. Tim was not talking to the reddish-haired girl who was sitting between him and Pete. They both seemed to be trying to listen to Pete and the attractive brunette.

"It gets pretty wild down here," Glen said. "It's been getting more and more crowded all the time. When it gets dark out they race."

"Really?" the light-haired girl said. "Where?"

"Over there." Glen pointed to an area of the other lot. He put his cigarette out in the grass and took another drink from his beer. "Oh—we have a whole case if you guys want one."

She didn't answer and glanced away, a slight grin still present.

"So—Ingraham can't be that bad," Glen went on, "can't be any worse than Lincoln."

"Well … It's kind of a jock school. The football team is like—the 'kings'."

"Yeah?—We sure don't have that problem at Lincoln." He grinned widely. "Pete—did the football team win any games last year?"

Pete looked over, slightly confused. "One," he said matter-of-factly and then went back to his conversation with the brunette.

"One," Glen repeated to the light haired girl, Julie; and he shrugged his shoulders and took another drink. Out on the water, several sailboats drifted slowly toward the nearby marina in the near windless air as the reddening sun continued its descent toward the mountains. "Hey, we know where there's going to be a party in Wallingford later. You guys should come."

"Yeah? … cool." She turned to her dark-haired friend who was talking to Pete. "Kim—they know where there's a party."

"Yeah? Really? You want to go?—Let's." She sounded very self-assured. Since they had sat down she had seemed to be enjoying herself, talking and laughing loudly.

"Yeah, let's," Julie repeated, and then to Glen, "Okay, we can follow you."

"All right," Glen said and held out his beer again but this time she declined.

A short ways over, two fast-looking cars were suddenly side by side, screeching their tires and engines, preparing to race. Everywhere people quickly began to stand as the long stretch of road in front of the cars cleared to make way. Then one of them gunned it and the other hit his and they shot up the road; and their engines screamed a deafening roar and thick smoke poured from the rear tires and they each hit second gear and then suddenly slammed their brakes and quickly slowed, both having known beforehand that they weren't going to get out of second.

"—*Shit!*" Tim yelled, grinning broadly as the ringing in everyone's ears slowly cleared.

They all stood up and fanned the thick haze of smoke that hung in the air.

"Look ... we'll pull out," said Pete, knowing that, with the exception of Tim, everyone was ready to leave, party or no party. The crowd grew noticeably more animated following the race and other modified vehicles began lining up.

"Kim's driving," Julie said. "Drive slow, there's a lot of traffic." She fanned some more. "Where in Wallingford?"

"Off Stone—not far from Greenlake," Glen said. "We'll go slow—follow us."

With the sun now behind the mountains, the mostly cloudless sky slowly reddened and darkened as the two cars left the crowded park and headed up the wooded hillside into the city. They moved steadily through the endless residential neighborhoods, Pete keeping the girls close behind in the mirror, and, reaching Wallingford, turned onto Stone where the traffic began to thicken within a few blocks. When he pulled onto Densmore he almost had to come to a complete stop from the amount of cars parked on each side of the narrow street.

The loud thump of pop music from a record player could now be heard coming from a house in the middle of the block and a few people were standing in the front yard. Pete crept slowly past and drove down to the next block where there were places to park and pulled over beneath a row of thick-trunk maples, their new summer leaves full and green. The girls pulled in behind and they all got out of the cars into the warm June air.

"Look, Peterson's here," Tim nodded toward a car across the street.

"Yeah—he was coming with Stacy and Chris is what he told me," Glen said.

Julie and Kim came up to where Glen and Pete stood in the darkening sky beside the car while the redhead with the glasses stood back a way. Then everyone went up the tree-lined street toward the house with the music; and through the brightly lit windows they could see the crowd inside, and, following Pete, they filed through the front door and into the packed living room.

Everywhere, small groups of high-school aged kids stood talking loudly over the music and drinking from cups of beer. A short, almost baby-faced kid in cutoffs and a wide-striped rugby shirt came into the room and, seeing Pete and the others, smiled broadly and went over to Pete. "Peter!" he said loudly. "I was wondering when you guys would make it ... Hey—'Junk'," he said to Glen, calling him by one of the seemingly dozens of nicknames he had acquired throughout his youth.

"We were down at the Gardens," said Pete. "Man, place was packed." He glanced toward the girls. "Hey, this is Kim ... and ... Julie?—Julie ... and ...?"

"Carol," said the redhead over the loud music and talking; and she lifted her glasses further up her narrow nose. All three of the girls were standing very near to each other in the crowded room.

"This is Darren," said Glen, finishing the introductions.

"The keg's in back," said the baby-faced kid. "It's a dollar a cup. But we got two more coming—at least."

"A dollar a cup," Julie said, turning to her friends.

They all paid and Darren briefly disappeared before returning with some large paper cups and then just as quickly disappeared again; and Pete led Glen and the three girls into the kitchen and out to the backyard while Tim stayed in the living room talking to some people.

There were at least twenty more people in the backyard, and, sitting upright on a picnic table on a corner of the patio, like a sacred alter, a keg of beer, its faded silver bulk badly scratched and dented from pilgrimages near and far of youth and alcohol. The fenced-in lawn stretched away from the patio and the evening light was fading but the air remained warm. Pete and Glen got through the small crowd at the tap and began filling theirs and the girls cups and then moved away.

"Kimberly?—*Kim!*" A girl called out loudly from across the yard and began to approach, her eyes open wide. Julie and Carol both laughed and moved with Kim toward the approaching blond-haired girl who was now also grinning broadly. The metallic gleam of braces showed from her wide smile. Her eyes, still wide, were clear and bright and she wore tight fitting jeans on her short frame. "What—are—you—guys doing here?" she asked haltingly, the wide grin still present.

"We came with them," said Kim, smiling almost as broadly as she motioned to Pete and Glen who stood a few feet back, watching with expressions of contentment. "We met them at

Golden Gardens ... What are you doing here? You don't know Darren do you?"

"Yeah, well, no. Chris knows his brother—do you know Gary?"

"No ..." said Kim laughing while at the same time sounding confused.

"Darren's brother," said the blond girl anxiously. "Chris goes out with him."

"God ... I don't know anyone from Lincoln," said Kim matter-of-factly.

"Yeah, I didn't," said the girl, sounding serious for a moment. "Neither did Chris ..." The braces suddenly gleamed again. "—She should be here later."

"Oh, this is Pete ... and Glen ..." Kim motioned toward where they stood on the lawn. "... This is Pam."

"Hello," said Pete, taking a step forward.

"Hi," said Glen, smiling and also moving up. He took a drink from his cup. "So, do you go to Ingraham, too?"

"Yeah—we're *Rams!*," the girl half shouted, grinning widely; and she seemed almost to bounce on the lawn as she drank again from her cup.

"Oh ... yeah—Rams," Glen repeated; and he laughed, but not as hard as the short blond. The sky continued to darken and more people came into the backyard and the loud sound of talking and laughter all but drowned out the scratchy rock music coming from the record player in the house.

"Do you want to sit?" Pete said, "—let's sit."

Tim came out of the house and made his way to the keg.

"—*Pam!*" Someone yelled out, almost shrieked to the short blond from across the lawn.

"I'll talk to you later," she said quickly to Kim, still grinning, and disappeared into the crowd.

"Let's sit down," Pete said again and stepped further back and lowered himself onto the grass with Glen and the girls following. At the keg, some younger looking kids were getting very loud, downing their beers as quickly as they could and laughing hard at each other.

Glen took a drink from his beer and turned to Julie. "That's a cool bracelet—is it silver?"

"Yeah, well, the plate is; this is just metal or something." She twisted the narrow band and Glen reached over and held her wrist for a closer look. She gave a slight grin and looked away.

Glen nodded approvingly and then let go and drank more of his beer and glanced around the yard. "So, Ingraham's a real jock school, huh? Actually, I think I have heard that before."

"Yeah, god, it really is. If you aren't like on the football team ... or going out with one of the players ..." She shrugged. "They just treat you like, you're nothing. God, I hate it."

With a slight grin, Glen shook his head. He pulled blades of grass from the lawn. "Nah ... Lincoln's not that bad. It's not big enough; it's just not that big a deal there." He looked over at Pete and Kim who were talking quietly a few feet away. Carol, the redhead with the glasses, leaned back on the other side, expressionless, her beer sitting beside her on the grass. "Hey, do you want to go inside?"

"Yeah."

They got up without saying anything to the others and headed toward the house with Glen leading. When it got crowded near the back steps, he reached back and found her hand and they weaved through the packed kitchen and into the living room where they stood to the side. The record scratched and boomed loud over the single speaker and a few couples danced on the floor where the rug had been rolled back. Still clutching hands, Glen and Julie cut quickly through the dancers to an open spot near the fireplace and stopped and took in the loud, crowded room. Tim was back inside and saw them from across the room and raised his cup into the air and they raised theirs in return. "I like this song!" Glen tried shouting into Julie's ear. "The Animals!"

"Who?" Julie half-shouted back over the crowd and the booming baritone of the singer that someone standing by the phonograph had just made even louder; and she squeezed Glen's hand.

"—*The Animals!*" Glen yelled again, now laughing. "They've been on KMR all month!" But he knew it was too difficult to try to carry on a conversation and shrugged his shoulders at about the same time she did and they each took a drink from their beers. Now a slower song came on and Glen suddenly set his and Julie's beers down and led her out to where the people dancing were embracing and slowly swaying to the singer's passionate voice. She moved her head toward his shoulder, and his face was very near to her smooth hair, and he pulled her closer. They swayed slowly in the crowded room as people continued to talk loudly and to move about; and the singer, his voice raspy and straining, pleaded emotionally: He did not know if he could make it, he sang, he did not know if he could go on since she had left. He had never known such pain, and whatever wrong he had done, it would never happen again, ever, of that she could be sure, if she would only just return.

Glen thought the singer probably knew a lot about things and that he was probably seldom, if ever, bored. He thought that the singer, who he had heard was from England, probably lived a very exciting life with many exciting experiences with girls, some of which would be painful, but that that was the price of such a life, and now he was releasing it all in his passionate, moving song; and Glen missed a half step just as Julie turned left instead of right, but he felt that it was probably his fault.

Then the singer let out a long final wail and the song ended and there was only the loud beer-fueled talk of the crowd; and Glen's eyes caught Julie's and they both stepped back in the now quieter room. And then over the heavily scratching record player came the loud clicking of drumsticks and the speaker blasted hard and a booming beat filled the room. But more people kept filing in—new groups who had just arrived; the little remaining space in the living room quickly disappearing; and Glen pushed Julie toward the kitchen, grabbing their beers off the table before going in. Now a fast moving Darren passed, his wide smile disappearing quickly after each brief greeting.

"Shit!" Glen yelled to Julie, "—place is packed," and he drank from his beer. Julie stood close, holding her cup, taking in the noisy crowd in the brightly-lit kitchen.

"—*Glen-o!*" A skinny kid with glasses and combed hair pumped Glen's free hand and laughed loudly. "*Heeeyyyyy!!*" he now drawled loudly with a wide smile to Julie who raised her cup and smiled. People were feeling good; they were happy, there at the residential party, talking loudly and laughing and drinking beer on an early summer night, almost everyone under age: it was exactly where they most wanted to be.

Now Darren was back in the kitchen and on the telephone: a neighbor had called, someone said; too loud, turn it down.

"—The cops are coming?" a woman's voice asked anxiously from across the room. And then quickly from others: "—*The cops are coming—*" and a few people headed for the door.

But only a few, and no cops showed up, and if anything it became even louder and the volume of the hi-fi slowly made its way back up, and the beer continued to flow.

Kim and Pete came through the kitchen holding hands and tipped their cups at Julie and Glen. "—*Eeeyyyyyyaaaahhhhhhhhh hh!*" Pete mockingly yelled, trying to imitate the general dialogue of the room.

"Yaaa ..." Glen started to respond but cut himself off and put his arm around Julie. He led her outside where the sky was now dark but for the faintest glow of red on the far western horizon. Beyond the fence, the dark distant outline of the houses and trees on the long ridge toward Northgate stood sharply against the faint western light.

There were still many people crowded around the keg and others standing and sitting about the quieter backyard and Glen headed toward a less crowded area of the lawn but stopped when Carol suddenly approached and asked Julie how much longer she wanted to stay.

"Gosh, I don't know," Julie said matter-of-factly. "What's Kim say? She's driving."

Carol headed toward the house without answering and Glen suddenly leaned forward and kissed Julie and she kissed him back and put her arms around his neck. There was a slight stumble as they stood on the grass, but they quickly straightened and kissed again. Julie shifted her head onto Glen's shoulder and held him tighter. Glen held tighter, too, and then they leaned apart for a moment and took sips from their beers which they had continued to hold in one hand. "How late can you stay out?" Glen asked in almost a whisper.

"Kim's got to have the car back by midnight."

"What time is it?"

She looked at her watch. "Almost eleven ... We probably have to get going before long."

"Look, give me your phone number, I'll call you tomorrow."

"All right."

Carol came across the patio from the house. A curly-haired kid in an open shirt stumbled into her path and asked loudly where her beer was. "Over there," she said, pointing behind him without slowing, and then was gone when he turned back around.

"Miss Carol," Julie called mischievously to her friend as she came up.

"We're going," Carol said, forcing a smile.

"Yeah? Where's Kim?"

"Inside. We're going to 'Sparky's—we're hungry."

"I've got to go," Julie said turning to Glen who had removed his arm when Carol came up.

"Phone number," Glen said.

"Let's go inside."

They made their way back into the house and Julie found a pen and wrote her number down and gave it to Glen. The house was still packed and loud and smoky, but there didn't seem to be as many girls as earlier; and the boys drank their beers and drew deeply from their cigarettes and talked pointedly.

Kim and Pete came in, no longer holding hands, but smiling, and everyone said goodbye and then the girls were suddenly out the door and gone; and Glen and Pete took sips from their beers. They looked around a bit but didn't speak and Glen shoved a hand into his pocket and Pete took out a cigarette. Glen drank some more and Pete wandered over to a small group of people who were talking loudly and animatedly between drinks of beer and long drags off cigarettes, and listened, but didn't say anything. He stood for a while and then came back over to Glen who was looking around the room. "Hey ... you ready?" Pete said, blowing smoke into the air.

Glen looked around some more, "Yeah, guess so." He motioned to Pete's cigarette and took a deep drag and handed it back. "Hey, wanna get something to eat?"

Pete belched loudly, paused, then said, "Yeah—I'm starving. Grab Tim—let's go."

They found Tim out by the keg and filled their cups one last time and headed for the street.

"Ah, shoot," Pete said, turning suddenly, but continuing to walk backward toward the car, "did anyone say goodbye to Darren?"

"Yeah, I said we were taking off," Glen said.

Pete sent his cigarette into the street and turned back around, now with a slight grin. "So, Tim … how was Carol?"

"Ahhhhhhh … She said she had a boyfriend. I tried talking to her." Tim paused. "Crap—she was only fourteen."

"*What? No shit? Fourteen!?* Holy Toledo … fooled me."

"Tell me," Tim said, drinking from his beer. "Crap—fourteen … Well, how old was Kim?"

"I don't know," Pete said, turning to Glen: "How old was Julie?"

"Well, they said they were going to be juniors next year," Glen said, sounding both a little defensive and confused.

"Right," Pete said. "So that would have made them fifteen or sixteen."

"—Crap," Tim said again, still drinking from his beer, his expression as though he had bitten something sour and eliciting grins from Pete and Glen.

They reached the car on the dark street and got in. "Hey, what say we go to 'Zekes'," Glen said, "get some food—eat."

"Yeah—food," said Pete, slamming his door harder than he had intended; and, turning the ignition, he revved the engine loudly and pulled quickly from the curb, his beer and the steering wheel in one hand, and reaching for the radio dial with his other.

* * *

"Hello? … yes, could I speak with Julie, please? Oh? … do you know when she'll be back? Yeah? … could you please tell her that Glen called? Thanks."

Glen hung up the wall phone and crossed the room and dropped back onto the couch, and resumed staring at the flickering light of the television in the corner. Out the tall glass of the sliding doors, rain fell lightly onto the patio and the yard from the cool, overcast summer day. Stretching out further on the couch, he thought of how he would have to get a ride home from the bus boy job at the local Elks club later that night if the rain didn't let up.

On the black and white screen, an already grainy Johnny Weissmuller was fading fast as he swung from tree to tree while hollering loudly at a herd of stampeding elephants, their quick, jerky movements indicative of the movie's age. Glen strained to watch for another moment and then pulled himself up and went over and tried adjusting the antenna on the top of the set; but the screen crackled static and more fuzzy lines formed, and, knowing by heart what happened next anyway, he turned the TV off—cutting off a knuckle-scampering Cheetah—and went back to the couch. There were stacks of magazines and volumes of old books lining the shelves on the wall above him: sets of Stevenson's classics and American Heritage; an Encyclopedia Britannica and his father's old engineering journals; and he reached up and grabbed a recent issue of *Life* and looked at the cover. There was a large color photo of a soldier holding another soldier who was either dead or dying. They were waist deep in water along the banks of a river, and the water was brown. There appeared to be a great deal of pain on the alive-soldier's face, to where he looked like he was about to cry. He appeared slightly older than Glen, but otherwise just like Glen or any of his friends; except for his extremely short hair and the mud on his face and clothes and that he was about to cry. Glen flipped through the pages, most of which were large black and white photos, some of which were more of the soldiers in the far-off place, some of whom were unmistakably dead. He flipped through the rest of the pages, some with articles and photographs of different parts of America, some with people who were very happy and smiling, and then stuck the magazine back on the shelf. He stretched out further on the couch and stuck a small pillow under his head and stared at the white tiles of the ceiling. Then, from another area of the house, his mother's voice called out, "Glen—*dinner.*"

"Yeah ... okay." He continued to stare for a moment at the ceiling and then swung off the couch and left the room.

* * *

"No ... no ... no.—No." The girl paused in the front seat of the car. "No," she now said softly and nestled her face into Glen's neck, snuggling up closer against him.

"What?" Glen half-mumbled, ignorantly and self consciously, and with just the slightest sigh, as the teseness in his body slowly dissipated. He reached over and turned up the volume on the radio, then leaned further back in the wide seat of the Buick as the guitars and singer crackled more loudly through the speaker on the dashboard. The car sat in the dark empty parking lot overlooking the choppy waters of the lake that stretched for more than a mile to the light-speckled hills on the other side. "Hey, I know where we could probably get some beer," Glen said from the driver's seat, in a more optimistic tone, one arm around Julie.

For a moment, she didn't answer, looking out over the dark water. "... Hmmmmm, well, sure. If you want."

"What time is it?"

She looked at her watch. "Ten to nine."

"Nah, it's probably too late." He pushed the button on the radio for another station. "But, there is a store in Roanoke that'll usually sell. It's Chinese or something." He adjusted the dial. "But, nah; I think they close at nine on weekdays. We'd never make it."

In her white blouse and long, snug jeans, Julie straightened up in the seat. "I could call my brother."

Glen looked silently out across the lake. The faint green and red running lights of a distant, late summer boat moved along the far shore. "Well, what do you think? Is he home?"

"I don't know. We could try."

"Nah, I should have just got some earlier." He reached up and moved his hand across her cheek and she snuggled in again. "Well, get something to eat?"

"Sure, yeah," she said, straightening as Glen turned the ignition.

"All right, Zeke's," Glen said, and he put the car in reverse.

SIX

"Hey, let's go—we're going to be late!" From the hallway, Glen called loudly to his mother who came out of a bedroom and headed once again for the bathroom.

"Oh ... I'll be right there," she said, a trace of irritation in her voice, but smiling nonetheless at Glen who stood near the door in his dark suit.

"We should have plenty of time," Glen's father said, coming in from the living room. "Why don't you go warm up the car, son?" He reached into his pocket and handed Glen the keys. Whereas just a year earlier, Glen's eyes would have been even with his father's. He now looked down at the slender, slightly balding man who was himself almost six feet tall. "Cindy—let's go," Mr. Gray called to his daughter who was watching television in the recreation room.

"I'm coming."

Glen went out to the Buick parked in the driveway and got in. He started the engine, pushed the throttle a few times, and let it idle. He turned on the radio and flipped across the stations for a moment, then turned it off as his parents and sister came out the front door. They looked like people on their way to church or a wedding, dressed in their very best clothes; and they opened the doors and got in.

"You look so good," Glen's mother said, sitting beside him in the front seat; and she brushed the shoulder of his dark jacket. "Can we see your bracelet again?"

Glen held up his arm to show the small metal plate, held with the thin chain that encircled his wrist. His grandmother had given it to him at the previous Sunday's dinner at her home in Shelton, fifty miles to the south, where Glen's father had grown up. His grandfather, a jeweler, had made the bracelet as a graduation gift for Glen, shortly before he had suddenly died the previous fall. A simple inscription read:

To Glen
Love, Grandpa Gray

Glen held it higher to show his father and sister in the back seat. "It's almost like the one your girlfriend has," Cindy said.

"Who?—Julie Thornton? Sheesh—that was last year." Glen tightened his grip on the steering wheel. "You know it was Linda Campbell who went to the prom with me. Besides, I hear she has a new boyfriend." His mother looked over with a reminding nod. He then held up his other wrist to show everyone the new watch from his parents; and Mrs. Gray, her light, below-the-knee dress, smooth, and her hands in matching gloves, smiled broadly.

"Okay, I think Highway 99 will be the quickest, Glen," his father said.

"Will Mr. Turner be giving a speech?" Cindy asked.

"That's what the program says," Glen said, backing out of the driveway and heading up the quiet residential street.

"My, he's been there for ages, hasn't he?" said Mrs. Gray.

"No one likes him," Cindy said, her dress and top shorter, but of a similar style and color as her mother's. "I hope he retires before I graduate."

"You'll do just fine with whoever is the principal," said Mr. Gray.

Pulling onto 99, Glen moved into the light Saturday-afternoon traffic, crossing over the high bridge that led to the downtown area from the city's north end, the calm waters of the lake and canal below the bridge at the base of several tall, tree-covered hills, stretching out dark and gray under the overcast sky.

Just before the highway disappeared into the tunnel under the buildings of the downtown area, Glen pulled off and moved toward the large, new, civic arena where the commencement ceremony was to take place. The arena was one of the new buildings left over from the recently held World's Fair, and as they moved past the remaining old warehouses and apartment buildings of the area, they approached the strange mix of futuristic-looking structures from the fair, the most famous, a slender, curving observation tower soaring many hundreds of feet into the gray sky. In the middle of it all sat the old National Guard Armory where the teen-fair had been held those many years before; and Glen suddenly thought about Karen Greene and wondered if she was still in California where her family had moved just months after that long ago summer.

Glen pulled into a covered parking garage across from the arena as a steady stream of neatly dressed families made their way from the parking lots surrounding the civic grounds to the arena. In each group walked a young man or woman in a long black or purple gown and square-topped mortarboard that he or she would soon throw into the air to mark the end of their days in high school.

The Gray family left the car and joined the flow of people moving toward the arena, and, with the crowd thickening steadily, for just the briefest of moments as they climbed the wide, outdoor steps, Glen reached down and gently touched the new bracelet encircling his wrist; and they entered the large front doors and disappeared into the building.

SEVEN

"*Glen!* Hey—Glen! Hey—hey, how'd you do, man? What'd you get?" The short young man with glasses in the heavy flannel coat ran across the courtyard enclosed by the aging brick buildings toward Glen who was coming down the wide steps of Stevenson Hall. Glen was wearing blue jeans and a heavy, blue wool coat over various shirts and sweaters in the cold January air. The end of a scarf, wrapped around his neck, hung down the back of his coat and at times flipped about in the brisk wind.

"A 'D' … A god damn 'D'," Glen said, making no attempt to conceal his disappointment when his friend, Randy, was beside him. He paused and stared at Randy, waiting. "Well?"

"'C'," Randy said, suppressing a slight grin, trying to sound nonchalant, remembering Glen's repeated questioning of his long hours of studying for what Glen had insisted would be an easy exam.

"Come on," Glen said. "Let's see if we can get into the Embers."

"The Embers?" Randy said, looking up. "Well, yeah, I guess we can try."

The trees in the courtyard were bare and small hard piles of snow from an earlier storm were scattered about the frozen ground. They cut across the campus under the gray sky and out a small gate to a residential street lined with older one-story houses and small apartment buildings, and, turning at the end of the street, soon came to the first buildings of the downtown area of the small college town, located near the Canadian border, a hundred miles north of Sealth. Beyond the town were the dark forests of the nearby hills and beyond the hills the bottoms of the snow-covered mountains that disappeared into the low clouds.

Moving down the main street, past the storefronts and parked cars and the few people on the sidewalk, they came to a large wood door with the word 'Embers' across the front and went in. The warm room air rushed quickly out, swiftly closing the door behind them, and the men at the bar turned to look.

They took a few steps forward and then saw the bartender, also looking, his arms folded, his head beginning a slow back and forth motion. "No ... no ... No—no—no. I told you guys last week—out. You're going to get me closed down.—Now out."

Back on the sidewalk in the wind, Glen walked swiftly down the block as he pulled the scarf tighter. "Shit, what an ass—I haven't been in there in a month. What's he talking about?" Randy half ran at times trying to keep up with Glen's long strides. "Ah, hell, it's freezing anyway. You want to get some coffee?"

"Yeah, sure," Randy said.

"Come on."

* * *

At Bocca's, they hung up their coats and slid onto the upholstered benches of an empty booth halfway down the long narrow restaurant, and Glen swung a leg up and faced the counter that was opposite the booths. Leaning slightly up, he could see the top of his head in the dirty mirror behind the counter; and he quickly ran a hand through his uncombed hair. The huge, stuffed head of a moose with wide, curving antlers stared out from a mount above the mirror and various other smaller fish and game from the surrounding forests and streams lined the high walls. Music from a jukebox came through the door of a windowless lounge in the back.

"Coffee?" The middle-aged waitress set two menus in front of Randy and Glen and filled their cups when they nodded and then went back to the cash register at the end of the counter.

"So?" Randy stared at Glen, who continued looking toward the counter. "What about econ'?"

"'F'. Flunked ... failed ... screwed up." Glen swung his leg down and looked at Randy. "I think this is it."

Randy took a sip of his coffee. His horn-rimmed glasses sat low on his small nose. There were the faint traces of freckles on his face. "So, what are you going to do?"

"Enlist, I guess." Glen stared for a moment then poured sugar and cream from a dispenser into his cup and stirred. A young mother with two small children came through the door and a rush of cold air blew through the room. An old man and woman, nursing cups of coffee at the counter, turned to look at the tightly bundled kids.

Randy poured sugar into his coffee. "Wow, enlist, huh?" He shifted in his seat and pushed the sleeves of his shirt and sweater up his skinny arms.

"I'm '1-A'," Glen said, "what else can I do? They're going to draft me, man. If I wait for that they'll send me down there for sure." He took a sip of his coffee. "Although, maybe it wouldn't be that bad. Anyway, at least this way I'd have a chance of going to Germany ... or Japan ... or somewhere."

"Wow—Vietnam. Have you seen where it is? It's like this little piece of land—way down by China." Randy shook his head and pushed his glasses up. He looked at the menu. "Hey, you got any money?"

"Couple of bucks."

"Crap, I got one buck for the rest of the week. You getting anything?"

"Nah. I got some spaghetti back at my place."

Randy put the menu down and took another sip of coffee. "Crap, the army, man. But who knows, maybe it would be cool."

Glen leaned back in the booth and glanced again toward the counter. His thick sweater covered his wide shoulders and chest and his large arms.

"Hey, how about the navy?" Randy said.

"Nope, they aren't taking anybody anymore. They said I might have a chance for the Coast Guard … But, no; everything's going to be army for at least the next year, until they see what's going to happen down there." Glen took another sip. "Hey, I can handle it. My uncle was in the army in Italy, and he says it wasn't bad at all."

"Yeah?"

"Yeah. Anyway, I got over a year of college so maybe I can keep out of infantry."

"Really? You think so?"

"Maybe." He picked up his spoon and began tapping it lightly against his cup. "But, crap, who knows—maybe I'd like infantry. I think you get out fastest that way."

"Yeah?"

"Yeah, I think so." The waitress, who had been talking with the woman with the children, came over with her pad. For an old, local establishment like Bocco's, she was actually somewhat attractive, although somewhat older than Glen and Randy, probably in her early thirties. She did not, however, look as though she had ever been a student at the college.

"I guess we're just having the coffee," Glen said, attempting to smile.

She didn't seem annoyed but didn't say anything and wrote out the check and set it on the table. They both glanced toward her as she walked away.

"What are your parent's going to say?" Randy said.

Glen shrugged. "What can they say? Sure, they'll probably wish I'd tried harder in school … But … shit." He shrugged again and looked off.

"What's your girlfriend going to say? Have you said anything to her?"

"Sure; we talk about it all the time. She understands. I think she's been expecting it more than me."

"Man—" Randy took another sip, staring at Glen. "There sure are a lot of people going in: Tim Cummings; Deegan. And, oh, that guy from Marysville who was going out with Diane—Craig. They drafted him, like, two weeks ago."

"No kidding? Crap, that guy was a riot. Remember him with Diane at all those parties up at Ron's cabin last spring? Christ—guy was crazy." Glen looked off, smiling. "So, see? It might not be that bad." One of the small children shrieked. They glanced over. "And look," Glen went on, "you gotta look at the big picture—my uncle was talking about this, too, just the other night—you know, it wasn't that long ago Khrushchev was saying how he was going to 'bury' us—"

"But in Vietnam? I don't know …" Randy faced the entrance and looked out the tall windows to the street. The light was beginning to fade and a few more cars were passing by as the workday ended and bundled pedestrians walked by on the sidewalk out front. "Hey, it might snow," he said casually.

"Yeah? Good—you're still coming up to the mountains with us this weekend, right?"

"Yeah, man."

Glen rotated his cup. "… So, was that guy ever actually enrolled here?"

"Craig? Nah, I don't think so." Randy took a sip of his coffee. "Nah, I think he was just hanging around town, seeing Diane."

"Huh, yeah, I can understand that," Glen said.

"Yeah, no kidding." Randy now grinned and pushed his glasses up again. "Yeah, he was just waiting for the final word … You know, once you're '1-A' …" The grin disappeared and he looked quickly at Glen.

"Yeah, but really Rand'—it might not be that bad." Glen leaned forward. "Crap; I tried, man. But I just can't cut school right now. I thought I'd really like engineering—really. And, you know, those classes were okay. And I really like all the science stuff. But all that other crap: history; German. Christ, I was studying all night for that stuff. And for what?—'Ds'?"

"Yeah, wow. So what'd you think you'd do? Electrical engineering or something?"

"I don't know; that's like the old man. I was even kicking around teaching."

"Yeah? Like your girlfriend?"

Glen shrugged and glanced toward the counter. "Hey, you ready? Come on, let's see what Daryl's up to. Maybe we can get some beer—make something to eat. The misses is still at the library; still has a couple of finals. But she's definitely planning on coming this weekend. Ready?"

"Yeah; all right." Randy finished the last of his coffee.

"Here, this'll cover it." Glen threw a dollar on the table and slid out the booth. He tightened his scarf and put on the heavy wool coat and gave a quick wave to the waitress, and, with Randy following, headed for the door.

Dusk was falling as they moved up the sidewalk into the wind and the overhead street lamps came on and with the headlights of the cars and the lights from the stores, and even a few leftover Christmas-lights from the recently ended holidays, a dull glow cast over the darkening town. When they turned onto Bayview they saw the first snowflakes whipping past the street lamps and when they came to the brightly lit courtyard of the east dorm the swirls were heavy and the ground had begun to turn white.

EIGHT

"Here, right here.—*Pull!*—Can you reach it?" Daryl Dubelli, owner of the red Impala, crouched low in the snow under the back of the jacked-up car as Glen and Randy tried to pull on the metal lever to tighten the chains that encircled the tire. Barehanded and pulling fiercely on the stinging clip with red, numb fingers, Glen's face contorted grotesquely.

"There, that's good. You got it!" Randy shouted as Glen rolled quickly out from under the car and jumped up and buried his hand into the armpit of his heavy coat and squeezed with all his strength.

"All right—we're set." Daryl quickly inspected the two chained tires, then cranked the jack down and the car sank into the snow. A few feet away, vehicles clanking loudly with half-broken chains rolled slowly up the snow-covered highway curving along the wide river valley into the cloud-shrouded mountains. Except for vast dark-areas of towering rock-cliffs, the white of deep snow covered all that could be seen. Rising steeply up the mountain slope beside them, the forest lay buried in snow, and everywhere along the shoulder were the white mounds of snow-covered trees bent to the ground. To each side, the rapid-fire bursts of voices from people working on chains at other cars sliced the frigid air of the otherwise silent valley.

A woman, heavily dressed in a thick ski parka and ski pants, having returned from wandering up the wide shoulder of the chain-up area, approached the car and looked down at the tires. "Well, how's everything going?" Mittens covered her hands and a wool cap was pulled down far over her light brown hair.

"We're all ready," Daryl said, throwing the jack into the trunk.

Glen pulled his hand out from under his clothing and tried to blow warm air over it. "Ahhhhhh!—I *hate* those things," he said, seemingly to himself, referring to the chains and the strenuous half-hour ordeal they had just endured. Then he turned toward the woman and grinned. "But I'm ready—let's go! You ready, Jules?"

"I am a–ready," Julie Thornton said; and she looked warmly at Glen and smiled.

Suddenly, a giant road grader used for plowing by the highway department came thundering up the valley. It slowed when it reached the chain-up area and a column of cars pulled onto the wide shoulder. "Let's go!" Daryl shouted over the roar of the engine, and, moving quickly, they jumped into the Impala and continued up the highway.

Flakes began falling again from the low clouds as the car swayed through the deep tracks before them. "Hey, all right—more snow!" Randy said mockingly from the front passenger seat, as if the winter's near-record pack wasn't enough. Julie and Glen sat in the back, straining to see out the fogged windows, Julie in the middle between Glen and a stack of bags that reached almost to the ceiling. Now the snow began to fall hard and the valley narrowed and to one side the shoulder dropped off steeply to the dark river below. They rounded a long curve and for a moment came out of the clouds; and the high ridge across the valley ended and a string of tall snow-covered peaks came into view and directly behind the peaks, as wide as three of them together, the enormous base of a single, glacier-covered mountain rose upward before disappearing into the clouds.

"Esmeraldo," Daryl said of that which they had each long been silently anticipating, as he watched both the road and the enormous cloud-truncated volcano.

They looked silently at the rising mass of glaciers until the clouds again covered everything and there was only white in every direction and the swirling snow began accumulating again on the just-plowed road. They had been rising steadily for the last few miles and the trees of the surrounding forests became fewer and smaller and all but disappeared under the snow and then the clouds parted again and suddenly the jagged peaks were everywhere.

Rounding a final curve, there was a sharp cutoff and Daryl turned and the car bounced over rutted snow along a narrow road and into a long parking area. An old lodge and several other snow-covered buildings sat silently at the base of a large slope, and Daryl kept going until he reached a row of cars near the lodge and pulled up to a high snow bank. Groups of people walked toward the lodge carrying skis and sleds, and some with inner tubes, and on the slope above the lodge, the tiny, slow-moving forms of skiers glided down the mountainside.

"All right—yes—look at this!" Randy jumped excitedly out of the car and stood beside the open door and looked up at the ski slope. The air was cold as the snow came down slower now and they all got out and began pulling on sweaters and jackets and Daryl opened the trunk. There were two pairs of wooden skis stretched diagonally across the large compartment and under the skis was an inflated inner tube and Julie came back and pulled out the skis, handing the longer pair to Glen.

"Yes, I will swoosh this peak," Glen said, clutching his skis and grinning widely. "I will be 'Killy' ... I will soar ... I will soar on this mountain."

"Here," Julie said handing him his poles, "you might need these."

"Holy mackerel!" Glen said as his eyes widened below the bright yellow cap on his head. "Look how long these things are! ... Aren't these kind of long, ma'am?" Julie nodded without looking as she grabbed a bag from the back seat. She opened it and began searching for something.

"Wow, there really is a lot of snow," Daryl said, stepping up to the nine-foot bank in front of the car. "A hell of a lot more than last year, that's for sure."

"I know," Julie said, looking at Daryl with an attentive grin as she stepped over to where the skis leaned against the car. "Christen's already been up five times."

"Hey, over there.—Oh yes, yeah, there's the sleds." Randy pointed to an area back in the trees where a small crowd gathered with sleds and inner tubes and the plastic lids of garbage cans to slide down a short, steep run. At the bottom they bounced hard before crashing in the snow.

"Oh, yeah, momma!" Daryl said grinning. "Get me there."

"You taking the food?" Glen asked Daryl.

"We can just leave it in the lodge," Julie said.

"All right; good idea. We'll meet you and Randy there at lunch, Daryl," Glen said as Daryl got the inner tube out.

"At lunch, okay," Randy said, and he looked up at the ski slope. "Wow, you guys going on the chair?"

"All the way up," Glen said. "I'm going to the top."

"It's a pretty short chair," Julie said. She removed her cap and shook her shoulder-length hair and pinned it up with a couple of clips and then tucked it carefully back into the cap. The faintest trace of red showed on her lips. Glen and Randy looked at her. "… Honest … I've skied it a lot."

"That's short?" Glen said, looking again at the distant string of chairs moving slowly up the slope and disappearing over a ridge.

"We can go over to the side," Julie said, "It's not that bad along the tree line." She watched Glen scan the slope as she continued to arrange items in the pockets of her jacket. "Over to the left, honey."

"Where—there?" Glen pointed.

"The left. I'll show you when we get up there."

"Ho–*kay!*"

"Oh, man," Randy said grinning widely as he pushed his glasses up. "We'll see you in the hospital.—Good luck!"

"Yeah, yeah," Glen said. "Hey, it'll be a breeze." He glanced quickly again at the chair.

"All right," Daryl said, "so we'll see you in the lodge."

"In the lodge," Glen said, arranging more things in his bag. "Just sometime at lunch. Just go there and look for us."

"If you aren't there we'll look for you at Ski Patrol," Randy said; and he jumped back when Glen grabbed for some snow. "—Come on, Daryl!" Randy yelled, laughing; and he and Daryl took off with the inner tube across the packed snow for the sledding area.

Julie watched them leave, then went quickly over to Glen. "What happened to Peggy?"

"I have no idea," Glen said, not looking up from his bag. "Something. All he said was she changed her mind. Didn't you talk to her after she left last night?"

"No, I didn't get a chance. All week she said she couldn't wait to come. Shoot."

"I don't know, something must have happened. He didn't seem to want to say much about it this morning. I didn't press him; you know Daryl."

"Yeah ... shoot." Julie reached down and adjusted the cable on one of her skis.

"Well, you ready?" Glen said.

"Yeah ... let's ski." And, gathering their things, they headed for the lodge.

* * *

When they were back outside the snow was no longer falling and the clouds were higher and the jagged tips of the surrounding peaks were visible everywhere in the crisp mountain air. It was a small ski area, high in the northern mountains, far from the large resorts near the cities to the south; and they got in the short line at the base of the chair and could see right away from the low pitch of the ramp the great depth of the snow.

With skis dangling in long 'V's', they rode the steep incline and watched the handful of skiers below starting and stopping in the deep, fresh snow. More snow-covered ridges and peaks slowly appeared as they ascended and they came to the top and suddenly there was Esmeraldo again, towering above everything; and they got off the chair and slid to a stop.

The air was cold and their breaths hung momentarily; and they pushed across the narrow saddle to the back side where the mountain dropped off steeply into another valley. Below the gray sky, for as far as they could see in every direction, mountains rose above the snow-covered forests and distant valleys, and directly opposite, rising toward the ceiling of clouds from the ridge across the valley and dwarfing everything, the glaciated-cone of Mt. Esmeraldo.

"Wow," Julie said, exhaling slowly, staring out at the white volcano. As was Glen a few feet away, she was stopped in a minor snowplow and struggling to pull the leather straps of her poles over her gloved hands.

With his straps now on, Glen continued to stare at the mountain and the string of peaks that extended to each side—those to the north reaching into Canada—and then slid over to Julie and put a heavily-clothed arm around her and tipped her toward him; and she grinned and stumbled, keeping her balance. "Ready?" she said in a muffled voice through his parka which pressed against her face.

Without answering, Glen let go and pushed off with his poles and began to descend the fall line.

* * *

The skiing had been excellent that day with Glen improving greatly and finally gaining confidence to where he could totally enjoy the many runs on the fine snow and keep control even on the steep parts. And Julie, who for two winters had greatly assisted his progress, could see the improvement and was glad that he could finally keep up.

They met Daryl and Randy in the lodge at lunch and sat at one of the thick wood tables in the old, high-ceilinged log building that had originally been built by the Forest Service in the 1930s. There had been a good crowd when they came in, but eating late, it had thinned out and they eventually had the table to themselves. And Daryl and Randy talked and laughed loudly about the inner tube runs at the sledding area and the many crashes that had occurred, and hearing Daryl tell it, they had all been Randy's fault, but Randy argued loudly that, in fact, they had all been the result of Daryl's great ineptitude.

"... If you hadn't kept sticking your foot out ..." Daryl said loudly through a mouth full of half-chewed sandwich.

"Crap—no way!" Randy said incredulously, then began laughing. "We'd be dead if I hadn't stuck my foot out.—You were supposed to be steering the damn thing. Glen, don't let him drive back, he can't even drive an inner tube."

And Glen and Julie listened attentively as they ate their sandwiches and bowls of hot chili, trying to discern exactly who the bigger coward had been.

"No way we were going to crash," Daryl said, trying for the last word, attempting to discredit Randy's testimony. "I was just taking the scenic route."

"Yeah, into the trees—moron."

"Glen's skiing was great," Julie finally said. "He skis—he's a skier. We went down everything. Even Thunderbird."

Randy looked up from his sandwich. "Wow, you guys did Thunderbird?"

"It was a gas," Glen said, smiling broadly. "I showed all those hotdogs out there."

"And for what, only your fourth time skiing? He was almost paralleling," Julie said.

"Fifth; that's five times now. The lessons helped a lot, though."

"Oh, yeah, you've got to have at least a few," Julie said.

"Hey, you guys have to do one inner tube," Randy said.

"Yes!" Daryl joined in. "We can all go. We can get all four on."

"Yeah ... right ..." Glen said.

"No, really," Daryl insisted. "We can do it; it's a blast."

Julie kept eating.

"Come on," Randy persisted. "You guys got to try it once, anyway."

"Okay—okay," Julie said. "We'll do a few more runs and then meet you over there." She looked at Glen.

"Yeah, okay. But I want to do 'Big Chief' at least once more, too."

"Okay, we'll be over in an hour or so," Julie said, sucking the last of her soda through the straw.

"All right, good," Daryl beamed. "—Really, you've got to try it. Just come up the tract through the trees. You can't miss us."

"All right. See you in a while." Glen rose from the table and he and Julie stowed their bags on the high shelf bordering the dining area, and, zipping their parkas, they headed for the door.

* * *

It was dark when Daryl dropped Glen and Randy off at their dorm, just after having let Julie off at hers. They had rendezvoused at the sledding area in the trees and tried once to go with all four. But Glen, although by far the biggest and on the bottom, put a quick end to it when the others piled on and, crying out that he couldn't breathe, rolled the tube over after just a few feet, and they stopped fast in the snow.

"Shit, man!" Randy cried out. "We were just getting going!"

"You get on the bottom, you little—shit," Glen yelled back as Daryl and Julie got up groaning out of the snow."

"Hey, no. No way. You're the biggest, Glen," Randy quickly answered.

"Jules … you want to be on the bottom?" Glen asked.

"Hey—forget it!" Julie said disgustedly, then stepped slowly back from the three figures all now looking quietly at her.

"Yeah—*Julie on the bottom!*" Randy cried, and they all tackled each other and the inner tube and tumbled the rest of the way to the bottom.

Later, driving down the mountain in the dark, they stopped at the Sportsman's lounge in Dukomish; but the waitress carded them and they trudged back out to the car and stood on the gravel under a single light bulb that was nailed to a tree and shared a sixteen-ounce beer that Daryl had found in the trunk.

"Place was weird, huh?" Randy said as they passed the beer in the cool mountain air.

"You see those people at the bar?" Daryl said, leaning against the car, one hand shoved into a pocket. "How old were they? Eighty? Shit, hackin' butts and nursin' beers at the local watering hole on a Sunday night."

"Yeah, Christ, those stools are probably shaped to their butts," Randy said. They finished the beer and got back in the car and Daryl started the engine and Randy, sitting in front, took a cigarette from the pack on the dash.

"Well, I know for sure that Christen's been served in there," a slightly chattering Julie went on from the back. She leaned hard against Glen as he vigorously rubbed her shoulders and arms trying to warm both her and himself in the cool air.

"And Christen looks like she's twenty-five," Glen said as he continued to rub.

"Christen gets served everywhere," Daryl said, taking the last cigarette and crumpling the pack.

"Let's get out of here," Randy said, and he cracked open his window and blew smoke into the dark.

With the cigarette hanging in his mouth, Daryl pushed in the lighter and pulled back onto the highway.

* * *

Now Glen took his bags from the back seat and thanked Daryl and walked with Randy toward the brightly lit foyer of the dormitory. He set a bag down at the large, glass door and pulled it open and they went in. A couple, talking to one side, looked up, and Randy and Glen walked over to the elevator and Glen pushed 'up'. The familiar doors opened and they got in, and, setting their bags on the floor, Glen pushed three and Randy four and they leaned against the walls as the doors closed.

Later still, after changing his clothes and washing his face and looking briefly at the biology paper that was due the next day, Glen went out to the pay phone in the hallway and called Julie.

NINE

In the spring there were parties almost nightly and although no one was seriously eyeing medical school, doing well academically was a true priority for the several-thousand student-body, especially amongst the men with the rapidly escalating draft, so the hardest drinking was saved for the weekends.

Port Crescent, where the small liberal arts college had sat for almost a century, was strict about serving alcohol, but just over the border in Canada, an hour to the north, was Vancouver, where you could drink at eighteen. So with increasing frequency in the spring, carloads of students would head up to Vancouver and the old Gas Town district and close the bars and clubs.

Also, the Canadians made their beer stronger.

* * *

"… This aint no Oly'." Randy, sitting at the well-worn bar just after six in the evening, read over the label of the dark bottle in his hand. He and Glen had left school at mid-afternoon with Tom Cambry and crossed the border and gotten to Gas Town by five. They had walked briefly around the restored, turn-of-the-century neighborhood, then gone into one of the large, cavernous bars, dark with wood and brick, heavy with the stench of beer and tobacco.

"Yeah, it definitely aint," Glen said from the stool between Randy and Cambry. "A buck a bottle; U.S. Shit, you can get a pitcher of Oly' for a buck in Port Crescent—who picked this place?"

Randy took a drink from his mug. "Jeez, you know, Glen, I think you did, as a matter of fact."

"No, no, I said—what's that place? Mulligans, yeah; remember?"

"Yeah, I think he did, Randy." Cambry leaned over from the other side. He was the only one not wearing blue jeans. He had on a kind of brown slacks and a nice sweater. His hair was short and he was clean-shaven and he was known on campus as a fraternity-type, although there were no fraternities at Western State. His family also had money, and he had a new car, and although neither Glen nor Randy knew him that well, Glen had told him he'd show him Gas Town sometime, and they had come up that afternoon in Cambry's new Oldsmobile, which for Randy and Glen was like riding in a limousine.

✳ ✳ ✳

Once, when Glen was eleven, his father, unannounced, had brought home a new Chrysler that he was considering buying, and Glen and his sister and mother had all gotten excitedly in, and, with his father, had gone for a drive. It shined, and smelled of new upholstery, and the transmission was automatic and the brakes and steering were power, and it cruised smoothly around the neighborhood.

Can we get it?" Glen asked repeatedly. "We can get it—can't we?"

"I'm just testing it out, Glen," his father said. "It's expensive, son."
"It's really awfully nice," Glen's mother said from the back seat.
"Will we get it, Daddy?" Cindy asked beside her mother in the back, barely able to see over the front bench.
"I'd like to," Mr. Gray said. "We'll see ..."

Mr. Gray had brought home two more cars in the next week, one a bright red Pontiac; but he didn't buy one of the new automobiles and never mentioned them again, and they continued to drive the old Buick. It was only a few months later that the first large-scale layoffs occurred at the engineering plant and Mr. Gray had had to accept a lesser paying position. In the ensuing years, it seemed, the plant never fully recovered, nor, in many ways, did Mr. Gray.

* * *

In Cambry's new Oldsmobile, with all of that week's school business behind them (if, in fact, what went on in the classrooms and libraries of Western State could be called business), they had talked loudly coming up Highway 100 to the border, the late-May afternoon sunny and bright, the mountains still snow-tipped and rising to one side with the dark waters of Capers Sound on the other. There had been only a few questions from the Canadians at the border and then they were cruising swiftly over the flat farmlands toward Vancouver.

"See, this is three-point-two percent," Randy said, reading from the beer label at the bar, squinting to keep his glasses where he wanted them on his nose. "American is two-five; maybe that's why it costs so much here."

"Yeah, it's stronger, isn't it? I can taste it," Cambry said, looking intently at his bottle. "We should really be able to get plastered—without having to drink so much."

"See? See what I was talking about?" Glen said, sounding proud and nodding to Cambry with a slight grin. "I'm still drinking eight, though."

"Eight?" said Randy. *"Eight?* Crap, I only brought enough money for six. That's it—six, man. Six of these, I'll be drunk as hell."

"Ah, Rand', really? You had eight when we came up for Peggy's birthday with Daryl."

"*Oh!*" Randy half-laughed, "I think I had nine for Peggy's birthday. But crap, we started at noon, remember?" His grin seemed to momentarily leave. "How'd we make it back, anyway? Weren't you driving, Glen?" Randy shook his head. "Shit, I don't remember anything coming back."

"Yeah, I think you're right; I think I did drive back." Now Glen sounded slightly puzzled, seeming to be recalling the details for the first time. He shrugged and took a drink from his beer. "—Ah, it wasn't so bad."

"Well if I'm too drunk you can drive back, Glen," Cambry said.

"Well, sure." Thinking of the new Oldsmobile, Glen attempted, unsuccessfully, to suppress a smile.

"Eight," said Randy, looking off. "Crap—eight three-point-fives. In one night. You're crazy, Glen." Randy lit a cigarette and looked around. Glen lit one and looked too. There were a few tables with some American-looking kids, but it was hard to tell. There were a few older people at the bar and a few tables of middle-aged couples who looked more Canadian. There weren't any girls.

"Hey, what's wine, anyways?" Randy said, looking back, smoke coming out of his nose and mouth.

"Four-one," said Glen.

"Twelve percent," said Cambry.

"Twelve percent?" said Randy. "What's the rest of it?"

"—Cool-aid," said Glen, exhaling.

"What you drink," Randy chuckled loudly and grinned. Glen and Cambry looked at him.

"Let's get out of here," Glen said.

"To where?" said Cambry.

"How about 'Mulligan's'," said Randy, tapping his cigarette on an ashtray.

"Nah, let's find someplace else," Glen said. "—More downtown."

"Hey, anybody hungry," Randy chortled, pushing his glasses up.

"I am," Cambry quickly responded.

"Get something to eat?" Glen said, looking at Tom.

"Yeah, I could definitely use something. I haven't eaten since breakfast."

"All right, sure; I guess I can eat, too." Glen raised his glass: "So—to Canada."

"To Canada," Randy echoed, clanking his glass into Glen's and Cambry's; and they raised the thick mugs to their lips and drank down the remaining beer.

* * *

Later, they were in an even larger, warehouse-size bar in an old neighborhood near Chinatown, with what seemed to be a crowd of older, blue-collar Canadian men with a few random, peroxide-like blonds sprinkled around and everyone drunk and smoking and talking loudly.

Going in, drunk from the two other bars they had tried but found lacking, finally guided to this one by an off-duty bartender at the previous place, Glen dropped the bottle he was carrying on the first table of women he passed and invited himself and his two pals to join them. But when a man quickly appeared, his weathered face not smiling, Glen quickly backed away, forgetting his bottle, he smiling broadly.

"You dumb fuck," Randy said, moving with Glen and Cambry through the crowd to a small empty table with tall stools against one of the high walls, "—you trying to get us killed?"

"Fuck, how was I to know? They looked like they were by themselves to me."

"I thought you had a girlfriend, anyway." Randy looked off.

Glen shrugged. "I was just talking." Taking in the crowd, they sat on the stools and lit cigarettes. "This is more like it, don't you think, Tom?" Glen smiled and tried to flag one of the waitresses working the busy floor.

"Crap; wait here," Randy said, indicating the futility of Glen's efforts; and he got up and headed for the bar.

"Place is wild," Cambry said. "Took long enough to find." He blew out smoke. "Man, did you see some of those streets we were coming down?"

"Yeah, no kidding," Glen nodded. "This aint no Gas Town."

"What is it? Chinatown?"

Glen nodded again and looked around. "… Yeah … I think we're right near it." Two girls went by. They were younger than what most of the few other women seemed to be, but still didn't respond to Glen's loud 'hello'. Glen looked at Cambry and shrugged. Over a ways there was a sudden crashing sound and some loud shouting. Someone had fallen down or been pushed. But the shouting faded quickly and now there was just the continuous noise of loud talking. They had passed an old jukebox on the way in but after only a few feet the crowd had drowned out the music. They had not recognized the song that was playing.

Now there was another commotion further down the long room and this time people seemed to move toward it; and the shouting sounded angry and even over the loud buzz of the crowd the sharp voices clearly reached the table where Glen and Cambry sat smoking.

A short, stocky man in his late-thirties with a wide grin and wearing a black leather coat made a kind of face at Glen when he squeezed past the table. Glen didn't respond and the man was quickly gone and Glen looked at Cambry and tried to imitate the face.

"Crap, what was with him?" Cambry said over the noise.

Glen shrugged and drew on his cigarette. At the entrance there seemed to be more people trying to come in; and Cambry stood up and tried to see toward the bar. He sat back down and looked at his cigarette and flicked the ash.

Now Glen stood up and strained to see deeper into the smoky room. "Hey, think I'm going to have a look around," and he suddenly left the table and pushed his way into the crowd.

Now by himself, Cambry glanced around, then at his cigarette, then watched the smoke blowing out, then looked around some more. The thick, wood table was old and scarred from numerous tobacco burns and carved letters, and the wall had faint yellowish stains and numerous holes and nicks. An old wrinkle-faced woman went by with a drink in one hand and a distant look in her muddled eyes; and Cambry took another drag and then looked at his watch before blowing the smoke out his nose.

Now a man began to take one of the stools. "Uh, someone's sitting there," Cambry said hurriedly.

"—Where?" the man said defiantly. "I don't see anyone."

"It's taken," Cambry said, his voice high and rising.

"Yeah; it is taken, mate—I'm takin' it."

"Hey!" Cambry half-yelled, but the man turned his back and left with the stool, at one point holding it high over his head as he moved through the crowd.

Cambry slid the other stool over and set his foot on it. He seemed to be sort of grinding his teeth and swayed his head back and forth, almost in a kind of jerking motion. He took a last drag from the cigarette and stamped it out on the floor.

A waitress suddenly appeared, pushing her way through the crowd, just a few feet away. Cambry quickly stood and waved his arms; but numerous others were doing the same and she ignored everyone and just as quickly was gone.

Now Glen suddenly appeared with a girl who looked about sixteen. "This is Carmen," he said, smiling, introducing the girl to Cambry. She was somewhat short, dressed very colorfully in a long, India-like cloth-jacket and snug burgundy pants with barely visible pinstripes. Well-worn black leather boots protruded from below the pants. She had a pleasant smile and clear eyes, and, looking closer, Cambry could now see she was older than sixteen. Her hair reached far beyond her collar and long ornamented earrings hung from the lobes of her ears. "Carmen—this is Tom."

"Hello," Cambry said, smiling; and she glanced at him, only half smiling, the smile, though, a seemingly permanent fixture on her soft, clear face. 'What?', Cambry thought, trying to understand how this seemingly sweet young girl could now be standing here at the table with Glen and himself in this place.

"Where's Randy?" Glen said.

"I have no idea."

Carmen took a cigarette out of the suede bag that hung from her shoulder.

"Where's the other stool?"

"Some ass-hole took it," Cambry said, making clear his anger with the word 'ass'. Now he took his foot off the other stool and slid it toward the girl.

Glen starred blankly for a moment as Carmen sat down, the unlit cigarette in her hand, then, turning quickly toward her, took out matches and held up a flame. "She's lost," Glen said, smiling again.

"—I am not." The slight, seemingly permanent smile leaving for the first time. She blew smoke out the corner of her mouth and flicked her head to move the long straight bangs hanging near her eyes.

"She was supposed to meet some friends but they haven't shown," Glen said, also lighting a cigarette. "She says she's not sure if this is the right place."

Now the smile returned and she seemed about to laugh. "We were either going to meet here or this other place.—'The Castle'." She laughed.

"What the hell's 'The Castle'?" Glen said.

"It's this bar, but ... I couldn't find it. That's why I came here. But maybe this is where we said ... I don't know." She blew out some smoke.

"So, are you Canadian?" Cambry said, the subtle difference in her English only very slight.

"Born and raised," Glen said before she could answer. He grinned and looked at her, then at Cambry. "Shit; where's the beer? Where the hell is Randy? Christ, I'm going to go find him." And Glen quickly left again, pushing his way toward the bar where the crowd eventually became impregnable. He headed down one side and suddenly glimpsed the back of Randy's small frame, squeezed up against the bar, the bartender handing him money. Randy turned with a pitcher of beer and three glasses just as Glen came up.

"Fuck, man," Randy said, a pained expression on his face. "It took for fucking ever—here." He shoved the glasses at Glen.

"We need one more," Glen said, knowing Randy wouldn't understand. Protruding above most of the crowd, he began to push again toward the bar but quickly gave up and fled with Randy back toward the table.

As they came up, Carmen and Cambry sat motionless, each looking off in a slightly different direction; and Randy set the pitcher roughly on the table, spilling some of the beer. With the table now wet and sticky, the glasses were quickly poured as Glen informed Randy, who was looking quizzically at Carmen, that they would have to share one of the glasses. "Oh, this is Carmen," he finally said.

"Hello," Randy said with a slight wave, not attempting with much effort to be heard over the noise. Carmen nodded. She was no longer smiling.

Everyone drank their beers; Randy and Glen, sharing, quickly drank two. "Now, what was that school you said you went to?" Glen eventually said.

With the perpetual grin, and the cigarette in a raised hand, Carmen glanced momentarily at Glen: "Fraser River Academy," she casually said, and then looking back over the crowd, "—of Arts."

Glen drank some more beer. "Yeah? Where'd you say it was?"

She took a deep drag and tapped the ash onto the floor. "It's just out of town—toward Haney."

Glen nodded. "Painting? You said you take painting, right?"

"Yeah … mostly." She blew out smoke and sipped her beer. "I mean, there's other classes, too." She looked around; the grin had disappeared. "Anyone have the time?"

"Ten to eleven," Cambry said, sliding up his Cardigan-like sweater and looking at his watch.

"Hey, I took art once," Glen said. "—Honest." He looked at Randy and slid the beer toward him. Randy, appearing stoic, glanced over and drank some beer and looked away.

"You know, it must have been the other place," Carmen now said to Glen. "I know it's right around here—somewhere." She crushed her cigarette out against the wall. "Look, I think I'm going to try and find it." She stepped off the stool which actually lowered her a few inches and took a last drink from her half-full beer.

"Hey, you want any help?" Glen said.

She adjusted the shoulder bag and blew her bangs away from her eyes. "I'm sure it's on this street; it's just like this really small door—hard to see." She suddenly seemed very young again; she looked toward the entrance.

"I thought it was a castle," Glen said. Carmen didn't say anything. "Look, I'll be right back," Glen said to Randy. "Don't leave."

"Hey—how long?" Randy grimaced.

"Few minutes," Glen said and quickly left as Carmen headed toward the door.

Cambry took a drink from his beer. "I thought he went out with someone."

"He does," Randy said, reaching for his beer. "I don't know … he thinks he's going in the army."

The night sky was clear and the stars bright and the sudden quiet and freshness of the air cleared everything the moment Glen and Carmen stepped outside. There were people standing on the sidewalk talking, and a few cars passing down the wide street, and Glen suddenly reached over and put his arm around her. She glanced at him but didn't pull it away and took a cigarette from her bag. Glen removed his arm and got the matches out again and lit the cigarette. "Look, maybe your friends can come back here," Glen said, tossing the match to the sidewalk.

"Well, maybe." She looked off, taking a long drag from the cigarette. "The problem is … one of them I kind of see."

"Kind of see?" Glen said.

"Yeah … George."

"George?"

She glanced at him and took another drag and looked away. "I don't know. We were, but not really … for a while."

"Were?" Glen said, now grinning, searching the pockets of his jacket for his cigarettes, now almost chuckling.

"Yeah.—Were," she said a little defensively.

Glen looked up the street. "Well … bring him along." He tried to smile.

She smoked some more, arms now folded in the cool evening air.

"Bring all of them," Glen said, trying, but failing, to sound excited.

She looked up. "I got to get going."

"You guys coming back?" Glen said. "Hey—bring 'em."

"Gotta go," she said once more and began backing down the sidewalk.

"—Carmen." Glen took a step toward her but she turned and strode up the walk. "Carmen—hey—bring 'em!" he called again; and she looked back once without breaking stride and then disappeared into the dark. From her shadow, the orange glow of a coal flew into the street.

Glen stood for a moment breathing the clear night air. He took a few steps up the walk, then stopped and looked at the faint lights of the neighborhood and breathed some more. Some men came up the walk and entered the bar and the noise briefly returned before the door closed and there was just the cool clear air of the dark night. Glen walked slowly toward the door and was about to enter when it suddenly swung open again and in a rush of heat and noise Cambry and Randy spilled out onto the walk.

"*There* he is," Randy said.

"Here I is," Glen said.

"Hey—where's what's-her-name?"

Glen glanced briefly at Randy. "Let's get out of here." And without waiting for an answer, he began walking in the direction of the car.

* * *

Later, after the border, speeding down the dark highway with the shadows of the hills rising on one side and the distant outline of Lummi Island on the other, a raccoon suddenly lumbered into the headlights; and Cambry slammed the brakes and swerved and Glen grabbed the dashboard and Randy, asleep on the back seat, flew onto the floor. And Cambry, breathing deeply, pulled the car to the shoulder and told Glen to drive.

* * *

"Congratulations, son; good news: you've been accepted into the United States Army.
"… Thank you, sir."

Part II
VIETNAM

ONE

"Hey, Mike—what you see? You see anything yet? Huh?"

"No ... Wait ... Yeah, some islands. No ... I think—that's got to be it."

The black kid leaned into Glen to look out the window and Glen pushed back in his seat to let him see but the plane went into more clouds and the kid bobbed for a better angle but gave up and leaned back. "Shit, Mike; it sure is cloudy out. Man my ass is sore ... think I'll stretch ..."

"—*In your seat, soldier.*" The sharp bark came from the green-clad sergeant in the back of the plane and fifty pairs of bloodshot eyes turned to watch Private Eugene Fischer of Indianapolis, Indiana, age nineteen, drafted, slowly lower himself back into his seat. There were close to eighty of them packed into the belly of the C-5 transport amongst the crates of war-supplies stacked to the ceiling; and with the loud vibrating of the propellers, the plane banked slowly left and continued its decent through the patches of clouds in the faint light of the newly risen sun.

"Yeah … we're coming in," Glen said to the helmeted-kid beside him, his voice rising above the roar of the engines; and he watched the narrow strip of beach approaching and the row of palm trees behind the sand and the dark asphalt of the runway extending straight inland from the shoreline; and in the far distance, through the haze, the densely forested green of lowland hills.

The plane floated now, aiming for the runway, tilting briefly to each side; and small buildings became visible along the tarmac and clusters of thatched dwellings in all directions beyond the buildings and, faintly, the tiny dots of people; and the plane touched down in a screech of smoking rubber and rolled in a loud roar to the end of the runway.

"Look at that, will you—just look at that!" Eugene pushed completely across Glen, his face to the window. "Man, we're here now—best of luck my man." And he clasped Glen's hand and shook it as the plane came to a stop.

TWO

Glen was sweating hard again as he shoveled into the red earth beside the twelve other shirtless soldiers in the late-morning sun. The blisters were mostly gone by the fifth day, having surprisingly reappeared after the brief layoff following the many strenuous months of stateside-training, and now, on the tenth, the heat and sweat were familiar enough that he felt he could somehow survive it; although he wondered how bad it would get when the dry season came and the temperature rose greatly.

They were digging what would eventually be a partially underground sleeping barracks—hooches as they affectionately called them—made of tin, to replace the rows of canvas tents where they now resided, as the base expanded daily to accommodate the rapidly increasing ground forces in the area. A small city was being constructed, and, like all the new arrivals to the quadrant, they alternated field-training and building every three days for the first month before they would ship out for the interior and possible fighting assignments in the war effort.

From everywhere came the roar of tractors and trucks and generators, and toward the runway the loud engines of the transport planes and helicopters, and throughout it all the shouts and voices of the green-clad soldiers hauling and hammering and digging and moving about. The ground was mostly flat and grassy with scattered clumps of trees, and a mile to their backs were the tall palms at the edge of the sea, and there before them, several miles inland, menacing in their minds, the first ridge rising upward from the green delta floor.

The other sound that was as constant as the tractors and helicopters, and closer and even more distracting, and had been there all morning as well as the previous two, came from the small village boy who stood with his sister a few feet behind the first line of digging men and asked for *'choc-o-let'*. All the hot morning they asked, except for when they were chased away by one of the staff sergeants; but they always returned within a few minutes.

"No more—none," Glen finally said, turning toward the boy and pulling his pants pocket inside out. This would generally cause their faces to brighten and for the two to creep slightly closer from their squatted position in the grass. Behind them were older children and young men from the numerous nearby villages; and they grinned and talked rapidly amongst themselves in reaction to Glen's response.

"Tomorrow ... More tomorrow," a stocky, sun-reddened soldier next to Glen called to the kids; and everyone stopped digging and turned to look, except to one side, where a group of the young black soldiers—the brothers—laughed and talked loudly.

"Come on, Dawson—give 'em something," another soldier called to the stocky G.I.

"No—don't," another called out. "It'll probably just rot their teeth, anyway."

"I don't have any, anyway," Dawson said, leaning on his shovel; and he pulled on the visor of his cap as the children inched slowly closer.

"All right—let's take ten." The only soldier wearing a shirt called out to the platoon, and everyone left their shovels and picks and walked over to where a large water barrel sat on the back of a truck and got in line to drink. The shirted-soldier walked toward the children who quickly stood and took several steps back. He then spoke in the local Asian dialect, firmly but without anger, and the kids began to move further back. The soldier then called out to the young men a few yards behind; and they at first grinned and laughed, and then called to the boy and girl who turned and moved slowly back through the grass toward them. Then together they all moved away.

THREE

"Moeller—Denton—Sweeney—Anderson, Robert—Sutter—Wolfe—." The mail clerk with the thick packet of letters barked out the names toward the forty squinting men gathered outside the green canvas tent in the late afternoon sun. "Murrow—Jerden—Eubanks—Grindle—." One by one they came up to the table where Pvt. Steven Lewis dropped the assorted envelopes and small packages. "MacCullum—Gray—." Glen gave a slight lurch when he heard his name and slipped quickly through the crowd and picked up the small white envelope; and his breath suddenly quickened when he recognized Julie's handwriting.

"Mundi—Deans—Emerson—." Lewis' voice faded as Glen walked across the hard earth of the camp toward the row of tents where his cot and pack and his rifle sat, and the small folding shelf that he shared with Pvt. Carl Pendras of East Trenton, New Jersey, age twenty-one, enlisted, in the next cot over, that held his other letters and books and the small unframed photo of his parents and sister smiling brightly in their Sunday clothes.

School is going okay but I don't know if Western State is where I want to be anymore, Glen read as he walked slowly in the late-day heat. *Paul and Don think they are going to get drafted so they are talking about enlisting. Jeff Hunt just went in but I don't know if he will be going down where you are or to Germany. They seem to be making it harder for people in college. They're thinking about raising the grade point average for deferments. I hope you did the right thing. I'm sure you did. I got your letter dated 10/25. It came about the 10th of November. It sounds really hot! Not like Port Crescent! It's been raining almost every day lately. People are still going mod. Even more than last year. You'd love it.*

I can't believe how far away you are, Glen. I think about you everyday and pray that you come back safely. Promise me you will. I don't know, everyday the news shows more fighting. Will you be around any? I forget what you said you'd be doing. Oh well.

All for now. Love you a lot. Jule's.

Glen entered the tent and walked down the row of cots to his and sat down and reread the letter. There was talking and some laughter from small groups at other cots, and at others were young soldiers quietly reading or trying to sleep. He laid down and stared for a moment at the canvas ceiling then opened the letter and read it again. Some of the sentences he would reread several times before moving on. He tried smelling the paper but it seemed odorless.

Glen sat up and removed the photograph of Julie from his wallet and stared for a moment. He reached for his pen and notepad, and stared again, but then put them and the photo back on the shelf and stood up. He began walking toward the door and passed a skinny kid with a flat-top and asked if he knew what was going to be for dinner.

"Number three," the kid said with a high voice, looking up at Glen.

"Three?" said an intense looking kid with piercing eyes lying on a nearby cot who had overheard the question. "Spaghetti—right? ... yeah."

"Meatloaf," the skinny kid said. "Spaghetti's six."

"Six?" said the intense kid, Pvt. Timothy Emerson of Akron, Ohio, age eighteen, enlisted. He was short and muscular with a medallion hanging across his tank-top. "I thought six was fish—right, Gray?" He looked over at Glen. "Whatever—hey, when you guys going to Dra Ming, anyway? They said yet?"

Glen looked at the kid lying on the cot. "Next week. That's what they keep saying, anyway. All of 'D' Company."

"Yeah?" said Timothy Emerson, and he rolled on his side. "Fuck—you walkin' or flyin'?"

"We better be flying," said Glen. "It's twenty miles."

"Thirty," said the high-voiced kid with the flat-top, Frank Krable of Owensboro, Kentucky, age nineteen, enlisted. Freckles, heightened from recent days in the bright sun, spotted his long, angular face. "That's what I heard, anyway."

"Any 'VC' doing anything up there?" Emerson asked.

"Nothing I've heard of," said Glen. "Nobody seems to know what's going on—even those guys hanging around outside the fence all day might be Cong. That's what I heard. No one seems to know anything."

"Well, you'll sure as fuck know when someone's shootin' at you," Emerson said, chuckling; and he sat up and lit a cigarette.

"Yeah ... I suppose. It's been happening more I guess, too. I've heard up around Pla Cu, and even around Kon Tum, they've been getting hit more and more ... surprise stuff. A lot of mines; booby traps."

"Mines ... Jesus," Frank Krable shuddered slightly and looked toward the open tent door.

"Well, we trained long enough for 'em," Emerson said; and Glen and Frank both nodded as Emerson drew deeply on his cigarette.

God, I'll miss you ... God, I can't believe this is actually happening ..." The long, tearful embrace at the Sealth train station with Julie and her near emotional collapse had been more difficult than Glen had anticipated. Once inside the car, he had waved and tried to smile at the small gathering of his family and Julie under the metal canopy of the platform, glad to be breaking away from the recent chaos of Port Crescent and Western State and what seemed the endless, restrictive, mundane-existence of home and youth. Embarking, finally, out into the world and the enormous unknown-journey. Through the foggy window, his mother's arm around a sobbing Julie, he watched them grow small as the train pulled away in the gray drizzle.

The training, also, had been longer and more difficult than he had anticipated—marching—marching. Two months of basic—marching—marching—marching—and then two more of advanced, having allowed himself within a few days of induction—actively seeking—to be swept into the near-deafening roar of the escalating war effort. The advanced—marching—marching—marching— marching—in the deep American south, with its attempts to replicate the Vietnamese environment: the hamlets, the snipers, the ambushes, and, yes, the booby-traps and mines; setting in concrete the reality of the impending one year war assignment.

War! In a far off land! The Army! The past five months, having all happened so suddenly, now seemed like a dream.

"But fuck," Emerson went on in the warm air of the tent on the other side of the world, "you been over by medivac lately? You go by there last Thursday?"

Glen and Frank listened.

"You didn't hear all those Hueys that kept landin' there all morning?" His stare conjured lethal potential. "Dak To. They were bringin' 'em in all morning. The real bad ones they were taking straight to the Chinook ..." Emerson cleared some mucus and sent it flying out the door. "Well, our radio man was over there, anyway. And he said it wasn't pretty."

"Nah, crap, we've only been here four weeks," said Glen. "There isn't nothing I haven't heard, though. The biggest bullshit is that they're going to surrender—that we've won."

"Fuck." Emerson snorted and flicked his ashes. "Yeah; you hear that one a lot during the first month. That LBJ's going to fake 'em with some fake H-bombs. Have 'em all runnin' to China."

"I did—I heard that," Glen said, his face grimacing. "That we're going to drop a few H-bombs ... Get the thing over with. Christ—what a bunch a horse-shit."

"Who knows?" Emerson said, a thick stream of smoke coming out his nostrils, "maybe it wouldn't be such a bad idea."

"Yeah, Christ—right." Glen's voice rose as he stared for a moment at Emerson, he staring back, then looked out toward the rapidly dimming daylight coming through the tent door. Numerous trucks, kicking up trails of dust, continued to move in the distance toward the sea. "Well, anyone going to dinner?"

Frank nodded and began tucking in his shirt.

Emerson laid back again on the cot. "Nah, maybe later ... I aint feelin' that hot. I think I got something."

"See you around," Glen said. The intense kid, staring up at the tent ceiling, blew out smoke without answering; and Frank and Glen stepped outside just as the horn blew for dinner.

FOUR

I had a girl her name was Sue
She left me for fat cat Lou
I got in good with her sister, though
She knew more than Sue'll ever know

    The forty soldiers made their way along the road up the wide valley toward the forested mountains in the mid-morning sun, Corporal Thomas Duncan of Redding, California, age twenty-four, enlisted, calling out the cadence's lead line and the double column shouting the response.

One day Sue came home with Lou
She threw me out and her sister, too
Now we got our own little place
With dogs and cats and a picket gate

The line of men and trucks stretched for a quarter mile along the dirt road, the road rising gently beside a shallow stream as the mountains grew steeper and the valley narrowed. Along with the whooping drone of helicopters that constantly crossed overhead (the imagining of those riding inside seeming to add to the weight of their packs) vehicles passed in clouds of dust in each direction, both military and civilian, the military mostly newer American transport trucks and jeeps with the occasional aging French half-track of the Army of South Vietnam, the civilian mostly older Peugeuot or Renault cars and buses. Local people on foot, many balancing large bundles of rice stalks or baskets of vegetables at the ends of poles, moved into the roadside grass as the column passed. From time to time they passed clusters of bamboo and grass dwellings as barefooted children followed excitedly along for short distances.

> *Now Lou's gone with a girl named Jean*
> *They left last night for New Orleans*
> *Sue don't know, don't understand*
> *She never should have left her Army man ...*

They repeated 'army—army man', rhythmically, over and over, in beat with the march, some voices rising above the rest, over and over, marching up the dirt road.

"*Take ten!*" The shout came from the staff sergeant in front and the soldiers stepped into the shade of the trees at the side of the road and slung off their packs and rifles and sat on the ground. Except for one private near the back, all forty men took out cigarettes and lit them.

The sun was high and the air humid and hot, and Glen bent with his cigarette toward Pvt. Robert Sandis of Chesapeake, Maryland, age twenty, enlisted, who cupped the flame from his lighter for the group who sat near him. A short ways over, a group of young black soldiers—the brothers—laughed and talked loudly. Everyone sucked on their cigarettes and most were squinting, even in the shade, and they leaned against their packs, sweating profusely in their flak-jackets and rolled up shirtsleeves.

"You know, I did have a girl named Sue," said a sandy-haired kid sitting beside Glen named Davis. "Tenth grade ... but she left me for this guy named Roger." The men around Davis grinned slightly. "Broke my heart," he said, letting out a long stream of smoke.

"Well, did they go to New Orleans?" asked a kid with several small bandages on his jaw from shaving nicks, as straight-faced as he could.

"N'awlins," said a smiling, round-faced kid in a thick southern-drawl who sat alone a few feet away. He was short and heavy and his shirt was stained dark and beads of sweat glistened from his face. He was no longer smoking, having taken only one or two drags before dropping it to the ground, his canteen resting in his lap.

"New *Ahlins.*" Several others tried to imitate the drawl.

"*New—Oh—Lanes,*" one kid said laughing as he smoked his cigarette.

"N'awlins," the round-faced kid said again, his smile even larger. "That's my home." He wore dark-framed glasses; and now his eyes were closed and he leaned back against his pack, still clutching the canteen. "I can smell the river-water ... the swamp-grass ... on a spring morning ..."

"I went there once," said a dark-complexioned kid beside Glen with a very deep voice. The round-faced kid opened his eyes and the others turned from the deepness of the young man's voice. His hair was dark and his sideburns long, and although he had shaved that morning when they had left before sunrise, there was already a shadow. His tall, lanky body—taller, even, than Glen's—rested against his pack. "My mother took our family down there," he went on, "from Minnesota. Father was down on business and Mother wanted my sisters and me to see the museum. She drove us all the way down to see the paintings."

"Oh, y'all went to the *NOMA,*" said the round-faced kid from New Orleans, Johnny Parker, age twenty, enlisted, smiling widely again.

"There was a showing of this Claude Monet's, and she took us to see them," said the tall, deep-voiced kid, Ben Archer, of St. Cloud, Minnesota, age twenty-two, enlisted. "We saw the French

Quarter, and everything else, of course ... but those Monet's. How she loved those paintings."

"Who the hell's 'Moany'?" said the kid with the shaving nicks.

"Monet," said Ben in his deep voice. "He was a famous French painter ... dead now, hundred years or so."

"A lot of dead French guys around here," said a muscular, older looking kid, Mullin, his sleeves rolled high, his helmet tilted forward above his sweat-smeared face. "A lot."

"Well, crap, what do you expect from France?" the kid with the shaving nicks said, smirking. His name was Tommy Walker and he was twenty-one years old; and he spoke rapidly, moving his head and jaw in jerks and flicking repetitively on his cigarette between deep drags. He was from Manchester, New Hampshire, where he had regularly been in trouble with the law. A judge had finally given him a choice between six months in jail and the Army. "That's why we're here," he went on. "'Cause they couldn't get the job done. Just like they had to have us come rescue them in World War Two." He flicked his cigarette ash and nodded and looked earnestly at the faces around him and then to the ground.

"I don't know ... You should get a history book," said Glen, leaning against his pack in the shade of the dense Eucal trees lining the road. "This country used to be ruled by France. But when they gave them their independence some of them tried to make it communist."

"Yeah—Ho Chi Minh," said the sandy-haired kid, Davis. He was twenty-one years old, from Santa Monica, California. It was rumored that he knew how to surf. He had enlisted.

"He's right," said Mullin, twisting his helmet up. "The French were trying to give them their country back but all these commies kept poppin' up."

"That's where we come in," said Tommy Walker.

"You got that right," said Glen.

"Well it don't surprise me we're finishing up for the French," Tommy went on, "—they should'a stuck to painting." He took a last drag from his cigarette and flicked it into the road.

"Hey, someone's got to do it," said Davis; "we stopped it in Korea, we'll stop it here."

"You think we'll find anything up here?" asked Bobby Sandis. Davis looked at him: "You know what Sarge always says: 'You got to expect the worst and be prepared'."

The soldiers looked at Davis.

"Dra Ming has been quiet for almost a year now, is what everyone says," said Ben in his deep voice.

"Yeah, but isn't that what they said about Kon Tum?" said Glen looking up, his face creased with sweat and dust.

"It's better if we do find something and take care of it," said Mullin. "It's all about getting the message across." One hand rested on the stock of his M-16 which pointed beside him toward the hazy sky. "They don't really understand they got the U. S. Army after them now."

"I don't know," said Ben. "You hear those jets screaming over every night? They've dropped a lot of ordinance for almost a year now, big stuff. And we've all seen what phosphors does—you'd think they'd have gotten the message by …"

"—*Fall in!*" The shout came from the front of the line. Cigarettes flew into the road and rifles and packs were flung onto backs. Over a ways, the brothers continued to talk and laugh loudly.

"—Ponchos," someone a few feet ahead said to Glen and the group around him. Word was coming down the line to prepare for rain and Mullin turned and passed it to the next group. The lush forest had grown thicker moving up the valley and dark clouds were now forming around the low mountains.

Bobby Sandis stood behind Glen: "Rains a lot where you're from, doesn't it Gray?"

"Yeah, it does. But it's just more this constant drizzle … not these cloud bursts."

"Shit, look at Parker."

The heavy-set kid was looking at the darkening clouds, his round face again with the dreamy smile. "… Jest lack 'ome."

On the road, the column (including the brothers as they continued in loud conversation) pulled green ponchos from their packs, and, as everyone began to march—many complaining of the heat from the ponchos—the first loud cracking from the thunderheads echoed down from the mountains ahead.

* * *

It was dark by the time they reached the camp at Dra Ming, the entire column soaked from sweat and the drenching downpours of the last few miles, their boots caked with mud. Then under the light of generators, the air humid and warm, they had set up their tents and cots and ate C-rations and gone to sleep.

They awoke early the next morning to clear skies and the sound of fighter jets streaking low overhead into the mountains and, for the first time since their arrival in country, the distant crack of bombs hitting the ground.

"You hear that?" Glen said, dressing in the tent next to Ben, the tall dark-haired kid with the deep voice.

"No ..." Ben mumbled as he pulled on his pants.

"—Listen." Glen stopped at the edge of his cot with one still-damp boot on. "There—hear it?"

Ben, too, stood motionless in the low tent. There was a sharp cracking sound in the distance and then the slightest tremor. "Jesus ... I heard that," he stared at Glen, "felt it."

They finished dressing and went outside where others were drifting out of the sprawl of tents and shelters, and scanned the surrounding hills and ridges in the early morning light. The air was warm, yet cooler than Tra Dien on the coast, and a mist rose from between the hills, and, now outside, the cracks of the distant bombs were clearer.

"Holy cow," Glen said excitedly, feeling for a moment like he was just on another camping trip in the American west, "look at this!" He stood beside the tent taking in the deep grasses and forests of the valley and surrounding hills, the last two hours of which they had missed, arriving nervously in darkness in the rain the night before. After hours of narrowing and a final steeper ascent, the valley had again widened, and flattened; and now in the morning light at least one large village could be seen further up the valley, and between the village and the American camp, a large military installation of the Army of the Republic of Vietnam, with it's swarming contingency of short-statured, dark-fatigued soldiers. There appeared to be many hundreds of soldiers between the two camps, and now with the sun rising, people were appearing all throughout the valley, moving about the two camps and the village and everywhere in between. Off to one side, a convoy of empty trucks that had been idling for half an hour—the nearby tall stacks of its contents being rapidly carted off by a swarm of South Vietnamese soldiers—began to pull out for the drive back to Tra Dien.

A few minutes later the jets came screeching back for the coast. Glen looked up at the vapor trails. "Shit ... do you think they got anything?" Glancing briefly at the sky, Ben turned without answering to find the mess tent, and Glen, tucking in the tail of his shirt, his eyes still fixed on the fading trails, stumbled slightly as he followed Ben into the camp.

FIVE

"You don't look left, Douglas—and you don't look right. You look straight—only straight. You understand that?" Sergeant Thomas Ross of Galveston, Texas, age twenty-nine, enlisted, was speaking forcefully to Pvt. Timothy Douglas of Mandon, North Dakota, age eighteen, enlisted, who stood at the head of the column on the narrow forest trail. Douglas had replaced Sandis at the point to scan for mines after Sandis had fallen sick and returned to camp shortly after they had left that morning.

Near the rear, Glen was glad to stop; when they were not moving he could take in the surrounding terrain more completely. They had mostly been in open fields throughout the morning, patrolling the same ground around Dra Ming they had been patrolling for the past two months, but this was a relatively new section where the forest spilled down from the hills into the flat valley, and although the trail was narrow and visibility limited within the trees, still, he could look.

In less than an hour they would backtrack to the hamlet of Phu Gan beside a small stream near the base of a steep ridge where they would stop to drop off bags of supplies for the CIA team that was operating out of the village on long treks deep into the mountains. It was uncertain what the specific objective of the mountain treks was about, but it was rumored that they somehow involved the recruitment of distant villagers for spying.

At the hamlet of Phu Gan, with its cluster of thatch huts, they would see Mr. Phen, a local farmer and businessman who owned a radio and wore expensive western clothing which he purchased in Hue, and who arranged for specially prepared bowls of rice for the patrolling Americans who visited at least twice a week, usually around mid-day. (It was rumored that Phen, more than a year before, having been bought off by the Americans, had provided the intelligence of an impending Viet Cong ambush, and in appreciation of the continued payments, provided the hot meals.)

There had been, however, almost no enemy hostilities in the area for half a year now, but abandoned tunnels were periodically discovered and destroyed, and land mines were still abundant, and at least once a week they found a trip wire, luckily, instead of it finding them. Five months into his tour and only twice had Glen encountered the enemy: as they patrolled in the first light of dawn near the hamlet of Kan Nack, two months in country, the charred corpses of five Vietcong (or were they?) still lying in the ditch outside of the village where they had been hit by a Navy Skyraider's phosphorous bomb the night before. The sight of a body; a once breathing, thinking human being, violently killed, slamming home the horror of where they were. And Glen, nauseous and covering his mouth, could think only of his parents and sister and prayed—begged—they would never have to witness such a sight. The other encounter being the first morning of his one and only *County Fair* (as the elaborate American PR operations were dubbed): A village was surrounded before sunrise to trap the Vietcong who came at night, then searched, amongst the panicked chaos of the awakening villagers, inch by inch, as daylight descended. There, in tiny Mang Ri, Mullen and Sandis had found them, three shirtless young men, trembling in their soiled pants beneath the floor planking of one of the huts. From a short distance away, Glen shot quick glimpses at them in between his nervous scanning of the crowd of anxiously-conversing villagers who surrounded them, before the men and the owners of the hut were led quickly away and given to the accompanying ARVN unit whose members were already detaching the gleaming bayonets they would use for the extensive interrogations that were about to come. But then very quickly the *Fair* would begin, and health supplies would be set up, and rebuilding crews with their truckloads of leftover munitions boxes would begin improving the local school. And cash and gifts for the village chief would be dispensed (usually upgrading or adding to his collection of pistols). And finally, with the area secure, to the boundless happiness of both the villagers (who seemed already to have forgotten the horror of how the day had begun) and the American troops, below the starry night, the evening's entertainment: and with generator and movie projector rolling, there in the Asian jungle-clearing of Mang Ri, in all its surrealism, Walt Disney's Donald Duck, dancing across the flickering screen, dubbed in Vietnamese.

Now, two months later, the valley and surrounding hills long before flushed out and secured, until receiving further orders, they would continue the daily patrols as part of the Division's efforts to control the quadrant.

When they got to Phu Gan an hour later Mr. Phen was not there, which struck Glen as unusual because he had been saying for weeks that he would not be traveling until after the main harvest before the start of the rainy season, to personally direct the flow of his crops to the market at Kehsahn. A woman in a flower-patterned dress and attractive shoes whom they had seen accompanying Mr. Phen before, and who everyone said was Mr. Phen's wife, greeted the platoon, and, with the help of several young girls (the girls barefoot and in more ragged shin-length pants; the older ones shielding the midday sun with wide, conical hats), served the bowls of rice to the hungry American soldiers, most of whom two months before had been reluctant to take, but who now looked forward to the hot meals.

Sergeant Ross, thick-boned and lean, and with the crew cut he was always removing his helmet to run a hand over, began speaking in halting Vietnamese to the woman, who pointed at times in the direction of another village, Qua New, as she responded rapidly to his questions. The CIA team, whom they had never seen, not surprisingly was also not there, and when Ross finished with the woman he sent Mullin with a padlocked duffel bag to the hut the CIA team occupied, where Mullin placed it inside.

As Glen and the others ate the rice in the shade of a group of palms at the edge of the village where they usually sat (beside them several of the brothers talked and laughed loudly—Ross having given up a month before with the no-cluster policy that had initially been enforced) the children of the village would gather a few feet away and ask for candy, which the mess private, Donald Chung of Portland, Oregon, age twenty, enlisted, would toss to them in a small bag they would scramble excitedly for, laughing and squealing in their high-pitched voices.

There were usually one or two women with babies or young children, and a few old men or women, who would gather around Pvt. Dunstun, the medic, and attempt to describe various pains and illnesses. Today, though, there was just one girl with a small baby in her arms whose mouth she was trying to show by pushing it open with her fingers as she spoke in both Vietnamese and halting French. Dunstun sat on the ground beside his pack with its red cross patch, eating his bowl of rice, listening to the young mother squatted beside him, at times also answering in broken French. When he finished the rice he took the baby from the girl's arms and looked into its mouth which was now open wide as the baby began to loudly cry.

"No sick—*non la nausée*," Dunstun said in both English and French as he held the wailing child. He handed the baby back to the girl who, adjusting the wide brim of her hat, did not seem convinced and continued to converse rapidly in Vietnamese. Then Dunstun opened his pack and wiped his hand on a cloth and took out a tube of gel and squeezed a small amount onto his finger and rubbed it lightly inside the child's mouth where there seemed to be a small rash. The mother rocked the child and the baby stopped crying and Dunstun closed his pack.

Glen, who had been watching from a few feet away in the shade of the trees, turned to Davis who sat on the ground beside him and Ben. He took out his cigarettes and handed the pack to Davis who took one, handing the pack back. "You should take a few," Glen said, leaning against his pack, his rifle and the empty bowl beside him. "I must have gone through half your pack yesterday—"

Two helicopters passed overhead, the loud woofing of their rotors temporarily delaying Davis' response. Squinting up at the sky, he struck a match and lit the cigarettes, offering the flame to Ben who shook his head. "Ah, don't worry about it—Hey, look at Phillips." Davis nodded toward a soldier who had gone over to where two village girls were washing clothes in large metal pans at the edge of the stream. Phillips, his rifle slung over his shoulder, his helmet on his head, was talking to them even though they didn't speak any English. He offered them cigarettes; he squatted down and examined some of the wet clothing. The girls talked nervously in Vietnamese between themselves, at times half laughing, at other times glancing quickly at Phillips. "Well, what, does he think he's going to come back here tonight?" said Davis.

"It wouldn't surprise me if he tried," Glen said.

"Christ—shoot and fuck," Davis said. "It's the shoot and fuck patrol." Now Phillips grinned widely as he held up a pair of women's underwear; and Tommy Walker, who had been observing and laughing a few feet away, came over to join him.

"Watch the Sarge," Glen said. "He's about done with Phen's wife."

Sergeant Ross was across the dirt ground of the hamlet, still talking with the woman in the flowered dress, along with 2nd Lt. Jeff Wilcox of Bakersfield, California, age twenty-two, enlisted, the radio operator, who had been busily making calls, and Ross was about to return to his men. Phillips, meanwhile, now joined by Walker, was still squatted next to the girls at the edge of the stream, smiling and talking; and he reached over to touch one of the girls, but she jumped quickly up and moved away and Walker laughed loudly and Phillips grinned and said something to her no one else could hear; and then Sergeant Ross saw them.

"Look out," Glen said to Davis and Ben, blowing out smoke in the pleasant shade of the palms, the broad fronds twisting gently overhead in the light breeze. Ross strode quickly across the dirt toward Phillips who jumped suddenly up and, with Walker, moved away from the girls; and many of the villagers now stopped to watch and the sixteen remaining members of the platoon all watched as Ross, his face reddening, continued toward the stream. But then he suddenly altered his path and began slowly veering toward where the trail picked up across the village, just as Phillips had begun repeating '*all right—all right*'; and then everyone was standing, and Ross, without breaking stride, called out sharply to move out, and packs were swung on and rifles picked up, and, leaving the empty bowls on the ground, they headed back into the forest.

SIX

"Come on, Unitas—let's *go*." Ben, in his deep voice, grinned broadly, as he spoke to Glen from behind, who was lying on his cot in the squad-tent reading a letter.
"Yeah, hey; I'm ready." Glen folded up the letter and grabbed his shirt. They ducked out of the tent and walked in the warm morning sun toward the mess-hutch where two idling trucks sat half filled with soldiers all talking loudly. Glen and Ben stood around conversing with the others for a few minutes, as more soldiers came up, and then everyone climbed into the trucks and the drivers ground into gear and they rolled out.
They left the camp and passed the sprawling South Vietnamese camp where numerous uniformed soldiers—many glancing up at the convoy with wide smiles and waves—moved about the assortment of tents and vehicles and supplies as others squatted in small groups around cooking fires. To one side, in a kind of field, several long rows of more men appeared to be training; and then the trucks were past the outskirts of the village and headed

up the forested valley. In a few miles they came to a junction and crossed a river on a one-lane bridge and then wound up the side of a ridge before reaching another larger, sparsely-forested plain where the road straightened and the drivers shifted into high. They went another five miles, passing small villages and assorted vehicles and numerous people alongside the road, and to one side an immense water-filled paddy where a lone farmer plowed from behind a water buffalo, and then came completely out of the trees and raced toward the outskirts of a small town with buildings and houses and many small huts and to one side another military base, more than twice as large as the base in the valley.

There was also a small airstrip a few hundred yards beyond the base where several planes and helicopters sat motionless; and the trucks pulled up to a long row of military tents and metal storage containers, and a short ways beyond the tents was a large field where groups of soldiers were playing football. The field was marked off with small flags and two games were going on as many soldiers stood on the sidelines or crowded around two open-walled tents and everywhere about the field.

The trucks came to a final stop near one of the open tents, both of which contained long tables of food and beer, and the men got out with the smoky aroma of grilling beef drifting over from the numerous barbecues beside the tents. Some went straight to the tables while the rest made their way to the soldiers along the sidelines; and Davis grabbed a football off the ground and Sandis took off on a short pattern. Someone said Glen's company would be playing members of Charlie Company of the 9th Infantry Division, at 10:30, on the far field, and Glen took off on a route and caught a pass from Mullin. Now Walker went deep with his cigarette in his mouth and Glen tried to throw long but it flew off his hand and into a group of the brothers who had to dodge. "Yo, Clark Kent!" one of them yelled. "You ain't on my team…" But another got it and threw it on to Walker.

"*Sorry!*" Glen yelled back, not knowing if they had really cared.

After a few minutes of warming up they gathered on the sideline and Mullin, who was the oldest and rumored to have been an all-state quarterback in high school, told Glen and

Walker to play ends and Davis and Pvt. Richard Hartz, who each now came up, mouths full, with a hamburger and ear of corn in each hand, to play on the line while Mullin took the snaps. Ben, drinking a can of Budweiser, volunteered to play center. "And let's play," Mullin said, "I want to beat these guys. We lost bad last time—no more of that crap. It was embarrassing."

"Yeah, and we got to block," said Hartz, born in Denver and raised in Colorado Springs, age twenty-one, enlisted, trying to finish the hamburger. He was big and heavy, the biggest soldier Glen had seen since his enlistment six months before, to where he thought someone somewhere must have made a mistake. All of Hartz clothes rode up high on his limbs, and although no one ever said it out loud, they had all had the troubling thought that if anyone was ever aiming at the platoon, they would aim at Hartz first. (On the other hand, Ross was always threatening to transfer him to a desk in Saigon whenever they cleared a tunnel and Hartz had to wait up above—*Fine; fine with me,* he would say contemptuously, *transfer my ass outta here*—and Ross would stomp off, his face red and scowling.) "Nobody blocked," Hartz went on at the side of the field, finishing the burger, chewing, licking his fingers. "If we can get Victor across the line we can run the crap out of them." No one anywhere had ever seen anyone as fast as Victor. Hartz was a big lineman but he wasn't dumb.

"Whoa—check the fleece at T-hut," Davis said, flipping the ball in the air and gazing at a group of nurses standing near some officers across the field beside a command hut. They were well over a hundred yards away, but their white uniforms and figures and movements stood out sharply from the many dozens of men around the field and the nearly hundred more visible about the base.

"Yeah—whoo-*eee,*" Drawled New Orleans Johnny Parker who had wandered up with a plate with two hamburgers, as everyone looked toward the nurses. "Ahm a-tellin' yew, I keep hearin' there's a whole buncha ladies posted here and at the C.O. in town." He looked gleefully at the others and took a bite.

"I heard there's a lady mechanic at the runway," said Ben, holding his beer.

"Nah—come on," said Davis, disbelievingly.

"It's what I heard," Ben said, not caring if he was believed or not, and drank from his beer.

"Okay, listen up," Mullin said. "We got to watch everything deep. Nothing deep—especially early. We don't want ..."

Just before the explosion some birds flapped their wings in a nearby tree and cawed in the pleasant late-morning air; and the earth shook and a roar cut Mullin off and sent everyone diving to the ground. It had actually come from the middle of town, a half-mile away; and thick smoke rose into the hazy sky above the buildings and then everyone got up and assembled near a wall of sandbagged bunkers. And half an hour later, the sky now filled with the swooping arcs of low-flying helicopters, the word came down: everyone back to base; no game.

SEVEN

"Hey! ... Red Hawk ... Everybody up ... *Red Hawk!* ... Twenty minutes at Blue Gate ... We have a Red hawk—*Everybody!*" The barking voice at the door was quickly gone and the generator light came on and Glen blinked at the dark canvas ceiling and then he was on the side of his cot pulling on his pants and boots alongside the eleven others in the tent. A Red Hawk meant they were heading out in a helicopter and then it hit him that this wasn't a practice Green Hawk and that it was very possible they could be going to confront enemy hostilities and a surge of blood rushed through his head. Throughout the tent the last articles of clothing were pulled on and packs were checked and the soldiers grabbed their rifles at the stand and filed out the door and into the dark.

When Glen got to the overhead light at Blue Gate there were another fifteen men from the platoon assembling and a first lieutenant was handing out Delta C-rations which were used for extended missions and checking with people on first aid and ammunition and then Sergeant Ross, and Colonel Zachary Wood of Durham, North Carolina, age forty-nine, two Purple Hearts, Korea, enlisted, the commanding officer of the brigade, came with his assistant from Eagle Hut. Everyone stopped what they were doing and stood at attention when they saw Col. Wood (except for a group of the brothers who talked and laughed loudly until Ross turned and yelled *attention*). Then Ross instructed everyone to continue as they were and five minutes after that suddenly told everyone to listen-the-hell up.

They had been assigned to a mission that would be flying to an outpost near the Laotian border where an apparent attack had occurred and three CIA operatives were missing, Ross told them. Two helicopters were going toward the nearest landing zone, six miles below the outpost, and a ground unit of the 101st Airborne would be hiking in to find out what had happened. Glen's unit would be staying at the landing zone to secure the Hueys until the 101st returned. When Ross finished, Col. Wood told them that they had been chosen from ten platoons from training scores over the past four months and they should be damn proud of it. '*We got some boys in trouble*' and he was counting on Glen's platoon to help bring them back.

After a last brief word with Sergeant Ross, Wood and his assistant walked swiftly back to Eagle Hut and two trucks pulled up and Glen and the others climbed into the back and they pulled out of the base and headed for the airstrip at Plei Ku. They stared silently at the dark outlines of one another and then in a low, soft voice, James Phillips said to William McCall, the soldier squeezed next to him on the hard, wood bench: "I told you not to always be walking so fast; you upped all our scores and now they're dropping us off in the middle of fuck-knows-where—China."

"With big U.S. Army patches stitched all over us," said Davis, drowsily.

"You afraid?" McCall said to Phillips, knowing they were all afraid, the truck bouncing in the darkness along the rough road. "Shit—I've been waitin' eight fuckin' months for this."

"Yeah, you've been here longer, too," Sandis said. "We're supposed to have been training for ground patrols right here—

War Zone C—Not this crap …" He muffled the word *crap* to be sure Ross didn't hear despite knowing he wouldn't be able to hear anything up front anyway over the loud whining of the engine. "And after what happened to Mr. Phen … It's not like we don't know they're around here again." The week before, another platoon patrolling the area around Phu Gan had found Mr. Phen hanging from a tree with his stomach slit open.

Now Ben's deep voice resonated out of the dark, the vague outline of his long legs coming up high on the low bench where he subtly rocked in the bouncing truck: "You really want to know? I've been climbing the walls since the first week at Tra Dien. And then sitting around everyday at Dra Ming when Con Thien was going on. And now they find Phen … Oh, don't get me wrong, we've had as much down time as anyone—but you start to wonder: is this all we're going to do?—But this, I don't know …"

"Yeah, well, we'll get to see some new countryside," said Glen with just the slightest trace of anger, his pack and rifle on the floor between his legs.

Phillips looked at Glen's shadow: "Christ, the hundred-and-first … man, that's elite shit."

"What's this, the third Hawk mission?" said Davis. "They never took us up into no mountains at night."

"Look, don't sweat it," said Mullin. They could see his dark outline and hear his voice, but they couldn't see his eyes. "They've been talking about night patrols for a long time—. Something's happened and we're going to go help straighten it out."

"Well, shit, something happened at Phu Gan, too," said Sandis. "We could be straightening shit right here."

"I think the one-oh-one's going to be doing most of the straightening," said Glen.

"I don't know," said Ben. "I never heard of any Zone-C Hawk-missions going out in the middle of the night either … and now you keep hearing about Laos more and more … and Cambodia.

"Look, did you see Ross?" said Mullin's dark outline. "He looked fine to me. I'm not worried. He's been here twice—more than two years. He's seen it all. Fuck, he was at Ia Drang in

'65—Ben Suc last year. He knows what the hell's going on ... he looked fine to me."

"Fuckin' CIA—those cocksuckers." Phillips yawned, as others also yawned, and gradually closed his eyes. Near the rear of the bouncing truck, Glen, wide awake, gazed up at the glimmering stars out the open back as, through the dust, the dark forest sped rapidly past.

* * *

"... Are they still there?" Davis spoke in little more than a whisper as he came up on Glen's post in the trees to relieve him from his position on the perimeter. The two helicopters sat behind them in the middle of the clearing with the circle of men dug in at the edge of the dense forest that spilled down from the steep surrounding hills. The late afternoon sun beat down hot from almost directly overhead, but at the higher elevation, close to four-thousand feet, it was not the stifling heat they had left behind at Dra Ming.

Glen shifted his helmet with one hand and with the other pointed his rifle at the hillside above. "There," he said quietly, "they seem to be moving toward the ravine." Davis looked into the trees above where a woman and a boy stood motionless in the shadows. Then slowly, at a barely visible pace, they moved a few feet through the thick undergrowth toward a narrow cut that led down to the remote mountain clearing. They had been there since at least mid-morning when Mullin had first spotted them and sent an adrenaline rush through the ring with word of movement. But Ross, with his high-powered binoculars, and hardened intuition, quickly identified them, and the perceived danger and level of fear gradually subsided.

Little was known of the area but it was thought to be the safest site below the Ashau ridge where for at least the last six months the CIA mission had been directing the Hmong food drops. The mountain Laotian Hmong tribes had been recruited to fight their ancient enemy, the Vietnamese, but the recruiting was more cruel manipulation of a mostly primitive indigenous people than political ideology. They armed the male warriors with rifles and grenades and then dropped desperately needed food supplies into suspected enemy positions and let them fight their way to the food. The war had taken away their farms and now it was feeding them with the currency that war used and something had happened high in the mountains three days before. The three CIA operatives had radioed an urgent warning and then went silent, and while members of the 101st climbed in to find them, Glen and Ben, and Davis and Mullin, and the fourteen others of 'D' Company, waited with the copters in the clearing below.

"Holy fuck—they are weird, huh?" Davis said in a tone as much confused as anxious, as the boy and woman stopped again in the trees.

"Real weird," said Glen, tensely. "This sure isn't like Dra Ming."

"It sure as fuck aint," said Davis. "This aint like anywhere I ever even heard of: boot camp—Tra Dien—New York City—the north fucking pole. Fuck—who the fuck are they?"

"I've heard of them. They're supposedly on our side; that's all I give a hoot about." Glen strained to see into the trees. "Besides, it's just a woman and her kid …"

"Yeah, but it doesn't take a brain surgeon to figure out where there's a woman and a kid … Shit, we made enough noise coming in last night."

"Yeah … It could have been worse."

The CIA had supplied the reconnaissance for the area, finding, with blind luck, a nearby natural clearing, instead of the usual procedure of air force bombers blasting out a landing zone in the dense, layered canopy. Trailing a decoy squadron of copters that was immediately preceded by two, blind, north-south air strikes, they had veered suddenly for the landing zone, following a long winding valley, then cut to drift propulsion and dropped without lights, hard into the clearing. And then the hundred-and-first was running up the hillside, cutting furiously into the thick vegetation as the second round of flanking air strikes flashed brilliantly on the distant horizon.

Glen squinted again toward the woman who had moved a few more feet toward the ravine. He reached for his binoculars and held them to his face. "Christ, look at that ... what's she got on?" Even from a hundred yards the brilliant bead-work cascading down from the woman's neck and the brightly woven shawl and pants were clearly visible through the trees to where Glen and Davis crouched in the grass.

"Let me see; yeah, shit, some kind of fucking necklace or something. Big sucker."

Glen slowly shook his head. "Okay, look, someone will be back at dusk ... I'll see you later." He took the binoculars and, in a low crouch, began to move slowly back through the grass.

* * *

There were three soldiers sitting in the flattened area between the two metal birds when Glen came up: first radio operator Wilcox, and Pvts. Brian Lewis and Douglas Guzzo, all of whom were eating C-rations from the supply stored on one of the helicopters. Sgt. Ross, meanwhile, had taken Ben and a second radio to the ridge behind them to try to track the 101st ascent of the mountain. Pointing in opposite directions toward the forest, the barrels of two 70mm machine guns protruded from the open copter doors.

Glen exchanged greetings and took a can of food and got out his mess kit and sat beside the others in the grass to eat. It was becoming late in the afternoon and darkness would fall within a few hours with the mountain shadows coming down quickly into the clearing, and Glen ate his uncooked food. "So, anything up?"

Wilcox shook his head. "Nothing. Sarge and Ben got a signal an hour ago but it was hard to read. He thought they'd made it up to some village—Det Tren, I think—and they could see Bolia at the summit. But it was supposed to take another four hours to get there. By dark is the word; if they're going to find anything it'll be tonight."

"When's Ross coming back?" Glen asked.

"Well, he better be back here by dark," Wilcox said. "It's hard enough hacking through that shit in daylight."

Pvts. Lewis and Guzzo, sitting in the shadows of the Hueys, silently spooned at their open cans. Glen looked toward the ridge where Ross had gone.

"Where's the woman?" said Wilcox.

"They're still moving toward the ravine."

"Shit—I wish they'd just come down."

"We tried," said Guzzo, looking up; "they ran."

"Lucky they didn't get shot," said Wilcox, scraping at the last of his can. He carefully licked his spoon and tossed the can into the grass.

Continuing to eat, Glen glanced at the hillside toward Davis and thought of the woman and child and then suddenly thought of Julie and the lunchroom tables at Western State their freshman year where they had spent many happy hours, the initial intoxicating freedom of being away at college, the passionate reuniting with Julie after the almost year of voluntary separation and her decision to come to Western, the whole of life before them.

"I don't like any of it," said Lewis in the clearing near the Laotian border, eating. He was stocky with a large jaw that moved from side to side as he spoke and ate. "If they're so sure those hills are clean what happened at Bolia?"

"Crap, Doug—it's Doug, right?" said Glen, sounding impatient, "—they just don't know. Maybe they were clean a month ago—or even last week. Anything could be going on out here."

Lewis slowly chewed. "Well, Sarge told me it was probably clean," he wiped his mouth, "but ..."

"... Expect the worse—be prepared," they said together, reciting Ross' most familiar refrain.

"Shit, why worry, anyway?" said Guzzo, still eating. He moved in jerks, at times adjusting himself on the grass where he sat Indian-style. "Hell, it could've been anything ... guy could just be sick. Or an accident—shit, we get enough of those around here."

"Yeah—right," said Wilcox, cynically. "If it was nothing they would have just dropped someone in to check it out ... instead of sending in the 101st, on foot, at night ... There wouldn't be all this crap over an accident."

"Yeah," said Lewis, now in a boisterous tone. "Someone knows more than we're getting told and it stinks. They let us watch all those bodies come in from Gia last month ... And they purposely keep us away from Dak Suh—or wherever the hell it was—where there's finally been some serious fighting going on ... And then bring us out here in the middle of the night." His eyes rolled upward. "Because our *test* scores were high."

"Right—to fucking *Laos!*" Wilcox half-snorted in a kind of frightened laugh.

"Shit—Laos," said Lewis, still chewing, seemingly more rapidly. "I don't know about you but I never heard nothing about Laos—I thought we were fighting Vietnam."

"No; no—come on. We aren't actually *in* Laos," said Glen. "We're near it."

"How the fuck do you know?" said Wilcox, getting out a cigarette and staring hard at Glen. "You see any signs?" He struck a match and lit the cigarette.

They all glanced silently out toward the deep forests blanketing the surrounding hills and Glen went back to eating as Lewis and Guzzo put away their utensils. And Wilcox, his cigarette in his mouth, began fiddling earnestly again with the radio that was spewing out the same static it had for most of the day.

* * *

'Wow! That was a big one!' Glen drove the car along the road beside the ocean beach as huge, towering waves roared in, crashing over the road both in front and behind, and flowing far up into the dunes on the other side. His sister, Cindy, smiled nervously in the passenger seat beside him as the deep, swirling water flowed heavily off the dunes and road and back into the sea. 'WOW!' Glen now said even more loudly: 'Look at that one—Good God!'. His voice suddenly changed from reassuring brother to confused, disoriented adult, as from the sea rose a massive wave that stretched in each direction for as far as they could see; and it floated slowly upward and above the car until it blocked out the sun and they were in semi-darkness; and Glen looked in utter terror toward Cindy as the towering crest began slowly to roar down from high above.

Glen awoke with a jerk in the darkness under the long blade of the copter as the fast streaking jets roared loudly overhead. With the loud beating of his heart, he lay on his back, listening: there were strange sounds now coming from the forest—small animals or nocturnal birds, hooting—and off to one side Mullin smoked a cigarette with his rifle in his lap, as the dark outlines of other soldiers, some also awakened by the jets and now leaning up, were faintly visible around him. Breathing more slowly now and rolling onto his side, Glen closed his eyes, and, almost immediately, he again saw the wave.

* * *

They arose before the sun in the morning with the noise of Ross and Ben leaving again for the ridge and the static of the radio and the sounds of the mess private making coffee. They ate and talked quietly as the sky lightened and the hills became brilliant green, and then Glen and several others left to relieve some of the perimeter posts at the edges of the clearing.

In the late afternoon there was a commotion at the base of the ridge where Ross had gone and then Sandis was walking swiftly around the perimeter with word that the 101st was coming out with a body. And two hours later, just as the sun was about to set, the heavily armed and camouflaged unit, carrying one man on a stretcher and another in a long black bag, came swiftly across the grass toward the copters, whose blades had already begun their slow, mechanical swoosh. And then everyone was scrambling on board and they lifted noisily into the air and began to rise above the clearing.

With the sun now sinking behind the distant horizon, they leaned toward the open doors and the rising viewpoint and below saw the woman and boy running across the trampled grass; and through the dense trees of the nearby ridge, their rifles protruding before them, the slow and steady descent of dark-clothed men toward the clearing.

EIGHT

"*Hartz!—Gray!* Get the fuck back out here! Everybody—fall *in!* Now we are staying *here!* Everyone—down. And hold your god damn fire." Sergeant Ross moved quickly in a crouch past several of his men, back in the direction from which they had just fled, violently, when they had suddenly encountered the swarm of NVAs a few moments before on the other side of the stream.

Unlike the patrols of the first eight months, these of the last two, since Tet, in the area around the new posting to Na Meo, had resulted in increasingly frequent enemy contact, several with long range engagements. The worst having occurred just a week before when for the first time since Glen had arrived in country, he and other members of the company had fired their weapons at visible targets where the objective outcome would be immediately known. (There had been numerous mortar firings at distant coordinates, and the ever more frequent rifle and machine gun discharges into real or imagined forest movements, but never with an actual face in the cross hairs). And also for the first time, someone had been shot, Peter Marshall of Vera Cruz, California, age twenty-one, enlisted, in the neck. Miraculously, it had missed everything in there that could have been fatal—which was about 95% of it—but he had gone into shock and been taken by helicopter back to the base at Ka Ban; and everyone felt greatly changed.

They were acting as a kind of safety valve; heavy engagements were occurring with increasing frequency near Ban Bo, twenty kilometers to the west, and any fleeing soldiers of the NVA (who were being largely routed by the American and South Vietnamese forces) were to be kept away from the area around Na Meo as they fled. Using their binoculars, they had been seeing some about twice a week in the far distance across the stream—short, ragged-dressed men with rifles, running through the forest—and now seemingly every other day. But they were almost always too far away to engage and so Ross would call in artillery or send off mortar rounds and then they would hunker down and cover their ears while the earth exploded in the near distance.

But today, for the first time, Glen's unit had crossed the stream to search for a rumored tunnel, and instead of a distant handful of fleeing enemy, they had come upon an organized battalion; and Ross quickly waved everyone back and radioed artillery. But Pvt. George Bailey of New Bedford, Massachusetts, age twenty, drafted, had suddenly turned and fired. So it was they who had done the fleeing, through the brush and back across the stream, a heavy barrage of fire coming from behind, and, surprisingly, Glen and Richard Hartz—besides Ben, the two largest men in the entire brigade—streaking in a near blur past everyone else, all of whom were retreating as rapidly as possible, and burrowing the furthest back into the forest growth on the other side of the stream, just as the artillery began pounding the just vacated position;—*running, running*—one more month—*running, running, running*—one more fucking month of this shit—*running, running, running, running*—until Ross had yelled for everyone to stop.

When he finally began to catch his breath, the adrenaline still surging, the beating of his heart still furious, one hand pressed down hard on his helmet and the other clutching his rifle, Glen looked down and saw the torn shirt and the long deep gash where the branch had caught his wildly swinging arm; and on his wrist, the bracelet from Grandpa Gray was gone.

Part III
LONGHAIR

ONE

When he returned to America that spring—the final months in Indochina in the aftermath of February's Tet Offensive a relatively quiet and uneventful posting to a supply depot near Da Nang before discharge in San Francisco via the Philippines—Glen resided for the first month at his parents home in Sealth, with most of the first week following the long journey home and initial shock of being suddenly back in the States and in the same house where it had all begun—as well as the battling of a nagging virus that had followed him home—spent sleeping in his bed. By the end of the month, however, he was ready to move back to the quieter and more comfortable surroundings of Port Crescent, and there found a small house to rent across town from the university. In Port Crescent, within a week, he began working in one of the large lumber mills—as many of the male students did during summers and vacations and as he had the summer before his enlistment—driving a fork lift, and loading trucks and train cars with the processed lumber cut from the trees that flowed steadily in from the surrounding forests.

Julie, finishing her primary education degree at Western State, was completing her student teaching and would graduate in June with tentative plans to teach third grade at a local elementary school. The long separation and extremeness of its conditions had made Glen's and Julie's reuniting difficult and slow, but the energy and flair of their youth carried it along until Glen made the initial re-adaptation to civilian America and Vietnam moved slowly into the past.

* * *

During that first month in Sealth, his own mother, who had written to him every week for the nineteen months he had been away, helped as much as anyone with his readjustment, supplying a continuous flow of relatives to the home, as well as large, specially-prepared meals, and long, frequent hugs—and simply by remaining close by.

In the evenings, though, within a few weeks (the virus having eventually subsided), after the large suppers and after any relatives or family friends had left, Glen would go to the bars around town and meet with old friends, or with Julie when she came down on the weekends, and talk and drink beer until they closed late at night.

One evening, accompanied by a few old high school friends, Glen went to someone's house who had marijuana, a substance he had tried once before in Vietnam, and, although fairly new to Sealth's middle-class youth, as the weeks began rolling by, it quickly became apparent that it was increasingly the fond object of their attention. This suited Glen fine as he seemed to take well to the kind of faint rush that pot created and the way it cut through the sloppy daze of alcohol.

Glen was well aware that large social changes had been occurring in civilian America while he had been away; there were the numerous magazines articles the soldiers voraciously read, and the letters from home, and, most vividly, the stories from newly arrived recruits. But only after experiencing civilian life first hand did it become apparent how much greater the changes were from that which he had envisioned.

And yet much seemed not to have changed at all. There was the daily regimen of the community: the mail that got delivered; the food and merchandise that moved in and out of the stores; the schools, banks, and offices that droned steadily on just as before. Northgate looked the same; the neighborhoods looked the same; Glen's father looked the same.

But other things had changed, or, in the case of the public's lack of support for the war, increased. And although public descent had only become vaguely apparent to Glen and his company leading up to the time of their departure a few months after Tet (high command repeatedly downplaying stories of stateside protests while plying their ears with counter stories of strong domestic support—which made many even more suspicious) now, stateside again, the tidal-change was greatly apparent, and after only a few weeks back, Glen stopped mentioning to people from where he had just returned.

His mother, however, did not stop mentioning it; she was constantly leaving newspaper and magazine articles on the kitchen counter about brave soldiers and returned veterans who were doing good things with their lives, despite the war's controversy. Such efforts helped greatly, providing much needed esteem; but mostly Glen was just excited about being back in the good ol' U.S. of A., and to have survived what had become an increasingly dangerous mission, and he tried to settle in as best he could. Often, if all else failed, he would simply retreat to the sanctuary of his bedroom to smoke a cigarette and play one of the new records from his rapidly growing collection, with music and words that seemed to both sooth and connect in ways the rest of the world could not.

TWO

"You won't believe it, Glen, it must be—what—how tall is it, Julie? Five feet? It's incredible—you'll freak." Randy drove up the dimly lit residential street with Julie and Glen beside him on the front seat and, at a small, single-story house, pulled to the curb.

"I'll what?" said Glen.

It was just like old times and had been all week. Randy and Julie were down from Port Crescent, Julie that afternoon and Randy a few days before, specially to see Glen. And there had been much drinking and talking and celebrating and visiting of old haunts around the city. And Randy had brought some marijuana and had been happily and enthusiastically sharing it with Glen each night.

"Five feet?" said Julie. "Honest, Randy, I have no idea—I haven't seen it. I saw some in Port Crescent that were—I don't know, three feet?"

"Really? You haven't?" Randy said as they got out of the car. "I thought you'd seen it, Jules."

"Nope."

As they approached the front door they could hear the booming base of a stereo and Randy knocked hard and the base was suddenly lowered and one of the curtains cracked and the door swung open.

"Hey, man." A large young man greeted Randy, wide-eyed and smiling, and looked at Julie and Glen and nodded, and then motioned them all inside.

"You've met Julie, right?" Randy said to the man once they were inside, who Glen could now see was not at anytime recently connected with the United States military. His look, in fact, was of a very non-military nature, with his head of long bushy hair, and thick beard, and the colorful shirt and reddish-tinted pants. Julie said hi and the man shook Glen's hand, and another young man, he skinny, sitting on a couch in the sparsely furnished room, also was introduced; and the stereo was turned back up, but not to the volume it had been.

"—Beer?" Randy said to the large man, Ray, extending the six-pack they had carried in, and then to the man on the couch, Tom; and Glen and Julie also each took one and they all sat on the various couches and chairs, except for Ray who stood beside the cabinet containing the expensive-looking stereo and carefully adjusted several of the dials.

"Yeah ... this is the part," the man on the couch, Tom, now said to Ray in a serious tone. He also had a very unmilitary air about him; although his hair was not particularly long—nothing like the after-hours group Glen had encountered a few nights before at the outdoor burger counter at Zeke's, to whom he had done a double take when he realized they were men; and then, surprisingly, had smiled—the young man's mustache was long and thick, and it curved far down on each side beyond the corners of his mouth. And like Ray his clothing was ruffled, yet strangely stylish and bright, and the pattern on his shirt bright, and he wore old boots and tapped his foot more aggressively to the music which had suddenly just changed in the middle of the song to a more unusual and upbeat rhythm, unlike anything Glen had heard before; and the sound flowed loud and hypnotically from the speakers as everyone listened.

The room was dimly lit with several lamps giving a slightly yellowish glow, and on the walls were several large posters of popular musical groups in unusual settings that seemed very different from the whimsical images Glen remembered from his old records; and all throughout, the air of seriousness was palpable. And like the late-night group at Zekes, and a few other individuals he had seen around town—and some of the recent photographs he had observed in magazines and newspapers—all of the men in the posters wore colorful clothing and boots, and they all had very long hair; some as long as women's.

"Oh—so you're the dude just back from Vietnam?" Ray said, looking over to Glen as the song faded, with the expression of someone who has just recalled something they had been struggling to remember.

"Yeah," said Glen, looking first at Ray, then Randy.

"Yeah," said Randy, nodding, reassuring Ray that he was correct; and he reached for his can of beer and took a drink.

Ray nodded and smiled and looked at both Randy and Glen. "Wow—no shit?"

"Yeah … yeah …" Glen repeated, and then once more, "… yeah."

"Wow," Ray said again, and drank from his beer. "Well, shit, how was it?"

"Ah … not real great. I mean, shit, it could have been worse … I survived." Glen took a drink. "I'm alive—fuck."

"Yeah … fuck," Ray said, leaning forward from where he sat at the edge of the couch. On the small coffee table before him were several small boxes and a small plastic bag partially filled with a dark, green substance; and he took two cigarette papers from a rolling pack, and, licking the papers together, rolled up some of the green material. "Shit," he went on, as he continued working on the joint, "well, any fighting? … I mean, I don't mean to like, pry, or whatever, but shit, man …"

"Yeah, well, I know …" Glen drank more of his beer. "… No, not really. I mean, Tet, but everyone was getting hit then."

"What about the ambush," Randy said. "You guys got ambushed, right?"

"Well, we didn't get it. But we went into some heat that was hitting some guys before us …" Glen glanced at Julie who listened expressionless from one of the chairs. "I don't know—it all seems screwed up now."

"Whew ..." Ray shook his head. "Fuck, man, I couldn't ... just couldn't. I got 4F anyway; my eyes are all fucked up."

Glen drank from his beer.

Ray looked at the oblong-shaped joint in his hand and struck a match. "It's pending—you know?" He lit the end and inhaled deeply. "My doctor thinks it'll go through, though." His voice turned high and strained as he held in the smoke.

"Remember Daryl Dubelli?" Julie said to Glen from the chair. She wore a wool sweater and her brown hair hung far past her shoulders.

"Daryl? Yeah, where's Daryl?—I've been meaning to call him."

"He's here in town, somewhere," Julie said. "But Christen says Daryl knows some doctor who can get people 4F. It's supposed to be real secret, though—like real secret. The guy would go to jail in a second if he ever got caught—banned from medicine, everything ..." She looked at the others in the room.

The joint came to Randy and he inhaled deeply and the coal glowed bright and sparked and burned unevenly up the paper.

"Wow—so what's Daryl up to?" Glen said as Julie took the joint.

"Well, he's still in school ... sort of. Still going out with Peggy ..." She began to inhale.

"Yeah? ... no kidding." Glen smiled, "what do you know ..."

"Yeah, I guess they might be getting married ..." Julie blew out the smoke, "... she doesn't want him going over there."

"Shit, I just couldn't do it," Ray said, shaking his head again; and he reached over and pulled out more rolling papers.

"A lot of people going over the border." The other man, Tom, sitting low on the other couch, spoke slowly and for only the second time, as he pulled on one side of his mustache. He glanced at everyone and then back toward one of the large floor speakers across the room where his gaze had seemed permanently fixed, legs crossed, a suspended foot swaying to the beat. The multi-component system appeared very expensive and complex, not unlike what Glen had seen of the bustling, Asian electronics trade he had witnessed on the streets of Saigon and Manila.

"... Yeah, a lot," the man on the couch went on. "Port Crescent's full of 'em ... Waiting to cross ... They come up from California by the car load ..." After Glen, Tom was next for the joint and they reached long to each other for the exchange.

"Yeah?" said Ray, glancing up and nodding as he finished the new joint. "A lot—huh?" He held the joint to his mouth and moistened the yellow paper while still nodding to Tom.

"Hey," Randy said, "so I told Glen you'd show him the plant." He pushed his horn-rimmed glasses up and looked eagerly at Ray and took a drink from his beer.

"Yeah?" said Ray, lighting the new joint, "yeah, sure, man." He sucked hard and held his breath, struggling to keep in the hot smoke. When he finally exhaled, the bluish stream flowed thick across the room, settling into the drifting layers already floating about the dim light. "Yeah, sure ... sure, man," he repeated, nodding. "Yeah ... she's about ready for pickin'."

"Yeah?" Randy said, now smiling broadly, almost laughing, "—no shit?"

"No shit, man," Ray said, and he did laugh; and the wide smile spread to the creases of his face and eyes, and exposed the dull white of his large teeth. "Yeah ..." he continued to grin, nodding, "come on."

With Ray rising first and the others following, they filed into the kitchen and out to a small, porch-like enclosure in back where the vague, uneven outline of something large filled one corner of the darkened room. He waited until everyone had crowded in and then reached up and pulled the cord on the single overhead bulb. And smiling broadly, he stepped back as the sudden light filled the room and glowed brilliantly off the thick, bursting tangle of glistening green that spewed up and outward everywhere into the surrounding space above the dirt-filled bucket on the stained linoleum floor.

* * *

Later, when they were on the couch in the basement at Julie's and suddenly heard her mother walking upstairs, Glen sat quickly up and grabbed his shirt and listened to see if he would have to run into the bathroom to dress. But they heard her go back to the bedroom and it was quiet again and they leaned back on the couch.

"I don't want to get caught," Julie said, her shoes on the floor and the wool sweater off to the side.

"Yeah, I should probably go," Glen said.

She reached over and put her hand behind his neck. "… I just said I don't want to get caught." She pulled him closer and he kissed her again.

Later still, Julie awoke with the first light of dawn and woke Glen and after he dressed she walked him to the door and kissed him goodbye and then rushed up the stairs to her room before her mother got up.

When he pulled up to his parents house it was light and they were already up and he said only a quick good morning on the way to his room when he caught a glimpse of them sipping coffee and reading the paper in their bathrobes in the kitchen.

* * *

That evening, just before dinner, Glen sat in the recreation room with the TV on while his sister, Cindy, sat at a table doing homework between glances of the old '50's rerun Glen was watching as he casually tossed a softball from one hand to the other. Then he got up from the couch and turned the station and adjusted the rabbit ears on the top of the set.

The war raged on and the news was filled with the stories and images of the fighting and the growing American opposition, and of the noisy, head-turning clatter (or was it simply amplified music?) of something even louder and deeper, yet not as readily identifiable, which filtered up from somewhere within the youthful opposition's increasingly loud voice that emanated largely from college campuses around the world.

"Tra Dien!" Glen suddenly said as he watched the flickering images and listened to the reporting correspondent; and Cindy looked up from her papers and books. "That's where we spent the first month …" He leaned over to turn up the sound as the scanning camera swept across a field of military structures and tents and fencing, and soldiers passing in jeeps, waving. "Come on ..." Glen said anxiously to the screen, trying to coax the camera to sweep just a little more broadly to the sides, just a little deeper into the faces.

"Where's that?" Cindy said, looking at the TV.

"This town, along the coast—where they do a lot of staging into the central highlands. Pretty place; nice beaches."

"You went to the beach?" Cindy said.

"Yeah," Glen said without looking up, "... once."

THREE

By early June, Glen was back in Port Crescent and into his house and working at the mill. Julie had finished her student teaching and was about to graduate and had decided to stay in town for the summer and wait tables again at the Thunderbird Inn where she had worked on and off over the past four years while going to school. She had secured the elementary teaching position for the fall.

* * *

The work kept Glen busy and as best it could his mind occupied; but the memories of the war were never far away and throughout the day the images of what he had experienced would appear. (Often, as much as the horrors of the battlefield, the raw harshness of the distant land he had been sent to would burst through the antiseptic veneer of everyday Port Crescent, bringing cognitive dissonance, physical discomfort, and a cornered-rat-like-urge to flee.) The initial excitement and celebrating of his first weeks back in Sealth eventually gave way in Port Crescent to quieter evenings at home; and he occasionally wrote letters to scrawled addresses he had collected from various company members, and, after a couple of weeks, he came home from work one day and found a letter in his mail box from Ben. Glen had invited him out from Minnesota to visit and Ben had responded that Glen could expect him within a few weeks.

Glen continued to closely follow the war; but he felt now that it was a lost cause and probably had been from the start. And he, too, thought that it should end; but he also knew the inevitable kinds of problems that that kind of civilian thinking would have for the soldiers still there.

"I know it's fucked ..." Glen spoke into the receiver at the kitchen table in the bright sunlight of the Port Crescent Saturday morning. Ben's deep voice, on the other end, had seemed to lift a great weight from Glen's shoulders the instant it had crackled over the line: it was someone who understood. "... But in the long run it'll be best to get out," Glen went on animatedly, between the deep drags of the cigarette he held in his hand, "even if we lose the south ... Well, for us it'll definitely be better in the short run ... I know, I know—not for the AVN ... Right—right ... Anyway, look, I'll pick you up at the station ... Great ... Right—5:30, Friday ... Great—see you then, man."

* * *

Glen watched excitedly as the passengers disembarked from the silver Amtrak onto the platform. When he saw Ben, towering above everyone, he walked quickly toward him; and they embraced in the crowd and both beamed widely. He grabbed Ben's army duffel bag out of his hands before Ben realized it and slapped him again on the back as he led them through the station.

"Mother fuck ..." Glen said repeatedly between his questions about the two-day ride, feeling as much peace as he had since his return three months before, the great weight even more removed from having a brother in his presence who knew of the war experience first hand.

"Xin chào!" Ben finally boomed in Vietnamese in his deep voice, slapping Glen back for each he received.

"Xin chào! ..." Glen boomed back, and they walked off for the car, arms around shoulders.

FOUR

"Here—try this." Glen tossed Ben one of the old heavy coats he had brought up from Sealth for the camping trip. Spread out across the small living room floor were sleeping bags and clothes and boxes of food, and cooking supplies and flashlights and maps; and Ben tried on the coat and it fit well. "My old man's," said Glen. "A Redwood—like you."

"What about the pants?" Ben said, holding up two pairs of old wool pants. "Look at these things ... both?"

"Both—bring 'em," Glen said, and then attempting to sound serious: "—it could rain the whole time."

"No ..." Ben said with a look of confusion and concern. "Really?"

"*Naw*—" Glen suddenly laughed. "I think we've got sun at least through Thursday. But, hey, you never know. Bring 'em ... Sarge would say bring 'em."

Ben grinned. "No, Sarge would know ahead of time if it was going to rain or not, then he'd say what to bring—how much food, bug juice."

Glen worked contentedly at his pack, tightening straps, rearranging. "Sarge would know whether it was going to rain; how hot it was going to be; how many mines we'd find; if we were going to get shot at—and when Phillips would start bitching about the food."

"Anybody could predict that," Ben said, laughing; and he stuffed the pants into his pack.

They finished packing the rest of the boxes and the packs and carried them out to the car which already had the tent and the stove and the cooler and then took everything out again to try once more to make it all fit and finally with a hard slam closed the trunk.

"Room to spare," Glen said as a car pulled to the curb. The driver's door opened and a broadly smiling Julie climbed out.

"Holy moe!" she called out coming up the driveway, "—have you guys got enough stuff? My God, Glen, how are you going to carry all of that?"

"You wait, we'll be wishing we'd brought the badminton; you've got to be prepared."

"What? ... You didn't bring the badminton?" Ben said, attempting a straight face, his lack of acting skills brutally exposed.

Julie began to laugh: "Get out of here."

Ben laughed, too, and threw some more sweaters into the back seat.

"So, have you decided where you're going?" Julie said. She stepped toward Glen and they each leaned forward and kissed.

"Looks like Nooksak, at least to the base of Shuksan."

"Really? Great. I've never been all the way into Nooksak ... just around Sulpher."

"Sulpher's good, too," Glen said, still adjusting the contents of one of the boxes. "Good hot springs at Sulpher." He looked at Ben trying on some heavy leather boots they had rented from a supplier in town. "Those going to be all right?"

"Should be; they seem big enough." Ben sat on the grass and pulled on the laces. "I guess I'll find out."

"Yeah, well, you better find out before we get on the trail." Glen knew that Ben, a combat veteran, would be well aware of the dangers of ill fitting boots.

"You guys have a great time," Julie said, putting an arm around Glen, "and be careful, honey-pooh," she exaggerated a pout, looking up at Glen.

Ben tried to make his deep voice high: "Honey-pooh ...", but failed again; and they all laughed.

Now Glen smiled broadly at Ben: "We will conquer—divide and conquer. We will conquer Nooksak."

"I hope he knows what he's doing," Ben said with half a wink, looking over to Julie.

"So do I ... No!" she laughed. "I'm kidding, he knows— You'll be careful, won't you Sweetie? ... hmmmmm?"

"Of course—of course," Glen said, working again at his pack. "Always careful, always careful. It's just a hike, anyway. It'll be easy ... believe me."

Across the tree-lined street, some dogs barked as they romped through a neighbor's yard. Glen and Ben kept loading their packs as Julie glanced quietly at the dogs: "... I believe you."

* * *

"So this guy—real hard-core freak—tries to get me to be one of the speakers at the thing ... Jesus-shit!" Ben rolled the passenger window the rest of the way down and, clearing his throat, spit toward the rapidly passing shoulder of the road. Beyond the shoulder the forest rose steeply up the mountainside until it disappeared over a tall ridge. Out Glen's window, the bank dropped quickly down to the gray-green glacial-silt of the swiftly flowing river that cascaded over the boulders and rock-cuts of the mountain valley. As they rounded a long curve, distant jagged peaks loomed before them in the late morning sun. From the open beer can in his hand, Ben took a drink.

"Christ—did you?" Glen said behind the wheel, a beer between his legs on the seat.

"No!—shit," Ben said disgustedly. "I have a hard enough time just going to the fucking store. No way I was going to be some converted vet for those guys. Most of those goons hate our guts, anyway ..."

"Yeah, shit," Glen smiled, his eyes on the curving pavement, "what the fuck do they know, anyway?"

"Not a fucking lot," Ben said, "believe me."

"Yeah, I know—I know."

Ben took a drink from his beer and gazed out the window. The early summer green of the mountain valley gleamed in the bright sun and air rushed into the car. "... I went, though," he said after a while. "Fucking crazy, man ... big, crazy-ass crowd. Mostly students, hippies. Cops all over the place, everyone just waiting for something to happen.... Lot of nice ladies, though."

"Yeah?" Glen said.

The road came over a rise and moved slowly away from the river and flattened and stretched straight into the distance as the dark, thick-trunked trees rising up on each side closed in on the shoulders. A wide spot approached on the right and the dark log-walls of a ranger station appeared in the trees and Glen pulled in and shut off the engine. Outside, the forest was silent but for the faint rush of the river flowing beyond the road, and everywhere in the filtered sun, thick moss covered the ground and the fallen trees on the forest floor and the split-cedar roof of the small log-building.

They left the car and went into the one-room structure and Ben walked toward some of the artifacts hanging on the walls and Glen went up to the counter and bent over the large topographical map under the glass and smiled and nodded to the ranger at the single desk who stood and came to the counter's opposite side. They each said hello and the trim elderly ranger stood straight and silent in his neatly pressed uniform with the many patches and insignias of the National Forest Service and Glen asked about the trail into Nooksak and the snow line and the number of hikers in the limited cirque of the upper basin. And Ben moved slowly about the historical displays of the region's early settlements covering the walls—the rusty mining pans and picks, the eight-foot long double-handed logging saws, the grainy black and white photographs from the turn of the century—and then around the three-dimensional model of the area's mountains displayed on a large table in the center of the room. And directly in the middle, rising high above the other peaks in the model, the white-painted cone of Mt. Diablo. And Glen talked quietly with the ranger who had spread another map onto the counter as they leaned over closely from each side and pointed to tiny trail lines and talked more.

Then Glen was standing straight and thanking the ranger and walked over to the model where Ben stood and looked at the steep-rising mountain surfaces. And he pointed to Nooksak and the trail and the high cirque and they bent down low and briefly followed the route. Then they were both standing and waving good bye to the ranger and went out the door and into the soft sunlight that filtered down through the trees to the mosses and ferns covering the forest floor.

Off to the side were aging moss-covered outhouses they each used; and they wandered briefly about the quiet roadside area before getting into the car and pulling back onto the highway.

✶ ✶ ✶

It was mid afternoon before they finally reached the trailhead, having stopped for lunch and a final food purchase in the tiny mountain village of Kokomish, with its aging filling-station and store, and half-dozen cabin-like houses. Then the long drive on the narrow logging road that wound for miles through the dark forest into the increasingly steep mountains.

At the trailhead, there was a final rearranging of the contents of the packs with several items being left behind upon realization of the extent of their over-preparedness and the extreme weight of the packs. Then the first awkward steps with the great weight on their backs and shoulders; but after the long hours in the car and the excited anticipation of their destination, it felt good to be outside in the clear mountain air, despite the weight, standing and moving again. But mostly it was the enormous vertical east face of Mt. Diablo that had come suddenly into full view after rounding the final bend on the road—and now remained in view through the trees across the river, towering high above the other peaks on the facing ridge—that had lessened the pain of the packs as they stepped into the silent forest.

* * *

"… But, really, even if they had known every NVA and Cong position—every weapon, tunnel, backup, ammo dump, sympathizer, in the whole god damn province, it still wouldn't have meant shit in a place like Gan." Glen spoke animatedly from the slab of rock at the edge of the small cascading stream where he leaned beside his pack amongst the towering firs as Ben, a few feet away, bent down and scooped the cold water into his hands and drank. There had been numerous small streams and waterfalls, many they had stopped to drink at, splashing down the steep mountainside and crossing the trail, which had risen steadily as it followed the river in the deep gorge below. Since moving behind a high ridge a mile up the trail, they had not seen the face of Diablo now for almost two hours.

"… But Phu Gan was ours to take," said Ben, standing and wiping the dripping water from his mouth. The stream splashed loudly after the long silent stretches of the forest where there were no streams, with only the low roar of the unseen river coming up through the trees, far below. The tee shirt Ben wore was streaked wet and patches of dirt clung to the sweat on his face. "Christ— there was a whole battalion just sweeping floors in Dra Ming that entire month. If anything had come in from behind, just even to cut off the upper valley, it would have fallen."

Glen pulled his sweat-soaked shirt away from his chest and then arched his back and pulled at the wet material there. "I don't know; I suppose. Assuming the recon hadn't found anything first … But, sure, it would have made things a lot simpler." He sat straight-backed on the slab of rock, the pack and trail taking their toll after the many inactive months back in Port Crescent (with the exception of the lumber mill), well aware of what was still to come, his face grimacing with a dual expression of concern and disgust, as though he had just bitten into something sour. "Yeah, without Phu Gan they would have been forced to divert their entire southern flow another fifty miles west—at least. And that would have put them right at the edge of the Troung Sons … And we all know what that would have meant." He grimaced even more and pulled again at his shirt.

Without answering, Ben looked over from his pack where he worked on a zipper and slowly shook his head.

"But still," Glen went on, "even if the Eleventh Groundcorp had somehow gotten back there ... well, the sixth would have been in the same position—at least initially."

"Yes—soldier—they would have," Ben spoke from beside the stream, his voice strained and rising: despite his pained expression and the vague knowledge of what lay ahead, he felt good; the exertion of the trail and pack clearing and focusing his mind more so than at any time since his return, "—but they wouldn't have had to rush. They could have waited them out for six weeks if nothing else."

Glen stood and reached for his pack. "I don't know ... I don't know ... They may have been waiting for longer than six weeks. Da Nang wanted to get moving on the whole thing—they sure as fuck weren't going to wait that long."

"Maybe, if they'd known what was going to happen ..."

"But that's just it, man—they couldn't. Nobody knew shit about anything." Glen looked at Ben, grimacing again, from both the memory and the pounding of the trail, and took a long drink from his canteen. A few feet away, on the thick moss of a fallen tree, a chipmunk darted to a stop and rose on its hind legs, its tail quivering in the cool mountain air. Glen glanced at it for a moment before looking up the trail to where it disappeared into the trees. The sun continued moving toward the ridge beyond the river and the shadows of the mountains ascended slowly up the valley. "Come on, we better get going," and pulling on his pack, he stepped across the stream, as the chipmunk suddenly darted back into the trees.

* * *

When they finally broke out of the forest it was across a wide, ancient rock-slide where only low underbrush grew; and the jagged tips of the peaks were suddenly everywhere and the trail flattened as it entered the lower cirque of Nooksak. There were more patches of tall forest, some long and deep, followed by more rock slides, until it was almost all rocks; and the valley widened and continued to flatten and the river, which was the same river they had been following all afternoon, was beside them again for the first time since they had parked alongside it at the trailhead more than five hours before. High above were quarter-mile wide glaciers, clinging to the steep sides of the peaks, from which, after the late afternoon sun, chunks of ice would occasionally break off and plunge onto the snow fields below. Above and to the sides of the glaciers were near-vertical rock faces that rose a thousand feet up the slowly curving cirque wall, sometimes to jagged points, sometimes to saddles, all in the blue sky above. Wisps of clouds spilled quickly over one of the saddles, then drifted slowly above the valley before dissipating in the cool mountain air. Around the trail, the dull green of the new season grew amongst the rocks and the remaining clusters of trees, which were shorter and fewer in number; and heading into the upper cirque it became almost all brush with the trail winding and rising and flattening through the endless piles of glacial moraine and the massive boulders that littered the valley floor. From time to time the wind blew down the cirque, swaying the taller brush and trees; and the trail moved into a final stand of firs in a flat area near the river before fading into the rocks and terminating at the base of the cirque, another quarter mile beyond, below the thousand-foot faces of the wide curving wall. Amongst the last grove of firs were the bare patches of ground from old camps, and in a final push they plunged into one of the camps and threw off their packs.

"Oh—man!" Glen called out, collapsing on the bare ground and reaching back to his pack for the metal canteen dangling on the side. His chest rose and sank under his sweat-soaked shirt as he struggled for oxygen in the thin mountain air. He drank from the canteen, then handed it to Ben.

"Thanks," Ben said, breathing just as heavily as he raised the water to his lips. Now the wind came down the cirque and blew through the fir grove and the straight narrow trees leaned and creaked and the brush surrounding the camp ruffled, and then everything grew quiet again, except for the low roar of the river, now only a few feet wide, tumbling over the rocky channel just beyond the camp. "*Whew,*" Ben said, wiping his mouth with the back of his hand and passing the canteen back to Glen. "A killer—Man, that last half mile …"

Glen looked over with an acknowledging glance as he put away the canteen, his breathing now slower. He stood up, stumbling briefly, and began digging into his pack to change his shirt.

Ben stood, too, and pulled off his wet shirt and dug for warm clothes as the mountain air chilled their now bare skin. "Yes!—man oh man, we are here!" he boomed excitedly in his low voice from the half-spilled contents of his pack, and pulled on a fresh shirt and sweater.

"Yes—we are here," Glen repeated, not as loudly, in a more serious tone, working his arms through the sleeves of a sweater he had pulled from his pack. "… Looks like we're the only ones, too." With great effort he finally got his head through, his damp hair matted and rumpled and his face streaked with dirt. He scanned the peaks that towered around them. "Man, look at this place—unbelievable.—Hey, any firewood?"

"Look." Ben pointed to an edge of the camp where the ground was littered with the fallen twigs and branches of the surrounding trees.

Glen observed the thick layer of combustible material. "Great, all right, let's set up, then get a fire going."

"Roger," Ben said, "—agreed." With his heavy shirt back on and a cap pulled over his head, he began to lightly jog in place. "Man, it's chilly up here."

Glen glanced over but didn't answer and then together they began to unload the equipment and spread out the tent.

* * *

"Charlie Elwood went to the Rose Club? Get out of here, Gray—*get out of here!*" Ben stuck the end of the stick into the campfire and a plume of sparks shot into the dark night. The heat of the coals and the burning wood warmed the area around the fire where they sat on the ground, the flickering light dancing off their faces. There was darkness beyond the trees, and the sound of the rushing stream, and the wind continued from time to time to blow down the cirque, building slowly before fading again to the stillness of the night air.

"I was there, well, I was there the next morning ... well I saw him the next day anyway." Glen poked at the fire from the other side with his own stick while glancing over at Ben. They were wearing most of the clothing they had brought: the heavy wool sweaters and shirts; the heavy jackets. A small metal flask—a quarter full with bourbon—and a half-full bag of Oreos sat on the ground between them.

Looking off with a wide grin, Ben reached over and took the bag of cookies. He had been laughing hard at times listening to the story. Still grinning and reaching into the bag, he looked suspiciously over at Glen. "But, you don't know what actually happened."

"Come on—he danced with her, he drank with her—they walked out the door together." Glen began to laugh. "So this lieutenant and his buddy—eighth—ninth—I'd seen them in there a hundred times before—knew all the whores—they line him up with this ... god ... old ... fucking ..." Glen's face contorted. "... *Bag!*"

Ben fell back on the ground, laughing, almost in tears.

"She must have been *forty! ...* " Glen blurted loudly, laughing just as hard, his eyes beginning to water.

"Jesus Christ ... well ..." Ben, his eyes moist, partly from laughing, partly from the bourbon and the shifting smoke of the fire, raised himself back up, grinning widely, and through his laughter tried to talk. Small twigs and bits of dirt clung to his arms and back, "... well, did anyone see where they went?"

"Sandis said he saw them get into a taxi."

"And then you talked to him the next day?"

"Well, I didn't actually talk to him," Glen said, calmer. "But, Christ, I don't doubt it in the slightest. Crap, it's still funnier than hell." He laughed again and then reached for the flask and took a sip. "—*Whoosh.*" He puckered his mouth and shook his head as he swallowed the smooth liquid.

"God almighty," Ben said, also calmer, his eyes still bright and moist in the firelight, "that little bastard; he never stopped moralizing in what—eight months? That he'd go to the Rose Club. Christ—that he'd even walk down that street ... Crap, he used to wake everybody at five in the morning trying to get to that Sunday service in Plei Ku." He shook his head, his grin smaller, growing more reflective.

"Yeah … yeah," Glen said, quieter. "Crap … I'm glad I got that over with early." He stared at the fire. "But I don't know … fuck, it was weird. Actually, I don't remember a whole lot … she sure seemed hot at first. Fuck—at least I didn't get robbed like half the first-month grunts that go there." He poked again at the fire and his face grew distant as he thought of Oscar Lewis who the Danang MPs had found curled up in the corner of the filthy, back-alley room, staring at the bare, gray wall with the girl he had stabbed to death lying a few feet away on the blood-drenched bed. Glen pushed a burning log further into the fire. "But shit, yeah, then it's eight weeks of penicillin and god-knows-what," he shifted on the ground, "… I still get these weird itches."

Ben poked at the coals and slowly shook his head. "… Charlie Elwood." He gave a final sigh and stood up and stretched, and with a slight stumble made his way to the edge of the camp where the furthest of the firelight hit the slender trunks of the trees. Swaying in the cool air, he unzipped his pants and began to piss. When he finished, he grunted and took a few steps further into the darkness to where he could see the faint outline of the peaks above the camp. He continued slowly on, stumbling at times on the uneven ground, until he was out of the clump of trees surrounding the camp; and the sky was clear with the canopy of stars shining brilliantly across the heavens and a sliver of moon glinting just above the cirque. Then, raising his hands to his mouth and taking several deep breaths, he yelled a deep, bellowing holler; and after the shortest silence it bounced once—sharply and loudly off the nearest wall—then again only slightly less so, and then again and again.

Glen stood up from the fire and made his way unevenly over to Ben and looked up at the bright, night sky. Swaying slightly, he raised his hands and hollered as long and deeply as he could; and together, motionless in the chilled air, they listened to the sharp distant echo which bounced repeatedly before fading and was then replaced by the low rushing of the stream and the gentle creaking of the trees from the light breeze blowing down the star-lit cirque.

*   *   *

In the morning the air was crisp and cool, and, unzipping the nylon tent door, they looked out to the greens and grays of the cirque floor, and through the trees, the walls of the peaks and the snow and ice of the glaciers clinging to the sides of the cirque, all below the bright blue of the morning sky. They dressed and got another fire going, and made breakfast and coffee, and wandered down to the stream and, later on, sometimes together, sometimes alone, everywhere about the rocky area surrounding the camp.

Late in the morning, with their lunches in knapsacks, they hiked the rest of the way up the cirque floor to the base of the peaks, and began climbing toward what appeared to be a low saddle at the top. But by early afternoon they reached snow and after another quarter mile of scrambling to whatever bare spots they could find, the snow became steep and the bare areas of rock on either side almost vertical. Everywhere along the curving cirque wall were enormous rock slides and the cracked, blue and white faces of the glaciers, motionless on the steep walls. Far below, on the cirque floor, they could see the clump of trees surrounding the camp and a corner of the bright red tent and part of the line they had hung up to dry towels and clothes.

"Whoa, Glen—where're you going?" Ben leaned back into the steep rock side as Glen put one foot onto a snow chute that rose a hundred yards above and dropped two hundred below to where it plunged over a rock face that fell to the floor of the cirque. They had been climbing all morning, scrambling up steep rock and snow chutes, following bare areas of mountainside, toward the narrow saddle on the curving top of the cirque. They had gained a thousand feet and the glaciers that had been high above them back at the camp were now directly across, and to each side, hugging the near vertical walls. They had rounded the narrow sides of a steep gully that extended up to the saddle, and the camp was no longer visible, but for hours they had risen directly above it and watched the tent and the packs grow smaller until the tent was just a spot in the trees. Downstream, beyond the entrance to the cirque, the forested valley stretched into the distance, with more valleys beyond, and endless rows of pinnacle-sharp peaks rising everywhere, all fading off hazily into the horizon.

"Look," Glen said, slowly digging his other foot into the snow, testing the step, "we get over to those rocks and we can be at the top in twenty minutes."

"Jesus, Glen, I don't know—you slip on that sucker and you're gone."

"Come on," Glen said, sounding serious and yet, strangely, as though he were about to laugh, focusing intensely on each step, moving further out the chute, continuing to talk, "… it's not too bad … you dig in … you lean in …"

Ben went to the edge of the chute and faced the slope and put one foot into Glen's track as Glen moved slowly out to the middle. "Shit!" Ben snapped; "we have to come back, too, you know?" But he kept going, leaning far into the chute, his hands in the snow above him.

Without answering, Glen continued to kick into the snow as he moved slowly toward the other side. He stopped once and looked up the chute which became almost vertical before it ended at a rock face that rose straight up to the top with the blue sky above. Thin wisps of clouds spilled over the saddle and to one side the sun glared down. "It's not bad—just follow my tracks." He continued on without looking back and crossed the last few feet to the other side.

It was another hour before they reached the last steep, outcrop of rock that led up to the narrow saddle; and they could hear the wind blowing above and began to feel the coolness of the high altitude as they found hand and foot holds to climb to the crest. And just below the lip the wind blasting hard as the horizon, which for the past two days had always been above them, was first even, and then, as they made the final roll onto the saddle and the wind hit full, everywhere below; and they looked for a hundred miles over the range of mountains that extended in all directions, and to the distant valleys and lowlands, some with large, dark bodies of water. And extending both north and south were the half-dozen string of snow-covered volcanoes that rose high above the rest of the mountains, each one fainter and seemingly smaller in the distance until the furthest, in a neighboring state, was just a faint point of white.

Straddling the narrow saddle in the full force of the wind, they pulled on clothing from the knapsacks while making slow, three-hundred and sixty-degree turns. And a moment later, before completing even a second turn, without need of discussion, they stepped to the edge and headed back down.

FIVE

Ben stayed in Port Crescent after the camping trip for almost two more weeks—twice as long as he had originally planned—and they took several more trips both near and far: one with Julie and Randy up to Vancouver; another a camping trip, this time to a remote beach on the rocky Pacific coast; and once down to Glen's family's home in Sealth.

* * *

It was quiet the first few days around Glen's house after Ben took the train back to Minnesota, but Julie came over more frequently and sometimes spent the night, and Randy came around almost daily; and Glen worked long and hard at the mill, sometimes overtime, and he came home in the late August evenings after work tired but content. The money from the mill was good in that summer of 1968; and they drank beer until late on the weekends and more and more frequently went to different houses around town and out into the countryside to smoke marijuana and experiment with other sometimes more potent drugs. And the occupants of the homes they visited were subjectively—and, given the sometimes isolated location of the dwellings, objectively—moving further and further away from what had been the cultural mainstream of the 1950s and early 1960s, towards a vague, loosely-visionary lifestyle that was largely the polar opposite of their parent's post-World-War-II domain. And the increasingly loud and passionate opposition to the war heavily galvanized and fueled the emerging new culture, resulting in an almost schizophrenic-like essence with its extremely serious and intense sense of mission, accomplished at times by a circus-like atmosphere of the bizarre and absurd. It was not, however, the opposing of the war alone that drove the emerging new culture, but an almost across the board rejection of the traditional American way of life and materialistic forces of capitalism that seemed to drive it.

But the passionate opposition to the war was the movement's strongest unifier; the very real threat of being killed, or having to kill, as a kind of surreal yet persistent and undeniably loud reality for the young men who had, to that point, known only the greatest physical comfort and security of any generation in the history of the world. With the exception, that is, of the non-white races, who had, historically, received the brunt of the republic's injustices and thus were largely the least exemptible from military service.

So the young men grew their hair long—the exact opposite of the short-haired GI's of this and earlier wars—and dressed and acted more loudly and flamboyantly, refusing to conform to an order that appeared to lead inevitably to war and a repression of the spirit, all with the desirable result of seeming to scare the older mainstream generation, the source and soul of the nation's military and social fiber.

* * *

"So whose place is this?" Glen stared out the window from the passenger side as Randy drove the old Ford Falcon up the narrow dirt road, deep in the countryside out of Port Crescent.

"Bagley," Randy answered, "—you remember Tom? It's his older brother. He's been up here for at least a year."

"John; no Jim—was that his name?" Glen kept one hand on the dash as the car bucked and bounced over the increasingly rutted track.

"George ..." Randy said, inhaling on a marijuana cigarette rolled in dull yellow paper which he held to his lips in one hand, while tightly gripping the wheel with his other, which pulled viciously to either side with each rut and hole they encountered. Randy handed the joint to Glen as sparks burst from the end and fell into his lap. "Shit!" he half-gasped as he finished the exchange and shot his hand down to the seat and brushed frantically at the smoldering material while continuing to drive and trying to keep the burning smoke in his lungs. The car bounced hard and his head almost hit the ceiling as he exhaled long and fully in relief from the hot, expanding smoke.

"Christ!" Glen said, inhaling on the joint, "—slow down."

Randy turned and grinned, thinking that was probably a good idea, yet having also partly enjoyed the bouncing.

"Crazy ass—" Glen said, also sort of grinning, thinking that Randy was so stoned he was laughing about realizing he had almost destroyed his car from the fun of bouncing.

The road entered a clearing and a farm house appeared with an old barn to one side and they drove up to the house and parked beside two other vehicles, one of which was abandoned and partially covered with grass and weeds. "Whew—shit!" Glen said, grimacing from the rough ride as he quickly got out of the car and slammed the door. Randy also got out and studied the house. There was no sign of activity in the slightly-overcast, afternoon light; and he began walking toward the porch as Glen, still grimacing, remained beside the car and scanned the surrounding countryside.

It had once been a functioning farm, with acres of open fields spreading out beyond the house and the barn to where the second-growth forest began, but the fields were now only weeds and wild grasses, with the remains of some fences, except near the barn where the fencing appeared new and largely intact. Glen looked up and saw Randy almost at the house where a small, non-menacing dog had come from somewhere and was barking and prancing excitedly at his feet; and Glen began to walk toward the house.

Now the door opened and a woman appeared in a flowing floor-length skirt and denim blouse, and with thick brown hair that extended almost to her waist, and stepped onto the porch where Randy stood; and the dog pranced higher and leaped at the woman's feet as she reached down to calm it. "Hey, Glen—this is Kathy." Randy nodded toward the woman as Glen came up and reached down to the dog that now leaped wildly at his feet.

"Hello," Glen said, smiling; and he shook the woman's hand and they all went into the house. There was dark wood and beams everywhere, and old furniture, and a large, oval rug which took up much of the wide living-room floor. A bearded man who had been sitting in a large stuffed-chair reading a book under a lamp looked up as Glen and Randy and the woman came in. He was wearing faded jeans, as were Randy and Glen, and boots and a flannel shirt, and his bushy hair and beard billowed outward thickly, and Kathy introduced him as Jonathan. Then another man came in from the rear of the house and smiled when he saw Randy and was introduced to Glen as George; and with a friendly passive demeanor he shook Glen's hand and they all sat on the several couches and chairs. And after a moment Randy took out the marijuana he carried in a small plastic bag in his front pocket, and rolled a joint, and after lighting it, passed it around the group which sat about the large living room exchanging small talk as the light of the autumn-afternoon filtered in through the windows.

"So, I heard you were in Vietnam?" George said after a while, whose younger brother, Tom, both Glen and Randy had known back in Sealth where once, long before, they had all grown up.

"Yes—yeah," Glen said, sitting beside Randy on one of the couches.

"Made it back in one piece though?"

"Oh, yeah ... somehow. Yeah, what a fucked up mess."

The people looked at Glen.

"Probably should never have gone ... But what did I know?"

"Yeah—really," Randy said, nodding.

"Huh, well." George shook his head, collecting his thoughts.

"I was reading just the other day," said Jonathan, looking up from the chair under the lamp, "that when Ho Chi Minh lived in Paris, he had a French girlfriend whose father was a Marxist—and that's what first converted him." The people in the room looked at Jonathan. "This family took him in and became, like, a surrogate family, and that's when he first started seriously organizing with the other Vietnamese, students and laborers, all living in Paris." On a small table beside his chair were a number of thick paperback books.

"Yeah?" said Glen. He had not shaved in several days, and light patches of hair grew from his face. He had not cut his hair since a small barber shop near the dock in San Francisco where an elderly barber, now accompanied by a son, had been cutting the hair of returning GI's since World War II. American flags and VFW banners had covered the walls, along with several framed, in-flight photographs of the Blue Angles; and the man had smiled often and spoken admiringly of Glen's service and sacrifice. Admiring his reflection in the barbershop mirror, Glen had wanted to look good for his mother when he returned to Sealth, who, understandably, had worried greatly throughout his absence.

"I think he knew members of Mao's family in France, too," Glen said in the dim light of the farmhouse room, "at about the same time ..."

"The Chinese?—really?" said Jonathan. "I'm surprised. I thought they were mortal enemies ... But, maybe not then"

Kathy took the joint over to George and sat on the wide arm of the stuffed chair and draped her arm around him as she handed the pot to him. "Well, it makes sense to me," George said. "He falls for a woman and starts a revolution." He grinned and nudged Kathy who nudged him back.

"Yeah!" Randy half-burst. "No kidding ... shit." He grinned widely and pushed the same glasses up his nose that he had worn for as long as Glen had known him.

"Did you have to fight?" Kathy asked, now in a serious tone.

"Fight? ... no ... well, not much. I mean, it was going on everywhere, but ..." he trailed off.

"We're trying to get Jonathan over the border," Kathy went on.

Glen looked at the man in the chair.

"There's a Jesuit school in Blaine that's been taking people over when they go up for field trips. They make like counselors—the people going over—with the bus full of kids, and then—" She stopped and looked matter-of-factly at Glen.

"Wow—no shit?" Randy said, handing the joint to Glen.

"Hopefully," Jonathan said, shifting in his chair.

"Where are you from?" Randy asked.

"Oakland."

"Yeah? Wow, I'll bet it's wild down there. Got to get down there one of these days."

"Very wild," Jonathan said. "A lot going on."

They listened.

"Berkley, the whole bay area ..."

Glen had passed quickly and uneventfully through San Francisco, spending one night in a downtown hotel (also on good terms and favored by returning military), too exhausted after dinner and fighting the virus to go out on his first night back. And then directly to the train station early the next morning for the two day ride back to Sealth.

"So," George said, looking at Randy, one hand clasping the chair and the other Kathy's leg. He, too, was in blue jeans and an old flannel shirt. He was clean shaven but for a thick mustache. His wavy brown hair hung far past his shoulders. He was somewhat older than the others, which was how he had missed the draft. "How many did you want, Randy?"

"Oh, yeah, let's see—how many did you say you wanted, Glen?"

"Well, I guess three."

"So I hear they're pretty strong," Randy said, looking over to George.

"Real strong; you can split them—take a whole. Take a whole and you'd be flying, though. I don't know too many people who've taken a whole one. Some people have taken a third and said it was the strongest they'd ever had."

"Yeah?—no shit?" Randy said, nodding, "wow ... purple, double ..."

"Dome," George said. "Purple-double-dome." He got up from the chair and left the room.

"They're strong," Randy said quietly to Glen on the couch beside him. "I know Peterson took a half and said he couldn't leave his chair for four hours." He raised his eyebrows while lightly moving the fingers of one hand; he grinned and pushed his glasses up his nose.

"Yeah?" Glen nodded. "I don't know. I just took it that one time. I have no idea how much I took—but, god, it was incredible." He stared at Randy.

George came back and from an envelope removed several small tablets, each with a slight purplish color. Randy reached over and examined one of the tablets. "See, it's sort of dome-shaped." He showed it to Glen. "So, let's see, four—yeah, four," he said to George and took out his wallet. Glen also got out some money and handed it to Randy who gave it to George who put the acid in another envelope and handed it back to Randy. "All right," Randy said smiling, "let's smoke another joint." And he reached again for the marijuana and the rolling papers.

* * *

"Really; that's all he does—sell dope?" Glen spoke from the passenger's seat of Randy's Falcon.

They were on the highway heading back to Port Crescent in the evening darkness. They had spent the rest of the afternoon at George and Kathy's, staying for a large dinner Kathy had prepared (many of the dishes with unusual grains and sauces they had not tasted before) that they had eaten around the heavy, wood dining-table. They had smoked marijuana almost continuously throughout the afternoon and then again around the table after the meal. Earlier, they had all taken a walk across the field to a path in the forest that led to a small waterfall that splashed down from the high ridge extending into the mountains. All about them, the last yellow and gold leaves of the fall foliage drifted to the ground from the numerous patches of birch and maple sprinkled about the mostly fir forest. At different times throughout the afternoon, George and Kathy, and to a lesser extent, Jonathan, each individually asked Glen more questions about his experiences in Vietnam. Glen was the first veteran of the war in Indochina any of them had ever met.

"Oh, and the soapstone … the pipes," Randy went on at the wheel, leaning slightly against the door to rest the muscles that had tired from the long day's walking and driving. "I know he sells some of them … Or sometimes he just trades them for things."

George carved pipes out of soapstone at a small shop at the back of the house. He cut them out of blocks that came from the plentiful veins in the nearby mountains and carved them into different sizes and shapes, before polishing them to a smooth, shiny gloss. From time to time, he ventured down from the mountains to the increasingly frequent arts and crafts fairs that were held in the cities and larger towns of the lowlands to display his wares. Lately, he had been including the rough outline of a spider along the sides of the bowls as a kind of signature.

"And I guess Kathy's a nurse," Randy continued. "I think she works part-time at the clinic in Blanchard …"

"… Oh yeah?" Glen stared out the window, seemingly only partially aware of Randy's answer, he also low in the seat, yet still unable to rest his head on the top of the bench.

"… Yeah, that's what Tom tells me."

Glen tried to slide lower and then looked to the fading light of the distant horizon where the sun had gone down behind the mountains across the sound. Coming out of the foothills of the Cascades from George and Kathy's there had been mostly forest beside the highway, but now as they approached Port Crescent there were more farms and open fields, and then houses and a few small businesses; and they rolled swiftly down the dark, empty pavement.

"Hey, you want to stop for a beer?" Glen asked after a while.

"Yeah, sure."

"There's a place up on the right."

Randy nodded and they kept rolling.

* * *

'I thought you were going to call?' Julie's voice came through the receiver Glen held to his ear. He had noticed it was almost midnight when he walked into the house a few moments before and then hurriedly dialed the phone.

"Jeeze, I'm sorry; they didn't have a phone." Glen lay sprawled on the couch in his front room, the room dark but for the light coming from the kitchen.

'They didn't have a phone?' came the voice on the other end.

"No ... I know, yeah ... they were way up past Skykomish, pretty remote. Randy—he say's they're just out of town—it took a fucking hour and a half to get up there. Half hour on this dirt road! ... yeah ... I'm sorry."

'We were going to go over to Mike and Judy's—remember?'

"Ah, shit, I'm sorry ... They invited us for dinner, and Randy wanted to stay ... I'm sorry."

There was no response.

"Are we still going tomorrow night?" Glen spoke into the receiver.

'I hope so—we've paid for the tickets.'

"Well, I got the stuff ... so, maybe ..."

Julie didn't answer.

"Look, I'll be over in the morning, about ten, all right?"

"All right ... " Julie said, and he thought he heard a sigh.

"Goodnight," Glen said, sinking deeper into the couch.

"Goodnight ... "

SIX

It was ten-thirty when Glen arrived in his Plymouth Valiant at Julie's apartment the next morning, and after a brief discussion, they elected to take Julie's VW beetle—the more reliable of their two automobiles—for the two hour drive down to Sealth. In Sealth, they planned to have lunch at Julie's parent's, and then go later to the Gray's for dinner, before finally picking up Greg and Ann and going to the concert.

As usual, the lunch at the Thornton's, Julie's home, went well, as Mrs. Thornton in particular had always liked Glen, and always been friendly toward him; and she was very intelligent and interesting and tried to engaged everyone in stimulating conversation. And she spoke very supportively and in an aggressive manner of Glen's military service, while at the same time clearly not backing the war; just Glen and whatever he did. She also chain-smoked—even during the meal—which was not totally unusual for a World War II housewife; and Glen thought she smoked more than anyone he knew, male or female, young or old: even more than Bob Sandis in Vietnam, or David Petrocelli at the old Friday night card games at Western State; and they both smoked like venomous fiends.

"—I'm just not sure we can trust Nixon to honestly bring it to an end," Mrs. Thornton said at the dining-room table as they finished eating the chocolate cake she had served for desert after the tuna-fish sandwiches and milk. She had taken only one bite of her small slice and then set her fork down and lit another cigarette. "He's just so much more of a hawk than Humphrey; much worse than Goldwater. And I'm afraid he's even more bound up in the military complex than LBJ ever was."

"I don't believe him, either," Julie said, the fall sunlight streaming through the tall windows and faintly illuminating the layers of drifting smoke. "I don't think he has any intention of getting us out. Vietnamization—give me a break. What's that supposed to mean?"

"He's certainly not going to pull out quickly if it makes him look bad," Julie's father said from one end of the table, dressed in his casual, Saturday-afternoon clothes. "We've known that about him for years." Mr. Thornton was much quieter than Mrs. Thornton. Glen didn't know if he smoked or not, had never seen him, nor did he recall Julie ever mentioning it. He also didn't seem overly friendly toward Glen, unlike Mrs. Thornton. He made Glen feel slightly uncomfortable, at times slightly guilty, as though he were not going to be very outgoing toward someone who may be sleeping with his unmarried daughter, sexual revolution or no sexual revolution. Mrs. Thornton, on the other hand, had actually told Julie on several occasions that she was glad her daughter was growing up in a time that was more sexually open than when she had been a young woman. She had told Julie she was glad she was on the pill.

"You're right—he won't," Julie said, picking at her cake with her fork while looking wide-eyed at her father. "You think he'll just pull out and be the only American President in history to lose a war? No way—never. That's where you get this Vietnamization bullshit."

Mr. Thornton looked at his daughter disapprovingly for her choice of words.

"Oh, it is bullshit, though, Arthur," Mrs. Thornton said. Along with smoking a lot, she also swore a lot. Mr. Thornton dug into his cake. "I just don't think we're going to get out of there anytime soon if he gets into office." Mrs. Thornton stubbed out her cigarette. "—What do you think, Glen?"

Glen swallowed his mouthful and wiped his lips with his napkin. "I don't know … it's hard to say." He looked at the others before going on. "Well, there's no way the south is going to stop the north without help. But even with a full military campaign—a total U.S. effort—you still won't be able to eliminate them completely. I mean, they're too hard to find.—It's hard to explain. They're everywhere. It's not like a regular army that's like all congregated on one side, where you can just go in and shoot them all. They're all over the south; families in the south have ties in the north—and vice versa. They're all mixed together; it's almost like there are degrees to which side they are on. I mean, someone in the south might think of themselves as mostly south but also partly north. They might be more sympathetic to the south one month, and then the next month decide they are going to support the north … Actually, I don't think they care. They just want to run their farms—eat, live."

The table was quiet when Glen stopped talking. Everyone returned to their dessert except Mrs. Thornton who continued to look at Glen. "Well … we thought it was a good idea at first," she said. "Let's hope wiser minds prevail."

Julie grunted and pushed her plate away. She took one of her mother's cigarettes and lit it. She could not make a connection between the Republican presidential candidate and probable future Chief-of-the-Armed-Forces, and wiser minds.

* * *

Just before six, after having visited for most of the afternoon at the Thornton's (which, after a failed demonstration in the living room of the new color television due to there being no color programming on that afternoon, had consisted primarily of a tour and inspection of the vegetable and flower gardens, as well as the viewing of Mr. Thornton's new gas-powered lawn mower, which was rolled specially out of the garage for the occasion),

Glen and Julie drove across town to Glen's parent's house where they attempted to eat dinner despite still being somewhat full from the large lunch.

At the Grays, they sat around the dining room table with Glen's parent's and sister, and went through the motions of a casual Saturday evening meal that Glen's mother had not delayed serving, even though she had guessed that Julie, at least, would probably not be all that hungry. There was no talk about the war from a political standpoint, only in vague terms, and how grateful they all continued to be that Glen had returned safely. (That he had lost his grandfather's bracelet was bad enough as far as the Gray's were concerned.) They wanted deeply, however, to support the current president (was this not what a government was for, to know best how to confront and negotiate the dangers of the greater world?), but feared he might not have the best interests of the young men who were doing the fighting foremost at heart. There was still the lingering, 1950s patriotic-residual of sacrificing one's life to stop the danger of communism, which was perceived as divisional and threatening to the free world. There was a correct and moral path to follow, as the president laid it out, and Glen's parent's—and to a degree, Glen himself—wanted to follow that path; but they felt also the turmoil of their own gut and the increased nausea that resulted the more blindly they supported the government.

But now even parts of the government were speaking out against the war and questioning its morality: senators and members of congress were openly criticizing Johnson and the Pentagon, demanding more accountability and detailed intelligence as to exactly what was actually taking place. There was also a popular senator who had been conducting a bid for the presidency on an almost exclusively end-the-war platform.

"Cindy got A's in math again," Glen's father announced at the table; and everyone smiled and congratulated the blushing high-school junior.

"Good for you, Cindy," Julie said sincerely in front of her half-eaten hamburger. "Calculus?"

"Well; some." She grinned and shifted in her seat. "We started the tables—but just like introductory."

"Mr. Felton?" said Glen, clutching his hamburger with both hands, his mouth half full and chewing. He had not had a problem with the short interval between lunch and dinner. "Is Hubert Felton still gabbing his math lessons?"

"No—well; he's still there," Cindy said. "But I have Mr. Arren. He's new. He's really nice."

"Holy mackerel!—Felton's still there? Amazing—he must be eighty by now. At least."

Cindy grinned.

"Dessert?" Glen's mother said. "I have cherry pie."

"Oh, no—no thanks," Julie said. "I'm still stuffed from lunch."

"Sure, all right, Mom," Glen said. "I'll have a slice."

"You better, I made it for you."

"I know, Mom ... I'll be here tomorrow, though, too. You know it's not going to get thrown out."

"Pie?" Mrs. Gray said to the others at the table and after counting hands left for the kitchen with an armful of dirty dishes, as Julie followed with an armful of her own.

* * *

Glen and Julie left the Gray's shortly after helping clean up the kitchen and the quick viewing of some photographs of a recent weekend trip of Mr. and Mrs. Gray, and drove in Julie's VW to a neighborhood back across town at the edge of the tide flats on the city's east side. There they met Ann and Greg, old friends from Western State, who were waiting for them in the small house where Greg lived with a roommate. But before leaving for downtown and the old civic auditorium where the concert was scheduled to begin at nine, they went into the kitchen and cut into equal portions the small, purple tablets Glen had brought back from the house in the country. Then, placing the cut pieces in their mouths, they stood in line at the sink in the bright kitchen light and swallowed them down with glasses of water.

With a final rushed gathering of coats and sweaters and cigarettes and matches, they exited to the driveway in the warm evening air and piled into Greg's Chevrolet station wagon and headed for the concert.

* * *

With a lifetime of physical necessities taken for granted, and a relatively sudden unleashing of the parental chains of childhood (along with the increasingly greater and more rapid flow of unrestricted communication and thus ideas and information) the young people Glen and Julie's age, throughout America and the western world, were pushing hard on the boundaries of civilization and western thought, and seeking, as the young always had, the limits of what was possible. And with the luxury of a true abundance of life's basic necessities came the time to think and to imagine what might be possible. And with the continued and greatly increased separation of the mind from the body path that western science had been moving down for decades, if not centuries, came the union of that path with the paths of thinking and imagining.

And the result was LSD.

> *What will we do tonight?*
> *We will think and we will dream. But first we will assist our thinking and dreaming with these tiny pills that contain lysergic acid diethylamide; or this small capsule with its synthetic mescaline; or these dark, moist, mushrooms with their psilocybin.*
> *And then what? After we have fine turned our minds, after we have assisted them so that we are thinking and dreaming as we never have before, what will we do with the great clarity and vision that we will have attained, with the bursting forth of new thoughts and ideas that will come from deep within? What then?*
> *We will take those visions and dreams and we will change the world.*
> *For the better?*
> *Truly—And we will save the world.*
> *Save the world?*
> *For once and for all.*

* * *

"Where the hell is Ann!?" Glen was shouting into Greg's ear as he stood squeezed beside him in the pack of bodies that was to one side of the loud, booming stage.

"She's still in the women's room with Julie!" Greg yelled back: "She's still throwing up!"

"She's what?" Glen shouted again. On the stage in front of them, the half-dozen musicians played their instruments at a frenetic, sweat-inducing pace that blasted loudly from the tall stacks of speakers on each side, and swayed the ecstatic crowd in a foot-stomping frenzy.

"*She's still throwing up!*" Greg shouted as loudly as he could into Glen's ear. Suddenly he was knocked into Glen as someone large pushing through the crowd a few feet away had bumped into the bodies standing beside him. "Shit!" Greg yelled, turning angrily to the person next to him who he now saw to be a much smaller and younger girl; and she looked passively up at Greg and smiled. "Come on," Greg shouted to Glen and pointed him out of the pack of bodies; and they pushed their way to the side and through an opening and out onto the brightly lit concourse, away from the crowd and the loud blasting of the music.

"Christ—she's still sick?" Glen said dejectedly, his voice still loud, but no longer needing to shout; and Greg looked at him and nodded his head. "Man … this stuff …" Glen trailed off. "… Crap, at least I'm not as nauseous as I was, but … shit …"

"Yeah, I know," Greg said. "This stuff is fucking weird. It's got to be strychnine—or something. Shit, I'm still real off though."

Glen looked at the faces around him in the light of the concourse. There was an older woman in a clerks uniform selling sodas and snacks at a refreshment stand to one side. He thought she looked out of place, or at least different from the young concert goers who were all colorfully dressed and spirited. The concert goers were spirited, he thought, not like the heavy, slow-moving lady behind the counter; or were they? It was hard to tell at times with all the unusual movement everywhere in the very unusual light. The light made it difficult to tell exactly who was spirited and who, by-the-grace-of-god, was not. Back in the darkness of the main auditorium, with the loud beat of the music and the rhythmic swaying of the crowd—and the very strange swirling of the lights above the stage—it was very easy to tell who was spirited and who, by-the-grace-of-God's-God, was not: Everyone: Everything: All. Except possibly for the fellow who had gotten sick up near the front and had fallen down. It was hard to tell with him. And it was hard to tell with the two ushers who had carried him off. The ushers themselves had actually looked fairly spirited; even the man they were carrying had a vague sense of spiritedness about his somewhat ashen face. But several young people who apparently were with the man and followed him and the ushers out had seemed to have faces who's spirits were not as easy to detect. They had seemed to have somewhat concerned, un-spirited faces, Glen thought. But then some lights had briefly come on and the new shading had made the detection of the spiritedness of the faces of the two following friends, as well as the rest of the crowd, even more difficult to detect. Still, it was interesting to observe.

"Look, maybe we should check on them," Glen said.

"Yeah … let's."

Near an exit door there were four uniformed policemen standing and talking in a half circle, and Glen glanced at them and thought he could see a distinct spiritedness about their pale, shaven faces. They were oblivious to the young people moving about them and seemed to be talking and laughing loudly in a kind of spirited way. One of them, a tall lean fellow who had just been laughing very loudly, turned and glanced toward Glen and Greg as they passed; and his smile remained very wide from the just-finished laughing. Glen half-nodded at the uniformed officer, but only slightly, and then they were past and at the entrance to the women's room; and Greg began describing Ann and Julie to the women coming out and someone went back in and a moment later Julie came out the door.

"What's going on?" Greg asked.

"She's better," Julie said, not looking so well herself. "God; I feel so bad. We should never have taken that much. It's just way too strong."

"Jesus …" Greg shook his head. He was wearing the new wire-rimmed glasses he had recently purchased that had been made popular by several well known musicians. His brown hair was long and wavy, far past his shoulders. "It is incredible stuff... I swear I'm still hallucinating like crazy."

Glen looked at Julie's face and saw the spiritedness. It had a somewhat reddish glow (is it also humming?), all about her pale, moving face. He looked at Greg and saw some spiritedness, but not as much; it was more difficult to tell with the greater amount of reddish—no yellow (it's more a kind of uneven buzz than an actual hum)—what?—glowing that was all about his pale, somewhat moving face.

Stop it—STOP IT!

"What's she doing?" Greg asked.

"She's sitting in one of the stalls," Julie said. "—God; I feel so bad." Some more women went in the door and then it suddenly opened again and Ann came out, and, slowly, walked expressionless up to Greg and stopped. Greg put his arms around her and pulled her to him; and they stood in the bright light of the concourse and embraced. And Glen and Julie stood next to each other and put an arm around one another and watched Greg and Ann in their long, gently-swaying embrace. From the open doors of a nearby ramp, the loud booming of the band poured into the concourse as they played out the final songs of the concert.

"I think we're ready," Greg finally said.

Glen and Julie stood for a moment. "All right," Glen said, "let's beat the traffic."

And everyone turned and headed toward the exits.

SEVEN

In November a new president was elected and a great shadow seemed to descend over Glen and Julie and the people they knew. But there was also, breaking through the darkness, an almost overwhelming cultural excitement that had been exploding throughout the decade, and continued to; and there was a deep and profound sense of changing the world, at least socially, in a dramatically more progressive and freeing direction.

By then, Julie had begun her first full-time teaching position in one of the local Port Crescent elementary schools, while Glen continued working at the mill, thankful he could stay occupied as he tried, at times desperately, to blend back into civilian America. And throughout the long fall as the last leaves fell to the ground and the air turned cool and crisp, they traveled most weekends, alone or with friends, to walk in the foothills or mountains, or to visit with the increasing numbers of young people who were fleeing for the countryside to escape what felt to be the increasing strictures of the cities.

By Christmas, though, Glen decided it was time to begin looking beyond the mill, and, as he had always known he eventually would, enrolled in classes at the college for the upcoming winter term. And with government money from his service footing most of the bill, he began going full-time after the New Year, and on into the spring, while cutting back at the mill to just two days a week.

* * *

In the late spring, just after the first anniversary of his return from the war, Glen called Ben whom he had not heard from since a letter at Christmas; and they talked long about their lives of the past year and of the war and all the turmoil and pain it was causing people everywhere. They talked about the strategy of the new administration and of their deep distrust of for whom it was most intended to benefit, and their certainty that it was ultimately not the American Fighting Forces. They knew enough also that what they heard officially from the White House and the Pentagon was most likely not what was actually occurring. It was then, toward the end of the conversation, that Ben told Glen he had become engaged and would marry in late August.

* * *

That summer there were more and more bands passing through the state whose music and lifestyle were associated with the exciting new cultural changes, and concerts were held most weekends in Everett or Sealth, or at the college in Port Crescent, or sometimes at outdoor park-like settings. Then, in mid July, Glen and Julie traveled south with Randy toward a distant rural community near California where a new kind of multi-day, outdoor music-festival was being held for the second year in a row.

They arrived after the long drive in the late afternoon of the first day and followed the thick stream of cars, some hand-painted in bright, flowing colors, and all filled with young people and their increasingly long hair and even more colorful clothing and now, also, conversing with a partially separate dialect with its own unique cryptic phrases and words for expressing the new experiences and feelings of the times. And the back roads leading to the festival site became increasingly clogged until traffic came to a stop and crawled the last two miles; and just outside the entrance to the grassy parking area, a stout, middle-aged local police chief sat in a lawn chair with two deputies at his side—angry and frustrated by the local circuit judge's unwillingness to impose the last minute injunction to stop the swarm of itinerant, Dionysian invaders—and with clipboard and pen in hand, for reasons unclear to even himself, recorded the license plate of each vehicle that entered.

And once inside the gently-sloping, grass-trampled site, they set up their plastic tarps and sleeping bags in the tent area and began wandering about the many-acre, hastily-enclosed festival area. And they moved slowly past the ramshackle booths extending up from one side near the stage, filled with the small homemade trinkets and crafts that epitomized the spirit and direction of the new, independent, non-profit-motivated commerce, and which, other than getting stoned, was seen as the only truly worthwhile work. And at still other booths, the giving away or selling cheaply of various cooked and uncooked foods, before finally one stall, seemingly the most popular, with the hastily painted sign—like a child's lemonade stand—of *Drug Store*, written across the broken, plywood top, selling small amounts of marijuana and the more potent hashish along with a colorful assortment of pills.

And so for the next three days, together or individually, they were either resting up at the tarps, or down near the stage with the thickest crowds listening to the bands, or just wandering about the site; never going for long without inhaling some marijuana, or meeting and talking to people, or finding food or water or wine, or using the designated outhouse area, or choosing and taking various drugs to be high.

And when the light but steady rain came early in the morning of the last night and turned the sprawling site muddy, and chilled everyone without a plastic shelter or tent, they gathered their things and left just after dawn, along with most everyone else—

even though a few lesser-known bands were still planning to play—passing the same scowling officer on his lawn chair, now in full rain gear and sharing an umbrella with his deputies.

And finally, after leaving the back roads and congested festival traffic and moving freely up the central interstate toward Sealth and Port Crescent, the sun broke through and lit the surrounding hills and dried the glistening pavement; and the unlit joint sitting in the ashtray of the quiet car (except for the crooning troubadour playing at a low volume on the eight-track) that Randy had rolled back in the crowded, festival parking area, remained there for the entire ride back.

* * *

For much of the rest of the summer, Glen agonized over whether to make the trip out to Minnesota for Ben's wedding—he had been asked to be in the ceremony—but a few weeks beforehand he telephoned, dejectedly, and informed Ben that he would not be coming. Periodically, he and Julie had talked about trying to save money for a highly anticipated trip to Europe. Carefully weighing his options, Glen decided that with the summer's final earning days at the mill rapidly passing, he could not at that point afford a week long trip to Minneapolis.

EIGHT

With the new fall, the last of the decade, Glen again returned to school full time, picking up where he had left off in the spring, more determined than ever to complete a degree despite the new culture's increasing skepticism of following society's traditionally established paths. Julie, however, instead of returning to the school where she had taught the year before, accepted a new position she had aggressively sought at a school in the larger town of Everett, more near to her parents home in Sealth, and which was greatly more to her personal and professional desires. (Those desires being primary education: an established path where the new skepticism could be introduced and the enlightening ideas of the emerging new culture presented at an early age). At the end of August she moved into an apartment in an old residential neighborhood near the harbor, just north of the slowly redeveloping downtown area.

"This isn't going to be easy ... well, being this far apart."

"It won't be that bad," Glen responded, shortly after she had accepted the new position, trying to sound less disappointed than he was. "At least it isn't anything like before."

"Yeah ... I guess not," Julie said, lying beside him on the couch in Glen's living room in the late summer light, a Joni Mitchell album turning at low volume on the stereo.

"Look—maybe it will even help," Glen said, unconvincingly. "I'm going to be taking a ton of science this quarter. I've got to get it over with ... I mean, I'm going to have to get serious about it." He played lightly with her hair as she nestled into his side below his arm. "And you'll be able to really get into the new school."

She looked up at him. "Yeah ... I hope so."

"Plus, you know, this will help out money-wise if we're ever going to get to Europe." He reached for a cigarette as the music ended. "It'll work out; we've got to try, anyway."

* * *

And so the new term started and Glen moved from his house of the past year into a smaller, cheaper apartment, and buried himself into upper level physics and math. And Julie began her new position at the school in Everett; and they alternated most weekends between the two towns until the term drew to a close and Glen spent almost all his time at the library—unless he was over at the apartment of his new friend Russ, who, like Glen, was a veteran, and an older student, and who always had some of the best pot in Port Crescent. There, at Russ', after the night's studying, they would play records and get stoned and talk, sometimes until the early hours of the morning.

* * *

On the small campus of Western State, as the term progressed, there was again noise about the war—mostly symposiums and scheduled speakers proposing legislative tactics to legally stall or sidetrack the government's war efforts—but nothing like at the much larger university in Sealth to the south where the radical faction of the student movement regularly shut down the campus. Once, a march that had spontaneously swelled with youths from all over the city spilled onto the nearby Interstate and closed down three of the four southbound lanes, backing up traffic halfway to Everett, before the police, with tear gas and in riot gear, dispersed the raucous crowd.

Then in the spring, following an unexpected and bitterly received escalation of the war, the noise over the seemingly neverending conflict engulfed the country and there were large and violent demonstrations everywhere; even at relatively tranquil Western State where a drunk, log-ramming football player bashed down the door of the ROTC building. And yet through it all, the bursting reservoirs of uplifting intellectual thought already spilling forth from campuses world-wide, continued, sparking renewed life into the eyes of even the most despondent: a pair of new sideburns on an older businessman, where even just months before they would not have been, signaled, however subtly, the support and inner connection to those who had chosen to swim.

* * *

That summer, in between work at the mill for Glen, and waitressing at a restaurant in Everett for Julie, they began spending long periods of time with a group of people who had begun living together in a country house on Queen's Island, one of the larger islands in Capers Sound, a short ferry ride from the mainland. Striving for a new kind of independent community, the 'commune' (as such endeavors were called) had been started by a small group of long time friends from Sealth whom Julie had recently met, one of whom, Dwayne, had been given the old house and farm by an elderly uncle who had been in possession of the property for over forty years. And now, in the summer of 1970, it flourished as both a magnet and beacon for the seemingly newest and most progressive social thought and lifestyles of a broad-reaching band of young adults from the greater sound region as they moved further into adulthood.

The six to ten regulars, all with more or less middle-class, suburban roots, now attempted to live together under one roof, along with raising two pigs, eight chickens, and one cow, and grow a small vegetable garden. (Serious excited talk of becoming self-sustaining had flourished in the early days, and periodically continued still; although lately, with the recently increased summer hours of Parker's grocery in nearby Langley—with its greatly expanded snack section—somewhat less enthusiastically). There was also a continuous flow of marijuana, and its more potent cousin, hashish, in varying quantities—continuously smoked, and often sold or transferred—onto the property, which, especially for the men, was the greatest focal point of energy of all the commune's activities. But only slightly more so than the preparation and consumption of food, which was primarily overseen by the women, who put together elaborate and conscientiously-healthy meals (often with a decidedly Eastern bent that would try the palate and test the dedication of the uninitiated) which were eaten nightly in the dining room on a large table sitting just off the floor with the dozen or more daily diners seated comfortably on pillows.

And as the summer wore on, Glen and Julie (after having made the pleasant water crossing on the state ferry, during which, after exiting the car for the allowable twenty minutes, they would stand at the vessel's open bow with the wind and waves and the slowly changing horizon) gradually increased the length of their visits to where they would more and more often stay over in the small bunkhouse behind the main house, sometimes alone, sometimes with other visitors, crashing on one of the various mattresses and beds. Eventually, by August, they were staying every weekend, often shuttling in car-less visitors from the mainland, almost always bringing in various quantities of dope from Sealth or Everett or Port Crescent, the quality of their contacts a major appeal to the commune regulars.

* * *

"When it gets legalized they'll need people to run the stores—you know—to sell it." Dwayne Feloney, sitting in the small circle of trampled grass in front of the house in the early evening light with Glen and three other people staying at the farm that night, spoke matter-of-factly. The hair of all the men hung far past their shoulders and most of them had beards and they were all dressed in faded jeans and old, colored tee-shirts. A woman, Nancy, had long straight hair down to her waist. Only Glen was wearing any kind of shoes. They passed a pipe around and drew long on the burning hemp. "… They'll have to have people who know what the prices should be, too," Dwayne continued, stroking the thick hair of his mustache and beard away from his mouth as he spoke. Circular, wire-rimmed glasses with thick, smudged lenses rested on his nose, "… you know, and what the different kinds are from different places."

"It'll probably be a lot cheaper, too," one of the men said, leaning back in the grass.

"And stronger," said the other man, Ed. He wore a kind of suede-looking hat with a wavy, encircling brim. Glen had never seen him without the hat, even at night. The brown grass of the field sloped down from the house to the county road that ran below the farm. There were mostly fir trees beyond the road, tall and slender—a second or possibly third-growth forest—except to one side where the field continued, unobstructed, gently sloping into the far distance to where there was a small glimpse of the dark waters of the sound. Faintly visible across the sound were the low hills of the mainland, and in the fading light beyond the hills rose the mountains.

"Yeah—definitely," said the first man, Ken, nodding. "It should be a lot stronger." He was leaning back on his elbows in the grass with his skinny, barefooted legs stretched toward the center of the circle. Like a modern Huck Finn, a long stem of grass extended from his mouth, the end of which he periodically chewed.

"And think of how much cleaner it will be," Glen said, taking the pipe from the woman. "There won't be any seeds or stems … you know, all you'll be smoking is the leaves." He inhaled on the pipe.

"Yeah, and think of all the hash there'll be," Dwayne said, a slight smile forming. "I mean all the different kinds.—If you want Afghan, you get Afghan.—If you want Lebanese, you get that."

"You won't have to be so paranoid, either," said the woman, Nancy.

"Yeah, but even now it depends on how much you've got," said Ed, his hair spilling down from under the hat. "The cops don't even care about a few lids anymore … you know?" He looked at Nancy. "A lot of cops smoke now, anyway."

"No shit, man," said Dwayne. "What do you think they do with it when they take it from you? Shit—they just take what they want, all for free."

"No fucking kidding," said Ed, emphatically, and laughing. "Shit, you don't think they don't just go looking for freaks to bust? They see some heads on a bus or something and they know they're going to have their pick of whatever they want. And what can you do? '—Hey; you can't take that'. Shit, you just got to be glad they don't bust you in the gut."

"Mort says he gets pulled over all the time," said Ken, blowing out his breath of smoke before chewing again on the stem of grass.

"Mort?" said Dwayne, sounding somewhat astonished. "Mort always looks too stoned for the police to want to even bother with. Crap, they see Mort and think: why waste a cell?"

"No … no …" Ken went on. "He just says he's real polite. They check him out; they usually don't even search him he says."

"How are they around here?" asked Nancy. She was fairly new to the commune, having come up from Oregon the week before. Her blond hair was long and straight, and skinny, pale legs protruded from her frayed denim cutoffs.

"A lot of them knew my uncle," said Dwayne, looking over. "See, my aunt's father was from the island—like originally—so they know I'm the nephew. So they cut us some slack. It's not like a lot of the freaks who go into town and get drunk all the time. They're always busting them."

"Smitty was saying a guy got busted with a couple of pounds down around Langley a couple of weeks ago," said Ed, his tone now serious.

"Yeah?" Dwayne said. "—Fuck." He looked out toward the small patch of distant water, shaking his head. "So, anyway—yeah—I could probably run a weed store or something here on the island."

"To tell you the truth, I don't know what's taking them so long—you'd think it would have happened by now," Ken said, also in a serious tone. He tossed away the stem and sat up to free both hands as the pipe approached. "I even heard there's radicals on the city council down in Berkley now ... That's probably the first place it'll get legalized."

Everyone listened.

"You think so?" said Ed, handing him the pipe.

"It probably would be, wouldn't it?" said Nancy in a knowing tone.

"Shit—the cops probably don't want it legalized," Ed said, "'cause then they'd have to pay for it too. They couldn't get it free anymore."

"Really ..." Dwayne said, nodding. "That would drive them nuts: hippies with pot everywhere; and they couldn't touch 'em—fuck."

From the house came the sound of the screen door opening and Julie and another woman came down and joined the circle. Julie smiled at Glen as she sat down in the grass. The pipe came to him and he reached across and handed it to her. "That veterinarian's coming tomorrow to look at Sydney," the other woman said to Dwayne, having sat down beside him.

"Poor Sydney," said Ken. "I wonder what's wrong with him? I haven't heard him oink in two weeks."

"Oh, he does," said Ed. "You can just barely hear it ... you have to get right down next to him ... and you can hear something."

"Oh, poor Sydney," said Julie. "Poor Lois, too—I think she's worried about him."

"She goes over and kind of snorts at him every now and then," said the other woman, Karen, beside Dwayne. She was thin with a long, angular face and light, shiny hair. A thin leather band encircled her head. She was not unfriendly, but rarely smiled or laughed, emitting a kind of intenseness that scared some to a degree.

"He's going to look at Moose, too, isn't he?" Glen asked, looking over to Karen.

"Yes, for sure; I'm going to have him look at the chickens, too."

"Good—might as well while he's here," said Ken. He had the pipe and tapped the bowl against his palm and more smoke rose.

"You know, Moose doesn't seem to be eating as much either," Glen went on.

"He looks like he eats a lot to me," said Julie.

"He's a she," said Dwayne.

Julie looked at Dwayne.

"But I don't think it's that unusual for a cow," Ken said. "They kind of go in cycles—with what they eat."

The people looked at Ken.

"Well, she was only fifty dollars," said Julie. "What are we going to do with her, anyway—does she milk?"

"She will," Ken said. "Eventually."

"Yeah, good question," said Glen. "Hey, you know—maybe we could rent her out for rides."

"Cow rides!" Ed said loudly. "Ten cents a yard!"

The people looked briefly at Ed.

"Hey—I'm going to put her in the fair next year," Dwayne said. "She's going to make us famous ... We'll be known throughout the island as the owners of the lovely, the adorable—'Miss Moose' the cow."

Everyone looked across the field beyond the barn to where a cow stood, motionless, but for an occasional flip of its tail. They looked back at Dwayne. "Yeah; she's adorable all right," said Ken, knocking the ash out of the pipe.

"You know, you won't even be here for the fair next summer," Karen said to Dwayne in a serious, almost scolding tone. They had been talking alone a lot lately, at times taking off together; but no one was certain whether there was anything going on between them.

"Shit—that's right," Dwayne said, not sounding all that disappointed. "I'm going to miss the damn thing, aren't I? ... Oh well." He shrugged his shoulders and looked off again toward the dark patch of water and the last evening light of the late-summer day.

    Beside him on the grass, Julie and Glen glanced uncomfortably at each other, knowing why Dwayne would not be around next summer and that most of the others did not, and that that was how it was supposed to be.

NINE

"Listen ... can you hear it?"
"Yes—god; how terrible ... Christ."
From across the tops of the gray stone buildings of the central Turkish town came the crackling, amplified voice of a messenger of Allah, calling the brethren to the ancient mosque for morning prayer. It was 5:00AM.
"*Aaaaaaaaaaayyyyyyaaaaaaaaaaahhhhh...eeeeaaaaaaaaaay yyyyyyyyyyoooooooooooooeeeeeeeeaaaaaaaaaaaaaalllllllllllllllllllllllll lllllzzzzzzzzzzzzzzzzzyyyyyyyyeeeeeeaaaaaaaaaaaaaaa...*"
The muezzin's voice bellowed out over the dusty barren town from the loudspeaker at the top of the slender minaret that pierced the gray dawn from the dominating, dome-crowned mosque in the center of the town. On the street, below the open window of the second-floor room where Glen and Julie lay beneath the sheets of the small hotel bed, women with scarf-covered heads and dark billowing-pants guided cattle in the cool September air to the fields beyond the town, as men, riding mule-drawn buggies

laden with produce, occasionally whipped past the women and cattle. From within a crowded tea house a few doors down the dusty street, the noisy chatter of men, young and old, dressed in dark pants and jackets, drifted out the door as they finished small cups of chai before leaving for prayer.

Julie tossed off the sheet and swung her legs over the side of the bed and, naked, faced the tall open windows as the morning light, growing brighter, filled the barren room. Glen rolled onto his side in the opposite direction and pulled the sheet up and tried to cover his head with one of the pillows.

Aaaaaaaaaallllllllllllleeeeeeeeeeeeeoooooooooooooooolllllllllllllllleee eeeeeeeeaaaaaaaaaaaaaaaaaaaaaaaaaa…' The badly distorted voice continued from the loudspeaker over the otherwise quiet town.

"Ahhhhhhh—shit!" Glen threw off the sheet and pillow and turned toward the window and Julie. He put his arm on her bare back and then down around her waist; and she leaned back against him and reached back with her arms and cupped the back of his head and yawned. Glen also yawned, and stared blankly toward the dull light of the windows, his eyes red and baggy, and then nudged closer and kissed her neck and moved his hand up her waist and held one of her breasts. And Julie, swinging the long flowing trusses of her hair aside, turned and kissed him roughly on the side of his mouth and reached down with her hand.

* * *

"Coffee? … café?" Glen held his empty cup up to the young girl in the doorway of the dining-room kitchen who was clothed from head to toe in loose, light blue; and she came quickly forward and took the cup and disappeared back into the kitchen. When she returned with the cup full, she looked eagerly at Julie who shook her head, and the girl returned to the doorway.

"No more days like that," Julie said forlornly at the small, white-clothed table as she picked at the plate of cheese and cucumbers and olives in front of her. She tore off another piece of bread from the small loaf.

"That crazy ass is what you mean," Glen said, looking over in the fluorescent-lit hotel basement room.

Julie looked up. "Yeah ... at first he seemed cool; normal, or like ... I don't know." She spread butter on the bread. "Yeah; crazy ass."

Glen sipped carefully at the strong, hot coffee. "I'm just glad we were only going to Keyseir. Or we'd still be fucking out there driving around."

"Probably headed for Syria."

Outside on the street, the late-model Volkswagen bus sat caked with mud and dirt. Some children in long robes and pants, playing noisily nearby, ran over, wide-eyed, to look at the strange vehicle, then just as quickly ran off. Back inside the aging dining room of the Palaise Hotel in Konya, Turkey, Julie and Glen continued to fill their stomachs with as much of the breakfast as they could which had come with the one dollar room.

The time in Europe had been glorious with the summer flood of young travelers descending on the continent with its progressive cultures and exotic sights and seemingly endless supply of hashish. And rising up from it all, the deafening roar of social upheaval that radiated everywhere throughout the west, and, unknowingly then, around the globe. And everything was there: In London the markets in Kennsington for buying cheap clothes, and the pubs on Portabello Road for meeting other travelers and local British kids, and the potent hashish cigarettes cooked with tobacco, and the pads for crashing, finally, in the early hours of the London morning. And then on the last night, tickets and guidance to the Who concert at the outdoor Cricket Oval in King's Cross.

And later, the hitchhiking and rides to Copenhagen and Amsterdam and the crowded 'sleep-ins' with their wall-to-wall foam pads on the cement floors for fifty cents a night and the all night parties at the hash houses. And then, when paying fifty cents seemed questionable (as though any exchange of money was a suspicious triviality in itself), the sleeping bags thrown for free on the grass in Vondel Park; and the elderly Dutchman in his pressed suit and necktie—the memories of the recent brutal occupations of two world wars etched permanently into his soul—feeding the swans in the pond from a bench just a few feet away, seemingly uninterested in the vagabond children which the night had brought, when Glen and

Julie awoke in the morning, red-eyed and disheveled, and peered out from their bags into the bright Dutch sun.

But after the week in Hamburg, waiting for the Volkswagen with its false gas tank where the large quantity of hashish was to be stored (the ingenious tank secretly welded on back at the barn on Queens Island as Sydney and Lois squealed violently from the shower of sparks and flame) and which had been shipped to Hamburg from Portland, Oregon, a month before—after the week in Hamburg they had had to get serious about the van's delivery to Dwayne. A delivery which was supposed to have conveniently taken place in exotic Istanbul, but because of unexpected and—as details emerged—to say the least, mind-boggling complications, had been extended ten days and at least three-hundred miles further across Turkey, and possibly five-hundred to near the far eastern border with Iran.

So Hamburg had ended rather suddenly with the arrival of the bus to port; and so had the week long party at the German student's loft whom they had met on a downtown street corner, and where they had been staying with the traveler from Ireland, who had been with them since Belgium, and the couple from Wisconsin, who had been with them since Copenhagen. The week long party which started each day, gloriously, with a chillum of hashish (then, in northern Europe, blond Lebanese) the moment they arose from the previous night's sleep at two in the afternoon, and ended with more hashish and German beer back at the seemingly luxurious flat when they returned from the crowded discotheques and nightclubs at sunrise of the following glorious morning.

It ended in Hamburg with the late morning sun filtering in through the edges of the tightly closed blinds as Glen and Julie walked quietly with their backpacks out the front door, as the six others in the student's loft slept soundly on their beds, or the sections of floor where they had ended up after the previous night's party.

"Was he really going to try to sell the coke there?" Julie asked, looking up in the hotel dining room from the plate of cheese and bread. Some hornets had somehow made it into the basement and now hovered over the jam; and she tried to shoo them but they immediately came back.

"Christ—he was a crazy fucker," Glen said, sounding annoyed, "that's all I know. Shit, I should have known he might be carrying something like that." He looked off, the bags under his eyes still dark. "… But, well, actually, I guess it is a lot easier to hide …" He suddenly took a wild swing at a hornet. "God, what did he drink, anyway—five or six liters? In what—a day and a half? I've never been so scared in my life as that last checkpoint. I was sure that was going to be it. Christ; these are Moslems—I don't even think they drink alcohol."

"No, they don't," Julie said, also sounding annoyed, and shook her head. "If I'd known he had coke—no way. That could have been the end of everything."

A man with long hair and a beard, and a woman with very long hair and a headband, came down the stairs to the breakfast room. Glen and Julie could immediately tell they were European from the clothes they wore. They nodded to Julie and Glen who smiled back. A little boy and girl came hurriedly out of the kitchen and headed to the stairs talking excitedly in Turkish, their round, olive-skinned faces wide-eyed and animated. "Well, the stuff is sure weird, huh?" Glen said, sipping his coffee. "… Sure doesn't last very long."

Julie looked at Glen, grimacing profoundly, and rubbed her nose as though there were an itch. "No … it doesn't."

Glen ate the last olive and leaned back and looked around the mostly barren walls. There was an old color photo of a Turkish airliner, set aloft against a background of puffy clouds and blue sky, and on the wall near the stairs, a framed plaque with the exotic slashes of Arabic inscription. "Well," Glen said, "now we wait … If there's anyone we can count on, though, it's Dwayne … reliable Dwayne."

"I don't know," Julie said, shaking her head again, the hard swipe of her hand finally making contact with one of the hornets. She looked at Glen and spoke with a disgust that almost startled him: "It sure did not sound good. Jesus Christ—*Spiro Agnew?*"

They had talked to Dwayne by telephone at the Postal and Telegraph Office in Istanbul four days before, to make the final arrangements for the delivery of the van that was originally to have taken place on the outskirts of Istanbul, with Dwayne then driving on alone to Afghanistan to buy the one-hundred pounds of hashish. But, incredulously, without a word of warning, the border between Afghanistan and Iran had suddenly been closed to all traffic for the international birthday celebration that the young King of Afghanistan, Mohammed Zahir Shah, was throwing for himself. No one was being allowed overland into the country, primarily from American State Department security pressure, because the Vice President of the United States was scheduled to attend, to court the strategically significant Afghanis who were feuding, again, with their Soviet neighbors to the north. Ambassadors, presidents, dictators, and royalty throughout Europe and the Middle East were expected to attend. It was possible, Dwayne had said, that the border closure could last a month.

"If there's a way to get in …" Glen reached for the last piece of bread, "Dwayne will find it … I'm counting on him."

"A lot of people are counting on him." Julie tried to run fingers through her matted hair. "Spiro Agnew—Christ, this is beyond getting ridiculous; with all the money we went through in Italy and Greece? We're going to be completely broke." Her already existing grimace suddenly heightened when her hand caught some strands; and she tore them out and shook them to the floor. The little boy and girl came loudly back down the stairs with an overflowing basket of bread and rushed into the kitchen. "Crap," Julie said, one hand still in her hair, pushing her plate back with the other, "that guy was a lunatic."

"You going to eat that?" Glen looked at the slice of bread on her plate.

"No, go ahead … I'm going up to the room."

The payment for delivering the van to Dwayne and then picking it up again and taking it through customs back in Portland would more than cover the cost of the sloop. The very fine sloop: wood, double-mast, ocean going. And with the money left over they would be able to sail the world—and stay high—for at least a year, maybe two. At their age, the future beyond a year or two seemed extremely irrelevant and was nearly impossible to imagine.

"I'll be up in a while," Glen said from the table, reaching for the bread. "I want to get some things out of the bus." He began spreading butter. "Do you still want to try to find that museum later?"

Julie nodded, expressionless, as she left the table.

Earlier that summer they had taken the van, empty, over the Canadian border a few times, and then with just a few lids, to test the compartment, and were confident with the results. There had been a substantial investment of time and money to this point, and the border closure was unfathomable with all of Dwayne's significant and patiently cultivated contacts in Afghanistan. No one had heard anything beforehand about a birthday party for a king, let alone an entire country closing its borders for one.

* * *

"Oh, my god, Glen … it's beautiful."

"Yeah … it is … it's incredible …"

In the distance, down the brown, dusty street, piercing the gray sky above the billowing domes of the grand central-mosque and former monastery and the surrounding ancient buildings of the old town, rose the massive fluted tower of gleaming turquoise-tiles of the Mevlâna Museum. As large as a grain silo, an enormous cone-topped cylinder, gleaming in bright turquoise in the dull light of the day.

Here in the warm afternoon air, away from the van and the hotel and the difficulties of the previous few days, the light returned to Julie's face. "—It's supposed to be where the Dervishes retreated when they were driven from Constantinople—well, Istanbul.—In the thirteenth century." She smiled widely, a battered Fodors guide book in her hand, her face glowing in the afternoon light. "My god—it's spectacular!"

"Let's take a picture," Glen said, almost as animated. "Here, hold the bag." And he stepped out into the dusty street amidst the few cars and the horse drawn buggies of the central Anatolian town and pointed the camera at the glistening tower.

* * *

It was four more days before Dwayne arrived, his beard gone, his hair cut short, looking several years older instead of the two months that had elapsed since they had seen him last; and they knew immediately without him having to explain that Afghanistan was lost.

The border was teaming with security, Dwayne finally did explain in greater detail later that night in the dimly-lit hotel bar, and the Afghanis were not going to make an exception for some young Yankee and his Volkswagen bus, even for the thousand dollars cash he was offering. The transporting of the one-hundred pounds of high-grade black Afghanistan hashish the compartment had been designed for would not be taking place.

With the handful of other young travelers staying at the hotel: a Canadian couple; two women from New Zealand; another Brit; they spent the rest of the night in the hotel bar talking and drinking beer, but for the periodic trips out to the bus to get high from the various personal stashes that each possessed.

* * *

In the late fall of 1971, Glen, his hair cut short and clean shaven, picked up the bus at the Port of Portland in Oregon, and, under the buzzing rush of dexadrene (taken for only the second time in his life), cleared customs and drove up to the island and back to the farm without incident. Hidden inside the compartment were three pounds of red Lebanese hash that Dwayne had purchased in Italy. Little of it was sold, much of it was given away, and by the following spring, the last tiny piece was smoked by Dwayne in the van at the back of a rest stop on a cloudy afternoon while driving up the interstate toward Queens Island from a city to the south.

TEN

In the fall after Europe, Julie returned to her teaching position in Everett as she had originally planned—world sails were not to have begun until the following year—but Glen, disillusioned and uncertain about the path he most wanted to pursue, withdrew from the courses at Western State he had tentatively enrolled in the previous spring, and began working full time again back at the mill. But after only a month he suddenly quit and just as suddenly abandoned the house in Port Crescent and moved back down to Sealth, where, with the help of an old friend of his father's, he took an assistant research job at the university, working on campus in a rat lab in the psychology department. Despite the embarrassingly low pay, it was, at times, somewhat interesting work; but it was also part of an established traditional future he feared, with increasing anxiety, was becoming more and more inevitable.

Would there be no revolution?

(At the lab in Sealth, when he first saw the cages and mazes, he struggled with the extreme irony of his long obsessed drive to beat the 'rat race', and where he now held employment.)

But over time the job became an unexpectedly pleasant change—despite the daily disposing of rat shit (or, occasionally, following a graduate students' overly ambitious experiment, the rat). And it was warm inside during the cold winter months, and much more closely related to the math and science classes he had become increasingly interested in. And despite his still strong love for the small-town peacefulness of Port Crescent and its surrounding countryside, and the dearly held memories of his many years there, the large in-city university, with its used record and clothing stores and coffee houses and head-shops and the many neighborhood bars, became a comforting womb from the rest of the worlds increasing chaos.

By early spring, however, the grant funding the lab project was greatly reduced and Glen's hours were suddenly cut to just a few a week; and almost overnight his playful cuddly rats seemed like what they were.

* * *

"All right—so say you do finally get the degree, well, any ideas what you'll do then?" Julie's voice came from the receiver, still feeding off the topic Glen had brought up a half hour before.

"Well—yeah—I mean there's always teaching if nothing else, right? ... But that seems like it would just be going over the same things ... Sure, it would be noble and all that, but it would just be the same material over and over. I don't know how you do it, but then ... grade-schoolers ... I guess ..." Slumped in the torn, over-sized stuffed chair, Glen lit the stale remains of a cigarette he had taken from a can of butts he kept beside the chair. He continued when there was no response. "Or maybe if you were at a college you could do research or something ... Some of these guys in the lab—they're like these psychologists—experimental ones—This one guy, he's like a Fulbright from Berkeley—complete freak, hair out to here—he's got one whole lab wired with, like, two-foot speakers—nonstop music: he's analyzing brain circuitry with Led Zepplin blasting the walls; it's a complete trip ... But, anyway, all that means at least a masters, or probably a doctorate ..." Glen looked at the cigarette and crushed it out in the ashtray. The small rooming-house room was cramped, but quiet, especially then, with just the gentle sprinkling of rain against the window and occasional sound of the cars passing down the wet street in the darkness below.

"Well, I wish, Glen—but there's more to teaching then just going over and over the same thing." In her large Everett apartment, Julie looked across the living room toward the brightly lit kitchen. In the opposite direction, out the large living room windows, the lights of the city sparkled in front of the dark, distant waters of Capers Sound.

"Yeah—I know ... that's not what I meant ... But there's got to be something more like what Greg's doing ... only even more some kind of environmental science ... Some kind of technology or something."

"It's hard to see you working for some corporation."

"Well, no, but maybe some state agency or something ... or even some new company. There's new companies starting up all the time ... a lot down in California. All the advisors keep saying it's only going to get bigger."

"Whatever turns you on."

"Shit—what's that supposed to mean? I've got to do something ... I'm not going to work at the farm—or the mill ... Especially if we're raising kids."

"Glen—I thought we agreed we weren't going to talk about that sort of thing for a long, long time. Until we both know what we really want to do."

"Yeah—well ... I know. Hey; we'll figure it out ... we always have."

There was a pause as Glen waited with the receiver pressed against his ear, and then: "... It's late ... I'm going to bed ... I'll see you this weekend."

In Glen's upper floor apartment, the gentle sound of rain continued against the window. "Yeah; okay ... I love you ... good night."

There was a pause. "... I love you ... Good night ..."

* * *

In the fall of 1972, Glen officially transferred to the university in Sealth, and again began taking classes full time, as well as continuing a few hours a week in the lab. After the many years of the small town feel of Port Crescent and the state college, Sealth and the university felt enormous, and he seemed often to withdraw into the crowds of both the campus and city.

There was, however, a much greater assortment of activities in the city: the numerous concert halls and movie screens; the vibrant, budding theater-community; the many sports teams that played in the numerous stadiums and arenas throughout the area, some of which he would frequent with his father. (With his parents home again nearby, there were also the random Sunday dinners, and now, the periodic phone calls from his sister regarding various boyfriend ecstasies and disasters.)

But with the much larger campus and student body, and the decidedly liberal slant of the school and faculty and surrounding community, the radical factions of the anti-war movement continued their noisy efforts, as did the now hopelessly mired American forces in Southeast Asia; and that fall Richard Nixon was reelected to the presidency.

* * *

Outside of class, Glen spent most of his time in the library, or at the lab, or in his small room off campus; and when moving between classes and a gathering or demonstration of some kind was unavoidable, he walked quickly around the outskirts and caught only fleeting glimpses or distorted fragments of amplified speech from the distant speakers perched on a bench or platform or wall at the foot of the crowd.

Figuratively, the noise faded—the government and society at large had withstood the at times fierce domestic uprising—even as the war continued; although its purpose and direction drastically and permanently altered.

There really isn't going to be a revolution ...

There was, however, even better dope in Sealth—fuck the war—dealers like Fast Eddie and Uncle Tim had tightly packed clumps of pot they called 'buds', which actually glistened with resin. They came from somewhere in South America—or was it Central?—and Glen learned quickly that they were best saved for weekends. And then only when there was nothing serious planned for the next few hours. But mostly he studied and read and on weekends made the hour drive up to Julie's in Everett.

* * *

One late-winter night, after the new year, the phone rang and a familiar voice invited Glen to a small bar at a nearby restaurant just a few blocks away. When Glen entered the well-lit establishment with the many hanging plants and dark, wood beams, he began to smile widely when he saw the familiar face reading a newspaper at a corner table. "Randy?—man, is that you? Man—how have you been?"

"Glen ... Glen you mother—hey, man."

"Shit—I thought you were living in California." Glen grasped Randy's hand and then lowered himself into the opposite chair at the small, wood table. "What's it been—two years?"

"Two and a half, man," Randy said, reaching a hand over to the beer in front of him.

"Wow, where's Rachel?—You guys have a kid, right?"

Randy's gaze brightened. His hair was short and neatly combed and the horn-rimmed glasses he had always worn sat low on his small nose. "Yeah, Casey. She's a year and a half—walks like crazy now, almost talks; a real trip. She's with Rachel back in Redding."

Glen smiled then motioned for the waitress to bring him a beer. "You look good, man. What's up?"

"Oh, nothing, really. I just thought I'd look you up. I came up to get this car my brother's giving me. You remember Dick? Straight arrow? Works for Boeing now—he's an engineer."

"Dick?—shit yes. He bought us beer a few times, like when we were freshmen—didn't he? Yeah, he's what, four or five years older isn't he?"

"Yeah, five." Randy nodded and took a drink. "Yeah; he's got this old Plymouth—perfect shape—was going to trade it in; he's loaded. But he decided to just give it to Rachel and me."

"That's cool." Glen nodded.

"Yeah, so what the fuck—I took the bus up—pain in the ass; the old 'hound. Visiting my folks for a few days. Decided to give you a call."

"Well, shit, I'm glad you did, man." His beer came and he paid the waitress. "So, how's Redding? What are you doing down there? Working?"

"Oh, yeah … Believe it or not, man, I'm working in a mill." Randy laughed and drank from his beer.

"Oh, no," Glen laughed, "you too?"

"Yeah, well—there's a lot of logging down there. But wait, don't tell me," he looked earnestly at Glen, "you're not still at the mill … no, you couldn't be—or one down here?"

"No—no. I was last summer for a while, up in Crescent. But, no, I'm still the student." Glen smiled and drank from his beer.

"Yeah? Still hitting those books?" Randy looked at his beer. "Yeah … I almost graduated. I probably could in about a year if I ever went back … but …" he shook his head, "nah, I couldn't afford it now. Not with Casey. The mills not bad, though. Mostly freaks."

"Yeah?"

"Oh, man; everywhere. Communes everywhere—all over."

"Yeah? Wow."

"Oh, yeah—yeah." Randy nodded. "So … how's Julie?"

"She's good, man—she never stops: the pillar. She's got more—she knows more people than I can even think about." Glen drank from his beer. "Still teaching …"

"Elementary school, right?"

"Yeah. Up in Everett now."

"Cool." Randy took a drink. "So, did I hear something about some trip to Europe? … Like last year?"

"Yeah—yeah, two months. Oh, man, it was wild. But we were just the straight tourists."

"Yeah, yeah, sure—*sure*, I'll bet," Randy laughed and drank his beer.

Glen took a cigarette out from the pack in his coat pocket. Randy took one from his pack on the table. "So," Glen said, flicking his lighter, "what, did you talk to Greg or something?" They lit the cigarettes.

"No ... no but I heard something about some little side trip—to Iran or someplace. Holy fuck, man, Iran?—no shit?"

"Wow; yeah.—Actually we made it to Turkey." Glen blew smoke to the side. "Wow, word gets around—all the way to California."

"Ah—no—you know."

"Yeah—yeah I know," Glen gave a slight laugh and drank more beer.

"So, what's up with you?" Randy said. "You going to graduate?"

"Man, I hope so. No, I will; probably by next year."

"Yeah? Then what?"

Glen blew out smoke. "Good question; I don't know. Maybe go for a masters. Maybe some kind of environmental science ... something."

"Yeah?" Randy drew on his cigarette. "And Julie's doing all right, huh?"

"Yeah, real good. It was kind of rough last year for a while; but she's just really getting into the teaching. The school loves her—a lot."

Randy blew out smoke and took a drink. "So, what's with you two, anyway? ... You guys have been together since—shit—before Western."

"Ah, you know—the big step ... I don't know ... I mean, I hope we get married—or something. Shit—what's marriage, anyway? But Julie's unbelievable. She's just really amazing—well—she puts up with my crap anyway, which must say something." Glen looked at Randy.

"Yeah? ... huh." Randy looked across the quiet room. There were plants hanging everywhere from the beams of the ceiling; dark, drooping ferns, and along the wall toward the bar. "So, how's the family?"

"Good ... they're all right. Cindy's at Central now. Loves it—big party school. Sounds like it's just crazy.—Crazier than

Western. Mom's doing good. The old man still doesn't know what to make of me: his hippy-veteran-son."

Randy chuckled and nodded. "Yeah? Good ... good."

A group of students came in from the winter street and sat at a table across the room. They looked to be freshmen or sophomores, not long from high school, and although they were only five or six years younger than Randy and Glen, they bore an air of being from another lifetime. They looked socially aware, and contemporary, and with the unmistakable look of students; and the hair of all the males was very long and the females all had long hair and wore jeans; but they seemed awfully young and innocent. The waitress served them beer. Randy looked at Glen. "Well, man—my sister is supposed to be coming over to my folks place in a while ... I said I'd only be an hour."

"Yeah? ... Yeah, I should crack some books." Glen put out his cigarette. "You can never catch up. Hey, good to see you man ... Glad you called ... Glad things are working out."

Randy nodded and drank the last of his beer. They got up from the table and walked out the door to the street. There were still a few stores with Christmas decorations, and the lights of the buildings, and a few cars that passed in the dark.

"If you ever come south, man, look us up ... The place is a trip. And Rachel would love to see you."

"I will," Glen said. "And tell her I said hello." He reached out his hand but Randy pulled him in for a brief hug.

"Take care, man," Randy said. "Say hi to Julie."

"Will do. You too—take care."

Randy turned and walked up the street. Glen stood for a moment in the dark and listened to the quiet. There were the faint shapes of low clouds moving swiftly past in the night sky above, and an occasional star appeared between the clouds. Up the sidewalk, another group of students approached, talking and laughing loudly; and Glen glanced at them briefly and then quickly turned in the cool night air and strode off in the opposite direction.

ELEVEN

The rest of the winter was particularly dismal with the endless weeks of clouds and rain, and difficult, with the increasingly cerebral and competitive upper-level science with the older stuffy professors (the exception being frail, bow-tie-adorned, Professor Edwards, whose presence and manner, and unmatched enthusiasm, left one transfixed and in awe of the presented physiology, and seemingly enlightened, while totally unaware of the passage of time) and the younger arrogant ones, and all the extremely ambitious younger students who thought they should all be in medical school and felt their lives would end if they weren't.

But the spring came and the skies cleared and the days lengthened, and the hills turned green; and even the physics and calculus, and the chemistry and statistics, mysteriously and wonderfully, entered a period of relative ease. The war, though, continued, now with the American involvement winding down greatly, and simply seeming more and more like annoying background static. And through the remainder of the spring Glen pushed forcefully yet contentedly through the most difficult of his classes and on toward the degree he hoped soon to receive.

✳   ✳   ✳

But then one day the phone rang and although she could not say so right away, the distance in her voice said it for her; and it was a distance far greater than the forty miles that separated them physically: and it brought forth from somewhere deep inside a fear that greatly overshadowed the most harrowing episodes of approaching danger and uncertainty in the darkest bowels of Vietnam. So when Julie began explaining the details about the man she had been secretly seeing for the past three months, and that the hiding and immense confusion, and the enormous guilt, had pushed her into an abyss of darkness from which no spring on Earth could ever hope to enlighten, and that they would be moving in together by the end of the month, the small room on the shady street where Glen sat began to move, but stopped before one full rotation; and a dog barked across the street and there were children playing near the dog and he now heard his father talking very gently to his sister when she had asked, tearfully, when she too could get a bicycle, that warm, sunny spring day long, long ago. And then came the roar; but it, too, quickly became fascinated with the barking dog, and the children, and now the flurry of tiny birds that streaked into the brilliantly bursting Dogwood out the open window: and Sergeant Ross smiled mockingly at the sight of Phillips finally getting his god damn mess kit to fit into his god damn pack before the Equaya vines growing on the ground at his feet encircled his legs and torso and blossomed beside his cheek. But didn't Ross know that there were people up that road; we'd been hearing about it all week, and because it hadn't been reckoned in over a year, we were going to be the first ones in; but the flowers on the Equaya vines are actually quite interesting with the very thin white ribbing across the soft, velvety blue.

"Jesus, Julie—why?" Glen said from the sun-filled room. "Can we talk? Julie … I'm what? You're getting upset with me?

Oh—great. Thanks ... Oh, come on—what? All right, all right, all right ... Oh—shit. All right!.... Good bye. All right—Jesus."

He talked with her once more that summer, but had known from the moment of the phone call that she was gone; and after hanging up he got immediately into the car and somehow found the interstate and began driving east toward the mountains. And except for one brief stop after the pass to fill the tank and use the bathroom, he continued on across the arid eastern sage for six more hours until the sun disappeared behind him and the distant, dark borders of Idaho and Montana slipped quietly past.

* * *

In the fall, Glen entered the University in Sealth for the final three courses he would need for his undergraduate degree, and on a cloudy afternoon of the week before Christmas, turned in his last exam and then went with several older students and another veteran to a popular bar near campus and drank beer and played pool and darts until it closed late that night.

TWELVE

"Hey, where is she? Ahhhhhhh, there she is—hey sis." Glen entered the bedroom and put his arm around Cindy's waist and, pulling her and the flowing, wedding-dress toward him, kissed her on the cheek. She grinned and made a kind of exaggerated dorky face and then grabbed the brush off the bureau and began stroking her long, wavy hair. When she was through, she took a flowered band and placed it carefully over her head.

"Wow—look at you!" Glen beamed, standing behind his sister in front of the mirror, observing her reflected image. "The flower princess."

"God—don't ever get married. Just don't." Cindy dropped onto the bed and began adjusting her sandals.

"No?—Never?" Glen turned from the mirror wide-eyed and with an exaggerated look of deep shock.

"No, it's too much work."

"Ah, kid … I thought the rehearsal was fun … this'll be even more fun."

Cindy rolled her eyes, then smiled again. "Well, unless it's to a sweetheart like Tim.—Hey, is your friend coming? What's her name?"

"Leslie? Oh yeah, she'll be there." Glen took a cigarette from the pocket of his suite and leaned against the bureau. He had grown his sideburns long again and now had a mustache as his hair spilled over the back of his collar.

From the hallway, Mrs. Gray called out to Cindy: "Honey—we're ready."

"Be right there, mom." Cindy took another look in the mirror. "All righty, I'm-a-ready." She reached out her hand toward the cigarette and after a deep drag handed it back. "Let's go," she said, blowing the stream out her nostrils with smaller whiffs coming from her mouth, and Glen smiled and followed her out the door.

* * *

The lawns were brown from the August sun, and children ran through sprinklers in front yards as the Grays passed along the city streets in the old Buick toward the Episcopal Church. White puffs of clouds floated high above in the deep blue, and beyond the city hills, the hazy outline of the mountains creased the distant horizon.

Mr. Gray pulled into the parking lot where a few groups of people who had gathered on the shady walk beside the church turned and smiled. "There's the Holmgren's," he said, coming to a stop and waving to the older couple near the walkway. They got out of the car and greeted people and then another group, all Cindy's age, came excitedly up; and Cindy exchanged long hugs and they talked with her for a moment before going into the tall, stone church.

Off to one side, from beneath the shade of a large, billowing willow, a woman with long dark hair and a short skirt approached with a smile. "Hey; there you are," Glen said, leaning over and kissing her cheek. Her smile grew and she nodded to the Grays.

"How are you, Leslie?" Glen's mother said. "You know Cindy—and this is Phil." She introduced Mr. Gray.

"Hello," the woman said, continuing to smile as she held her hair back from her face in the gentle, afternoon breeze.

"Well—are we ready? Ready sweetheart?" said Mrs. Gray, giving Cindy's dress a final light brush with her gloved hand.

"Ready," Glen said before Cindy could answer, and they turned and walked toward the tall wood doors of the church.

* * *

Afterward, at the nearby reception hall, with Cream blasting *'Sunshine of Your Love'* on the stereo and empty champagne glasses littering the white-linen tables, Glen began sneaking up on people and taking surprise photos with his father's camera, the flash blinding everyone for an instant before they burst into inebriated laughter.

And later still, in the back seat of a car belonging to one of Cindy's friends, a hash pipe moving quickly amongst the smokers, with Glen randomly handing it out the window to Leslie who had not wanted to cram into the crowded, beat-up car.

And then finally, in a corner of the hall, with most of the guests gone and a scratchy low-volume record playing and a clean-up crew in full swing (consisting primarily of the two mothers and a few of their friends), Glen, wide-eyed, with a bottle of Rainier in one hand and the other deep in the pocket of his dark trousers, talking with Tim, his young new brother-in-law, about the best cabins on the isolated Pacific coast, where he and Cindy were headed shortly. And with key stabs of the bottle, Glen emphatically explained—almost lectured—that if they walked from the small store at Toleka back to the highway and crossed the footbridge over the river so as to continue northward up the wide, sandy beach, they would come after a few miles to the rocky headland with the narrow tunnel that at low tide emerges out the points' seaward-side, to watch the heavy surf pounding the protruding rocks and seastacks.

* * *

"I had a great time—your sister's a doll. And Tim really seems like a nice young man."

"Isn't she?" Glen sat smiling in the passenger's seat of Leslie's car where they had parked in the late-night darkness in front of his apartment. "Yeah; she's a good kid … oh hell, they'll give it a good shot." He sat low in the seat and looked off to the dark street. "You coming in?"

"Well … sure … for a while. But I have some things I have to do in the morning." Leslie drew in her shoulders and leaned forward. "Well … I don't have to do them right in the morning."

"Come on. I've got some beer."

She took the keys from the ignition and grabbed her purse and they got out into the warm August night.

THIRTEEN

"Anything?" Tom dropped a pile of two-by-fours on the ground where Glen stood painting a row of long trim boards spread across two saw horses. A newscaster's voice droned over the radio that played at the end of a long, bright extension cord that stretched across the uneven ground of the construction site where Glen had been working for the past month. Occasionally the announcer's voice crackled as power saws randomly screeched about the half-completed house frame, drowning out the words.

"They're saying one day," Glen said, looking up at the foreman, "… if even." The foreman, Tom, was tall and lean and had a close-cropped beard and wavy, collar-length hair. He was in his mid-thirties, six or seven years older than Glen; and he stuck out his work boot and attempted to straighten the two-by-fours. "They're almost to Saigon," Glen went on, the bucket of paint in one hand, the wide battered brush in the other, his jeans and tee-shirt soiled and spotted with paint. "It's sounding like the resistance has completely collapsed … they're probably in there as we speak."

"… Jesus," Tom kicked lightly at the two-by-fours again. He had served in the Ninth Marine Expeditionary Brigade out of Da Nang at the war's outset in the mid-sixties, leaving at about the time Glen had arrived. He had been grazed in the helmet by a sniper near Quan Tra whom they had later killed and discovered was a fourteen year old boy from a nearby village. Later, near the end of his tour, he had been superficially wounded in the calf by a land mine that killed a fellow marine. He had returned home just before his unit's bloody engagement in the Yen Bai offensive with its eighty percent casualty count and wondered ever since if before the age of twenty-five he had used up his entire life's allotted share of luck. But then he had only to think of his beautiful wife and two small children and it made him want to get on his knees and pray.

Although the calf wound had been very minor, he had immediately shown Glen the still clearly-discolored skin upon learning of his tour.

"They—are—*screwed*," Glen said, pronouncing the words slowly and clearly. He reached down and stroked the white paint across the boards. "All those officers and support? … Christ."

A scruffy, muscular looking kid came up to Tom with a set of blueprints. He wore work boots and frazzled, cut-off jeans and a tee shirt; and his hair hung down to his shoulders, encircled with a red bandana that crossed his forehead. He pointed with Tom to an area of the plans and they exchanged a few words and then he left.

"Jesus … well … at least they new it was coming," Tom said. "Maybe not this damn fast, but … Christ … The entire ARVN has probably known all along that it could very well come down to this."

"God, if it happens fast enough—it could be a god damn bloodbath." Glen looked over at Tom. "Man, there's no way they're going to evacuate all that support."

"They'd never even try," Tom said. "It'd be impossible."

"Better pray they saw this coming two months ago."

Tom shook his head. "Hey, give Danny a hand when you're done with those, okay?"

Glen nodded and kept painting.

* * *

"Well, I'm hoping to get into nursing school ... maybe by the fall." The woman speaking sat across the table from Glen at the large urban bar.

"Yeah?" Glen poured more beer into his glass from the pitcher in front of them. "That's good—they always need more nurses."

The woman nodded and drank from her beer and glanced around the crowded room. She was somewhat short, but attractive, with long brown hair. Her sweater fit tightly and had caught Glen off guard when she had removed her jacket as she had worn loose-fitting tops on their previous two dates. Despite his strongest efforts, his eyes constantly darted across her front.

The wood-beamed ceiling was high and the bar crowded and noisy, even on this Wednesday April-night, and the band that had been playing earlier began gathering again on the small stage. The singer, in particular, looked the role of the jaded rocker with his long, shaggy hair and the tight pants on his skinny frame; and the two guitarists were both skinny, and, hunching over their instruments, they tuned the strings in the low, tinted-lights of the stage.

Then the singer, who had been huddling off to the side with one of the bar employees, took the microphone, and, suddenly looking much more animated, said he had a very important announcement to make. "Yeah—good *neeews!*" he said loudly into the PA, dragging out and exaggerating the word 'news'. "The war—people—is over! ... Saigon fell today ... it's over ... it is all *over!*" And the heavily beer-fueled crowd began to holler and whoop; and the two guitarists plucked some strings and the band drove loudly and fiercely into a new song as the crowd roared again.

To one side of the crowded room, still at the small table, Glen sat silent and expressionless. Then he gestured to the woman, Denise, toward the dance floor; and they each took another drink from their beers and headed out into the packed, fast-moving crowd.

FOURTEEN

Throughout that summer of 1975, with his hard fought, now eighteen-months-old physics degree folded neatly into the billfold of his back pocket, Glen helped frame houses, mostly for Tom, in the endless new developments that pushed eastward toward the mountains from the small cities bordering Capers Sound, like a slowly unrolling carpet that left split-levels and smoothly paved cul-de-sacs where there had been forests and farms just a few months before.

In late August, while again at the placement office at the university (his now more or less permanently adopted home-away-from-home) checking on job listings and inquiring about graduate programs, he noticed a table set up by a Peace Corps recruiter, with a large spread of photographs and brochures. One photo album showed young volunteers in mostly tropical settings in third-world villages engaged in various Peace Corps projects. Glen looked closely at the pictures, many with an eerie resemblance to the terrain of Vietnam, and spoke for a while with the young man at the table and then left with several of the brochures.

A few days later, back on campus again (his route usually passing the Student Union building where out front there often gathered a group of black students talking and laughing loudly), after earlier having been scared away from both the mathematics and physics graduate programs (with word of their numerous, Einstein-like applicants), Glen was in the graduate department of anthropology, talking with a smiling, middle-aged assistant professor who, after looking over Glen's transcripts and evaluating his background (his expression turning serious only following the reference to Glen's service in Vietnam, and the ensuing questions), explained the most appropriate degree, and then happily informed Glen that he would indeed be a strong candidate. The middle-aged bespectacled man then spoke enthusiastically about the program's many exciting and challenging aspects, and that on the west coast the department was second only to Stanford and the University of California at Berkley, and the professors were all highly respected and in some cases world-renowned. He also mentioned to Glen that, unfortunately, however, it was extremely unlikely he would actually be able to find a job in anthropology when he finished. None-the-less, it was a highly interesting field.

As he left, Glen passed the door to the astronomy department and took a half-step toward it before veering abruptly off and continuing down the hall.

FIFTEEN

"Hit it!—*HIT IT!* Ah—*fuck!*" Glen let the ski rope snap out of his hands as he wavered precariously on one foot at the top of the dock piling, trying to keep his balance, his other foot in the binding of the custom-made, mahogany water-ski, the boat now circling loudly back to again toss him the rope.

Come on Gray!—that was your big chance. Here, you want a beer to take along?" The bare-chested man driving the boat, a smirk across his face, held out a can of beer as he pulled back up to the dock. The lake was crowded with boats of every size and description, and the water choppy from all the wakes; and the voices of people in the water, and on other nearby docks, filled the warm, Indian summer air.

A thin woman in a two-piece bathing suite sat on a bright towel below Glen on the dock and smoked a cigarette. She stood up as the boat pulled up and took the rope from the woman riding in back. The driver tried to hand the beer to the woman on the dock, who smiled with a look of confusion, not knowing whether to take it or not.

"No—*no*," Glen said in an annoyed tone, still balancing on the pole, an old, oil-stained life-preserver encircling his bare waist just above his very short, badly tattered cut-offs. "Shit, throw me one after I get up."

Jim, the man driving the boat, his eyes hidden behind dark sunglasses, laughed and headed out again as the slack slowly left the rope. There was another loud cry of *'Hit it!'*; and the boat roared off again and this time Glen leaped from the pole just as the rope pulled tight; and he slammed onto the water hard and immediately flew onto his face in a tremendous splash before the rope again snapped from his hands.

"All right!—All right!—Throw me the god damn beer," he yelled to the woman on the dock, Pam, when he surfaced; and she took a can from the cooler on the dock and tossed it out to where he floated in the warm water.

They had driven up to the country lake that morning, Pam and Glen, Pam having come into Glen's acquaintance a few weeks before from a mutual friend on the softball team he had been playing on throughout the summer, leaving early to beat the weekend traffic that poured from the urban centers for cooler locales in the gently rolling countryside. Jim, the man driving the boat—an old acquaintance from Western State—and Carol, the woman riding shotgun, already there, having come up the night before to the small, lake-side cabin owned by Jim's parents, then early that morning getting the boat ready for the day's skiing.

So by the time of the much anticipated arrival of Jim's little brother, Dan, and his friend, Mark, later that afternoon, the two couples had been out on the water for most of the day, and had drank most of the beer, and were well sun-burned and intoxicated, but still going strong, as they had been determined to ski long and hard to make up for the summer's unfortunate string of rainy weekends.

But it had been unseasonably hot this week, and it was hot now, and everyone was in or near the water; and Dan and Mark came straight down the yard to the boat beside the dock where Jim, who had in particular been anxiously awaiting their arrival all afternoon, had yelled out a loud 'finally' when they had first appeared moments before up near the cabin.

"Finally," Jim said again, in a noticeably less-than-friendly tone, when they reached the boat, his tanned, muscular arm holding the craft away from the dock as the many waves pushed hard against the side.

"Traffic." This was the single word Dan said in response, expressionless and without eye contact. Both he and Mark, in dark tee-shirts and long pants (apparently the only people within miles not wearing shorts), were bean-pole skinny, and, for the middle of September, as pale as ghosts (this due to the extremely rare daytime leaving of either their or their friends basement bedrooms where the record collections and dope supplies were kept). And they each had long, shoulder-length hair and looked to be barely high school age, although they were each a year removed.

"Well—all right!" Jim suddenly cried out, and just as suddenly seeming much happier for the first time in hours. "Let's take a ride!"

And the people on the dock climbed into the old fiberglass outboard and Jim pushed off and the six of them headed out onto the wide, blue lake.

* * *

Later, after the half gram of cocaine and the South American marijuana that Dan and Mark had brought were gone, Jim headed up the lake in the late-afternoon sun in a slow cruise in the direction of the nearby mountains. Seated on the back bench beside Pam—the noisy whine of the old Mercury inches behind them, the wind blowing hard into their sun-burned faces and an occasional sheet of spray accompanying the wind whenever the boat struck the face of one of the larger wakes moving silently over the deep, blue surface—Glen, his eyes hidden behind dark glasses, looked silently off at the distant mountains rising hazily above the forested hills beyond the lake.

SIXTEEN

In the fall, with the local economy continuing to recede as it had for the past year (rumors circulating of its acceleration due to recent worldwide oil shortages), the previously steady construction work slowed, then stopped, and Glen, now in his late twenties, was suddenly out of a job. Soon after, however, for reasons no greater than attempting to keep busy and have at least a few dollars coming in, he pursued and acquired a part-time delivery position at a large furniture store near the sprawl of aging warehouses at the edge of Sealth's downtown. But after only two weeks, with orders slow and most of the time spent sweeping and dusting, he abruptly quit. He then inquired about his old research position at the university and was informed that it was now reserved solely for graduate students, due to recent departmental restructuring. He poured through the federal listings at the veterans center for which his military service provided priority status, but other than the laborer positions in various western national parks (which actually held the greatest appeal) the only even semi-professional positions were all out of state, and more so, oozing with the ridiculously bloated and questionable establishment-bureaucracy that Glen, no matter how hard he tried, could simply not bring himself to pursue. And then a few weeks later, as much out of frustration as desire, he answered a classified advertisement for a part-time clerical position at a downtown Sealth paralegal firm, and was hired on the spot. And the very next day, deep within the windowless-bowels of a cluttered, office storage-room, he began his assignment: reviewing huge stacks of litigated construction documents for the technical information his supervisor requested.

As the winter wore on, Glen finally got around to taking the Graduate Entrance Exams, and later still, again at the university (the sprawling campus and neighboring streets with its crowds of students and wandering long-hairs, and the nearby record stores and cheap restaurants and avant-garde film houses, his now long-adopted neighborhood) he inquired about a masters degree in psychology, an undergraduate degree in journalism, and a masters degree in education. And through it all he continued to drive his aging Dodge Dart from the university flat through the usually wet Sealth streets to a downtown parking lot and trudge through the city office crowds to the paralegal position in the old Vance building on third avenue. And despite its being part-time and low paying, and excruciatingly monotonous, after the months of house framing and employment futility, it seemed at times comforting; and it was warm inside and the coffee pot was always full; and he briefly had what seemed at the time the absolute ultimate sexual-fling with a slender, dark-haired female co-worker from Virginia who was more-or-less just passing through town.

* * *

One particularly dark evening after work in the dead of January, while leaving the downtown library where he sometimes stopped to browse through the numerous periodicals (as well as to read the newly emerging books and journals about the final years and months of the war) he passed another poster for the Peace Corps, with its nostalgia-invoking village setting, pinned to a reference wall near the door, and, almost feeling the warmth and tranquility of the tropical local, stopped and wrote down the local recruitment number. When he got back to his small studio apartment—old clothes and beer cans scattered about the floor, the sink full of days-old dishes, the ashtray overflowing with roaches and cigarette butts—he began searching for the brochures he had brought back from the university the previous summer, but gave up in a panting fit after looking obsessively through every box, drawer, file, cupboard, and shelf that he owned. He then carefully placed the newly recorded phone number on the small, cluttered desk beside the phone, and then, briefly, thought about calling his mother with whom he had not spoken in several weeks. But instead he took some leftover food from the waist-high refrigerator and turned on the tiny black and white television and settled into the torn, stuffed chair that he had been hauling around since his first days in Port Crescent.

* * *

"Vietnam? Yes, we've had several veterans inquiring about different assignments. I think Don had one going to Peru just last spring; I'll have to ask him when he comes back from lunch." The woman in the Peace Corps recruiting office sat at the cluttered desk opposite Glen in the downtown office and read through his application. Her thick, brown hair hung long and wavy, and round, wire-rimmed glasses protruded from her face; she wore a bright, colorful, woolen-like top of obviously foreign origin. There were several other extremely cluttered desks and a few partitions; and on the walls about the small room were more large posters of mostly tropical settings with various Peace Corps slogans in large print across the tops or bottom. To one side, from out the windows, the sounds of city traffic rose up to the sixth floor office. "We've gotten leaner," she went on, thumbing through an enormous binder with photocopied pages; "we're more technical now. Not like the Kennedy years. But, let's see … there are a few math-science programs … Teaching … Let's see … West Africa: Sierra Leone and Asombo; those are English speaking…both former British colonies…There's English-as-a-Second-Language in Korea. With your physics degree, though, that's going to be about it—teaching: math or science."

Glen edged up closer to the desk, twisting to see the listings in front of the woman. He thought briefly about that first long-ago Army recruiter in Port Crescent: the American flag in the corner; the photographs on the wall of Lyndon Johnson and General Westmoreland; the short trimmed hair and sharply creased uniform of the lieutenant behind the desk. And then he thought about the hot road to Kon Tum and he suddenly wondered about Mullin and Davis and then Ben. "… What about India?" Glen said, looking up; now with an image of the Beatles seated with the Maharji appearing just as suddenly.

"India …" The woman grabbed another thick binder. "Let's see … Health; health; engineering; management. No—if you were a nurse you could choose your spot." She adjusted the glasses on her nose.

"Hmmmmm … well, okay, so we're looking at spring or summer?"

"Right; all the references would have to be in by mid April … the medical exams … oh, and your service record."

Glen pushed the chair back. "Well, all right … Thank you, I'll keep in touch." The woman nodded and Glen got up and left.

* * *

"Ah, Jesus … sure, some. But it was the sixties." Glen shifted in the large chair and glanced toward the elderly man sitting in the chair opposite. There was a desk to one side and soft lighting and several impressionist-style paintings hanging on the walls beside the numerous framed certificates and degrees.

This was the second meeting and Glen doubted deeply now that there would be a third. It had come at the suggestion of the career counselor at the university who had pushed Glen into talking more and more over the past few months, which resulted in her becoming concerned that perhaps there were some difficult-to-pin down, unresolved inner conflicts that maybe,

maybe, a trained counselor: a social worker; a psychologist; a, god-forbid, psychiatrist, could successfully tackle.

"What about in Vietnam?" Dr. James Mitchell, Clinical Psychologist, asked gently, peering above his bifocals, continuing with the drug history as he occasionally made notes in the writing pad on his lap. He had served as a gunner in the Air Force on flying fortresses over Europe during the second world war.

Glen looked at him for moment: "Oh, you know—heroin, marijuana—diesel fuel—anything to improve aim."

The doctor stopped writing and folded his hands on the pad.

"Look—" Glen said sharply with an expression of anguish. "I don't know what Colleen at placement was thinking, but ... It's just ... never mind."

"No, go ahead."

"It's just ... I don't think this is going to work."

The doctor set the pad aside and removed his bifocals. He looked at Glen. "There are some good VA counselors ... Perhaps that would be worth a try."

"Well, maybe ... maybe; I'm going to be taking a physical there in a few weeks."

"It's hard to say now what we could accomplish here. Change occurs very slowly." The doctor glanced toward his desk. "I'm afraid it's time to stop for now. Please, if I can be of any help, do let me know."

"Sure," Glen smiled, "thanks."

* * *

"Dwayne? ... Dwayne?—*DWAYNE!* Holy fuck, man! What the fuck, dude?" Glen, wide-eyed and mouth open, switched the milkshake to the hand that carried the burger and fries and extended the now free hand toward the man standing in front of him.

"Glen? ... wow ... hey." Dwayne, also staring, but more so like a deer in headlights, slowly raised his hand and shook Glen's. He held his half eaten burger in his other hand and leaned away from the metal outdoor-counter where his drink sat along the side of the city, drive-up hamburger stand. A few people stood eating further down the counter, and others stood in short lines at the windows of the brightly-lit establishment. Toward the street, the large, fluorescent 'Zeke's' sign blinked slowly on and off at the top of the rusty metal pole where it had been blinking since the mid 1950s.

"Man—how you doing?" Glen said. "*What* are you doing?" The wide grin remained on Glen's face as he beheld the semi ground-shaking sight before him: Dwayne Feloney was wearing a suite. It fit horribly; but there was no mistaking it: dark slacks; some kind of actual sports-coat; a white-shirt buttoned firmly at the neck; and, unbelievably, extending downward from the collar—it pulled at Glen's eyes like some strange sort of anatomical magnet—an authentic necktie. Very slowly, Glen forced his eyes downward toward Dwayne's feet, digging deeply into the last of his psychic reserves to prepare for the Wing Tips that he was sure would be there, and then exhaled in relief when he saw the casual, gray loafers. Surprisingly, Dwayne still had his old wire-rimmed glasses, and the thick beard he had had for as long as Glen had known him was still bushy and long. "Man," Glen said, still smiling, "how are you?"

"Good ... good ... Not bad ... working a lot."

"Yeah?"

"Yeah ... real estate. Yeah, I got my license about a year ago."

"Yeah?"

"Yeah ... Hey—hey, how about you, man?" Dwayne finally grinned. "Man; long time, huh?"

"Hey ... yeah," Glen said. "Ahhh ... Not bad—not bad ... Finished school—finally."

"Yeah?" Dwayne's smile grew and he took a bite from his burger. Yeah?" he said again, his mouth half full, "Julie still around?"

"Julie? Nah ... no, we split up a few years ago." He looked at Dwayne. "... Yeah, I don't know ... I've been looking at graduate school. Working here and there ... even thinking about joining the Peace Corps, if you can believe that"

"No shit?—the Peace Corps? It's still around, huh? ... wow."

"Yeah ... Hey, how's the farm? Man, I tell you, I've been going to come up. Every month—every month I go: 'I've got to get up there'." Glen grinned widely.

"Yeah? ... well," Dwayne kept chewing, "most of it's still there ... at least right now, anyway." He reached for a napkin and wiped his mouth.

"Most of it?"

"Oh, hey, the island is hot, man. I could get fifteen, twenty lots out of it."

"Ah, Dwayne, really?" Glen sighed and set his bag and drink on the counter. He took out a cigarette and lit it. "Well, shit, man—tell me, what's there? Is the house there? The house is still there isn't it? Dwayne—tell me the house is still there."

"Oh, yeah, sure ... I mean, I rent it out ... Hey, can I have one of those?" He gestured toward the cigarette and Glen extended the pack and Dwayne took one and set it on the counter. He bit into more of his burger and reached for his coke. "You wouldn't believe the barn, though," he grinned and shook his head as he chewed, "yeah, the barn's almost gone."

"Really?"

"Yeah, well ... it wasn't really getting used anymore. We really weren't planning on it staying anyway."

"Ah, no kidding? Shoot, I don't believe it," Glen reached over and took a drink from his shake. "That's too bad, Dwayne—I had really hoped the farm would have lived."

"Yeah, well, you know—thing's change."

Glen looked toward the blinking orange sign at the top of the pole. "Yeah, I guess so. Well, hey, you ever see Mort—or Karen? What about Ed? What's Ed been up too?"

"He's here in the city, last I heard. Crap, I haven't seen Ed in probably five years ... Longer than you." Dwayne grinned and drank more soda.

"Well what about Mort or Karen? How about Duncan?"

"Let's see; Karen—she married some guy a couple of years ago. I think they're in East Sealth somewhere. Duncan—I don't know. Mort—Mort hasn't changed a bit; got a place on the island—same old Mort."

"Yeah? Wow—Mort." Glen shook his head.

Dwayne finished his burger and wiped his mouth again. "Look—come up sometime; I'm in the bunkhouse with my girlfriend."

"Yeah? ... Yeah, I probably should." Glen leaned back against the counter. "So, what brought you to the big city?"

"Oh, the company on the island has contracts with Everett Trust ... I come down once a month or so."

"Everett Trust ... Shit, Dwayne, what a trip."

Dwayne grinned. "Come up ... anytime. I'm in the book—give a call. Hey, gotta run, man—take care." He held out his hand again.

"Yeah, you too ... take care."

Dwayne began to turn, then reached back and took the cigarette off the counter. He smiled and nodded again and then walked over to a newer model sedan and got in. Glen opened his burger and took a bite but grimaced when he realized it was cold. He threw it into the garbage and carried the rest of the shake and the fries over to his aging, mighty-fine, Dart, and got in.

SEVENTEEN

"Well, dear, are you sure? ... Africa is an awfully long ways. Two years?—my."

"Your mother's right, Glen. Did you see *Time* last week? A tremendous amount of disease there."

Glen sat on the couch of his parent's home and skimmed a section of the Sunday newspaper. His mother stood in the doorway of the kitchen, her arms folded in front of her. His father sat in the large stuffed chair where he always sat and read the section he held at arms length in front of him. The pungent smell of pot roast, cooking in the kitchen oven, filled the main floor of the house.

"What about the graduate program?" Mrs. Gray said. Her hair had begun to whiten and the lines of age creased her face.

"Which one?" Glen said, flipping quickly through the pages.

"Oh—have you been looking into more than just the one?"

"Actually; yeah," Glen said casually, "yeah, a few of them."

"Well, I'd just think having been away for so long before, you'd want to be extra certain before going off somewhere again." She turned and went back into the kitchen. Near the doorway, the dining room table was neatly set for the birthday dinner that was being held that evening, jointly, for his sister and father, both of whom had birthdays within a few days of each other.

"Your mother's right, Glen—it's an awfully long ways." Mr. Gray stared at the paper. "... What got you interested in the Peace Corps, anyway?"

Glen flipped rapidly through the final pages and tossed the section aside and stood up. Extending his arms almost to the ceiling, he stretched and yawned. "Oh, I don't know, why not? They said I could be a teacher ... maybe do some good for a change. Besides, it might be fun." He looked out the window toward the trees in the backyard. The ones on the side, blooming with spring buds, towered high now above the fence; and he remembered when he and Cindy and his father had planted them as saplings in the barren backyard when they had first moved into the house. Everywhere, tall trees and bushes and shrubs filled out the neighboring yards. "Anyway—it couldn't be any worse than what I was doing in Vietnam. Might even make up for some of it." He looked into the afternoon light.

On the living room chair, his father continued to read the paper.

* * *

"Glen? ... hello, there ... Glen, how are you?"

"Good ... pretty good ... Not bad—wow, you look great."

Julie stood in front of Glen in the dimly-lit foyer of the Northgate restaurant, smiling broadly as they waited for the hostess to seat them. She leaned forward and kissed his cheek. "It's so good to see you."

It was mostly older women meeting for mid-week lunch, with a few businessmen in suites sprinkled about the large dining room. Out the tall windows to the side was part of the vast parking lot that surrounded the mall, and toward the street rose the old, familiar Northgate totem pole.

"This way ..." The hostess took them to a table where water was already poured and silverware set and placed two menus on the table.

Julie continued to smile broadly as they sat down. Her hair was short and slightly styled and traces of makeup were visible and Glen marveled again at her good looks. Earrings dangled from her lobes, and an attractive necklace hung below the open neck of her blouse. "I'm really glad you called," she said, continuing to smile. "God—I can't believe we haven't run into each other in all these years ... I mean at least once."

With a slight grin, Glen sighed and gently shook his head. "Yeah—really."

Julie, making herself more comfortable in her chair, leaned forward. "So, god, the Peace Corps—I couldn't believe it when mom said you'd called ... I'm glad you called her."

The waitress came and they each ordered a beer.

"So—I hope this is all right," Glen said.

"Of course—of course. I just said to Tom I was meeting this old boyfriend for lunch and he just—'huh'—shrugged." She grinned and took a drink of water.

"Yeah? ... well, so, how are you?"

"Really good—school's great ... Tom's wonderful. You'd really like him, Glen. He gets a little nutty at the bank every now and then, but, really ... he's just very mellow." She took another drink of water. "So, what about you? Tell me about the Peace Corps—wow, the Peace Corps. You hardly ever hear about it anymore ... where are you going?"

"Asombo."

"Asombo?"

"Yeah ... yeah, it's in West Africa ... you know, the bulge?" Glen made a kind of curve with his hand. "It's right along here ... right, like ... here ..." he pointed with his other hand.

"Yeah? ... yeah." With a quizzical expression, Julie studied his hand. "Oh, wait—isn't that the Gold Coast?..."

"Yeah, right. Yeah...believe it or not I'll be teaching."

"Oh—wow; really? Good for you. That sounds exciting—are you excited?"

"Well—yeah. Yeah, I kind of am." The beers came and they tipped their glasses and filled them. "Yeah, it's time to get out of here—the old U.S. of A." Glen drank from his beer, the foam dampening his lip. "Yeah; time to hit the road."

Julie continued to smile. "Oh, I know ... I don't know what to make of anything anymore." She leaned forward again, her eyes widening. "It's like—what happened?" Glen looked at her. "But, oh, I'm envious." She leaned back and drank from her beer and looked out the window. "Amazing ... Africa ..."

Heavy traffic passed on the four-lane street beyond the parking lot, and a tangle of utility poles and wires hung in every direction above the street and in front of the endless cluster of box-shaped stores that had sprouted up on the other side, like fungi on an old log. Facing the street, it's weathered, unpainted back toward them, the tall, thick totem rose into the gray sky, like a disoriented old woman who had lost her clothing.

"How long will you be gone?" Julie asked.

"The programs are all two years—yeah, two years."

"Wow. I'm envious."

"Well ..." Glen nodded and drank from his beer and glanced around the room. More diners continued to come in and the waitresses hurried about, serving the afternoon lunch crowd. "Yeah, so I just thought I'd look you up before I left. I've tried to get a hold of a few people ... the old gang."

"Well I'm real glad you did."

Glen drank more of his beer. "Hey, I couldn't believe it—I ran into Dwayne Feloney."

Julie's eyes widened. "No ..." She reached for her beer.

"Yes—just last month."

"No!"

"Still lives on the farm—he's selling real estate!"

"God—*No!*"

"*Really!*"

"Oh—god ... Dwayne." Julie set her beer down and wiped her lips with the cloth napkin in her lap. She looked off, shaking her head. "Oh ... I saw someone who used to go up there—who was it? ... Let me think ... oh—Ken—Kenny—what was his name?"

"Oh—uh," Glen nodded, "Olson—Olston."

"Ken Olston—he came by the school. Had a couple of kids— I didn't even recognize him. We were having an open house; they were looking at the school." Julie smiled. "But I don't think he knew where Dwayne was. I'm sure he hadn't seen Dwayne in years."

"Jeeze ..." Glen leaned back, "yeah—old Dwayne, selling real estate ... still lives in the bunkhouse."

Julie shook her head again and sipped her beer. "How are your parents doing? I miss them ... I should have called."

"Oh, the same ... the old man's about to retire; finally. Christ—Capers Electric. Actually, Dad's had some health problems ..."

Julie listened.

"Yeah, they think he may have had a minor stroke ... but, otherwise, they're the same," Glen took another drink of beer. "—Oh, hey, Cindy got married."

"Really? How exciting—good for her."

"Yeah—yeah, nice guy. Works for a heating distributor. They live down in Olympia."

Julie smiled. "Wow," she looked off again through the tall windows, "my ..."

Glen nodded. "Yeah ... yes sir."

After the sandwiches, and the bill, which, without discussion, they split fifty-fifty, they stood on the walk in front of the restaurant with the mall pedestrians passing in each direction, and the rush of traffic loud on the busy street.

"Good luck, Glen. I'm really glad you called."

"Yeah ... good luck to you."

"I really am envious."

"Yeah, hey, I'm ready to get out of here. I'm pretty psyched. Shit, Africa ... it's a dream ..." He looked again into the afternoon light. "... a dream ..."

PART IV
AFRICA

ONE

"Kobina—Akwaba! Wo-ho-te-sen?"
"Yooo—Kaurachi! Nyame adom, me-ho-ye. Na-wo-nso-e?"
"Yoo, me-ho-ye. Yeda Onyami ase. Ah!—*Glen-o!* Welcome back! Yeda Onyami ase pa-paa. We did not think you would be coming back. We hoped it went as well as could be. Did it go well? We were sorry. We worried greatly."
"It went well, Kaurachi. No worry. I arrived in Accra last night. I came straight here on the first transit this morning. Yes, it went okay. Ah—Kaurachi! I'm glad to be back. Glad-pa-pa-pa-paaa!"
"Yoo, Kobina. We are happy you returned. We are sorry about your father's death. *Ah*—we are happy today. Is your family well? Your mother?"
"Ani. They are well, considering."
"Yoo, Glen. Yeda Onyame ase."
"Yo, medasi."

As they released their tightly clasped hands, Glen put his arm around the short, smiling African and they walked across the sunny courtyard of the teachers college in Sekondi, toward the conference block and auditorium where the late morning lecture was about to begin. They entered the crowded room and sat at a table facing the speaker who placed a graph on the plate of the overhead projector and, when the room was quiet, began to outline the squaring properties of absolute numbers for the audience of teachers attending the Asombo Western Region Mathematics Conference.

Afterwards, they ate lunch in the school cafeteria, Glen—who was also called by his African name, Kobina—and Kaurachi, and the fifty or so other secondary-education math teachers who had traveled to the central coastal town for the conference from schools sprinkled about the Western Region as far away as Dunkwa, in the valley below the Abona escarpment, eighty miles inland, to Sambreroi, a hundred miles north and west on the Ahofa river on the border of the Ivory Coast. Glen and Kaurachi representing Assini Secondary School in Assini, a hundred miles due west along the sun scorched Atlantic, also at the Ivorian border.

But they had not come together on the grueling two day bus ride, Kaurachi and Glen, as they had originally planned when they had first joyously learned that the assistant headmaster (known at the school as 'The Assist') had made funds available for them to attend the bi-yearly conference, just as he had for the biology teacher and the two physics teachers to attend the science conference in Tarkwa the previous Christmas. That—the joint bus trip along the dirt track to Sekondi that passes as the coastal highway but in the rainy season, as it was then in late May, resembles more a swamp on the stretch between Axim and Sunama, and approaches a threshold of eminent danger when the rivers draining the highlands become raging torrents and are crossed by the multi-ton vehicles (but if the rivers are too high everyone will get out and cross the bridge on foot and board another bus on the other side)—the plan was scratched—Glen and Kaurachi's traveling together—when the confidant from the embassy appeared unannounced in the Land Rover at the remote school one warm morning two weeks beforehand and, taking Glen aside, told him that his father had died and then drove him back to the capital—another two-hundred miles east of Sekondi—and to the airport and put him on a plane for home. And now, three weeks later, after having returned to the U.S. and Sealth for the first time in almost two years, and attending the delayed funeral and consoling his mother and meeting for the first time his new baby niece whom his sister had bore more than a year before, as well as consulting with the lawyers and banks and seeing to his mothers needs, he was back in country, and at the conference, having been slammed the night before by the now familiar wall of coastal humidity upon disembarking at Kotoko International airport before leaving early this morning for the seemingly smooth ride of the tarmac linking the capital, Accra, with Sekondi.

And after the afternoon workshops (Glen attending polynomial and constant factorial applications to pre-calculus theory) and the closing seminar and keynote speech by Dr. Kofi Prempeh, Distinguished Professor of Mathematics at the University of Asombo, Legon, on the future needs and challenges of the Joint West African Mathematics Council, Glen and Kaurachi had joined many of the other attendees for cold beers on the breezy hillside patio overlooking the wide blue Atlantic with the two anchored Liberian freighters in the deep water harbor of Takoradi a short ways down the shoreline.

"This Matron," Kwesi Andoh of Aboso Technical School continued at the table in the shade of the patio where Glen and Kaurachi sat with the three other Western Region teachers, the late afternoon heat more bearable because of the ocean breeze, Andoh's finger stabbing the air for emphasis, "she has two months school rice in her bedroom—*three hundred students!* The inspector found it under her bed! I'm telling you!"

The table erupted in high-pitched moans as they stared wide-eyed at Andoh while rapidly drinking the strong Asomboian beer.

"It is the *truth!*" Andoh cried.

"Ah!" said Kaurachi, sitting beside Glen, "these matrons—they will steal and steal. They cannot be trusted. I am telling you, they will take the foods."

The older, graying Arthur Asam of nearby Takoradi Boys School filled his glass with the amber bubbling beer from the large bottle in front of him and poured the last into Glen's. The deep, horizontal tribal gash of the coastal *Fantis* that crossed his left cheek below the eye glistened with perspiration as he leaned his heavy body back into the chair. "Oh—they will take and take," he said, the others turning to listen. "They are not caring about the welfare of the students. It is no wonder they riot."

"We've been lucky," Glen said. "They've only rioted once."

"*Uhhhhhhh,*" the others at the table uttered in acknowledging unison as they turned toward Glen.

"Well—or whatever the hell it was." Glen looked at Kaurachi and drank from his beer. "Remember? They marched late that night to the headmaster's house and demanded more meat. I was at my house so I didn't really see anything … But I sure as hell heard all the noise coming from the school."

"They had sticks," said Kaurachi. "It was their complaint that meals were insufficient for basic health. It was girls, too. Ah—these students!"

"They will not riot with Peace *Corpse,*" said Victor Akim from across the table, vividly pronouncing 'corps', '*corpse*'. He was tall and slender with a short beard and sat casually in his chair dressed in slacks, a shirt with a wide-open collar, and sandals. He taught fourth and fifth form math at tiny Awaso Secondary School in the heart of the rainforest below the Adele Plateau where he had been assigned for his obligatory governmental service after completing university three years before. He was a *Lobi* from the far Upper Region, toward the sahel, below the Saharah, and although the area was predominantly non-imbibing Muslim (as opposed to the Christianity, which ruled the southern regions) he drank long from the strong smooth beer. The long, viciously deep *Lobi* tribal scar curved across his black face from high on one temple to the corner of his mouth. "They like the Peace Corpse," he went on. "Riots—two years running. Then Mr. Thomas of Nashville, Tennessee, arrives in Awaso, and—nothing—*Atall!*" He clapped his hands loudly and reached for his beer as the others nodded in unison.

"*Ahhhhhhh*—these Asomboians," Kaurachi said, laughing in the warm humid air.

Victor Akim spoke again: "Mr. Glen; Kaurachi says you were just in States ... we are pained to hear of your father's passing. Was the funeral well?"

"Oh; yes—yes. They are not like here, though."

"So?" said Victor, refilling his beer.

"Oh, yeah. People just sit around, quiet. They don't talk much. Then they go to the cemetery and bury the casket."

"*Uhhhhhhh,*" the table hummed in unison and nodded.

"No dancing. No music—No beer." Glen raised his glass.

"My sister's husband," Arthur Asam now spoke up, "he once traveled to New York. Ah—the stories he told!" He looked at Glen. "Are you in New York?"

"No—no," said Glen. "West coast."

"Ah—California," said Arthur, grinning.

"No, north ... Washington State."

"Ahhhhhhh—Washington," said Arthur, and although Glen knew he was thinking of D.C., he did not bother to correct him.

"I would not be in New York at this time *atall*," Victor Akim now said in a serious tone. "Mr. Glen, tell us the truth—Is the 'Son of Sam' the 'forty-four magnum killer'?" The table looked wide-eyed at Glen.

"Son of Sam?—*Son of Sam?* How the hell do you know about Son of Sam?"

"*Uhhhhhhhhh,*" the table responded loudly.

"We are knowing him!" Victor said. "We are knowing he is the forty-four magnum killer! *It is the truth!*"

Glen shifted in his chair and drank from his beer. He shook his head. "I don't know—I guess. But actually, I've never been to New York. Never been and don't want to."

"Ah—if only," Victor said. "I should like to attend university there. Or, what's this place? Vir-gin-ee-a. Very fine." Victor grinned.

Another group of teachers talked and laughed loudly at a nearby table as the late-afternoon sun filtered down through the wide fronds of the tall palms that lined the edge of the patio. Two small children, walking with there mother who balanced a bucket of water on her head, laughed and squealed excitedly at the sight of Glen and his pale, god-forsaken skin.

"When are you traveling?" Glen turned to Kaurachi.

"Ah, in the morning." Kaurachi was short, even by Asomboian standards, barely five feet tall. He would often disappear within a crowd of students at the school, most of whom were taller. "First Assini bus—But I will be at my brother's again tonight—Kobina, come and join us."

"No. Sorry—I can't," Glen said. "I'm going to see the Peace Corps at Takaoradi Secondary; Miss Patty."

"*Uhhhhhhh,*" several at the table hummed.

"Do you know her, Arthur? Miss Nelson? Patty?"

"Ah—let me think. Yes, I know of her. I have heard of this woman."

"So, I won't be back in Assini until later," Glen said to Kaurachi. "It may be as late as Tuesday."

"Mr. Glen," Victor said, "we are going to be taking chop, just now. Come with us."

"Oh—I would like to," Glen said. "I am hungry-o. But I want to get the tro-tro for Takoradi before dark."

"Ahhhhhhh," Victor said, nodding. He raised his glass. "So, Kobina, to your health." And he gestured to Glen as the others raised their glasses and they all drank the foamy beer.

TWO

"Pat ... Patty ... Ah-go—*AH-GO!*" Glen stood in the rapidly darkening light before the screened door of the bungalow amidst the long row of teachers' quarters in the middle of the school compound. He began to open the door to the brightly lit room when a student appeared from another part of the house. "Wo ho te sen?" Glen greeted the slightly surprised boy in dialect. He looked to be at least sixteen, maybe older, and wore the traditional Asomboian secondary-school uniform of blue shirt, brown shorts, and sandals. When the boy smiled, the brightness of his teeth showed sharply against the blackness of his face.

"Me ho ye," the boy said to Glen, still grinning. "Na wo nso e?"
"Me nso me ho ye. Yed Onyami asc."
"Yoo," the boy grinned widely at the verbal exchange.
"Patty ehe no wotee?" Glen now spoke rapidly.
"Ahhhhh—Patty ko ana-we nyeh jom."
"Ahhhhh," Glen uttered and nodded to the boy.

From behind came the sound of footsteps and a voice called out from the darkness of the walkway: "Glen?—Glen Gray?" Glen turned to see the faint outline of a woman approaching the steps and, as she began to climb, the widening of her eyes. "*Kobina!*" she called out excitedly. "Glen—my god!"

"Yoo ... Ama ..." Glen stood smiling for a moment, then raised his arms to the woman who, raising hers as she climbed the last steps, embraced Glen in a long, gentle hug. "Wo ho te sen?" he said.

"Yooooo. Me ho ye," Pat said with a wide grin. "Oh—this is Kofi." She gestured toward the boy. "Kofi ... Kobina." Glen and the student clasped hands and snapped fingers as they released.

"Gosh—Glen—come in, come in." Her smile remained wide and she pushed through the door and they entered the brightly lit flat. There were wood chairs and a thin sofa on the linoleum floor, and several lamps and bookcases along the walls. Down a short hallway was a bedroom and bathroom and in the other direction a narrow kitchen. The boy spoke briefly in dialect with Pat and she gave him some money and he left. She turned to her visitor. "Glen, god, how are you? Paul told me about your father ... I'm really sorry ... When did you get back?"

"Oh, last night. Long night, too long ... Then we had this conference at the college so I came straight here this morning." He looked at Pat. "Yeah, it's been kind of a rough few weeks."

"Here—sit down." Pat took the pack slung over Glen's shoulder and he sat on the couch. She wore the familiar wire-rimmed service glasses of the United States Government, and a cotton blouse and a long skirt that hung past her knees toward the cheap rubber sandals on her feet. Her light thin hair was shoulder length and streaked with gray. She was a few years older than Glen and together they were two of the older volunteers in country—in their thirties as opposed to the vast majority in their twenties—except for the handful of retirees in their sixties and seventies. "So, gosh; you went back. What was it like? Please; tell me."

Glen reached over from the couch and guided the heavy pack Pat was still holding onto the floor. His shirt remained open and the ceiling fan spun overhead, partially moving the thick, humid air. "Well," he began, "aside from the circumstances—weird, the pits. I take that back; I got to see my kid sister's new baby. That made it worth the trip. Although she kept trying to convince me not to come back—got real serious about it. But, that's another story. Otherwise, like just weird … I couldn't wait to get back here. I was like: 'get me on that Pan Am—*please.*'"

Pat lowered herself onto the edge of one of the chairs. "Now, Glen … you were in Vietnam, right? … That is right, isn't it?"

"United States Army; Second Division; Eleventh Brigade."

"All right, so, you've done this before then. You know, where you are out of the States for a long time—in some foreign country—and then you go back, right?"

"Oh, yeah. Yeah—but that wasn't the same. You couldn't get me home fast enough then. Christ, that was a fucking war—excuse my French. Although, actually, I got out of there before it got really screwed up."

Pat shook her head and leaned back in the chair. "Jeeze … I still can't believe you're actually sitting here. It's been what, a year? No, longer than that. A year and a half—at least. And look at you, you hippie. Isn't there anyone out there who cuts hair?" She grinned and shook her head again.

"*What?*" Glen laughed, mockingly. "Christ—I just got it cut for the funeral."

"Well, we missed you at Christmas. Everyone was like, 'where's Glen? Has anyone seen Glen?' I think Zabrisky was going to send someone out to look for you."

"Hey, if you had to take the Axim road you'd never go anywhere either. I mean, crap, you've got tarmac—*tarmac*—all the way to Accra!" Glen grinned and shifted on the couch. "Besides, Patty, I love it our there. And the school needs me, badly—Christ, this funeral screwed everything up. 'O' levels are starting this week. I'll never catch up." He looked off. "Anyway, with the beach it's paradise."

"Glen …" Pat continued to stare wide-eyed at the man before her. He seemed much thinner than she recalled. His faded levis hanging loosely, the faint outline of ribs beneath his shirt. "… I go crazy here in Takoaradi sometimes—And this is a *city!*"

"Oh, and I'm re-upping," Glen said. He brushed the hair that had somehow grown long again away from his face.

"You're kidding—you're kidding, right?—Glen—are you really?"

"I'm ninety-nine percent sure."

"Jeeze." Pat shook her head, lightly biting her lower lip. "Well, good ... I guess." She stared again. "So, really, tell me, what was it like? I mean, I think I'm actually looking forward to it. Now that I've surrendered myself to returning. I mean, as much as I do love it here, I actually think I'm looking forward to those Vermont falls."

"Yeah? Yeah, there are some things I miss ... but ..." He looked off.

"But really, Glen, just—what was it like? I mean, it must have been crazy."

"Oh, it was—it was." He gently stroked the light beard that had grown during the recent days of travel. "Worse than ever—rush, rush—buy, buy. What can you say? They don't know any better."

Pat shook her head.

"Oh, and disco—it's like this big thing now."

They both shook their heads.

"Want some water?" Pat got up and headed for the kitchen. She returned after a moment with an old wine bottle filled with chilled tap water from the refrigerator and filled two glasses. "Honestly, Glen," she sat again in the chair, "sometimes I can't believe how long we've been here."

"Two years," Glen said, drinking the cool water. The overhead ceiling-fan droned on, the slow-spinning blades waging a losing battle with the thick air.

"I mean, I confess," Pat said, "sometimes I just get terrified thinking about going back."

"Oh, yeah, the first days are the worst ... the *very* worst." He looked off again. "No, wait, I take that back. It was crazy the whole time."

"Oh ... gosh ..." Pat said reflectively, setting her glass on the low table between them and leaning back in the chair. There was a stack of school folders and some papers and a few well-worn paperbacks at one end of the table. "... Two years ... Remember the bus ride to Cape Coast the day we landed? People were ready to go back the first day."

"Hey, some did; remember that kid?—Kid—that guy from New Jersey? He took the first flight back."

The woman shook her head and drank from the glass. "God, Glen—how about training? Remember the language lessons with Ossei? Just me, you; Don and Nancy? And Ossei going nuts when we'd keep screwing around?"

"*Screwing around?*" Glen said as he continued to grin. "Christ, I had the runs the whole time. The *whole* time."

"Well, we all had the runs." Pat grinned slightly. "Oh, god, and then Ossei would take us out onto the lawn trying to get the breeze from the ocean, hoping it would calm us down ... it was so beautiful with the sea."

"It was hot enough. But wait—didn't Ossei bring a blackboard out there once?"

"The last week—my god, that's right! Everyone was, 'where are you going with that blackboard'?" Pat grinned widely and laughed. She looked off, continuing to smile, and adjusted her glasses. "... I still think Don had a crush on Nancy."

"Don had a crush on every girl."

"True. True."

Glen drank more of his water. He glanced down at one of the paperbacks on the table and turned his head to read the title. "So, I got a letter from Bob, that you went up north, into Mali. To Mopti?"

"Oh, Glen, it was just spectacular ... breathtaking. I went with Lisa and Mike. We were in Ouga for three days. We saw David in Bawku—Joannie in Bolgatanga. It was the middle of Ramadan so it was hard to get food. But Mopti, Glen, it was incredible. They build the mosques out of mud. We didn't get to Djenne—but the central mosque in Mopti; this kind of soaring, brown-mound ..." Pat raised her arms into the air. "With the spires it must have gone up three stories—all mud, or clay, or whatever it is ..."

Glen listened under the spinning fan.

"We were going to take the barge to Timbuctu, but we ran out of time. Oh, Glen, the heat—even at night. At least during the dry season. It blows down from the Saharah. The compounds are all circular and thick, thick mud ... so they stay cool. But David, Joannie—even the Asomboians living in the cinder-block houses up north—they would all drag their mats outside at night and sleep on the ground." She looked to the couch. "Glen ... have you been to the north?"

"Ah—Jeeze, Patty." He shook his head. "I went up to Damongo with the school bus once. Horrible ride. But really, that's one of the reasons I'm re-upping: I want to get up there—at least once."

"Oh, Glen ... It's so beautiful ... It's barren; but the expanses, the openness. And the *people!* My god, so *mellow.* Nothing like here in the south. You can actually walk through a village and hardly be noticed."

"Really? God, I'll have to go ... How was transport?"

"Well, the worst of it was getting to Bolga—that was a killer. Fortunately, Mike was along to entertain."

Glen grinned. "Mike—ol' Mike-o."

Pat smiled. "But then after Bolga it was all Peugeuots. Except for the train to Bamako—but that's the best part of the trip."

"I've heard about the train," Glen said. "Even in Assini."

"It's like this brand new *Amtrack,* or something, only better. Huge seats—fast. Nothing like the Accra line ..."

"Oh—I died once on the Accra line. Died, and went to hell—and never came back."

Pat drank from her water. "So, anyway, yeah ... nice, fast, Peugeouts, all the way to Mopti. We'd stop in villages along the way and the girls would come up to the car windows selling food. Then we get to Mopti and we hike out to the Dogon villages ... all day ... Mike takes us out to the first escarpment with the villages built into the cliffs. The higher ones—they're abandoned now—they've been there for like—*centuries.* We met a British volunteer in Mopti and she said they take scooters out to the farthest villages—clear to the border of Niger."

"Got to get up there," Glen said. "Got to get myself up there." He picked up one of the paperbacks. "So, how was Christmas?"

Pat finished her water and set the glass on the table. "Well ... better than the first year. They had us in the mission again. I stayed with Betty and Bret at this 'AID' guy's house. He was more into the local chop than Mr. Olson—"

"*Ha!—god!*—that crap was *horrible!* ... That was the sickest I've ever been. The mission; how do they eat that crap?"

"The party was at the Zabriskys. It was fun—roasted a goat—got drunk—sang Christmas carols ... Everyone wondered where you were."

"Yeah, I thought about it ..." The fan slowly spun. "We were behind at the school—as always. But, hey, I went the first year. And it's not exactly a real Christmas-like setting ... Ah, it would have been fun to have seen everyone ... I'll go this year ... Shit, Mr. Olson." He shook his head. "Hey, see any game up there?"

"My god, I completely forgot—yes, just below Ouga. About three or four elephants—just off the road. The driver pulled over and we tried to take some pictures, but ... they were gone ... like that ..." she snapped her fingers.

Glen looked off for a moment. "... I saw a gazelle in Assini once ... Weirdest thing, it was just standing their in the student's maize field...bizarre..."

"That is, I didn't think they came down to the rain forest. All I've ever heard of them being is north of here, up around Molé."

Glen poured more water and turned another of the paperbacks over. Without reading, he stared at the bold-faced accolades splashed across the back as his face seemed to darken. "So ... What happened to Steve?"

"Oh, Glen ..." Pat leaned forward into her hands. "Did you read the letter?"

"About two months after the fact."

"I guess they weren't going to print it until the medical staff had a chance to respond. A few people said they saw him when he came back to get his things ... He showed them the scar."

"Well ... it sounded like it was partly his fault ..." Glen spoke with a trace of anger. "Christ—he waited too long before he went in to get looked at."

"But, still. They send him to the Abochi Clinic instead of the *mission?* I mean, give me a break. And then when it hemorrhaged it was all they could do just to keep him alive."

"Christ ..." Glen pushed the book aside. He slid lower in the couch and crossed his leg. His sandaled, suspended foot shook rapidly. "How long was he in Hamburg, anyway?"

"I guess, like a month."

"Christ ... So it was pretty bad?"

"Well, you read the letter. But yeah, it starts almost at his groin ... and like curves up to the middle of his chest ..." Pat moved her hand across her front.

"Jesus. That's fucked." Glen slid lower.

Pat sat quietly in her chair. "So ... how was the conference?"

"Ah—good. Actually, it was a blast. They had this one speaker—an Ewe; Eastern Region—guy had a masters from Oxford University and a doctorate from *Columbia*. Little guy—smaller than Kaurachi. You could barely see him. And he's up there talking away with all these calculus tables. Didn't understand a thing he was saying, but ..." Glen grinned and threw his hands in the air. "It's just something about being in a room with all these Asomboians from all these little bush schools where half the classrooms don't even have books, and here's this guy from *Columbia!* ... Wailing away about polynomials and co-sins. It was a trip. And man—those guys know how to come up with the beer. There must have been fifteen cartons stashed in the kitchen."

Pat grinned. "I wonder if Mr. Aburi was there ... I remember him talking about it last week."

Glen shrugged and picked up another book. "So, what about you—how's the teaching?"

"Good ... good ... They're finally used to me ... after two years. Which is kind of amazing seeing as I'm about the twentieth *Obruni* to teach here."

"*Oh*—they still talk about Mr. Jimmy out in Assini," Glen said. "The guy was there *ten years ago.* British guy. I guess he stayed, like, four years."

"Really? Wow ... Four years in Assini?"

Glen shrugged. "It grows on you, Patty."

"Well," Pat poured more water into her glass, "yeah ... I guess so."

"Come on, you have to admit, Assini is a lot more the kind of thing you were expecting, huh?"

"I don't know, Kobina, I was only there three days. Anyway, I like it here in Takoradi: twenty-four hour electricity; pipe-born water. Oh, and we have food here." She looked again at Glen. "But I do have to admit, the beach was spectacular. But then again, Busua is only an hour from here, so ..."

"The beach is pure heaven," Glen said. "... Although, I probably haven't been down to it in over a year ..."

"A year? A *year*? *It's two-hundred yards away!*" Pat shook her head in disbelief and reached for her water. "Well, what about you? Did you ever get electricity?"

"No. No—no electricity. I don't think that generator has worked in five years. But it's just a couple of hours to the border so we have plenty of kerosene—Beer, too."

"Really? Don't you need a visa for the Ivory Coast?"

"Nah—If you go up to Awaso you can cross for a few cedis. Just as long as you stay right there."

"Hmmmmm."

"Gets expensive, though; you have to convert from cedis to dollars and then to CFA ... Kalibulis everywhere ... Ripping off everyone."

"My ..." Pat drank from her water. "It was a breeze going into Mali. You should have seen Mike—" She laughed and wiped her mouth with her hand. "He had every Kalibuli at the border crowded around: bidding—shouting—yelling. Lisa and I just stood under this Baobob drinking fantas, watching the whole thing." She laughed again and drank more water.

"Mike ..." Glen shook his head. "Guy threw a mean softball ... those games back in training ... Always made me ground out ... always."

"He always asks about you."

"Yeah, I wrote him a few times."

"I think he thought Assini was much closer to Takoradi, that you'd be dropping in more."

Glen set the book back on the table. "Yeah, well, it will be when they finish the road and get a few bridges built."

Pat leaned back in her chair. "Ever hear anything from Donna?"

"Donna? Nah ... Nah, she's somewhere around Boston, last I heard ... Grad school or something ... Nah—ol' Donna. Jeeze, she left the first Christmas, huh?"

"Yeah ... yeah, she didn't like it at all."

His expression darkened again. "That's the problem with a lot of these sites. They send someone out there by themselves— especially these young girls—fresh out of college, never been out of the states before, and—poof—gone at the end of the first term."

"Yeah ... they should have sent someone with her."

"Definitely—" Glen looked hard at the woman across from him. "That place—where'd they send her?—Ahofo. It's further out than any school in the Western Region—no food. *By herself* ... Idiots." Glen folded his hands behind his head, his foot moving vigorously.

"Yeah, it might have been all right a few years ago—"

"But not now—you've got to eat, you know?"

Pat shook her head.

"Morons ..."

"Katie's doing good."

Glen continued to sit low on the couch. "Yeah? ... Katie ... Katie would do good in Dagotu. Katie should be running the whole god damn program."

"She's extending," Pat said. "They've got her teaching upper sixth."

"She is? No shit. Good. Good for her ... Someone I can go see next year. Good ... Christ, upper sixth, huh? Wow."

"So, back tomorrow?" Pat said.

"Back tomorrow. Buy a few things in the market. Get out of here by noon."

"Want any books?" Pat gestured toward the bookcase against the wall. There were large binders and textbooks on the bottom shelf, and dozens of battered paperbacks above. "They're all going in the library if no one takes them."

"Sure, yeah, I'll have a look." Glen tried to lower his head onto the back of the couch. Above, the bare bulb hanging from the wire in the ceiling glowed brightly beside the spinning fan.

"Speaking of food," Pat said and glanced toward the entranceway just as there was a knock on the screen. The door opened and the student, Kofi, walked in carrying a cloth-covered basket that he took into the kitchen. "Kenkey," Pat said with a slight grin, getting up from the chair.

"Oh, yes. My favorite." Glen scrunched his face, the standard reaction to the cheapest and foulest tasting street food in Asombo. And, pulling himself up from the couch, he followed her into the kitchen.

* * *

In the morning, Glen threw off the sheet that covered him on the couch and, as he slowly awakened, stood up and stretched. He pulled on his jeans and shirt and sandals and went into the kitchen and began to heat the pot of water on the stove. Daylight came rapidly out the windows, and the sounds of roosters crowing and a few people calling out and walking nearby on the school grounds echoed about in the already warm morning air.

Later, after the breakfast of instant coffee and fresh bread with ground-nut paste, and the two eggs fried in palm oil that Pat had forced him to eat, he was nearing the top of the roadway leading out of the school when he stopped and looked back down at the small bungalow nestled in the trees, and was pleasantly surprised to see Pat, still on the front steps, looking up from where they had just embraced and said their long good-bye. And she slowly raised her hand and waved; and Glen, expressionless, raised his, and then quickly turned and disappeared out the gate.

THREE

'I wonder, wonder, wonder, wonder, who wrote, who wrote the book of ... Wonder, wonder, wonder, wonder, who wrote, who wrote the book of ... A-maz-ing Grace, how sweet, the sound, that saved, a wretch, like meeeeee ... Wonder, wonder, wonder, wonder, who wrote ...'

"O-bruni—wo ko he?"
"Me ko Assini."
"Ahhhhh—Assini. O-bruni, oh te Twi?"
"Me te Twi ka kra."
"Ahhhhhhh—o-bruni! Yefre wo sen?"
"Yefre me Kobina."
"Ahhhhh, Kobina—yes, yes."

'I wonder, wonder, wonder, wonder, who wrote, who wrote the book of ...'

"Kobina—wo ho te sen?"
"Me ho ye. Na wo nso e?"
"Me nso me ho ye."
"Yoooo, yeda Onyami ase."
"Yooooo—Ah! O-bruni." The young assistant who walked the aisle helping the driver clasped Glen's hand with a wide grin and snapped fingers as he stood above Glen in the middle of the packed, jarring bus. The people in the rows around Glen laughed loudly at his dialect and the assistant grinned wider.

'Tin soldiers and, Nixon's coming ... We're finally, on our own ... This summer I, heard the drumming ... Four dead in, O-hio ... Four dead in, O-hio ... Four dead ...'

"Kobina, wofiri he?"
"Mefiri America."
"Ahhhhh—America." The assistant laughed and the people around Glen laughed and the bus lurched and swayed and a woman in a brightly patterned dress turned and held an infant up to Glen; and the baby began to cry and the mother laughed and the assistant laughed harder and the people, packed tightly, shoulder to shoulder, all laughed loudly.

'Wonder, wonder, wonder, wonder, who wrote ...'

"Kobina, woye adwuma ben?"
"Mekyere adee."
"Yooooo—adee ... *Ah! O-bruni!*"
Out the window, the Nyema Escarpment began to disappear in the distance and the lush forest spilled down toward the road from the low hills and then beside the road and then across and down the valley toward the Tano River. In the distance, briefly, the white-capped expanse of the ocean suddenly came into view when the road turned south and the forest gave way to the grasses of the coast.

'A-mazing Grace, how sweet, the sound, that saved ...'

When they reached the Agori bridge, they slowed and crossed the swirling waters of the Tano and then sped beside the lagoon until they came to Owabi and the driver stopped beside the market. When they left again, the many clouds against the Iwabu Ridge drifted toward them and the sky darkened and it began to rain; and then it opened in sheets and lightening flashed and the road turned quickly to mud. The people who got on in Asim, a short while later, were very wet, but they laughed when they saw Glen, and the baby began to cry again.

'I may not, have a, lot to give, but what I got, I'll give, to you … I may not, have a. lot to give, but what I got, I'll give, to you … 'Cuz, I don't care too …'

"Bruni, wote he?"
"Mete Assini."
"*Ahhhhh*—Assini."

'Tin soldiers and, Nixon's coming … We're finally …'

When they broke into the sun there was steam rising from the road and the grasses alongside and they heard the thunder behind them and another bus approached rapidly from the other direction with a goat strapped on top amongst the high piles of luggage.

"You are going to Assini?" A man with thick sideburns and black glasses leaned forward from the row behind. He wore an open brown shirt with a wide collar and brown slacks. The people looked at Glen.

"Yes … Assini … Assini Secondary."
"*Ahhhhh,*" the man uttered. "Teacher?"
"Yes," Glen said.
"Peace 'Corpse'?"
"Yes."

"*Ahhhhh,*" the man said and grinned. "You are coming to help. You are coming from your home to Assini to make the children clever. Where is your home?"

"America."

"*Ahhhhh*—America. It is fine. But we are not having much in Assini. I think you must find it difficult. How can you stay?"

Glen shrugged. "To help."

"Ahhhhh—The children will be happy."

'Four dead in, O-hio ...'

When they crossed the last few hills that flanked Assini to the east, the sun completed its rapid descent and then it was dark and the people along the road on the outskirts of town returning from the farms stepped into the tall grass when the headlights approached.

'Wonder, wonder, wonder, wonder ... Wonder, wonder, wonder, wonder ...'

As he stepped from the bus in the center of town the assistant threw his pack off the top and yelled good-bye and Glen bumped into the man with the glasses who told him to come to Salomey's Bar for beer and Glen told him tomorrow and two small-boys approached in the dark and chanted '*Kwesi-Bruni—Kwesi-Bruni*' before running back to the dull light of the lanterns amidst the food stalls bordering the crowded lorry park.

When he left the park, Glen moved quickly past more lanterns glowing in the windows and doorways of the mud-brick houses and the people walking about the red clay earth and reached the row of houses at the edge of town. He turned up a narrow lane to a small, single-story cement compound behind several houses and crossed the small yard and entered the front door of his home.

FOUR

"Come on, Bonfu—don't you understand? It is these electrons that bond with this nucleus. And when they bond, they react with the corresponding portions of the atom to produce heat. Do you see?" Glen pointed with the chalk at the form-two blackboard while the young African stood in the aisle beside his desk. The other thirty students in the cement-block classroom listened in the humid morning air.

"No, sir."

"What do you not see?"

"All, sir."

"All?" Glen stared at the young student. "Bonfu, here, read this; it will explain everything."

"Yes, sir. Thank you, sir ... Sir?"

"What, Bonfu?"

"Sir ... are they coming?"

"That's what Mr. Ocansey says," Glen said. "He says they are coming."

"Thank you sir. I am sitting."

"Yes, sit." Glen turned again to the blackboard as the students worked silently at their desks, books open, pencils in hand, scratching on paper the answers to the questions they had been assigned. Beyond the classroom windows the lush, green forest rose at the edge of the school grounds, and in the distance, the tops of the inland hills radiated heat into the hazy, humid sky.

When the elders from the town, draped in the bright patterns of their traditional cloths, finally came up the dirt road leading to the school with the goat, all the classrooms emptied and everyone stood about the short grass in front of the several buildings to watch. The elders and the headmaster and a few other officials from the school grounds, including Mr. Ocansey, the agricultural teacher, took the goat down to the small stream that ran at the edge of the school, and there, as one of the elders began to recite the ancient prayers, they began to sip and sprinkle about small amounts of the distilled liquor that the farmers made from maize. And then the man with the machete inserted the point into the goats neck; and the front legs quickly buckled and the stream turned red and a sudden loud murmuring arose from the students back where they watched from the knoll, and, like an incoming tide, they surged forward a few steps toward the stream.

"*Ah!—grazee a go!*" Mr. Ocansey said angrily to the headmaster along the bank near the back of the group a short time later. He had wanted an all white goat but the town elders were warring again with the school and had brought a brown one that, it was well known, did not have the same protective powers as a white goat. And so the scourge of illnesses that had been leveling the students for the past six months could be expected to dissipate at a much slower pace than had it been '*grazee a bwa*'.

When it was over they carried the goat away in a burlap bag for future cooking, and everyone returned to their classrooms except for Glen and a few other teachers, and several men from the village who had come with the elders, who all stayed in the hot sun by the stream and continued to drink the liquor.

* * *

"Tell me, Janet, when did this class not have the teacher?" Glen stood at the form-four blackboard with the young girl moments after the class had let out. She clutched her books and notebook to her chest, the sleeveless blue dress of her school uniform extending to her knees.

"First and second form, sir."

"Two years?"

"Yes, sir."

"So what did you do?"

"We read the book … Unless a student came from upper form to teach us."

Glen looked at the girl in the light of the open windows lining the classroom walls. "All right, look, these are decimal points."

"Dez–mul–points."

"They are just like fractions. This is one half—this is point-five. They are the same."

"Yes, sir."

* * *

Glen stood in the midday heat with the tall fifth former on the grass below the boys' dormitory. To one side, a column of girls carried buckets of stream water on their heads toward the girl's dorm for afternoon bath. The student, the tail of his blue school shirt hanging over his brown shorts, patiently awaited Glen's request. "Abbey, please … won't you take me there?"

"Ahhhhh, sir—it is a bad place. Very bad. Since I was a young child. The tree has hurt my family much." The boy looked yearningly at Glen, tiny beads of sweat glistening across his forehead.

"Okay, Abbey—if I go on my own, how far from Kurua is it?"

"Oh, it is just there, at the edge of the forest, where the ancient trees are. They are afraid to log there. You cannot miss it, sir. If you ask for '*Aya gwa*', they will point ... But, sir, they will not like you going there."

"Just to look?"

"It has harmed many in the village, sir. I would pray that as my master, you did not go."

* * *

"Ocran. Who was Sykes?"

"Sykes, sir—he was a *bad* man ... Who wanted Oliver only for his own greed."

"And why did Oliver go along with Sykes? ... Grace?"

"Sir. I don't know."

"Boateng?"

"Sir. No Idea."

"Bonfu?"

"Sir. Oliver was in need of food. Sykes gave him the foods."

"Good, Bonfu. That's good. —All right, tomorrow, chapter four. And don't forget the paper due on Friday."

* * *

"Mr. Glen; I'm telling you—he is gone. He offended the matrons beside his stall and they have sacked him. He can't be found."

Glen walked swiftly with his young friend, Afful, in the stifling market heat toward the row of yam and cassava stalls beside the central shed where the canned goods from Tema were sold at the beginning of the month. He moved quickly down the narrow corridor as the matrons laughed and called for him to examine the fine tubers they were almost willing to give away to the tall, humorous *O-bruni*. When he came to the stall he believed to be the one the old *Wolemie* had sold his small piles of root-powders and ground animal teeth and the tiny dried monkey paws—like those said to have been eaten by the Great Asanthene before leading his warriors in the battle of Agwam, a hundred years before—he stopped and starred at the tall stacks of shirts and cloth and locally woven handbags, and the rack of plastic sandals, that now filled the stall.

Finally catching up from behind, Afful, almost out of breath, stopped beside Glen as numerous children and the merchants in the neighboring stalls crowded around. "See? He is gone, Mr. Glen. Gone—Ah bin nye ho."

* * *

"Look, Mr. Awere, I saw the god damn books on the station platform—with my own god damn eyes."

"Yes, Mr. Glen ... You have to understand. The destination of these books ... whatever you saw ... was not to have been Assini Secondary School."

"Bull *shit!*—Where are they? I god damn know you know what happened to them, Mr. Aware. Just like the last shipment that disappeared—I god damn *know* it."

"Mr. Glen—you must control yourself. These books, they come on the train to Ogobo every few months or so. And besides—who had authorized you to travel to Ogobo? As a teacher of Assini Secondary, you are responsible for the classes assigned. Now, I will instruct the messenger to write to Education Service to inquire as to the whereabouts of these books.... And I will be making a report of your absence."

FIVE

"Yoo—Kobina. Ohnom nsa fufuw?"

"Kwami ... Yoo, wa me pa paa. Me nom nsa fufuw."

The raggedly dressed farmer set the large bucket of palm wine on the ground in front of the porch where Glen sat in the wood chair in the late afternoon sun. The farmer, Kwami, who lived in the house next door, dipped a small bowl-shaped gourd into the milky liquid and raised it to his lips. When he was through, he filled the bowl for Glen who rapidly drank the pungent, lukewarm drink. When Mr. Amoah, coming from the school, walked up the dry grass of the yard, Kwami waved, and then set off again for the nearby plot and the palm tree from which he was tapping today's wine, to refill the bucket. Later, just as he arrived back at the porch, his wife, wearing a bright, floor-length cloth that wrapped around her lower body and a cotton blouse and small cloth wrapped over her hair, came over with a steaming pot of plantain and okra she had been preparing next door for the now hungry men.

"Ah ... Josephine. Meda ase pa paa," Glen said to Mrs. Essuman as she set the pot and bowls on the cement-block railing of the porch.

"Yoo. Onyame ase," she said and grinned, and took the lid off the pot; and the strong, steamy aroma escaped into the thick, humid air. Several small, bare-footed and shirtless children, their bulging navels (the permanent mark of village delivery) protruding from their bare round stomachs, stood shyly at the foot of the yard to watch Glen and the others on the porch as a solitary goat wandered beyond them down the narrow lane. Other people occasionally passed, mostly from the nearby mud-brick houses with the corrugated metal roofs that spread in every direction over the grid of dirt streets, or from the few cement-block houses with the long porches like where Glen lived at the back of the town, also glancing at the men on the porch. The small, one-story house had become his home after the large two-story teachers quarters at the school had almost collapsed during a rain storm the previous year, and the twenty or so teachers of Assini Secondary had been reassigned to temporary housing throughout Assini and the two neighboring villages of Banda and Aowin.

"Ah ... Kwami, it is sweet," said Mr. Amoah, a *Wasa*, who taught upper and lower form English and had been born in Assini and lived there his entire life, to Kwami, also a *Wasa*, and Assinian, for generations eternal. Kwami now served fresh calabashes from the new bucket. "Kobina," Mr. Amoah turned in his chair beside Glen and grinned widely, "it is sweet pa paaa."

"Always," Glen said, leaning back and drinking from his gourd. "Kwami's trees are the sweetest in Assini ... Eye de pa paaaaa."

"Ah, hnnnnn," Mr. Amoah uttered knowingly. "But in fact, it is true. The trees are fine pa paaa. But Kwami knows the exact best time of day to tap. I'm telling you, he knows it!"

"It is the truth," Glen said. "When I see Kwami coming from the forest with his bucket, I know—I *know*—we will be ending the day properly. *Properly.*"

"Ah, hnnnnnnn," Mr. Amoah uttered; and he grinned again at the fair-haired, white-skinned man beside him. "*Ah*—This Glen!" he said to Kwami and his wife and slapped his thigh.

Mrs. Essuman grinned and began to dish the food into the bowls. She stopped after a moment and called back toward her house and then grinned again and tugged on the bright cloth wrapped around her torso, tucking it back into the fold below her arm. Momentarily, a skinny, barefooted-girl appeared with another pot and carefully handed it to Josephine who spoke rapidly to the girl in dialect and then handed her the now empty first pot which the girl took from the porch. Off to one side were the forested hills that extended down from the long ridge behind the town, and, barely visible through a narrow gap between two houses across the lane below, the distant hazy row of coconut trees bending inland at the edge of the sea.

With the last of the food served, Josephine left, and the men, sitting in the chairs, silently and rapidly ate from the bowls, forming the doughy contents into small balls with their hands and then dipping into the thick sauce before raising the balls to their mouth's.

"Eye de paa," Glen finally said.

"Eye de pa pa pa pa pa paaaaa," Mr. Amoah answered, and they scraped at the steaming food.

Out front, a boy approached in the blue uniform of the students, and, carrying several books and notebooks, stepped onto the porch.

"Owusula," Glen said casually, leaning over his bowl.

"Sir," the boy said, and he exchanged greetings with Kwami and Mr. Amoah.

"Owusula, what happened?" Glen said as he continued to eat the food, "I waited all last night."

"Sir ... Mr. Ocansey. He instructed me to attend to Miss Amoako's laundry ... Ah—sir." The boy grinned shyly, his mouth partly covered by a hand. He was older for a third former, which was not uncommon for the more remote rural schools, his muscular body more physically developed with traces of facial hair below his temples.

"Owusula," Glen continued, "last week it was cutting grass—the week before something else. You beg me to tutor and then you don't come. It is you who has to pass the O-levels. Not me, Owusula."

"Sir, I'm sorry—I beg. If we can only go over problems now—I beg."

"These students," Mr. Amoah said, glancing at Glen, rapidly chewing his food, and then to the boy. "Owusula, mebaa ha enkyeree, madi abosome mmiensa pe."

Owusula's face turned serious and he responded rapidly to Mr. Amoah in dialect.

"Ah, hnnnnnnn," Mr. Amoah uttered casually and looked off as he continued to eat from the bowl in his hand.

"Owusula," Glen said, "clean the kitchen floor and we will study tonight—half an hour."

"Yooo, meda ase." Owusula grinned and gave a slight bow and walked quickly to the small kitchen room off the end of the porch.

Glen looked at Amoah and shrugged and continued to eat. Now several more children gathered on the lane in front of the house and looked toward the men on the porch; but they ran suddenly and noisily off when Glen looked up from his bowl. Several women with huge bundles of cassava balanced on their heads walked past in loud conversation; and Glen could hear the word '*O bruni*' repeated several times and saw the wide grins on their faces as they twisted their eyes toward the porch. "Kwami ... Ma mee pa paaaaa," Glen said to his friend beside him, telling him how full he was, and set his empty bowl on the rail and patted his stomach.

Kwami grinned as he finished his bowl and Mr. Amoah echoed '*ma mee*' and set his bowl aside and reached for the gourd of palm wine.

Dusk was coming, and Glen stood and walked down the porch toward the kitchen and glanced out across the tops of the jumbled quilt of tin roofs toward the sea. As the sun disappeared behind the hills, more voices drifted up from the lane and the nearby houses and compounds; and he went into the kitchen where Owusula had lit a lantern and was sweeping the cement floor. He spoke briefly to the student and then lit another lantern and brought it back out to the porch as the sky began to rapidly darken. The small girl from next door, Amma, one of Kwami's daughters, was back now to retrieve the remaining pots and bowls; and Glen reached suddenly down and lifted her high into the air; and she grinned widely and Glen laughed and Kwami and Mr. Amoah laughed and he set her gently back down. Looking to her father and then gathering the bowls, she left with Kwami for their house next door, as Kwami carried the now almost empty bucket of palm wine.

Mr. Amoah, still grinning, stood and stretched and patted his stomach and repeated '*ma mee*', several more times, thanking the great *Onyami* and informing *Him* of his very full belly, and then looked toward the street just as a woman turned into the yard. Now Amoah's smile grew very wide and he called out her name just as she called his, and, grinning broadly, and carrying a small basket, the woman stepped onto the porch. She walked directly over to Glen and stopped in front of him; and Glen leaned quickly forward and kissed the side of her mouth as he set the lantern on the railing.

"Okay," Mr. Amoah said, "I'm going …" And he grinned as widely as he had all afternoon.

"Okay," Glen said. "I will see you tomorrow. Bye-bye-o." And the woman, Lizzy, said good bye to Amoah, and Amoah, still grinning widely, crossed the yard to the street and disappeared into the village as Lizzy flopped into one of the empty chairs.

"Where were *you?*" Lizzy said, her smile now gone, her eyes darting between Glen and the darkening lane she faced from the chair. There were more people now talking and walking about the narrow street, with an occasional goat wandering past, and lanterns glowed in the windows and doorways and on the few outdoor tables that had been set up toward the nearby corner for the evening selling of small servings of cooked food.

"Ah … Lizzy,' Glen said and leaned over from behind and wrapped his arms around her; and she grinned widely again and reached up for his face with her hands. Her name was Elizabeth Afia Azim, Lizzy to her friends, a *Dagati* who had come to the school from the Upper Region the year before to teach home economics to the lower form girls. And when she was not at her flat at the school, or at the flat of her best friend Alice Appiah, who taught middle-form geography and who had also been assigned to Assini Secondary the year before, in part, to accommodate Miss Azim on the all male faculty (this being one of the Asombo Education Service's near futile attempts to stave off the ceaseless flow of Asomboian teachers who fled the small bush schools like Assini for nearby countries like Nigeria—or, in some instances, then, clear across the continent to Libya, to work for Mr. Khadafi—where they were paid in hard, exchangeable currency, as opposed to the useless Asomboian Cedi)—if Lizzy was not at Alice's or at the school, then she was at Glen's.

"Don't Lizzy *me,*" she said, her grin rapidly disappearing as her expression darkened.

"Well ... Did you go?" Glen asked quizzically, standing back up. Now it was dark across the town and the first glow of a half moon shown above the hills behind them. On the street, dark figures moved by, some illuminated by a lantern swinging at their side.

"Of course!" Lizzy folded her arms. The white of her eyes showed brightly against the blackness of her face and the black grid of tightly spun braids of hair. The flowery print of her dress danced over the silky material, which ended, as she sat in the chair, near the top of her thighs. "Obo *Addy?*" she now said in disbelief. "*The greatest singer in all of Asombo?* Ah—Glenny." Raising her shoulders, she pursed her lips and shook her head. "I would travel a hundred miles to see Obo—A *thousand!* And, by the grace of god, he comes to Assini—*bush-town Assini!* ... Ah!" She grunted and crossed her legs.

"Ah, Lizzy," Glen said, trying to sound apologetic as he again tried to put his arms around her, which she immediately removed; and she got up from the chair and stepped toward the railing. "So, it was a good show?" Glen asked.

Lizzy leaned against the rail and looked out over the village, her face slowly brightening and the white of her teeth gleaming brightly within her smile. "Oh, Glenny—we danced the whole night, me and Alice. Just at the stage. We did not sit for even one minute ..." She turned back around. "Oh, Glenny—why?"

"I went with Rodney to the bottle factory."

"*I wen' wit' Rotney to bo'le fac-ree*" she said, mocking his voice. "Oh, Kobina, wo ko he?"

"Oh, fuck," Glen said. "I forgot—Okay? I'm sorry. Rodney knows the manager. It was fun—*they were fucking serving Bier Benin.*" He looked at her in the soft glow of the lantern. "Maybe he'll come back."

Sitting again in the chair and sliding low, she folded her arms across her chest. Lanterns glowed everywhere now and the half moon rose brightly over the town. "Come back—hmmmph … He is on his way to Ivory Coast and then France. He will not return ever again to Asombo, less Assini—Hmmmph" From the kitchen, Owusula emerged and stood before them.

"Finished?" Glen said.

"Yes," he said; and he greeted miss Azim.

Glen looked at the woman in the chair. "All right… we won't be long." And taking one of the lanterns, he headed with Owusula into the house.

"Remember," Lizzy called out. "Ocran will take us to find Bonfu on Saturday."

SIX

The walk in the morning with Lizzy to the school at the outskirts of town, as always, was warm and humid, and when they arrived the students were just breaking from morning assembly where they stood in rows on the grass in front of the two-story main classroom block, to hear announcements from the headmaster and the Assist. It was also then that the students learned of the day's allocations of weeding, which was doled out as punishment for various disciplinary infractions. There were no canings today.

After the first two classes came the morning break, and the students filed into the makeshift cafeteria which had been thrown together from sheets of tin and laminated pulp, while the new cafeteria, like much of the slowly evolving school, sat to one side, the large cement shell half completed within a ramshackle cage of bamboo scaffolding. The teachers, meanwhile, retreated to the upstairs teachers' lounge, which, with chairs and tables and a sofa, had been converted from a vacant classroom. There, the nineteen teachers (fourteen today as five were absent for various reasons) sat about drinking *Milo*—the national hot-chocolate breakfast beverage of Asombo—and eating fresh bread and orange slices and shelled peanuts and talking loudly (one particularly boisterous group violently slapping the remaining battered cards of a playing deck onto the small table around which they huddled, at times screaming with enthusiasm, indulged in the national street game of *spar*), all in the brief period before the next class began shortly after ten.

At lunch, Glen joined Mr. Amoah and several other teachers under the bamboo shed, where the school cooks prepared the three meals they served daily to the students (most of whom were borders and lived at the school) and to the staff, and there in the shade of the wide, overhead palm-fronds, they shared gourds of wine a farmer had been bringing at lunch each day for the past several weeks. When they were done with the wine, they ate their lunches of rice and canned fish that the cooks simply served them from the large cooking pots that sat over the coals of burning wood just a few feet away.

By the time the last class ended in mid-afternoon, the sun was almost directly overhead, and the heat and humidity were sauna-like, and Glen's clothes and the students clothes, as well as the clothes of the rest of the teachers and staff, ranged from damp to soaked, and the energy levels of everyone—whether from the heat or the chronic lack of protein in the rural areas, or both—for the most part, were very low.

But instead of riding the bus for an hour to *King Solomon's Bar* in Tarkwa Junction with Mr. Attah, the music teacher (who sometimes brought along the old accordion he used during classes and harmonically filled the passing forest with the sounds of the bellowing reeds), where they had been selling beer daily for the past two weeks, or going with Rodney to the hillside bottle-factory in Oboso with the pleasant second-floor balcony bar that overlooked the lush, narrow valley with the several large houses of the well-to-do factory managers sprinkled about the forested ridge—instead Glen stayed at the school and reviewed math with his form three students who had been begging him for extra revision all week; but when he entered the classroom there were only ten of the classes' twenty-four students present.

"Look at *this,*" he said in dejected disbelief as he entered the room, those in attendance beaming widely with the self-knowledge that the white teacher's extra instruction might very possibly (through means never fully understood by anyone) push them over the proverbial fence into academic success and advanced education with the resulting life of wealth that all imagined would surely follow. Still, he accomplished more in one hour with those who were so inclined than he had in the previous three weeks; and the students left laughing and happy and talking loudly and thanking Glen profusely.

It was then, in the late afternoon, that the heat laid most heavily over Assini and the surrounding hills, and even along the shoreline where the surf crashed suddenly on the steep-sloping beach; and the students rested in their dorms after their late lunches and bucket baths, and Glen, today without the dulling effects of beer, made the agonizing walk back to his house over the short, horribly exposed stretch of baking tarmac that connected the school to the town.

* * *

That evening, by the time it was dark and Lizzy came over, Glen was lying on his bed under the mosquito net, sick from the batch of palm wine that Kwami had brought over before dinner. (Although it was difficult to know for sure whether it was the wine or that night's dinner a student had brought from the school, which had been made with the leafy aburoo, purchased in the Assini market, instead of the previously planned cans of mackerel that the school had mysteriously run out of—very mysteriously as six cartons, a full month's supply, had arrived from Ogobo just the previous week).

But whether it was Kwami's sweet, sweet wine, possibly the sweetest in all the Western Region, or the aburoo, or even the rice and beans Glen had eaten at Tarkwa Junction the day before, or, perhaps, a new strain of malaria that even the weekly, bitter, corlequin pills couldn't stop (or, *Onyami* have mercy, the dreaded tree at Kurua that Glen had yet to visit), whatever the cause, he was sick, and nauseous, and sweating and shaking one minute, and chilled the next. And Lizzy pulled back the hanging net and sat quietly on the side of the bed and gently touched his arm.

"Ah ... Kobina," she said softly, leaning closer and sounding concerned, although due to the extreme chasm of cultural differences, Glen was never a hundred percent sure. "Look at you ... All sick ... Mr. Glen is not good. *Ye ya ri pa paa.*—Don't you have aspirin?"

Glen looked at Lizzy through cloudy eyes, and, grimacing, shifted on his back. He removed her arm and tried to sit up.

"Oh, Glenny—where you going?"

"To the bathroom ... Ah, fuck ..." He lay back again and rested his hands on his stomach.

"Ah, Glenny." Lizzy touched his forehead. "Where is the pain—here?"

"Everywhere—shit, fucking aburoo." He sat up again and rubbed the back of his neck, then, suddenly, turned to Lizzy, and, attempting to smile, said hello and kissed her cheek.

"Ah, poor soldier ..." Lizzy said, rubbing his arm; and Glen stared hard, his smile quickly disappearing. "Oh—Glen, don't do that. You were a good soldier ... Aspirin?"

"Aspirin is gone," Glen said. He was shirtless and shoeless and sat in his underwear on the side of the bed. He drank the last of the water in a glass on the nightstand and then stood up, swaying for a moment on the cool cement floor of the small room. To one side were several chairs and a couch and a desk that sat covered with stacks of paper and numerous folders and books. A partially opened drawer was stuffed with letters from home and friends in Asombo. Shaking and with waves of goose bumps forming on his bare skin, his hair matted and protruding in various directions, he looked for a moment at Lizzy and then left to go to the bathroom as Lizzy leaned back on the bed.

Later, when he finally came back, Lizzy was sitting in one of the chairs, thumbing through Glen's enormous hardcover dictionary, which came with small diagrams and photographs in the margins; and she glanced quickly at him and then back to the book. "Ohhhhh, Glenny," she said in another difficult to decipher tone as she rapidly turned the pages, her eyes skimming swiftly back and forth.

"*Mi ya ri pa paaa*" Glen said, and Lizzy glanced up quickly and pursed her lips as she continued to flip the pages, occasionally stopping when something caught her eye. Moving slowly and with muddled face, Glen pulled on his jeans and a tee shirt and sat on the couch. From the porch came a sound and then the deep voice of Abby Quay, the student who had brought the dinner that afternoon, asking if he could take the bowls back to the school. "Yes—yes—I'm finished," Glen called out, failing to dampen his irritation, while knowing that Abby had simply transported the meal of aburoo. "Take them—take them." He slid lower on the couch, looking off, seeming to grow darker, more distant.

"Vietnam …" Lizzy said, stopping at a page near the back of the thick red book. She leaned closer to the lantern burning on the table beside her which lit the room, sparingly, with a yellowish glow. "A country on eastern coast … southeast Asia peninsula … Divided from 1954 to 1975 into Democratic Republic of Vietnam … 63,344 square miles … population twenty-one million. *Ah!*—Twenty-one million! Kobina, it is big-o."

Glen, expressionless, looked at Lizzy, who glanced quickly up and sheepishly grinned and then flipped the page. Turning slowly, he looked back across the room to the far wall where an aging poster of Che´ Guevera was taped, the words, *'Viva La Revolution'*, emblazoned across the bottom below the bereted-guerilla.

"Oh, Glenny—Go to bed," Lizzy said; and she closed the dictionary and set it back on the desk. She went over to the couch and stood above Glen, straddling his outstretched legs, and reached down for his hands. "Bed … bed," she said again and began to pull on his arms.

"Sir," Abby stood at the screened door with the plastic tub of pots and bowls from the school, "I'm going."

"Okay, Abby … Thank you," Glen said.

"Sir … You are not well?"

"Not well, Abby—Sick."

"Sir … I'm sorry."

"Thank you, Abby."

Africa 253

"Okay—I'm going."
"Okay—Bye-bye," Glen said.
"Yeda Onyami ase."
"Yoo."
"Bed," Lizzy said and pulled on his arms until he stood up. When he was out of his clothes and back on the mattress, she covered him with the sheet and kissed his cheek and lowered the mosquito net. Moving over to the table, she turned off the lantern, casting the room into darkness, except for the faintest slivers of moonlight around the shuttered windows, then went quietly out the door.

* * *

Glen had no classes until after the ten-o'clock break the next morning, and felt revived enough to teach his schedule, and by the day after that he had all but forgotten about the illness.

That is how it was then in Africa: each day the same as the day before; the rhythm of life having emerged from the land as slowly as a sapling from the soil; the present indistinguishable from the past; yesterday disappearing into each of the yesterdays before it, like the repeating reflection in two mirrors growing smaller and smaller until they disappear into infinity.

On the following Friday, when the Headmaster came noisily into the teachers lounge after school with a full carton of the glorious *Star* beer (glorious indeed as it was brewed in Accra by a plant that had been constructed by *Heinekens International* during World War II), Glen quickly joined him and several other teachers, including Amoah and Mr. Ocansey and Mr. Attah, and even Lizzy and Alice, to drink the golden brew. With the bottled *Fanta* sodas hard to come by lately, and pipe-born water again coming inconsistently from the bore hole at Tarkwa Junction (which, when it was available and running, was randomly visited by the school bus to transport the clean, clear water back to Assini in large plastic barrels)—and with kerosene-boiled stream water taking half the day to cool (and still tasting unusual)— the smooth, bottled *Star,* pleasantly and safely quenched one's thirst, and fought the late afternoon heat, as well as conveniently assisting in the retrieval of the near bottomless reservoir of unique and exceptional ideas that rested always within the subconscious of the young.

And afterwards, walking with Lizzy and Amoah back to town in the equatorial sun, the heat, after several of the strong beers, now somewhat strangely seeming more interesting than uncomfortable; and the young children who still after more than two years ran daringly up to Glen to speak, miraculously seeming very delightful and sweet (as opposed to the bothersome pests he perceived them as most days as they annoyingly called out '*good morning*' in the evenings and '*good evening*' in the mornings). So today Glen laughed, and Lizzy and Mr. Amoah laughed, and the children ran off squealing excitedly, just as quickly as they had appeared.

SEVEN

A month earlier, Francis Kodjo Bonfu, the class proctor of form four and most popular and beloved student at Assini Secondary (that is, after Gloria Addy, who was to the isolated and nearly exclusively male student-body what Rita Hayworth had been to the American G.I.s of World War II) had mysteriously disappeared. The disappearing in itself was not unusual; all of the students and staff of Assini Secondary disappeared from time to time. But that it had gone on for more than three days was highly so. By the fifth day, Glen had begun to casually inquire as to Bonfu's whereabouts, and was told simply that he was ill, and by the seventh, after pushing more forcefully, that he had returned to the village he was from, apparently, to recover there. In Assini, there was a clinic run by a Dr. Kwaku Aware, where Glen had once sought treatment for a serious foot infection after the pills administered by the Mission nurse in Accra had failed to work. (The injection in the buttocks he received at the clinic with the plastic-sealed WHO syringe had almost immediately cleared up the infection). But after speaking with Dr. Aware, Glen learned that Bonfu had never gone to the clinic.

"He is in Aberde," Ocran, Bonfu's best friend had said that second week when Glen had asked. "It is just off the Dunkwa line. Do you know it?"

"No," Glen had responded, "I know the Dunkwa train, but I don't know Aberde."

Compared to most of the students at Assini Secondary, who tended to be on the lean or skinny side (despite the school's carbohydrate-rich diet of rice and yams and cassava), Bonfu was short and stocky. But even more so than his physical stature, from Glen's very first encounters, he had stood out from the others with his particularly clear and accurate English, his exceptional maturity and intelligence, and his seemingly innate ability to grasp the basic underlying concepts of classroom discussions. And Glen's observation of these traits occurring more than two years before of a barely fourteen-year-old second former, and now, in the fall of 1978, he was even more mature and refined, and excelling masterfully in his studies, and Glen worried greatly as to the boy's well being.

"Mr. Agee, have you heard anything about Bonfu? Anything?" Glen asked the Headmaster by the third week.

"Ah—he has returned to his home in Aberde," the Headmaster had said that day after school in the late afternoon heat on the veranda in front of his office. "We know only that there was a fever and the family has brought him home."

There actually were other students who scored higher on various tests; even Janet Yeboah (*'Oh, Onyami! A girl!*', the villagers would exclaim) had beaten Bonfu on the math exams at the end of form three. (As serious a gender offense in secondary school Asombo as any). And he was anything but the best footballer on the team: Issac Kirby of form two, from neighboring Ghana, would be the next *'Pele'*, all were convinced. But Bonfu carried a great dignity and pride and caring that was inspiring and uplifting, and seemingly contagious; even if the perceived absorption was more imaginary than real.

"You know, Lizzy, if he misses much more it will be extremely difficult for him to pass the exams," Glen said at home to Lizzy one evening as the absences continued to mount. "Ocran went to see him last weekend and said he is still not well. I really think we should go check on him."

"Then we will go, Kobina—I am worried, too. His cousin is in my form one class and she is upset. Ocran will take us. We will go."

EIGHT

With the first distant clanking of the approaching train from down the long curving tracks leading into Dunkwa-Station, an hour inland from Assini, Glen quickly rose from the cement platform where he had sat for the past hour reading a well-worn paperback, and waved to Lizzy, who was off buying some fried plantains near the ticket booth; and Lizzy, also hearing the train, called to Ocran, who was further away still, buying some small bits of chocolate from a seller near the road at the edge of the station. They had met at the school with the first light of dawn and traveled from Assini by Datsun-car to bump-in-the-tracks Dunkwa, arriving well before the scheduled 8:00 A.M. departure, knowing it was possible the train may not arrive before noon, or at all.

Pushing their way into one of the half-dozen cars of the aging Southern Line, they stood shoulder to shoulder with the crowd of travelers who took up every square inch of available space, everyone loudly arguing the legitimacy of their presence, particularly the colorfully-clad market women who now lowered to the floor the large produce baskets they had gracefully carried in on their heads. As the train chugged slowly from the platform, black smoke billowing from the stack of the ancient locomotive, Glen, Lizzy, and Ocran felt lucky they had managed to actually get inside one of the cars, as opposed to the people who clung to the open doors, their bodies outside hovering over moving ground as they waited for the crowd to settle and allow them the necessary few feet they would require to squeeze inside.

"Three stops?" Glen yelled to Ocran, only inches away, yet straining to hear because of the loud metallic clanking of the tracks and engine, and the adrenal-fueled buzz of the crowd.

"Yes—three," Ocran yelled back, his slender arm stretched past several people to a closed window in an attempt to retain his balance as the train, swaying from side to side, slowly gathered speed. With permission to travel for the weekend and no longer on the school grounds, Ocran, skinny and tall for a sixteen-year-old, was no longer dressed in the uniform he was required to wear daily throughout the term, and instead stood in an open-collar shirt, the sleeves rolled up, the tail hanging out, and possibly the cheapest denim pants in all the developing world. (The price which for he, no doubt, was a small fortune). On his feet were a pair of old black leather shoes, the backs flattened down so as to be conveniently slipped on or off.

Lizzy, although in her mid-twenties as skinny as Ocran, and whose height fell several inches below Glen's shoulders, stood beside the two of them, her feet spread as far as the crowd would allow, using those she was pressed against for balance, her arms extending straight down in front of her short, sleeveless jumper, clutching firmly with her hands the leather bag she had brought along for the weekend journey. She looked up at the tall, increasingly slender figure of Glen, who, with one hand stretched all the way to the swaying ceiling, and wearing a short-sleeved shirt, the collar open, the tail also hanging out (however for him over the tops of his badly faded but authentic and highly coveted American *Levis),* looked down at Lizzy. Everywhere around them faces strained to look at Glen as frequent voices uttered '*O-bruni*' within the rapid bursts of local dialect.

"Sir ..." Ocran had somehow managed to pull one of the small, now melting pieces of chocolate from his pocket and offered it to Glen who shook his head and bent down to look out the window. There was mostly tall grasses on each side of the tracks moving swiftly past, with the thick vegetation of the western rainforests beyond the grasses; and the train, now at full speed, lurched and swayed as the loud clanking of the cars almost drowned out the combustible roar of the fiery engine.

They stopped once, and then again shortly after, at two small villages with small platforms; and at each a rush of people poured off and a new wave swarmed on. And during the second they were able to move to a small section of wall against which Lizzy could lean, and where Ocran and Glen could more comfortably brace themselves; and with a sudden lurch the train started forward again. Soon they were alongside a river and the muddy water swirled past and the forest was tall and thick along the banks and then the river was gone and it was just the forest and the train slowed and slowed, and slowed some more, and then stopped, but there was no village or platforms, just the deep lush green on each side of the tracks.

"What? ... Why the hell are we stopping?" Glen asked, bending toward the window to better see; but all he could see was the thick, green tangle of the dense forest. And inside the vintage 1940s German-built cars, without air rushing through the partially opened windows, the temperature began to rise. "Ocran, where in the hell are we?"

"Ah, sir ... I am not knowing as to why the delay. I believe we are just at Kumavu."

The people in the car were quieter now, with only an occasional voice spoken softly between companions; and Glen looked down at Lizzy who raised her eyes to meet his. Now someone was talking near the door to the next car who seemed to know what was going on, but neither Ocran or Lizzy could pick up on the discussion, and then the man was laughing, and Glen tried to wipe some of the sweat from his face.

"This train," Lizzy said, sounding annoyed. "It breaks down too much—I *don't* like it."

"Is it broken down?" Glen asked in disbelief. They could no longer hear the engine. "No ..."

"I think we will be going just now," Ocran said.

"No ..." Glen said again, very slowly, and seemingly to himself; and he leaned again toward the window.

It was pretty outside with the dense tangle of vines and plants that rose up through the first layer of trees that spread around the thick, white trunks of the towering hardwoods that rose above everything before bursting with green at the high, high tops. *Could you walk out there? Are there bush-paths like in the forests around Assini? Or are we in the middle of nowhere? Probably not ... There are probably paths everywhere, and villages and farming plots and palm wine and people eating and drinking ... and fucking ... There is probably someone—someone—two* people, *out there somewhere, right now, fucking ... There's got to be ... Probably in some little house or hut, right now ... Fucking, fucking, fucking ... Somewhere.* He glanced down at Lizzy who looked back just as she had the last time; and he looked again out the window. *But it's really quite pretty out there. It would be worth coming back to hike around. Maybe for a day or even just half.* He continued looking into the thick forest. *I wonder ... I wonder how close by, this very second. Jesus it's hot. Almost as hot as fucking 'Nam. What am I saying 'almost'? The 'Namer was cool compared to this place. We had mountains there. Fucking cooler ... Fuck-fuck-fuck ... Fuckty-fuck ... Come on ... Come on, let's get this thing going ... We haven't got all fucking day ... Fuck ...* He looked down at Lizzy again who this time didn't look up. *Don't know—Dizzy-Lizzy—just don't know ... Really, sometimes, honest to fucking-god—just don't know ... You want to come back to the States with me? ... You don't know ... you just don't fucking know. Come back and make babies? Never see Asombo again? Mommy, Daddy—brothers, sisters? Go off to big USA? ... Eat steak?...Fight there?...Fuck...* The train suddenly lurched.

"We are going," Ocran said, and a murmur arose from the crowd.

"Too hot," Lizzy said and rubbed the back of her neck.

Glen bent low and looked out the windows as the forest again began to slowly move past. "About time," he said and reached for the wall as the train picked up speed.

It was another unexplained stop and two more hours before they reached Kumavu, and, *pushing, pushing, pushing*, they got off the train and then pushed some more through the crowd on the platform. Ocran led swiftly through the dirt streets of the village to the footpath out the other side as people stopped everywhere to look at Glen, and to laugh, and call out *'O-bruni'*; and by the time they reached the trail the swarm of children running beside Glen was most of the total that lived in the village.

The path was wide and the area around it had once been logged so the trees were short, with dense green growing everywhere. There were also numerous small compounds of mud-brick and bamboo houses scattered within the trees, and in cleared areas, and also within the many long rows of cocoa trees that were everywhere in the south. Coffee had recently been introduced as well, and banana and orange and plantain trees were common—and out of Tarkwa the enormous *Firestone* rubber plantations with the miles of perfectly aligned rows sweeping up the hillsides and disappearing into the hoizon—but it was the short, wide, cocoa trees with the clumps of dark cocoa pods below the wide green leaves that were everywhere.

Ocran led, followed by Lizzy and then Glen, and occasionally they passed someone from one of the houses—usually a man or woman with a large bundle of yams or cassava or cocoa pods on their heads—and they all called *'O-bruni'* when they saw Glen. And Glen would smile and greet them; and the many small children playing noisily in the dirt around the houses would suddenly stop, and stare, when they passed.

"Two miles?" Glen said, reconfirming with Ocran the distance from the train to Aberde, for what must have been the tenth time since they had left Assini early that morning.

"Yes," Ocran said in the same gentle tone he had used for each of the earlier inquiries. "It is not far."

Before long there were no more huts within the trees and the path narrowed and began to climb a ridge and the wide stumps of some of the old hardwoods began appearing more and more frequently in the thick, sloping undergrowth. This led Glen to believe there must be a road nearby—*unless they had just dragged the logs down to the tracks*—and they came to the top of the ridge which put them, Glen figured, at least a mile and a half from the station. "Half mile?" Glen said to Ocran; but Ocran didn't seem to understand and didn't respond, and he continued to lead them along.

"Hold it," Glen said a short time later from the rear, breathing deeply and stopping in some shade. "Let's have a drink.—Lizzy, here, drink some water." He took the plastic hiking bottle from his shoulder bag and unscrewed the top and handed the bottle to Lizzy who took a few sips. Beads of perspiration dotted her face, and she looked up at Glen and squinted in the afternoon light and handed him the bottle. "Here," Glen said, handing it to Ocran who drank, then gave it back to Glen who took several large swallows. "We must be close," Glen said, and drank some more.

"*Krow no ben ha anaa?*" Lizzy said something quickly in dialect to Ocran who answered in dialect and pointed up the trail.

"All right," Glen said, putting the bottle away, "ready?" Ocran nodded and they continued up the trail.

* * *

"Sir!—*No!*"

"I am telling you, Ocran—*the bear took the pack!*" Glen had moved ahead of Lizzy to where he trailed Ocran by barely a step. Lizzy walked a few feet behind in the humid afternoon air, listening to the story as she watched the ground at her feet.

"Sir—The food?—*All* the food?"

"It took it all, Ocran, every damn bit we had. We had to leave and go back to our homes because we had no more food."

"Ah!—*Sir!*" Ocran, wide-eyed and grinning, occasionally twisted to look back as he continued up the path. They had been following a small stream for the last half mile and the undergrowth was thick beside the trail and along the banks, and dense groves of timber bamboo towered everywhere around them.

"Oh, it was no fun," Glen said, almost bumping into Ocran. "No fun a-tall." He turned, grinning, to look at Lizzy who looked quickly up and faintly shook her head.

"But in fact," Ocran said, "I have seen photos of these creatures—this *grissly* bear—"

"—No," Glen said, "this was a black bear, Ocran, black."

"But they are very dangerous, I think."

"True, true ... But the pack was high in a tree, away from the camp. So we weren't much afraid."

"*Ah!*" Ocran said. "I think I would not want to meet one by any means!"

"What do you think, Lizzy?" Glen turned, still grinning. "If you come to the States and go into the woods, well ... maybe ..."

"No *WAY!*" Lizzy said with disgust and stopped. "I will *never* go in woods—*Never!—Never!*"

Glen laughed and continued up the path.

"Big bear—n*o!*" Lizzy could be heard at the back talking to herself.

"We have been lucky," Ocran said after a short ways, "no snakes."

"Yes," Lizzy now said adamantly from the back. "So far, no *aboatsena*—Yet!"

Glen looked at Lizzy and then Ocran.

"Ah," Ocran said. "*Aboatsena*—very big—very bad."

"*Ohhhhh,*" said Lizzy, "very bad. *Bad—bad—bad.*"

"All right ... okay," Glen said, "I comprehend-o ... I'm scared ... *Scared—scared—scared.*"

"It is fine, sir," Ocran said. "We will drive *aboatsena* back to his house in the trees. No worry."

"Yes—yes," Glen said continuing up the trail. "You know ... I've seen one snake in two years. You remember, Ocran, the one the students and Mr. Kiti found in the science lab?"

"Ah—sir, it was big-o."

"Before you were here, Lizzy. Big 'ol Black Mamba—Big guy. I thought the school was falling down, there was so much commotion."

"It is true, they are about," Ocran said. "But we killed it."

"Sure did, Ocran. Had what, ten students pounding on it?"

Ocran turned and smiled widely.

"You just watch that path," Glen said. "Lizzy and I are right here." Lizzy moved up closer and they continued up the trail.

* * *

It was late afternoon when they began to encounter people again along the path, and small mud and bamboo houses under the trees, and then a footbridge crossing another stream and a large clearing and the first mud-brick houses of Aberde.

When they entered the grid of dirt streets Ocran was called to and greeted by several people, and there were wide smiles and gasps at the sight of the tall, ambling Glen. Everywhere, wandering goats scurried quickly out of the way, and children began to come up, at first just a few, and then more until they surrounded Glen in a noisy swarm.

At each of the many houses people appeared at the door to look, often a mother with a small child on her hip, and they all pointed and smiled widely and laughed loudly and spoke rapidly in dialect, as Ocran led them up the street.

"Sir," Ocran finally said as they approached the center of town, "… I think we must first go to the palace." And he turned up one of the many side streets and after a few houses passed through the entrance of a large cement and mud-brick compound and stopped in a courtyard that was surrounded on all four sides by low, interconnected rooms.

An elderly man in one of the brightly-patterned traditional *Akan* cloths that hung from one shoulder and draped around his body came from a room smiling widely and greeted them, his eyes opening wide within the deep creases of his face when Glen responded in dialect, and learned happily that Glen, too, was '*Kobina*', born on the same day of the week as himself. A cloth hung over another door and was pushed aside and they entered a room with several chairs and tables and a large clay water-vessel in a corner and one of the brightly patterned *Adrinka* cloths hanging on a wall and some tiny brass figurines lining a shelf against another wall; and sunlight streamed in from several of the small windows opening back into the courtyard.

Then from another room entered the chief and an assistant, also draped in traditional cloths, the chief looking much younger than most of the others Glen had met over the past two years in rural Asombo, and after greeting his visitors, and also smiling widely at Glen's use of dialect, led them back to the courtyard where a tray holding a glass bottle filled with the traditional, locally distilled liquor and several small shot glasses was produced. And the assistant chief, closer in age to the elderly first assistant, recited the prayers and sprinkled from one of the glasses a few drops of the *apeteshie* onto the hard-dirt floor for the ancestors, and a few more for *Abezee,* the great Earth god, and then drank down the last as the rest of the glasses were handed out to Glen and to Lizzy who declined.

As it always did, the clear liquid burned Glen's mouth and throat and tasted like lighter fluid—which it probably more closely resembled than not; but he smiled anyway and thanked the chief in dialect.

When they were back in the room and sitting and drinking water from the clay vessel and the chief stopped from his brief discussion with Ocran, he asked Glen in English how his journey to Aberde had gone and how long he had been in Asombo.

"Oh, not bad—Ocran was an excellent guide," Glen said. "And I am now in my third year at Assini Secondary."

"Ahhhhh,' the chief said, smiling, "it is fine. And you have been Bonfu's teacher all this time?"

"Yes," Glen said from his chair, nodding; and Ocran spoke rapidly in dialect and the chief and the two elders nodded and uttered the long guttural, *'ahhhnnnnnnnn',* response of understanding.

"So," the chief said. He looked to be not much older than Glen and was clean-shaven and his hair of a modern and contemporary style, and it was obvious from the clarity of his English that he had been educated through at least upper sixth form, and more likely the university. "Bonfu," he went on, "he is having what we say in Asombo—'*atta-kre*'—bad spirits." The chief grinned and his perfect, white teeth showed brightly. "But here, in Aberde, we do not have the necessary medicines that you, the European, would use if it was one of your own. So, perhaps, you can be of assistance?"

Glen glanced at Lizzy. "No—no, we didn't bring anything—I don't have any medicine." He looked at the others. "But I was very concerned. I wanted to come—to see Bonfu. I wanted to see how he is doing. Hopefully he is getting better … he is getting better, isn't he?"

"Well, I have not seen him personally. But I know several of his brothers." The chief spoke rapidly in dialect again to one of the elders who responded loudly in the rapid-fire bursts of the *Twi* language. "So," the chief went on, returning to Glen, "if you like, we can go see Bonfu just now."

"Yes," Glen said, nodding. "Yes, I would like that."

* * *

When, after a lengthy discussion with the chief regarding his desire to acquire any spare American dollars Glen may have had in his possession, in exchange for grossly inflated quantities of the local currency (the impossibility of which Glen patiently explained due to his own lack of any foreign monies), they finally left the mud-brick palace compound, they discovered that a small crowd had gathered outside, noisily awaiting Glen and his companions. But now, along with Ocran and Lizzy and an older brother of Bonfu's who had come down to the palace to accompany them, they were in the presence of just one of the elders, as the chief had elected not to come after all.

As they moved up the dirt street toward Bonfu's at the outskirts of town, the houses joined more closely together, with split bamboo becoming as common as the tin roofs that were nearer the palace, and everywhere the long mud-walls of the houses waved subtly from years of settling. Leaving the crowd outside, they soon entered a small house and passed through the front room where a young woman sat on a woven mat with two small children; and she grinned as they entered and the children quickly moved closer, clutching her arms as Glen passed through. Everyone stopped in a short hallway toward the back that connected the front room to the rest of the house, except for Ocran and Glen, who, pulling a cloth from a doorway, entered a small, darkened room. In a corner, barely visible in the dim light, a thick cotton mat lay on a low wood frame, and as they came in, a dark figure on the mat swung slowly around and sat on the edge of the bed.

"Bonfu?" Glen said softly, his eyes adjusting to the darkness.

"Mr. Glen? Ah, sir, it is true ... you have come to Aberde. They have been saying you are here ... But, sir, why? Why have you made the journey to Aberde?"

Ocran went to the window and opened the wood shutter letting the late light of the day into the small room. Bonfu pulled on the sheet wrapped over his shoulders and squinted. "I have come to see you," Glen said. "I have come to see how you are doing—Bonfu, how are you doing? Look, Miss Azim has come too—*Lizzy.*"

"Ah!" Bonfu said, now seeming to brighten. "Sir, I am not believing my eyes—it is really you. Yeda Onyami ase."

"Yoo, yeda Onyami ase," Glen said.

"Heyyyyy—Bonfu," Lizzy said entering the room, smiling. "When you coming back to Assini?"

"Yeah, Bonfu," Glen joined in. "When?"

"Sir, ah, my strength ... it is not good ... And at school I am behind ... I am far behind ... Ah!" He lowered his eyes.

"All of form four," Ocran said from the side, "we will not pass the exams without you—A-tall."

"Ah, I think Mr. Glen will make you pass exams." Bonfu looked up, again with the faint trace of a smile. His face was puffy and his eyes glassy but he seemed, amazingly, to have kept most of his weight; and he pulled again on the cloth.

"No—no, Bonfu," Glen said. "You help the students with the tricky mathematics. When there is a story problem that is tricking all of form four, it is Bonfu who surmises the answer."

"Yes," Lizzy said, grinning; "these math problems—I don't know them."

Bonfu slowly grinned wider and edged closer on the bed. He spoke rapidly in dialect to Ocran and grinned some more.

"Bonfu, what do you have?" Glen asked. "Is it fever?"

"Sir ... I don't know. Yes, fever ... pains. My neck, my sides. Badly ... Sir, can you give me aspirin?"

Glen shook his head. "Dabi—' he clapped his hands, "aspirin me nyi bo bio."

For a moment, Bonfu looked distant, then smiled again. "Ah ... I am happy to see my master. You have come to Aberde—*Ah!*"

"So, when will you return to Assini, Bonfu?" Glen asked.

"I am feeling better this week. Now I am feeling better more … I can return soon. Next week … I feel I can return next week. I feel stronger."

His brother who had stood quietly in the doorway now spoke rapidly and forcefully to Bonfu in dialect. And before his brother finished Bonfu responded forcefully and then his brother spoke again, more rapidly, and Bonfu grew quiet.

"We hope you can come back soon," Glen said after a moment. "We hope you are well again, soon."

Bonfu had lowered more now onto the bed. He looked up at Glen. "Sir … I will try."

The others looked on silently. "Good, then we will let you rest," Glen said. "We are staying at the palace tonight so we'll come by before we leave in the morning."

Bonfu looked up at Glen with the faintest trace of a smile. "Sir … I am happy."

"Okay," Glen said. "Then in the morning."

"Sir … Meda ase. In the morning."

NINE

"Kobina—wo ho ye?"
"Yoo, Kwami, me ho ye. Na wo nso e?"
"Me nso me ho ye. Yeda Onyami ase."
"Yoo, Onyami ase."
"Sir, what will you grow?"
"Lettuce ... cucumbers ... tomatoes."
"Ahhhnnnnnnn."

Glen squatted in the soil beside his house burying seeds that he took from packets in several short rows. He had removed the weeds and grass and turned the hard dirt with a shovel, and now he planted. To one side, a short row of sporadic green protruded faintly from an earlier effort with onions. A small boy and girl from a neighboring house stood silently beside Glen with a bucket of stream water, which together they carefully poured over the freshly planted seeds the moment Glen signaled with his hand. Kwami, on his way to his farm, looked on from the brown grass in front of the house a few yards away. "Sir, the sun ..."

Kwami said, pointing up at the great sphere of *Ewia*, "... sir, too much, they will burn."

Glen looked up at the sky and shrugged and planted some more. He stood and pointed toward the earlier plantings and toward the onions and the children gently rushed to pour the water. He pointed again to another area and then another and together they poured the last of the bucket. He squinted again toward the sun. "You are right, Kwami. I should have planted over there. Right beside Mrs. Appiah's house." He shrugged again. "Oswea yen ko," he said to the children, and they ran off with the bucket for the stream.

"It is fine ..." Kwami said; "they will grow."

Glen looked again at the onions that had not done much. "I will not be selling at the market, Kwami. I can tell you this: I will be going to the market, but I will not be going there to sell."

"Sir, they will grow."

"Ask Onyami to make them grow."

"In fact, I will pray to Onyami to make them grow," Kwami said, and he squinted in the bright sun and grinned before turning for his farm.

When the children came back with the full bucket—struggling together with all their strength, yet spilling nothing—with Glen's help, they carefully poured the water over the plot of planted seeds, and the ground darkened as the water quickly disappeared into the soil. They emptied the bucket and proudly watched the rest of the water disappear and then Glen squatted down between them and patted their heads and hugged them tightly in each arm; and, releasing, they left to return to their home, grinning widely. Glen stood and walked to the house and crossed the porch and went inside. The bed was unmade and a pile of dirty clothes lay on the floor—including those he had worn to the funeral—and he turned and looked out the open window toward the sea. Through the small gap he could see the distant tops of the arching palms along the shoreline as several goats wandered in the afternoon heat up the lane below the yard. He sat for a moment on the edge of the bed and looked again at the clothes—including the shirt he had worn: the nice, pleasant, dirty green shirt—where they had been lying on the floor the past two weeks. He began to lie down but instead arose and went to the desk in front of the window and sat in the wood chair. Rummaging through the scattered heaps of paper and books, he stopped and held up a single paper which, after clearing a space and picking up a pen, he set on the desktop.

'*Unfortunately*', he began to write on the back of the form letter that had sat half-completed on the desk for over a month, '*I will not be able to attend Baker Company, Twenty-Third Battalion's tenth anniversary reunion at Fort Lewis this January. Please send my love and warmest greetings to Commander Thomas; First Sergeant Ross; and all attending personnel. Sincerely, Private Glen Gray*. He turned the letter over and looked again at the series of questions he had earlier answered regarding his activities since discharge. He looked once again at the note on the back, then placed the letter in an envelope, sealed it, and set it back on the desk. Then he opened the drawer of old letters and dug into the pile until he found the one from Ben. He took it out of the envelope and skimmed the first page and then began reading the second. '*... and am still shocked to have gotten a letter from Africa ... have heard from Peter Duncan a few times. He says O'Donnell—short guy from L.A., Ross was always yelling at him—was killed at Trong Den in his second tour in '69, and someone, Vincetti—I don't remember him but I recognize the name—was killed near Da Lot in '70 ... the kids are growing too fast ... Susan is doing great ... We can canoe and camp in Voyagers if you ever come out ... disco is still ruining the country ...*' Glen put the letter back and began to close the drawer when he noticed a corner of Julie's letter. He moved his hand toward it but stopped and closed the drawer completely and got up from the chair. He grabbed his shoulder bag off the couch and went out the door.

By the time he reached the inlet at the edge of Assini his shirt was soaked from the humidity; and he weaved through the dugout canoes and fishing nets spread about the white sand and the fishermen repairing the nets who all called *O-bruni* when he passed, the heals of his sandals kicking up the sand. He headed toward the rock point and the crumbling white-walled remains of the ancient Portuguese fort that had stood at the entrance to the tiny bay for over four-hundred years, an ancient shrine to the gold and slaves that had once funneled down from the interior on their way to the New World. He passed stray goats and huge piles of garbage and the endless parade of women with huge baskets of fish and produce on their heads as he moved along the sand in front of the long row of ramshackle houses strung out toward the point from Assini. The sea had taken half of the fort and the sun and wind most of the rest; and Glen crossed the narrow isthmus of wave-battered rocks in front of the ancient steps leading to the seaward entrance and remaining walls perched on the rock point, and dropped down onto the sand on the other side and started down the long ocean beach. He veered down toward the surf which came up suddenly on the steep sand, and a light mist hung over the beach from the crashing waves and the faint offshore fog; and a sudden, far-reaching tongue washed over his feet. He passed a lone woman far down the beach who carried a huge bundle of firewood on her head and a child strapped in cloth to her back and they greeted each other in dialect and Glen followed her footprints in the sand until the waves washed them smooth. He stopped for a moment and looked out over the rolling swells and traced the distant curve of the wind-whipped horizon and then cut up to where the lush forest came down to the sand and sat on the long, scaly trunk of a fallen coconut tree. But he quickly noticed the foul stench of feces and knew what this area of the beach was used for and jumped quickly up and jogged back down to the surf. He let another wave wash over his sandals and ankles and then began to jog again: at first slowly, and then faster, until he was sprinting across the damp sand; and his arms and legs pumped furiously with the shoulder bag flopping violently against his back, until he gradually slowed, and stopped, and, breathing deeply, bent over with his hands on his knees. But the bag began to slip off his shoulder and he straightened again and walked a few more feet, still breathing deeply the humid coastal air. He thought he saw something out in the sea and stopped and squinted toward the wide swells, straining to see into the shifting surface. But after several moments of intense searching nothing appeared and he walked back toward the trees. He approached cautiously this time, sniffing deeply with each step, and concluded the area was safe and sat down where the sand abruptly met the soil and laid back and rested his head on the earth. He stared for a moment into the hazy sky with the fingered end of a wide green branch above protruding into his view, and then he closed his eyes.

TEN

Since the October coup', with its newly installed *Armed Forces Revolutionary Council* (known as the AFRC), the number of soldiers roaming through rural Asombo had increased noticeably; although their efforts to force the matrons in markets such as Assini's, and the shop owners in the surrounding stores, to sell their goods at the now government-imposed prices simply drove everything underground, or to the nearby borders of the Ivory Coast and Togo, where transactions were conducted in hard currency. Of the extra troops that did wander into Assini, being as they were so removed from the capital and the small main forces and top commanders of Accra (three-hundred miles and two days to the east), they were no more organized or taken anymore seriously than before; unless the drinking they spent most of the day doing got too out of hand and they pointed a rifle at an angry merchant whose hidden goods they had accidentally stumbled upon and were now giving away to a delighted and swarming crowd as the merchant protested bitterly. But even of the new troops, almost all were from Assini, or nearby, and had families in the area; and soldiers in rural Asombo as a whole were taken less seriously than the police who were taken even less seriously than the young, ragged driver's assistants of the numerous buses that plied the country's dirt roadways; but the sight of a loaded rifle was still unnerving.

And so it was not totally unexpected when a tall, tooth-pick-skinny, middle-aged soldier suddenly began living in a house a few doors down from Glen, and, upon discovering that Glen had once been in the United States Army, began dropping by almost every afternoon to salute and have Glen inspect his aging, battered, Russian AK47 which, if properly cleaned and oiled, might actually fire once every six or so squeezes.

"I should not be showing you this, Kodjo—this is not what *'Peace Corpse'* had in mind; but I don't want you hurting someone ... or yourself," Glen said one afternoon as he removed the bolt and clip with the butt of the rifle on the cement porch floor and the barrel pointed at the ceiling. "But if you pull this down and then slide the bolt in ..." the mechanism snapped and the hairpin caught the chasm, "... the holding-chamber will stay tight against the stock."

"*Ahhhhhhh* ... yes, fine," Kodjo said, grinning in his aging fatigues. "*Otuo obaa pa paaaaa!*"

* * *

Early in the evening a few days later, with the sun still high and the waves of heat still rippling off the tops of the metal roofs, one of Mrs. Essuman's daughters brought from next door a plate of two balls of the pungent, fermenting kenkey to the shaded porch where Glen and Kodjo sat talking (or more so, Glen talking and Kodjo listening) and waiting out the late day heat; and they took the plate from the girl and began to eat the starchy balls.

After a while, Kodjo, his rifle leaning beside him against the rail, looked up at Glen: "So ... this Vietnam, sir ... I am hearing it was a very bad war."

Glen pulled a small piece from the doughy ball and placed it in his mouth. "It was, Kodjo." He chewed for a moment, then wiped his mouth with the back of his hand. "But—all wars are bad, Kodjo ... They just are."

Kodjo smiled in agreement and ate some of his kenkey. Along with the horizontal gashes on his cheekbones of the Wasaw tribe, the deep creases of age and equatorial sunlight had chiseled themselves everywhere about his dark, perspiring face, as well as behind the faint, spotty wisps of a beard. For reasons unknown to Glen, perhaps from the lack of morrow that most Asomboian villagers sucked from animal bones resulting in the almost universally strong white teeth of the area, Kodjo's were yellowed and with several missing, which seemed, strangely, to add to his harmlessness. "But it was the *communists!* ... " he went on animatedly in his high, scratchy voice. "I think you were beating them back with very big bombs. It is known—The Americans are not liking the communists."

Glen glanced at Kodjo and continued to chew the kenkey. "Yeah? ... maybe ... I don't mind them, though."

He thought back to the first Christmas in Asombo, two years before, and the week long stay in Accra and the hot afternoons when they'd go to the one, sure, guaranteed place in the crowded, sprawling city to have beer: the Russian Cultural Center. The fragile Asomboian economy had by then begun it's fatal plunge (spurred largely by OPEC's recent crippling oil-embargo of the West) and along with the disappearance of the basic necessities of soap and rice and cooking oil and meat, the breweries were no longer able to import hops, and whereas only a few short years before there had been endless quantities of beer flowing in every corner of the country, now there was none. Except, that is, for the outdoor bar in the pleasant garden of the Russian Cultural Center, a short walk amongst the large homes of the shady residential Accra neighborhood of Cantemonts, where there was still plenty of the only somewhat weaker and less tasty, *Red Knight,* served, instead of in bottles, as was almost all Asombian beer, on tap.

And Glen remembered the very pleasant afternoons after the crowds and heat of central Accra and the enormous, exposed Makola Market with its endless maze of stalls and open sewers and piles of rotting garbage, sitting in the shade of the Center's covered patio at the edge of the lush, meticulously-maintained gardens at one of the dozens of empty tables with David and Mike, and Joanie and Tim, and, back then, Donna—oh *yeda Onyami,* Donna—drinking and talking and laughing and toasting until the impending reality of the six or twelve or eighteen hour bus or car or train ride back to one's terribly remote, desolate village in the harsh, isolated, Asomboian interior became, miraculously, an almost exciting and highly desirable endeavor that would not be missed for even a steak and movie and paid room at the *Ambassador Hotel* with Donna. Well, perhaps with Donna. And, of course, with the exception of Tim, who worked in Accra and didn't have to go anywhere, except to walk home, and who, like Pat in Takoradi, lived in housing that was the Asomboian version of a Park Avenue penthouse.

But he also remembered the Russians from the Soviet Embassy who were the sole other patrons of that expansive, shady patio on those sunny afternoons that long ago December week. And how at one table, in their torn and faded levis and flowing multicolored Asomboian smocks and somewhat long hair, and in the case of David and Mike, long, scraggly beards, the just-in-from-the-bush American Peace Corps Volunteers, clanking glasses and sloshing beer, while at another randomly chosen table, sometimes just a few feet away, the middle-aged Russian men from the nearby embassy in their brown slacks and plain blue shirts and neatly trimmed hair, each group talking loudly and boisterously in their native tongues and each essentially oblivious to the other—no greeting or acknowledgement ever occurring between either party (nor, though, the belaying of even the slightest overt or covert animosity of any kind)—and yet, in fact, a kind of peculiar, unspoken unity, and mutual bonding from being light-skinned foreigners far, far from home and loved ones, living and surviving on a daily basis in the harsh, contemporary chaos of equatorial Africa.

"—I like their beer," Glen said from his chair on the porch.

Kodjo grinned widely and nodded and chewed his kenkey, knowing only that Glen had said something about beer, and that he, too, by all means, enjoyed the smooth, fermented hops (although he could not recall the last time he had drank any other than the bitter village-brews of the north) and that regardless of the context, the subject deserved a grin and a nod.

Glen finished as much of the pungent ball as he could and leaned back in his chair as Kodjo continued to eat. "Sir," Kodjo asked, "did you do battle?"

"Battle? No."

"Were you not on the battle lines?"

"In Vietnam? There were no battle lines."

"Ah—so?" Kodjo tore from his ball as he continued to chew. "I think there were these things: hello-copters—you were flying in them."

"I did, Kodjo; sometimes I did."

"Ah, they are very big machines. Very fine ... In fact, one came to Kotoko when I trained, long ago. Yes—U.S.—very much noise. *Ah!* The noise! But we are not having them in Asombo. Just the fighter jet planes ... Like what Rawlings travels about in."

The October coup' had been spearheaded by a low ranking member of the Asomboian Air Force: Flight Lt. J. J. Rawlings, the mulatto child of an Asomboian mother and Scottish father, who, from time to time, flew his aging F16 down the coast from Accra and over Asisni to the delight of the tens of thousands of people in the towns and villages below. Like all the previous coups' in Asombo, and most of the neighboring countries in West Africa, they were essentially bloodless and confined to a limited number of strategic sights in and around the capital, with the daily rhythms of rural life in the rest of the country uninterrupted. With the minor exception, that is, of every male in every village and town in the country being glued to every available radio or short-wave (which also meant all the teachers of Assini Secondary) for the latest word out of Accra; and in a letter soon after from Katie she described being at Tim's the day it happened and sitting that night on the balcony of his third floor apartment with everyone else who had been in Accra that day and watching in the darkness the tracers of the distant fire fight at the army barracks on the outskirts of the city.

"I have not heard Rawlings since last week," Glen went on.

"He is busy—" Kodjo said, eating, chewing, "very busy man."

Yes, busy, Glen thought, and he could still see the front-page photo that had appeared that first week in the *Asomboian Times* of General Ignatius Acheampong, the previous military ruler, and five of his closest aids, hooded and slumped at the poles to which they had been tied and executed by firing squad in the hot Accra sun.

"But, no?" Kodjo went on. "Even with the bombs and soldiers and the hello-copters, still, these Vietnamese, they don't give up?"

"They don't give up," Glen said.

"And you don't shoot any?"

"No, Kodjo … I don't see any to shoot."

"Ah, it is so?" Kodjo finished the last of his ball and took out a piece of cloth and wiped his mouth. "I would not want to fight them … by any means."

"Good," Glen said, searching the street in front for Kwami who was due back with the evening's palm wine. "By any means; don't fight them … Or anyone else."

"I will not fight unless Rawlings orders me to fight. Then I will fight for Asombo."

Glen looked at the man before him. "Kodjo, you are how old?"

"Ah—just this thing: forty-five years."

"Do you have a family?"

"Ah—my wife is in Banda. Many grown sons and daughters." He smiled widely from the chair.

"Then you should be with them and not go off fighting anywhere," Glen said.

"I will fight—For Asombo, I will fight."

Glen shook his head and searched the street. "Fine, make sure the bolt is down."

ELEVEN

With each new régime came a new constitution and Rawlings and the AFRC quickly emerged as less authoritarian and greatly more democratic, and after the initial consolidation of power quickly established a peoples governing body with local representatives from each major town and jurisdiction in the country reporting to Accra. And chosen to represent Assini and the surrounding district, comprised mostly of the Wasa people of southwestern Asombo, but spilling also into the eastern edge of the coastal Fantis, was Leo Aketti, a former biology teacher at Assini Secondary, who still lived in town and whom Glen knew well from various people connected to the school.

And as November gave way to December and Christmas approached, word spread through Assini and the school that a large celebration would be held for Leo, who, after an initial series of exploratory sessions in Accra, had been selected as a member of a new national legislative council and would be returning to Assini at Christmas before going back to the capital on a permanent basis after the New Year for the start of the new constitution's first term.

* * *

"Oh.—They have decided on Dr. Appiah's house," Mr. Amoah said on Glen's porch one day after school during the last week of the term, where they again sat drinking palm wine with Kwame in the late afternoon heat, discussing the location of the upcoming celebration for Leo (as well as life in Assini in general including the excellent goat kabobs being roasted by the new seller near the entrance to the market and the very short skirts of the two young sisters selling soap at a table toward the back near the racks of dried fish).

"Dr. Appiah's?" Glen replied, leaning back in his chair. "Really? I'm surprised ... I thought Appiah had ties to the régimes of Afful and Acheampong ... I didn't think he'd be associated with Leo seeing as Leo is now signed up with Rawlings."

"*No!*" Amoah said, animatedly, correcting a serious technicality on Glen's part. "This Acheampong was the worst. He disposed of *Appiah's* people—And Rawlings disposed of him! So they are friends—Appiah and Leo. Appiah will help Leo."

Glen drank from his gourd, unsure if he could even remotely comprehend the enormous web of tribal and political affiliations of Asombo. "Really? So when will it be?"

"Christmas Eve," Amoah said. "All of Assini will be there—I'm telling you all!" He drank down the last of his gourd in one long drink.

"Kwami, will you be coming?" Glen said, his hair and beard uncut and long again and wet with perspiration. "Will you be bringing *nsa fufuu*?"

Kwami, in his ragged farming pants, frayed at the ends above his bare feet, grinned and nodded. "Ani ... I will begin searching for the tree just tomorrow—I will find the best tree in Assini!"

Glen and Amoah looked at each other and grinned and Glen drank from his gourd and Amoah, reaching for the bucket, refilled his. "The matrons from the school will be making the meal," Amoah said, his eyes seeming to sparkle as he leaned up from the bucket. "There will be many goats—not one, not two—*many!*"

"*Ahhhnnnnnnn,*" Kwami uttered in understanding and he drank the rest of his gourd.

"And beer," Amoah said, his eyes now widening as he playfully inflated his cheeks with air. He exhaled long and slowly. "I'm telling you!—the headmaster has ordered the school bus to Awaso for a full supply—*Ivorian!*"

"*Ohhhh—whooooooosh!*—You hear that, Kwami?" Glen said. "Beer *piiiiiii!*—Ivorian."

Kwami grinned widely and nodded.

"But Kobina, you will not be traveling to Accra? ... To see your friends?" Amoah asked. "I think they will be celebrating Christmas fine."

"*Ah!*" Glen said emphatically as he lowered his gourd. "My friends are here!" and he clasped first Amoah's, then Kwami's hand, loudly snapping fingers on release. He raised his gourd again: "*You* are my friends," and he drank the milky wine."

"And I think Miss Lizzy," Amoah said, grinning broadly.

"And Miss Lizzy ..." Glen said, his eyes narrowing. "*Ohhhhhhh,* Miss Lizzy ... She is fine-o ... She is fine-o pa paaaaa."

"Sir," said Kwami, grinning as broadly as Amoah, "I think Miss Azim will make you fine wife—She will make *strong* babies."

"*Ahhhnnnnnnn,*" Amoah uttered loudly. "Very fine—Strong-o." And he clasped Kwami's hand and they laughed hard and snapped fingers.

Glen sat quickly up in his chair. "Oh, no ... No, no, no. I don't think so. I—don't—think—so." And he looked hard at Amoah.

Lately, when sober, especially since a particularly loud argument between Glen and Lizzy that was heard by much of Assini, Amoah had been more and more frequently talking— no, lecturing—to Glen, about the fierce pride and loyalty of the Dagahti, a once powerful tribe of the north. In the old days, in the harsh, arid plains of the Sahel, as a sign of bravery and strength, a man had to kill before he could seek a wife. If, as proof, he did not show her the dried trophy from his castrated victim, she would mock him: *I am a woman and you are a woman so why do you approach me?* The old ways were gone, but the pride and fierceness remained. Swamped with work from the school, Glen would often brush these lectures aside, and then think of Pat in Takoradi after her trip to Mali, marveling about the mellowness of the people.

"At night, the tail of the lion looks like the stalk of the cassava plant," Amoah would persist. "Yeah, yeah, Amoah," Glen would testily respond, "—go kill two birds with one stone, will you?—I've got *work* to do!"

On the warm Assini porch, Kwami, his face contorted, was laughing loudly now, his half-buttoned shirt hanging over the ragged pants. "*Strong!* ... Asomboian babies are *strong!*"

Amoah, wide-eyed in the other chair, also laughed convulsively; and Glen quietly lowered in his chair and shook his head, and they all drank more of the wine.

* * *

"*No!*" came the response sharply. "Glenny drunk-o—*Tooooo* drunk." Lizzy, beside Glen on the couch, folded her arms across her chest and put her knees together as Glen nuzzled into her side, one arm loosely around her shoulders, his face on the bare skin of her neck. On the table in the corner, the lantern cast its soft glow about the room.

'Izz—jus'—me ... baby ... Jus' Kobina ..."

"*No! Tooooo* drunk! ... You know what I said ...and you smoking that hemp again...the farmers give you that...it make you crazy."

He continued nuzzling and moved his hand onto her thigh and then up to her hip; and she grew quiet and seemed to momentarily relax as though ready to let him begin, but then suddenly pushed him away, ending it while they were still fully clothed. And he emitted a long slurred *fuck* and rolled onto his side; and his eyes began to slowly close, and then shut, and with his mouth open, he was quickly asleep.

TWELVE

"Mail for Mr. Glen."

"Ah. Edward. For me? Two? Meda ase paa." Glen took the letters from the school messenger, Edward—middle-aged and neatly dressed—one of which was unusually large and padded, and put aside the stack of exams he had been marking in the teachers' lounge where he sat on one of the large cushioned chairs. The mid-morning sun was bright out the windows and the air warm and damp and the school was quiet and almost empty as the students and most of the teachers and staff, except for those who would be going to Leo's celebration, had vacated for Christmas break. Mr. Ocansey worked on exams in another chair, and the Assist and Mr. Attah talked quietly at the second-floor railing out the open door as a few students, late in leaving, strolled with large bags slowly over the grass below the classroom block. The greatest activity emanated from across the school grounds at the cooking shelter beside the temporary cafeteria where the matrons and their many helpers were in the early stages of food preparation for the celebration of Leo later in the evening. He had not seen Amoah for two days.

"Sir, your knee, you are hurt." Edward nodded toward Glen's legs, today protruding from shorts, to where a large, stained, hastily-applied bandage covered one of his knees.

"Ah, nothing, Edward, took a little spill the other day. — Onyami a paaa," Glen now said, smiling at Mr. Ocansey across the room, "two letters—one fat."

Edward grinned and left with the mailbag and Mr. Ocansey smiled as Glen studied the envelopes. The smaller, from his sister, he set aside, and then holding up the larger, looked first at the familiar destination:

Mr. Glen Gray
c/o Assini Secondary School
Western Region
Assini, Asombo
West Africa

Turning it over, he read the return address:

Pvt. Scott Burchett
24 W. Easton Ave.
El Paso, Texas
U.S.A.

He opened the envelope and removed a single, handwritten page:

Dear Pvt. Gray, Enclosed is one bracelet recovered near Don Doung on Dec. 2, 1972. I am as surprised at sending a letter to Africa as you probably are at receiving one from an unknown Nam Vet from Texas. I have been in possession of your bracelet since I convinced the woman I found wearing it with five dollars to give it to me that hot afternoon out of Don Duong six years ago. It sat in a box in El Paso while I regrouped my post-Nam life over the last five-odd years since discharge in '73. I finally got around last summer to tracking you down and got this address from a Fort Lewis directory for you in Asombo, West Africa. You were the only Glen Gray in highlands ground forces in the mid 60's. Man, how's friggin' Africa!? Hotter than the Binh Thuan Delta in March? I hope not! Hoping you receive this.

Peace and Love, Scott Burchett

P.S. The woman said her brother found it beside a stream near Kon Tum at the end of Tet in '68.

Glen reached into the bottom of the envelope and removed the bracelet and held it in his hand. The thread-thin chain was broken and half was missing but the curving bronze plate and inscription, though scratched and faded, was otherwise as it had always been: '*To Glen, Love, Grandpa Gray*'.

He flipped it over and stared at the blank back, and then with the tips of his fingers, slowly turned it end over end. He closed his fist around it, then opened and looked, then clutched it again. He reread the letter, stopping after each sentence to look at the bracelet, then dangled it by the piece of chain. He read the letter completely through once more while he lightly twirled the bracelet in his free hand. He balanced it on his wrist and took his hand away to look and then caught it when it began to slip; and he stood up from the chair. He looked again at the letter while lightly shaking the bracelet and chain in his fist, but stopped reading before the end of the first sentence and opened his hand and looked again. He shook his head and sat back down and held it up to the bright light streaming through the long row of windows along the back wall.

"Kobina get mails?" Mr. Ocansey said casually from across the room.

Glen looked over and, without answering, nodded, and then gathered his things and left.

THIRTEEN

It was not that he began drinking any earlier that afternoon; the palm wines of Assini often flowed freely even in the mornings amongst the teachers at the school. Or that the quantities he consumed were necessarily greater, or drunk more rapidly, or that the wine was any stronger than usual: although Kwami had mentioned that he would be tapping from the finest tree on his plot. Not even when he finally arrived at Dr. Appiah's compound with Lizzy and Alice just after dark, where the party for Leo was noisily commencing with the local chief and his council and the Headmaster and most of the teachers and staff, and even a few students from the school, and, of course, the wealthiest merchants of Assini and their families. It was not then that he drank significantly more beer from the liberal supply, or, again, more rapidly than on any other of numerous previous occasions; although it is well known that Ivorian beer is somewhat stronger than Asomboian; but not by much. It was, however, emphatically noted by the State Department when they finally did conduct their investigation with the assistance of the FBI, almost two weeks later (or, more accurately, attempted investigation; the decomposing equatorial jungle having taken for eternity the truths they sought), that by numerous accounts, more liquor had descended on Assini and into Dr. Appiah's compound than anyone could recall ever before being in one place for one evening. But perhaps more importantly, also noted, repeatedly, was the unusually loud argument with Miss Azim that had occurred when they had returned to his flat shortly before midnight—along with the fact that after the initial interview she disappeared from Assini before the scheduled follow-up and was never heard from again—which raised the most troubling questions and left the greatest uncertainty with regards to the movement of Glen's head, and whether something hard came toward it, or it toward something hard.

* * *

That he had sampled liberally that afternoon from Kwami's initial batch there is little doubt, nor that when Mr. Amoah showed up on his way to Dr. Appiah's, Glen had drank from the second, as Kwami had eventually taken the first bucket to the party and then stopped by with another before taking it, too, on to Appiah's.

So he was feeling nourished when Amoah left—somewhat suddenly, it seemed—just as Lizzy and Alice arrived; and they walked through the lantern-lit streets to Appiah's, where much of Assini that was not actually allowed to enter the large inner-compound had gathered on the streets and walls surrounding the dwelling, with radios blaring and people dancing and drinking the local wine and many children running about. And once inside and seated in the enormous ring that encircled the courtyard and must have involved every available chair in most of Assini, the bottles of beer were brought, nonstop, by women in brightly-colored floor-length dresses with matching head-scarf, along with plate after plate of peanut stew and palm-oil with the tenderly cooked goat meat and jollof rice and steaming yams and cassava. And to one side two car batteries powered a few electric lights and the early-'70s component-stereo where Edward, the school messenger (the dark glasses and bobbing upper torso the antithesis of his stoic, professional, daytime-self), spun a handful of badly scratched records on the aging turntable; and music boomed from the high-wattage speakers as people danced in the center of the ring. And Leo, smiling widely, sat on a raised chair on a step at an entrance to the large inner-house, with the chief, in his traditional shoulder-draped cloth, and Dr. Appiah, in a tie-less, open-collar suit, seated on each side. And before them sat a table covered with plates of food and open bottles of beer, while in a nearby corner rested a half-dozen buckets of palm-wine, two of which were Kwami's, joining the tappings of several other Assini farmers.

And extending further down each side of the ring of chairs from Leo were the Chief's elders and the Headmaster and the Assist, and Mr. Ocansey and Mr. Afful and several other teachers from the school, and the very wealthy Mr. Aquah who, aside from Dr. Appiah, was the only citizen of Assini to own and drive an automobile that was not a taxi. And when Glen came in with Lizzy and Alice there was a loud cheer from the crowd, both inside and out, and many greetings, and three chairs were quickly produced and they joined the circle just down from Mr. Amoah. And Glen waved at several more people in the ring, including old friend Kaurachi, who had lately been spending long periods away from Assini at his family's home in Sekondi; and quickly one of the tall bottles and a glass was produced, and, smiling, Glen filled the glass and raised the foamy beer to his lips.

* * *

"Sir ... Akwaba."

With the music blaring and the courtyard now jammed with perspiring bodies, Glen turned from his conversation with Arthur Amable, a brother of Leo's and local poultry farmer who now sat beside him, to the slender young figure before him in the dim courtyard light; and his face suddenly brightened. *"Ocran!"* Glen said loudly, clasping the young man's hand, "you are here!"

"Sir ... yes," said a grinning Ocran. "I am knowing Dr. Appiah's son—Kofi. We are friends."

"Ocran," Lizzy said, smiling widely as she leaned forward from the other side of Glen. Ocran greeted Miss Azim and then turned back to Glen, his smile even wider.

"Do you think you did all right on exams?" Glen asked.

"I am hoping so—Sir, I am praying."

"Oh, you will do fine, Ocran—Fine," Glen spoke proudly, the music continuing to blare, the crowd loud, the dancers bouncing wildly. It had been mostly flowing, rhythmic West African Highlife, and disco, coming through the speakers, but now suddenly Mick Jagger was singing *'Miss You'*, and Glen looked quickly up. "God damn—The *Stones*," and he turned to Lizzy, raising his glass.

"Sir, you are not traveling home for the Christmas?" Ocran said.

"No—*no!* ... God no ... No, I'm staying right here ... Right in Assini," and he tried to drape an arm around Lizzy as he continued to drink his beer, but his arm pulled her off balance and away from her conversation with Alice; and she squirmed quickly out of his hold and stared at him briefly before turning back to Alice. *"Ooohhhhh* ... Oh—well ..." Glen said in mocking disappointment, at first wide-eyed and grinning, and then not; and he drank more of his beer.

"Okay," Ocran said, "I am greeting ... Now I am going."

"Yooooo—bye-bye-o," Glen said, again clasping Ocran's hand and snapping fingers; and Ocran turned and disappeared into the crowd. Glen stared for a moment into the swarm of dancers and then glanced at Lizzy who continued in her conversation with Alice, before turning back and aggressively tapping his foot to the crooning Jagger while drinking long and deeply from his beer.

* * *

When the speeches were about to begin, Glen quickly got up, momentarily stumbling, and went to the beer table for an extra bottle in case he ran out during what he knew would be a lengthy period of sitting and couldn't get the attention of one of the servers. When he returned, Lizzy was looking at him; and he set the new bottle on the cement floor and looked hard at her and she turned curtly back to Alice. Suddenly the music stopped and Dr. Appiah rose from his chair beside Leo and the courtyard grew quiet, the excited groups of playing children, dressed in their finest clothes, with sharp reminders from any who were older, the last to be still. The elderly Appiah, with his London-acquired doctorate in economics and past high-ranking cabinet position in an earlier government, knew personally many of the politicians and powerbrokers of Asombo—both military and civilian—as well as the countries complex ethnic and political rhythms, and now with the courtyard's attention, he began speaking loudly and forcefully in dialect. He spoke firstly of a new beginning for Asombo and of high hopes for the young Rawlings and the AFRC, and in particular of his confidence that Assini's own Leo Aketti would be a strong and positive voice, not only for the people of Assini, but for all of Asombo. And he expressed particular pleasure that Leo would be our representative in the new government which, through means forever unknowable to Glen, Dr. Appiah had somehow had a role in bringing about. And in between the sharp barks of Appiah's words, the voices and sounds of the Assini night drifted over from the crowd on the street and also from the busy kitchen area off the courtyard where numerous women and young girls continued with their preparation and serving of the food and beverages. And Dr. Appiah, turning from side to side, continued to talk in dialect in the mostly lantern-lit glow of the courtyard of the greatness of Assini and its historical importance as the Western Regions liaison to the capital during the long struggle for independence from colonial Britain only one generation before. And to one side an elder of the Chief's called out the rapid 'Asim' request of ancestral compliance in the short pause at the end of each statement. And in the courtyard the crowd sat and listened and ate and drank under the starry night, and Glen, oblivious to most of the dialogue, drank the Ivorian beer.

Then Dr. Appiah introduced the esteemed Chief Olosula Boadure the IV, trusted protector of the sacred spirit of the *Wasaw* tribe of Assini, who, adorned form head to foot in cascading bands of gold, stood in the bright patterns of his draped, traditional cloth, and, in even more rapid and forceful bursts of local dialect, began a long tribute to his great, royal ancestral family and their many great victories and accomplishments, both in battle and diplomacy—including their key strategic compliance with the neighboring Ashanti and Dagati empires in the late-nineteenth-century-battle of Koforidua against the invading British, which greatly enhanced the Wasaw's wealth and consolidated regional control for another fifty years—all throughout Assini's long, storied, and sacred past.

The pace of the speakers dialect was much too swift for Glen's moderate mastery, but leaning over from the chair beside him, Amoah would from time to time inform Glen—in what seemed to evolve into an almost lecturing manner—as to the general topic, to which Glen would then nudge Lizzy and convey the information, who would turn and, after a brief, penetrating stare, exclaim in a hushed, incredulous voice: *"I know!—I am a Dagati!"*

* * *

And so the evening went, with several more speeches, before short and thin forty-three year-old Leo, in his slacks and short-sleeved shirt and with his thick mustache and long side-burns, stood to much applause and cheers, and, in a more humble and subdued tone, began to speak to the attentive crowd. He described his simple upbringing in nearby Banda and education in local schools before going off to the teachers college in Kumasi, which led to postings in several Western Region schools before the eventual return to his beloved Assini and a long and distinguished career at Assini Secondary. And he spoke of Assini and the school with great emotion and of his eventual rise to Head Science Master and then smiled as he recounted from so long ago his former colleague and fellow biologist, the wondrous Mr. Jimmy, Assini's first foreign teacher. And then turning to Glen, his voice low and deep, expressed his sincere appreciation and gratitude for this latest overseas acquisition. And Lizzy, having now moved closer, elbowed Glen—somewhat more vigorously, as he conveyed with an icy glare, than Glen felt was necessary—and the crowd turned toward them and cheered loudly and Glen smiled and nodded and raised his glass; and the elder beside the Chief continued his *'Asim'* request of acceptance at each pause.

When Leo concluded in a voice-rising, finger-stabbing, patriotic crescendo, which had gradually built over the final ten minutes, the courtyard erupted in ecstatic cheer and applause, and then the stereo immediately scratched loudly back to life with another popular Asomboian high-life artist crooning melodically over the speakers, and the dancing began again.

"*Dance—Glenny!*" Lizzy suddenly jumped up and pulled on Glen who said '*no*', but Alice and Amoah coaxed him also, and he reluctantly stood with his glass of beer in his hand and followed Lizzy into the gyrating swarm. He moved at first only minimally, but Lizzy punched him in the chest and cried '*come on!*', and he began to sway more vigorously, and then suddenly with great theater—or perhaps not—to flail his free arm and legs wildly about. Then he drained the glass and someone took it away and he leaned over and wrapped an arm around Lizzy's waist and held her free hand out and swung and jittered even more wildly as the high-life blared and the crowd watched and cheered. They bumped into numerous people who jumped aside laughing and cheering loudly and the students in attendance laughed and hollered hysterically at the sight of their two dancing teachers.

Eventually they sat again, this time Lizzy in Glen's lap; and Glen drank more beer, now straight from the bottle, and clanked glasses or bottles at every opportunity with Mr. Ocansey or the Assist, or Mr. Amoah, whose enthusiasm, oddly, seemed to diminish as the night wore on, or anyone else he recognized who happened by. Once, Leo came over and in his deep, pleasant voice, told Glen for what must have been the fiftieth time in the past two years how happy he was that despite Glen's having to endure the often serious and in many ways embarrassing hardships of everyday life in poor, humble, far-off Assini, he remained to teach our most fortunate children, just as the great Mr. Jimmy had done so many years before. And Glen, Lizzy in his lap, clanked his bottle against Leo's glass and swatted Lizzy's bare thigh and reiterated to Leo the god-forsaken-truth of his greatly trying and difficult life in Assini; and he drank more of the beer, and swatted Lizzy again.

Later, when he stumbled out to the wall on the dirt lane outside the compound, where the men were urinating that night below the brilliantly glowing-band of the Milky Way, which stretched fully from one end of the night sky to the other, he felt the bracelet in his pocket when he zipped up his pants, and, taking it out, held it up to the stars. But unable to clearly see it, he turned toward the very faint lantern perched a few feet down the wall and strained again to look at the inscription. But he couldn't quite focus, but knew well enough what it said; and turning it over several times he felt the smooth, cool metal before gripping it tightly once again and dropping it back into his pocket.

* * *

Although it was Christmas Eve, and in predominantly Christian Asombo Christmas was a national holiday, there was no indication anywhere in Assini that it was in fact occurring the next day. And except for the very small minority of wealthy or western educated, or, to a lesser extent, those associated with the school or the clinic or the one local (in those days of extreme economic stagnation, always empty) A.N.T.C department store across from the market, who were more or less practicing Christians, and did speak of its occurring, and actually planned a more elaborate meal (and in years past, before Asombo's great economic decline, actually exchanged small gifts) there was, again, no indication of its occurring.

Except for its occasional mention by various townspeople as it approached, Glen would not, as was the case anywhere else in rural Africa, be able to distinguish it from any other day of the year.

But Christmas was the next day, as Glen was well aware (the distant, emotion-laced memories visiting more and more frequently), and he earlier had been invited to Mr. Amoah's for a dinner with several others from the school, as well as having mailed cards home to his sister and mother a few weeks before; but under the brilliant canopy of West African stars at the increasingly Dionysian celebration for Leo, there was no mention of the next days celebration of the birth of Christ, our Lord Jesus and Savior.

That is, there was no mention until Mr. Attah, seemingly missing for most of the evening, suddenly appeared toward the end and, grabbing Glen, insisted that he accompany him to his house where he was in possession of a rare bottle of rum that he had purchased in Awaso, and which he would like now to share with Glen as a celebration of this Christmas Eve. And while saying nothing to Lizzy, whose absence from the vicinity he was only now somewhat aware of, he left with Attah, whom Glen now discovered was accompanied by two women that Glen had never seen before, whom Attah introduced as Ama and Rita. And once out of the compound and on the street, Attah put his arm around Rita, which Glen only vaguely and drunkenly took discerning notice of, as he had often heard Attah speak dearly of his wife and children at his home village of Nkfroful, twenty miles to the west; and the four of them walked with only a vague awareness of the observing murmur of people around them down the dark lane to Mr. Attah's flat a few streets away. And entering the small, lantern-lit room, Attah briefly sat on a couch with Rita, while Glen and Ama sat in chairs, and then, after turning on his small, battery-powered cassette deck, arose once again and produced from a cabinet the rum and two small glasses, to be shared amongst the four of them, and poured the rum. And from his chair Glen could see the very fine curving figures of both Rita and Ama, and the very fine faces with the high cheekbones and wide, dark eyes, and the smooth skin and long, slender legs. They were both wearing denim pants, which was somewhat unusual for Assini—although in Accra and other large cities, less so—and was usually an indication of a higher social and economic background, and worn almost exclusively to parties or celebrations; but it was also an attire not unfamiliar to Glen who had been noticing—no, studying—the very appealing western styles on young women throughout Asombo since his arrival in country.

"*Ah*—I was lucky-o," Attah said from the couch, sipping the rum and grinning, his arm around Rita. "You can't get spirits a-tall. Only Awaso. There my brother lives and he can get them. Oh, yes. He can." Attah grinned wider and pulled Rita around and kissed her on the mouth and then reached over and poured more of the bottle into the small, clear glass that Glen held, and they all continued to share the sweet, burning rum. "It is good, yes?" Attah said, and he lit a cigarette which Rita immediately took to smoke. "Oh, yes—It is a fine day for Assini. And, well, tomorrow?—Christmas!"

Glen took another sip and handed the glass to Ama and then nodded to Attah who sat with Rita across the dimly lit room. *"Eye—de!"* he now attempted to say enthusiastically, but in fact with great difficulty, as the rum heated, then seemed to slowly melt, while passing down his throat; and with eyes moist and wide, he puckered his lips and tried to grin as he nodded again.

Attah and Rita both laughed and repeated Glen's *'eye de',* and then laughed even more loudly as Ama, from her chair, with a look of embarrassment, tried to suppress her grin. She said something rapidly in dialect and Attah, smiling widely, laughed again, harder this time, almost doubling over on the couch. Then Ama shifted and Glen saw the curving denim and the slender exposed waist below the tight, short blouse and the very dark, smooth skin of her face and arms; and he slowly rotated in his chair toward her.

Then Attah put his glass down and took the cigarette from Rita and put it in his lips and pulled her off the couch and onto the cement floor. "Come on, Kobina," he said to Glen, the smoke curling before his face, his eyes watery and blurred, "it is Christmas, let's dance. Dance—dance—dance." And Rita smiled and retrieved the cigarette and in the dim light of the small room, slowly swayed her very fine Asomboian hips, very near to Glen's flushed, glassy-eyed face. But then her smooth round ass was no longer swaying and instead the room was: *swaying—swaying—swaying*; and Glen leaned quickly forward in the chair. Then someone pulled on him and he was standing and holding Ama and they were all swaying and the walls swayed and the couch and chairs and lantern that burned on the table in the corner swayed as well. And then the bottle of rum was in his hand and then just as quickly it was gone and he was half kissing Ama and the tape suddenly ended and there was a commotion outside.

And just before the room began to slowly turn, he thought he heard Lizzy, but he wasn't sure; and in the small dark room on the Assinian side street, that was the last conscious thought he had on this earth.

FOURTEEN

A woman drove a car at dawn over the damp pavement in front of Northgate, while in the backseat, her young daughter pulled a Christmas gift from her baby brother's grasp, causing the child to cry and the woman to turn angrily in the driver's seat and scold the older girl.

A few miles away, two dogs romped along the damp, dirt shoulder of a residential road and into the remains of an old field before crossing into the backyard of a nearby house.

Waves lapped the shore of the gray waters of the early-morning sound as a freighter crossed in silence in the distance.

* * *

Someone tried to help Glen home but he pushed them off and staggered up the street on his own, the few Assinians still up shaking their heads and commenting matter-of-factly in dialect as he stumbled along in the dark. He somehow made it back to his house and onto the porch and through the open front door, and, just before closing it behind him, thought he caught the vague outline of someone at the end of the porch.

The next morning, when Kwami came over to inquire as to Glen's well being—the hushed murmurings of the village rumors growing as he approached—the door was open and Glen was lying fully clothed and lifeless on the cement floor, a pool of blood surrounding his head.

He did not move when Kwami nudged him, nor for the longest while, before his haunting, primordial scream that was heard in all of Assini, did Kwami.

* * *

An old Fulani herdsman stood at the entrance of his hut in the small, Malian encampment at the southern edge of the Sahara, dust blowing from the dabunde Harmattan, and, observing his herd, called in dialect to his wife off to the side who squeezed morning milk from the teats of a cow:

("Katouche; look at this! Why has this gazelle come to stand with our cattle? Great Allah, it is like our children, brave pastoralists who go to the south to live with the agriculturalists, work fit only for slaves. They forget the only important things in life, Katouche: cattle, family, and skill at dancing and poetry."

"The gazelle is lost, Amadou; it is only looking for its home.")

* * *

Two screeching monkeys flew through the branches where the forest reached the edge of Assini, and a vulture dropped from a shed roof onto a pile of garbage in the center of the market, its narrow, drooping-neck and curving-beak lowering into the decaying refuse.

Along the rapidly warming West African coast, the villages and towns coming quickly to life with the rising sun, the surf breaking on the shore and the palms bending inland in the gentle breeze, lying face up on the cool cement floor of the back street of Assini, Glen did not move, he did not move.

EPILOGUE
Thirteen Years later

Carol Brighton emerged from the dirt-covered school bus onto the grounds of Lawra Secondary School in the scorching sun of the Upper Region in the remote northwest corner of Asombo, four hours northwest of her school in Kintampo, hundreds of miles inland from the West African coast. As the boys soccer team she had accompanied emerged excitedly behind her and began racing to the field for their match with Lawra Secondary, she did a double take toward the group of barefoot Lawra boys scrimmaging on the rough-cut grass as, amidst the blur of black legs and arms and faces, the pale skin of a young mulatto boy— his African features unmistakable even from a hundred yards, yet the light skin and wavy hair even more so—grabbed her gaze like an actor on a stage and forced the racing of her heart, as the young boys scurried after the checkered ball that bounced about the field.

"Ekow," she said to the boys proctor who had accompanied her on the long trip, he attending the match annually, she, six months in country, for the first time. "Who is this boy on the field? There—with the light hair?"

"Ah—I know him only as Kofi. His mother is at the school. I believe she teaches economics. They have been here many years. They came from the south. That is all I know." The slender African looked at the American woman. "Do you know him, Miss Brighton?"

"No—no, Ekow, I don't. I was just curious." She looked again at the boy who was somewhat larger than the others, scrapping furiously for the ball, his long wavy hair flopping about, yet his demeanor and aura at obvious ease amongst his teammates. Then, glancing briefly at the sun, and then seeing the shade of the teachers flats, she turned, and, at a brisk pace, continued over the hard red earth toward the school.

On the field, the ball suddenly flew out of bounds and play momentarily stopped; but it resumed again almost immediately upon retrieval, the players again streaking furiously about. Except for the boy, who, for the longest moment, stood silently to the side, his gaze fixed upon the woman walking toward the school. Then suddenly he spun back around, and, as fast as he could, ran back onto the field.

Thanks to Russ Chenoweth, John Prophet, and the Harwich Library writers groups.

CPSIA information can be obtained
at www.ICGtesting.com
Printed in the USA
BVHW041246080522
636346BV00002B/5

9 780595 497676